BEING 15 IS HARD. BUT BEING
15 AND PREGNANT IS EVEN HARDER.

A BUMP IN THE ROAD

NEW YORK TIMES BESTSELLER

MARGARET MCHEYZER

Editor: Debi Orton
Cover Artist: Kellie Dennis
Interior Formatting: Tami Norman, Integrity Formatting

www.facebook.com/authormargaretmcheyzer
email: hit_149@yahoo.com

A BUMP IN THE ROAD

MARGARET MCHEYZER

FOR MUM

Be Brave

Dear Mum,

Thank you for being brave.

You and Dad were brave when you decided to pack up your life, with two little girls –and travel across the world to a country you'd only heard of.

You and Dad were brave when in 1971, you spent two weeks travelling to a place where you didn't know the language, you didn't understand the currency, and you barely knew anyone.

You and Dad were brave when you decided to move to a small, hick town, where the Greek population was less than 0.01% and the overall population was just over seventy-nine thousand people. You were brave by planting roots in a suburb where you were only 1 of 894 European families.

You and Dad were brave for working the jobs migrant Australians worked. You had a family to provide for, and you chose to work minimum wage jobs to support us.

You were brave because you sacrificed to give us the life you didn't have the opportunity to live in Greece. You never gave yourself credit for your courage. If you weren't brave, neither of us kids would have had the prospects this rich land has showered us with.

If you weren't brave, I wouldn't have met the love of my life, my husband, and had my two beautiful girls.

If you weren't brave, we wouldn't be here, surrounded by acceptance, kindness and ultimately, love.

If you weren't brave, who knows where I would be.

So thank you.

Thank you for having courage.

Thank you for teaching me how to love my family.

And thank you for doing the best you were able.

It's time to be brave for one last time, mum. You and Dad are now free.

Thank you.

PROLOGUE

I'M THE GIRL at school every mother hopes their daughter will be friends with.

I'm kind, and courteous.

I make good grades.

I don't go to parties where drugs, alcohol, and sex are prominent.

My parents are loving and support me in whatever I want to do.

I love art. Painting in particular, but I do love sculpture, too. I want to be an artist when I finish school.

Well, I *was* hoping to be an artist. Now, I have no idea what's going to happen.

You see, I just found out something. That something is huge. And it's going to change my life. Not right now, but in the very near future. Like in about nine months.

I haven't told my parents, because I know they'll flip. Heck, I'm freaking out myself.

How did this happen? Don't answer that, I know *how* it happened. But why? Why me?

I'm only fifteen. And we only did it once. And he didn't, you know, *let go* inside of me, so how did this happen?

And now you're thinking I'm a slut who deserves the consequences of my actions. Problem is, I'm not a slut. And I've been with my boyfriend since I was thirteen, and this was the first time we've ever done anything.

This is going to change everything.

Absolutely everything.

CHAPTER
1

S ITTING AT THE dinner table, I listen to Mom and Dad talking. Mom's animated when she speaks. She likes to talk with her hands. There are two things you have to know about my mother. The first thing is she loves to feed anyone who comes over. Whether they want to eat or not, if we're having dinner, she's going to make them sit down and try whatever we're having. Second thing is she's part Italian, so feeding people is her thing.

Mom and Dad have been married since Mom was eighteen and Dad was twenty-one. High school sweethearts.

Dad's an all-American man. Red-blooded and a real man's man. He owns his own concrete business. And Mom runs the business side from the office. He's got a staff of five people, three of whom are female and two are male. He's kind, and open-minded. I'm not sure how he's going to respond to this, though.

I'm a sophomore and should be concentrating on what I want to do with my life. But now, I'm sitting at the dinner table, pushing my food around on the plate, thinking about the pregnancy test I took not fifteen minutes ago.

"You okay, bear?" Dad asks.

I look up to him and force a smile to my lips. "Yeah, just thinking."

"Don't you like dinner?" Mom asks, with hurt in her voice. Mom's super proud of her cooking skills. She's not a chef or anything, but she can certainly whip up a delicious meal.

"Yeah, it's nice." I push the meat around the plate again, feeling sick.

"But you haven't even taken one bite. How would you know?" she asks.

I lift my fork to my mouth, but the pit of my stomach churns. I'm not feeling sick. I'm more worried than anything else. But I force a piece of meat in my mouth, and chew. Mom smiles, but I notice how she keeps looking at me sideways.

"I just don't feel well," I lie, trying to give them a reason for my distraction.

"Andy, are you coming down with something?" Mom comes to me, and places her hand on my forehead. "You don't feel hot. Did you eat your lunch?" I nod my head. "Did you have a milkshake? You know too much milk upsets your stomach."

"Yeah, that's probably it. I had a glass of milk after school." I didn't, but I'd rather lie than tell them I'm pregnant. "Do you mind if I don't eat any more? I might go lay down for a bit."

Dad looks across to Mom, and she nods her head. "If you're gonna be sick, you need to let me know."

"I think I'll be fine." Standing, I take my plate over to the kitchen counter. "Thanks for dinner, Mom," I say, retreating to my room at the end of the hallway.

Slumping on my bed, I look up at the ceiling. So many thoughts are running around in my head, most of them are shadowed by fear.

What will my parents say?

What will Alex say?

What will Alex's parents say?

What will everyone say?

I live in a small town with a population of around fifteen thousand people. Fifteen thousand sounds huge, but when you've grown up here, your parents have grown up here and your grandparents have grown up here, fifteen thousand is actually quite small. I can't walk down the street without having to say hello to at least a dozen people.

Then there's Alex's family. Alex's dad has lived here for nearly all his life. Same for Alex's mom.

Alex is a senior, and I'm a sophomore. But we've been dating since I was thirteen. I think our parents have always wanted us to get together. It was no surprise to them when we went on our first date. But this is going to be a huge problem for all of us.

Placing my hand on my stomach, I gently rub my belly.

I'm not sure what to say. Or even if I should say anything. Should I try to hide it, then give the baby up for adoption?

Ugh.

Angrily, I stand and begin to pace. This is crazy. I'm only fifteen. I'm not old enough to have a baby. Why did we have sex? Why didn't we wait? Worst part, it wasn't even his idea. Oh, don't get me wrong, he was into it, but it was me who wanted to take it further.

Alex is going to freak the heck out. *I'm* freaking out.

I should tell him.

No, I shouldn't.

Yes, I should.

Ugh. Just tell him, Andy.

I'm trying to work up the courage to tell him, when an idea pops into my head. What if I'm just late with my period? Then I'd tell him, he'd stress him out for no reason, and I wouldn't actually be pregnant. "You're being an idiot," I curse myself.

"You're just late." Plonking on the bed again, I grab my phone, and send Alex a message.

Miss you. I write.

Miss you too. He replies within seconds. This makes me feel better. I know this is stupid, and a false reading. I'll probably wake up tomorrow, and have my period.

Yep, that's what's going to happen.

CHAPTER
2

"HEY, WHAT'S WRONG with you?" Zarita asks as she leans against the lockers beside mine.

"Huh? What?" I reply, shutting my locker door, and turning to walk away from her. I still haven't got my period. And I can't help but worry about what might be going on with me. Last night I barely slept. Instead, I tossed and turned the entire night, and when I felt a twinge, I'd jump up and run to the bathroom hoping to find blood in my underwear. No such luck.

"You. You're distracted." Zarita is larger than life. She's absolutely my best friend, and has been ever since I can remember. Zar has the most beautiful, wild, curly hair, and she refuses to tame it, which I love about her. She's short, shorter than me, and has a hell-fire spirit. Her skin is beautiful, like rich, dark chocolate; her eyes are wide and full of life and heart.

"No, I'm not," I quickly retort. But the reality is, I'm very distracted. Distracted by what's happening in my stomach.

"You'd better tell me what's going on with you. This whole 'let's be quiet' thing isn't working for me."

I clutch my books and computer closer to my chest, being careful not to drop my laptop. "It's nothing."

I can't tell her. Because what if there's nothing to tell? I just have to wait until I get my period and try to act normal until then.

"You're lying. I can tell. You've never been a good liar. So, just tell me. Get it over and done with."

"There's nothing to tell, except, we're going to be late to math." The bell sounds, and I know we only have a few moments to get to class.

I pick up my speed, and Zarita does too. "I'm gonna find out," she pushes.

"Zar, there's nothing. Will you drop it?"

"Drop it? So, there *is* something happening?"

"I didn't sleep properly last night, and I'm kinda tired. That's all. Nothing to tell. No massive secret. Nothing happening that I haven't told you about. I'm tired. That's it."

We get to class, and I turn to look at her. She narrows her eyes at me, and scrunches her lips together. Zar points a skinny finger at me. "You're lying. There's something happening, I just don't know what it is."

Rolling my eyes, I look away from her. "Good luck," I mumble under my breath.

"Good morning, class," Miss Haines says as she enters the classroom, and closes the door. "Who studied for the quiz? What quiz, I hear you ask. The one I'm doing this morning." She smiles at us, and we all groan. She never told us about a pop quiz. Hence the name, 'pop.'

"How do you think you did in math?" Zarita asks as we sit at our usual table at lunch.

Alex walks over, gives me a kiss on the top of my head, and

sits beside me. I look at him, but quickly turn back, because I can feel the tears starting to sting my eyes.

"Good," I answer Zarita's question. But my voice cracks, and I instantly look down at my lunch.

"Hey, beautiful. What's wrong?" Alex leans in and whispers.

My throat tightens because I don't want to tell him about what's happening. It's not something I should worry him with, not at this stage, because frankly, I'm probably late. The stupid pregnancy test has to be wrong. I can't be pregnant.

"What's going on?" Alex asks again, this time more concerned.

"Um." I force a fake smile, look into his eyes, then quickly look away. "I'm tired. I didn't sleep well last night."

"I'm not buying it. Not for a moment," Zar says over Alex. "She spouted the same crap before math, but I know there's something else happening." She taps her temple. "I have psychic abilities, you know."

"Don't you mean psycho?" I correct.

She picks up a carrot and throws it at me. But it misses, and hits Alex instead. "Death by carrot," he says as he picks it off his lap and places it on his tray. He slings his arm around my shoulder, and gives me a gentle squeeze.

"What are you doing Friday night?" Zar asks.

Trey, Hunter, Finn, and Elliot all come and sit at the table with us. Hunter sits beside Zar, and I notice how she slightly moves away from him and avoids looking at him.

"Hey, Zar," he says, adding a small head nod.

She doesn't even look at him. She just kinda smiles, not even in his direction. "So, what are you doing Friday?" she asks again, ignoring Hunter.

Hunter lowers his chin in defeat, but quickly looks away and starts talking to Alex and the others. He seems disappointed that she hasn't even acknowledged him.

"What's with that?" I jut my chin toward Hunter, trying not to make it obvious.

"What? Nothing." She shrugs one shoulder. But I can tell she's definitely hiding something from me. "What are you doing Friday?" she persists.

"Tell me about him, and I'll tell you what I'm doing Friday night." I indicate Hunter.

She rolls her eyes and looks away. Taking a deep breath, she replies in a soft voice, "Nothing. He asked me to the movies." Shyly she looks toward Hunter, and notices his attention is now with the guys, not on her. His back is to us, and he's laughing at something someone else said.

I lean into the table. "Are you into him?"

Zar's reply is non-committal. It's neither a yes or a no. She makes a low, grunting sound. But her mouth deceives her. Her lips slightly quirk up at the corners. "You so are!" I tease as I try to kick her under the table. Instead, I miss and kick Hunter. Wait, what are his legs doing all the way over in front of Zar's? Hunter's head turns to search for whoever kicked him. "Sorry, I um, meant to kick Zar, but got you instead."

"Oh." He nods his head but straightens his brows. "It's okay." Turning, he goes back to his conversation with Alex, Trey, Elliot, and Finn.

Zar looks over to me, and I can see she's desperately trying to keep me from saying anything. "You better call me tonight." I point to her.

She lowers her eyes, and smiles. "I will." She takes a bite of her wrap, chews, then takes another. "What are you doing Friday?" she asks me for the third time.

"Don't know." Probably freaking out if I haven't got my period by then. "Why?"

"I wanna go and see the new Marvel movie."

"Really?" I sag my shoulders, suddenly completely disinterested in going to the movies with her. "Marvel? Ugh." I grumble.

"Are you kidding me? Are you telling me you haven't watched any of those movies?"

"You know I'm not into super heroes and stuff."

She lifts her hand, and gives me the signal for stop. "Nope, I can't deal with you. Tonight, after dinner, you have to watch Iron Man. Just put it on, and watch it."

"You mean Boring Man."

"Nope, we are *not* going there. Watch *Iron Man*, then you can have an opinion. But until then, you can't be such a judgmental cow." She's smiling, so I know she's not serious. But, this is Zar. And *Iron Man?* Maybe she is serious.

I lift my wrap, and as it gets closer to my mouth I feel like I'm going to be sick. A waft of something that smells rancid drifts to my nose. "I think this is off." I throw it on my tray, and look away trying to settle my stomach.

"It looks fine," Zar says as she leans forward to sniff my food. "Smells okay too."

"No way. Can't you smell that?" The stench is burning the inside of my nose. Now I've smelled it once, I can't seem to get rid of the putrid stink clinging to my nostrils.

"There's nothing wrong with it." Zar picks up my wrap, and smells it closer. "Nothing." Lifting her brows, she looks bewildered.

"I'm not eating that." I point to the wrap.

Zar shrugs and tosses it on my tray. Just the sight of it is making me gag. It feels like the vomit is rising from the base of my throat. Gross.

"What's wrong?" Alex asks.

"It's off, and I can't eat it." I look at the wrap, and even though I'm hungry, I refuse to eat it.

"Here, have mine." Alex shares his lunch with me. "I got too much anyway." Alex pushes his tray closer to me. And the only thing I find appealing on it, is a banana. Picking it up, I peel it and start biting into it. I eat it so fast, and I want another one.

"Wow, you put that away." Alex looks at the skin.

"I'm hungry."

"Here, try something else." He nudges his tray closer again, but there's nothing on it that tempts me. Except the banana, but of course, that's now gone.

"It's okay." I scrunch my nose, turned off by everything he's left untouched.

"You okay?" Zar asks again. She narrows her eyes, concerned.

"Stop asking! I'm fine. There's nothing wrong with me. I'm getting my period, and you know how I get just before it."

"Ravenous." I nod my head. "Stressed." I nod my head to that too. "Bitchy."

"Hey," I object. "I'm not bitchy."

"Well, to be fair, not all the time."

"Thank you," I mumble under my breath. Zar keeps talking about something, but to be honest, I tune out. My imminent period looms over me. Because I might be pregnant, and if I am, I'm not sure what I'm going to do.

Tears prickle my eyes. I do everything I can to hold them back. I don't want Alex or Zar or any of Alex's friends to see me crying. If they do, then they'll ask more questions, and I can't answer them yet. This is too much for me.

"I need to go to the bathroom," I say while I stand and walk as fast as I can without attracting attention from anyone.

Heading into the closest female bathroom, I check no one is in here, then go to a cubicle, close the door, and burst into tears.

"What is going on with you?" I ask myself in a small voice. I'm all emotional. But my reality is, I'm terrified. Absolutely petrified of the 'what if' of being pregnant. Closing my eyes, I start to silently pray that my period is just late and I'm not actually pregnant.

"Andy, you in here?" I hear Zar's voice calling for me.

I slunk my shoulders.

I want to tell her to go away and leave me alone. But I also don't want Zar to worry about me. I wipe my eyes, and take several deep breaths, trying to calm my emotions. "Yeah, I'm here. Just feeling a bit yuck."

"Periods suck."

"Yep, they do." Opening the door, I head out, wash my hands. As we both walk together toward our next class, I try to avoid her eyes, because I know she'll see that I've been crying.

We walk down the hallway in silence. "Andy?"

"Yeah?"

"You'd tell me if something was wrong, right?" She's worried. It's obvious by her quiet tone and concerned gaze.

"Yeah, of course. You're my best friend. You know I would."

"I don't know. You seem different. Like something's really bothering you, but you're not ready to tell me."

Man, she's totally right. I do have something to tell her, but I don't want to say anything, because it could very well be a false alarm. "There's nothing like that," I lie. I hate lying to anyone. But in this instance, I just have to remain quiet.

For now.

CHAPTER
3

"ANDY, ARE YOU okay?" Mom asks as I pack the dishwasher.

"Yeah, why?" I know I've been quiet. I'm so damn worried. My period still hasn't come. And it's been four days since I did the pregnancy test.

"Because this entire week, you've barely touched your food, and haven't been joining in the conversation during dinner. What's wrong?"

"Nothing," I automatically snap back.

"Are you and Alex okay? Have you two had a fight?" Mom leans against the breakfast counter, crossing her arms in front of her chest, ready for a deep conversation.

"No, nothing like that. It's just that I've got a lot on my mind."

"What can a fifteen-year-old girl have on her mind that's so pressing?" Dad says as he dries the things Mom's washed and I can't fit in the dishwasher.

"Wow," I whisper and look away.

"Robert," Mom scolds. "Life is different than it was when we were kids."

Ugh, *kids*. That's how they see me. Just as a kid.

"Come on, Laura, what can she be worried about? She's got a roof over her head, two parents who love and adore her, and food on the table. Food that she hasn't been eating. Seriously, Andy, what's wrong? Are you on some kind of weird diet?" Dad snaps as he throws his hands up in frustration.

This makes me feel even worse. I really don't want to say anything. "Nothing. Sorry I've been so…" I try to think of the most appropriate word. "Sour." Is the best one to come to mind.

"Are you working tomorrow?" Dad asks. I nod my head. My one shift a week at the local coffee house. I like it there. It's really busy, because the owners offer all homemade baked goods and really good coffee — so the locals say. I definitely agree about the baked goods.

"Yeah, I start at eleven. Could you please take me? Or I can catch the bus. I don't mind."

"I've got to run into town tomorrow morning, so I'll take you," Mom offers.

"Thank you." I turn on the dishwasher and head into my room. Opening my laptop, I turn on Netflix. I want to be distracted by what *may* be happening with my body. Or should I say, what may be growing inside it.

I have to get another pregnancy test and double check. I can't wait until my period decides to come, because that may not be for many months.

I click on "Recently Added."

Are you kidding me? The first movie that comes up is *What to Expect When You're Expecting*. This has got to be some kind of sick joke. I let out a sigh, while looking away from the laptop screen. "Are you shitting me?" I mumble.

Frustrated, I close my laptop, and put it away. Lying on my bed, I grab my phone from the bedside table, and decide to put music on. That's a much safer option.

I hit one of my playlists, and settle into my bed.

I don't even realize when I close my eyes.

"Hey, you're going to be late for work," Mom says as she stands in my doorway. "Did you sleep in your clothes?"

I struggle to open my eyes, blinking fast I look down at what I'm wearing. "I was listening to music and I must've fallen asleep." I sit up on the side of my bed, trying to will myself to wake up. "I'll be ready to go soon."

"You've got forty minutes before your shift starts."

"Crap." I jump out of bed, grab some clothes and head for the shower. Quickly I strip down, turn on the faucets in the shower, and stand under the warm, pelting water. Closing my eyes, I take several deep breaths, trying to push the harrowing thoughts of pregnancy out of my mind. I don't want to think about it. I silently pray that by the end of the day I'll have my period. But a huge part of me knows I won't.

"What am I going to do?" I whisper to myself as I look down at the drain and watch the water running into it.

My heart is heavy and my soul is crying. This is the absolute worst thing that can happen to me. I let out a sigh. I suppose it's not just me this is happening to. It also involves Alex. He helped make this; I have to include him.

Ugh. My heart beats faster. What if he turns his back and tells me he doesn't want anything to do with me and this baby?

What if he leaves?

That's what happens, isn't it? The guys don't stick around. Which means it'll be me alone with this baby. My stomach roils, and without any warning at all, I vomit. Not much comes up, because I haven't had breakfast yet. But I instantly feel better.

"Oh my God," I say aloud. Is that what morning sickness feels like?

"Andy, you have to hurry up." Mom bangs on the bathroom door.

Quickly, I wash myself, then turn the water off, stepping out of the shower. Wrapping a towel around myself, I make a conscious effort to push it all as far down as I can. I just have to get through today and buy another pregnancy test on my break. I'm holding onto hope that I'm in fact *not* pregnant and all the pregnancy tests have been wrong.

"Andy!" Mom yells again.

I jump from her hard tone. "I'll be ready in five," I yell through the bathroom door.

Push *it* aside, Andy.

I rush into my room, towel dry, slide on my jeans, and t-shirt. Quickly, I wrap my hair into a messy bun, and slide on my shoes, now ready for the day.

"You haven't eaten," Mom says while I dash around trying to get my bag ready.

"I'll eat at work."

"Clarence is too good to her employees," Dad huffs over his morning coffee.

"You're in a great mood today, Robert," Mom snaps at him.

Dad grumbles again, but lifts his coffee and takes a sip.

"Bye, Dad," I say as I head over, give him a quick kiss on the cheek and start toward the door. Mom's already waiting with her bag and the keys.

"Bye, bear."

We walk out to the car, and I ask Mom, "What's wrong with Dad?"

"He wants a sports car. I said no," she replies bluntly.

I burst into laughter trying to imagine Dad in a sports car. He's really tall, and quite… solid. There'd be no way he'd be comfortable in a sports car. They're low to the ground and tight. "Why does he want a sports car? And what kind of car does he want?"

"A Porsche. I told him if we're buying a Porsche it's going to be a family car large enough for the three of us. He said he wants a sports car. Not happening, Robert, not happening." She points toward the house, as if Dad's listening.

I try to hold in the smile, but this is really funny. I couldn't imagine Dad behind the wheel of a car so small.

The ride to work is fairly fast. Mom pulls up at the curb, and I get out. "Thanks. I think I'll walk home when I finish."

Mom shrugs. "Okay. If you need a ride, call, okay?"

"Bye." I close the door, and Mom drives off to run her errands.

Walking into work, Clarence is already busy. "Morning," I say happily, making an effort to put the whole pregnancy thing aside.

"You're just in time. We're so busy, and Larissa can't make it in today. I'm afraid it's just you and me. But Arthur will come and be our busboy until we don't need him. Please tell me you can stay until we close?" Clarence is the sweetest lady.

"Of course, I can."

"Thank you, Andy. I'm really grateful for you."

"It's okay. I just need to let Mom know. But I'll text her when I can." I look around the quaint store, and notice all the dirty mugs, and plates left scattered around. "Wow, it's early, and you've been busy."

"You have no idea. And I'm not even sure why, because the annual Black Pine Town Strawberry Festival isn't until the end of the month. Usually, we're quiet leading up to it."

"Are you making your strawberry jam for the festival this year?"

Clarence puffs out her chest and smirks. "Best damn strawberry jam this side of the Canadian border. Heck yes, I'm making it. I need to win my ribbon. Fifteen years running, and I ain't losing cause I'm too lazy to make my strawberry jam."

Clarence is small, but mighty. She's a fixture in our town.

Everyone knows her, and everyone loves her. She started CCC, which stands for Clarence's Cakes and Coffee, when she was young, and has been here ever since. She's got short white hair, and is super slim. She's fast on her feet too, especially for her age.

"I think your strawberry jam is the best I've ever had."

"Damn straight it is," Clarence yells from the counter as I collect the dirty dishes from the tables. "Have you had cake today?"

"It's too early for cake," I reply as I stack the tray then wipe down the tables.

"Wash your mouth out, Andy. There's never a wrong time for cake. Red velvet? Or is it chocolate and orange flourless cake?"

"Yum, all your cakes are my favorite."

"I know. And I also know you like ice cream with them too. So which one? Or maybe a piece of each?"

I scrunch my nose. "Not both. But I wouldn't say no to the chocolate and orange cake you make. Will you share the recipe with me one day?" Walking out the back toward the kitchen, I catch Clarence shaking her head at me. "Is that a no?" I've asked so many times, and she always refuses. "'Granddaddy's recipes were passed down from his grandmother.' I know," I say the words before she has a chance to recite them to me.

She smirks at me. "Maybe, one day."

I start rinsing the dirty dishes, preparing them for the dishwashers.

"Hello?" I hear someone out the front.

Drying my hands, I rush out to take the order. "Good morning." I smile at Cassie, one of the locals.

"Morning, Andy. You're looking quite bright today. Can I have my usual please, but I'm in a rush, so I'll take it to go."

I enter her order of a skim caramel coffee and a piece of cheesecake into the system, turning to make her coffee.

"Hi Cassie," Clarence says. "You working today?"

"Not today. I've just dropped Simon off for an appointment over at the hospital, and I thought I'd come get my cheesecake and coffee and head back over."

"Everything okay?" Clarence asks as she leans against the counter while I finish the order.

"You know, just getting some things looked at," Cassie says. But I notice how sad she is. The sparkle in her eyes has become dull. She lowers her head for a moment, as if she wants to cry, but doesn't want us to see.

I look to Clarence, unable to find the right words.

"I'm sure everything will work out." Clarence reaches over and gives Cassie's hand a squeeze.

Cassie lifts her head, and this time I see a small glimmer of hope flash across her pretty, yet aged face. "Here's your order, Cassie." I hand her the coffee, and cheesecake I've put in a cardboard container.

"Thank you." Cassie takes them and leaves.

"Wow, that got heavy really fast," I say to Clarence.

"I thought Simon was in remission."

"I didn't know he had cancer."

"You saw Cassie. She's afraid, which means they've found something. Such a shame. They're a beautiful couple."

"How sad," I say.

Wow. I was happy-ish when I came into work, pushing my worries as far down as possible. But now, with Cassie's situation, it kinda puts everything into perspective.

I once asked Clarence why she has a male name. She looked at me and laughed. "Pot calling the kettle black," she said. She went on to tell me, "My father wanted a boy. Had Clarence set for him. But, obviously, I was a girl. He didn't care, and insisted I still be called Clarence." She shrugged. "Doesn't bother me any."

"Hey there, cute thing." Looking up from my remembered memory, I see Alex standing at the counter. He's smiling, and my heart skips a beat because I really do love seeing him.

"Hi." I look behind him to see the next rush of people start to drift in. "What are you doing here?" I ask, but keep an eye on the customers.

"I just came in to say hello, because you haven't replied to any of my messages. And do you want to come over tonight? Mom and Dad have some formal dinner for Lachlan's something that I can't go to. So… wanna order pizza and hang out?"

"Lachlan's something? That's as clear as mud! Um, yeah, sure. But we're busy, so I'll call you later, okay?"

Alex steps back and gives me a small wink. "What time do you finish? I'll take you home."

"She finishes at six tonight," Clarence replies to Alex.

"Thanks, Mrs. C. Bye." He winks at me again then turns to leave.

"I like that one. He's a good kid. Wasn't sure his parents would fit in here, but they do. Good people." She nods her head. "Now, get to work." I keep forgetting Alex's parents weren't born in the town.

And just like that, we're crazy busy.

CHAPTER 4

I CHICKENED OUT. I didn't tell him. How could I? The time wasn't right.

I bought another pregnancy test, choosing to go to a neighboring town where everyone doesn't know everyone, and now I'm waiting for it to have one strip or two. Two is bad. Very, very bad. So bad I think I'll cry.

I've peed, and now all I have to do is wait.

Again.

I can't be pregnant. I just can't be. We only did it once. Well, twice if you count Saturday. But I made him wear a condom then.

I'm not pregnant.

I'm not.

The timer on my phone buzzes, and my stomach knots in fear.

I take several deep breaths before I look to see if there's one line or two. Slowly, I shuffle toward the bathroom counter where the white stick awaits. Swallowing a giant gulp, I close my eyes as I pick up the stick.

I can't be pregnant.

Opening my eyes slowly, I see the result.

Stumbling back, my body finds the bathroom wall and I sink down to the ground.

"No," I cry. Dropping the stick on the ground, I cover my head with my hands, as I weep many tears.

I *am* pregnant.

Those two lines couldn't be any pinker if they tried.

What are my parents going to do? What am I going to do?

Oh my God! What is Alex going to do?

I look up, and knit my fingers together, balancing them on my drawn-up knees. The tears in my eyes have eased, only just. Taking several moments, I try and calm my thoughts. Whatever will happen, will happen.

"These are the facts, Andy," I say to myself. "One, you have to tell Mom and Dad. And two, you have to tell Alex." I count them on my fingers, as if I'm giving myself a pep talk.

Just when will I tell them all? Should I tell my parents first, or Alex?

Standing, I pick up the stupid white stick, and take it with me to my bedroom. I don't want Mom finding it before I have the chance to tell them. I need to be the one to tell them.

Closing the door to my room, I flop on my bed. My mind is working so fast that I can't keep up with all the thoughts. Most of them are fearful.

"Pull yourself together," I say as I sit up on the side of the bed. I reach over for my laptop. Opening it, I type into the search engine 'adoption.' I read the first few lines, and my heart sinks. I don't know what to do. I'm only fifteen, and I'm pregnant.

There's always abortion. But I don't think I can do that. Don't get me wrong, each person is entitled to make their own decision, but, I just don't know if it's something *I* can do.

What if I had it? Then I'd be a mom by the time I turned sixteen. What about my dreams? I want to travel the world, and learn new things, but is that really possible with a baby?

So many questions. And I don't have the answers for any of them.

I shove the pregnancy stick between the box spring and mattress, and go back to laying on my bed.

Bursting into tears again, I try to think of when the right time might be to tell my parents. Is there such a thing as the right time?

If I don't tell them, they'll eventually figure it out when my stomach becomes huge and I go into labor.

Maybe, I'll just leave it for now.

I'll wait for the right time to tell them. For now, I'll keep it to myself and deal with it on my own.

"Dinner," Mom calls from the kitchen.

Opening my bedroom door, I head out to set the table up for dinner. "Hey, what are we having?" I ask.

"Nachos. Everything's ready, you just have to set the table."

Silently I open the cupboard, take three plates out, and head to the table. Once I've helped Mom carry all the food over to the table, I call Dad.

"Smells delicious, darling," Dad says. Mom goes to her chair, and Dad pulls it out for her, waiting until she's seated before he sits next to her.

My stomach flips. I'm fighting with myself to tell them now.

But a small voice is telling me not say anything yet. The time isn't right.

"Hmmm, this is really good." Dad shoves some nachos into his mouth.

"This is one of your favorites, Andy. Don't you like it?" Mom asks.

"I do." I take a small bite and chew on it. The taste is really good, better than I've ever had before. My appetite returns, and I eat everything I dished out for myself, then I put some more. When I finish my second helping, I go back for a third. I've never been so hungry.

"I see you got your appetite back," Mom says as she sees me polishing off my third helping, and eyeing the platter to go back for a fourth.

"I'm really hungry."

"You training for a marathon we don't know about?" Dad jokes.

"Leave her alone, Robert. I was getting worried about her not eating. I thought she might be trying to lose weight in an unhealthy way. So many girls end up with eating disorders." Mom shakes her head.

"I'm sitting right here. I can hear you. I don't have an eating disorder. I lost my appetite for a few days, that's all. But now..." I point to my fourth helping. "I have it back again."

Mom watches me in amazement. I virtually finish off everything. There's usually enough food for Mom and Dad to take to work the next day, but not tonight. Today, I've demolished it all.

"What's happening at school?" Dad asks as we finish dinner.

"Not much. Just school stuff. You know."

"What kind of stuff?" Dad presses.

"I have a presentation due next week. I've nearly finished it. And then we have exams. You know, normal kinda stuff."

"How are you doing at school?"

"Dad, you get all my reports. You know I'm doing well."

"And Alex?" Mom asks.

My throat dries, and I look down at my now empty bowl. "He's good." I feel my face burning with embarrassment.

"You know, if you both decide to take your relationship

further, we'll have to do something about that to make sure you don't wind up pregnant," Mom says.

Oh crap. A boulder sits in my stomach, making me sick.

"You can't be serious, Laura. She's a child. She's not going to have sex for a while."

I feel my eyes widen as I tilt my head down further.

"It's going to happen sooner or later, and we may as well talk about it."

"She's not having sex."

Shit, shit, shit.

Definitely *not* the right time to tell them. Dad's losing his cool, and Mom wants to talk about protection. This is a conversation Dad prefers not to be around for. Because whenever Mom brings it up, Dad does what he's doing now. He reacts badly, then he goes quiet and leaves the room, unable to be in it while we talk candidly about sex. It's not a thing we do talk about frequently, but it's not uncommon either.

Zar's mom is super honest about everything. Sex and drugs are conversations that her mom will have regardless of where she is. For them, it's nothing to sit around the dinner table talking about the effects of crystal meth on a person's body and mind. No topic is off limits there. It's the same in my household. No topic is off limits, but nothing is talked about as candidly as it is in Zar's home.

Zar also has three older brothers who are super protective of her. Her oldest brother is bisexual, and he told them over dinner. Actually, I was there when he told his parents. His Mom looked at him and said, "Really, Hayden, are you telling us because you don't think we know? Doesn't matter to us. We love you and are proud of you, regardless of your sexuality."

And that sums up Zar's family. Open minded, and really accepting of everyone. Hayden told me later that he was grateful I was there, because he could use me as a shield. But as it turns out, he didn't need to.

"Well, we'd better talk about it because she's been dating Alex for two years, and it will likely happen sooner or later, Robert," Mom says to Dad, snapping me out of my fond memory of Zar's family.

"Then talk about it when I'm not in the room. I don't want to hear that my little girl will be sexually active. And while you're talking to her about sex, talk to her about all the infections she can get if she doesn't insist on a condom."

"You know I'm still in the room?" I snap at Dad. "You can tell me yourself."

"No. Not talking about this." Dad stands, and starts clearing away the table. "Go in the other room while I clean the kitchen."

"You're being completely ridiculous, Robert. If you can't talk about this, then what are you going to do when she *is* having sex? She needs to know she can count on both of us."

"She's fifteen. The legal age of consent is sixteen. We'll revisit this conversation when she's of legal age."

"You're being a moron," Mom snaps at Dad. She stands and begins taking things over to the kitchen counter. "She needs to know we have her back."

"Again, she's only fifteen," Dad roars.

"And she's a teenager. She's going to want to have sex."

I really should leave, and let them argue about when I'm going to have sex. But let's face it, this entire conversation is a total waste of time. Because I'm already pregnant, and I've had sex… twice.

"Having sex is going to happen when she's older!"

"Older? Like when? When she's married?"

"I'm not really interested in marriage," I say trying to defuse an increasingly tense situation.

"So, there we go. We have it sorted. Andy won't be having sex, until much, *much* later in life," Dad snaps back to Mom. This is my cue to leave. Because if I don't, then I'm probably going to tell them. And with emotions running so high, now's definitely not the right time to tell them.

Taking myself back to my bedroom, I flop on my bed and reach for my phone. There are several messages from Zar and Alex. I ignore all of them, consumed by my own self-pity.

Ugh.

What a screwed-up situation.

Fifteen and pregnant.

Great.

CHAPTER
5

I'M SO TIRED this morning. Last night was divided between crying, sleeping, and peeing. What is it with the need to pee every half hour? I'd cry until I'd fall asleep, then I'd be woken by the urge to pee. Which would set me off into the crying-sleeping-peeing pattern all over again.

I drag myself out of bed. Mom and Dad have both already left for work. Dad said this week is incredibly hectic, so he and Mom will be leaving early and getting home late. Mom usually does make it home at a decent hour. Dad though, he can work until quite late. As long as it's not dark, if the job needs doing, Dad will stay and work.

"I'm so hungry," I say out loud. My stomach rumbles, confirming what I already know. "Okay, okay. I need to pee." Once finished in the bathroom, I head out to the kitchen, and open the fridge door.

"Hmmm, what do I feel like?" My eyes set on the ketchup, I reach in and grab the bottle. Nothing but the ketchup is interesting in the fridge. Turning I spot the bananas. "Yum.

Bananas with ketchup." I peel the banana, and pour some ketchup in a bowl. Dipping the banana in, I inhale them together. So good. Yum. The banana is finished within a minute, and I peel a second one, devouring it with more ketchup. I eat a third, and finally, I feel full.

Looking at the evidence of the remnants of the ketchup smeared in the bowl, with the three banana peels makes me scrunch my nose. Bananas and ketchup? Really? But so damn delicious.

Quickly I clean the small mess I've made. Trekking back to my room, I get changed and ready for school. Packing my bag, I sling it over my shoulder and walk out the front door toward the bus stop.

I don't have to wait long before the bus comes to the curb. The ride to school isn't far, but the bumpy motion of the bus wakes my bladder up again. Seriously? I think to myself. Again? This whole peeing thing is already irritating.

The moment I'm at school, I go straight to the nearest bathroom.

When I'm finished, I try to find where Zar is. *You at school yet?* I message

Yeah. Locker.

Turning in the direction of the lockers, I walk past someone eating something that has the worst stench ever. It smells like a cross between rotting meat, and boiled cabbage. I barely make it back to the bathroom before I throw up. The moment I finish vomiting, I instantly feel better.

You have *got* to be kidding me! Is this what I'm going to go through? Throwing up whenever I smell something gross?

Washing my mouth out with water, I leave the bathroom and go to find Zar.

"If you're gonna make me wait forever, I'm gonna leave your skinny white girl ass behind," she snaps at me.

"Sorry, I had to go to the bathroom."

She casts a side eye at me. "So, what's going on?"

My mouth falls open. The way she asked that question, freaks me out. Like she knows what's happening. "What? Nothing." My response sounds nervous even to me.

Zar stops walking, grabs hold of my upper arm and drags me to a corner out of the way. Students are walking past, but the corridors aren't as busy as normal, because people are still filing into school.

"Spill it, and don't think I won't know when you're bullshitting me. I have a built-in bullshit meter." She lifts a questioning eyebrow.

"No, nothing. I have nothing to say."

"Liar!" she shrieks too loud, causing Finn and Hunter, who are walking past, to turn and look at us. I smile weakly, and turn to give Zar a 'shut up' look. Finn and Hunter keep walking, not saying anything to us. "You had sex with Alex, didn't you?" she asks in a low, but excited voice. "You dirty ho!" She leans against the wall, proud of herself for guessing what she thinks is wrong with me.

Feeling my face burn, I look away from her. "No, I haven't." My lie is so transparent. I wouldn't believe me if I was her.

"You're a terrible liar, and now a tart too."

"I'm not a…"

"I dare you, Andy. I dare you to stare me in the eye and tell me you haven't had sex with Alex." I look away. "Ha! See, I knew it. When? The weekend? Oh my God! Why didn't you tell me earlier?"

"Zar." I press my finger to my mouth, trying to get her to be quiet so no one hears.

"What? You don't want everyone to know you did the nasty with Alex?"

I let out a deep sigh, and lower my head. My head already hurts from Zar's inquisition. "Zar. Please," I beg.

"Tell me about it. Was it awesome?"

"Well. No, not really. The first time was really painful. And, neither of us knew what we're doing."

"First time?" Zar shrieks even louder.

"If you don't be quiet, I'm not telling you anything else," I warn seriously.

"Okay, okay. I promise, I'll keep my voice down. So tell me. What's it like?"

"First time was painful, and messy and really fast. Like, he was embarrassed."

"Did you orgasm?"

"Well, considering it was painful, and fast, the answer is no. But the second time was better. Not awesome, just better."

"You can only go up from painful, messy and fast." She blinks for a second, and we both burst into laughter. "You hope it can only go up," she says still laughing.

"Anyway." I peer down at the floor. My stomach twisting with worry.

"Wait, there's more? Oh my God, you're not pregnant, are you?" She laughs again.

I don't laugh. Instead I lift my gaze, tears welling in my eyes. Pursing my lips together, I feel them quiver. My heart is racing as I stare at Zar.

The smile fades from her face quickly.

Her mouth falls open, closes, and opens again. She narrows her eyes in question.

Before saying anything, she looks around.

Wiping the tears falling from my eyes, I follow her stare, making sure no one is near. "You're pregnant?" she whispers in a breathy, barely audible voice.

I don't have the courage to say the word. Instead I nod my head.

"Holy shit." She falls against the wall, letting it support her as she stares at me. "What have your parents said?"

"I haven't told them yet."

"What?" She shakes her head in a small disbelieving –almost shocked- gesture. "What about Alex?"

"He doesn't know either."

"I... um, I'm um, you know, um, well." She can barely form a sentence. "It's um. Like, um, are you like, um, sure?"

"I've done two pregnancy tests. Both of them have been positive. And I haven't gotten my period. I just threw up because something smelled off, and I ate three bananas with ketchup for breakfast because it tasted fantastic."

"Eww, gross." Zar screws up her nose.

"Which part?"

"The banana thing." She makes a fake vomiting motion. "Who'd eat bananas with ketchup? Only weirdos or pregnant women. Maybe you're not pregnant and just a weirdo?" She shrugs her shoulders. "You've always been weird."

"I have not," I say. I'm not feeling as tense as I was only moments ago.

"Nah, you're right. You're perfectly boring. The weirdest thing you do is read a lot. I mean, who reads these days? Well, who reads more than they're supposed to for school? You do, so maybe we'll go with the whole weirdo thing for now."

The bell sounds, causing us to look down the hall together. We both know what this means. We can't talk about this now. We've got class to attend.

"Lunch? Just you and me, none of those pesky, horny boys."

I smile at Zar. "Please," I start saying.

"Don't worry. Your secret is safe with me."

I let out a sigh, thankful for having such an awesome best friend, because I know she'll always have my back.

"So," Zar starts as she pushes her food tray toward me, before sitting opposite and leaning in.

"So," I say while I pick at the salad I've got on my tray. Dropping the tomato, I pick the banana up, peel it, and start eating. "Doesn't taste good."

"Want ketchup?" Zar says with a light-hearted tone.

"Yeah." I crinkle my forehead, knowing the combination is super delicious. "Would you get me some?"

Zar's mouth scrunches into obvious disgust at banana and ketchup. "Yeah, I'll get it if you want." She stands and gets some ketchup. Bringing it over, she squeezes some onto her plate.

I take a careful look around, making sure no one can see me. Quickly, I dunk the end of the banana into it and stick it straight into my mouth. "Yum," I moan with appreciation, and close my eyes to savor it.

"Yuck," Zar says the same moment. Lifting my eyes to her, I notice she's dry retching at my food combination. "That's one of the most disgusting things I've ever seen."

"It's good," I say through a mouthful of banana and ketchup. Zar's face drops. It's clear, she's got questions and probably concerns. "What is it?"

"What are you going to do?" She doesn't say any other words, but her gaze drifting to my belly indicates exactly what she's talking about.

"I don't know."

"What are you thinking about?"

I shrug. "I don't know," I say again.

"There are so many options. But you're going to have to tell your parents and Alex."

"What would you do?" I ask.

She shakes her head. "I don't know. I've never thought about it. I don't think I'd be able to do what I want if I had a…" Her eyes pointedly look at my stomach again. "I want to be an actress, and I don't think I'd be able to do something like that with a baby." She picks a spot on the table and stares at it for a long moment. I have too many thoughts traveling my mind, to make a coherent one stick. "There's adoption. But I don't know if I could do that. There's always abortion, but I might feel guilty for doing that. I could have the baby and raise it, but what kind of future could I give it? I'm not financially set; I don't have a secure job..." She lets out a huge sigh. "I'm not sure what I'd do."

"I've considered everything you've said, and more. What if my parents make me do one of those? What if they throw me out? What if Alex wants nothing to do with me and the baby? What if, *no one* wants anything to do with me and the baby? Everyone is going to think I'm a slut. I..." Tears well in my eyes. "I... don't know what to do." My breath quickens and I try to hold in how I'm truly feeling.

"I think the first thing you have to do is tell your parents. They'll take you to the doctor, and make sure whether you are or you aren't."

"I am."

"But you can't be one hundred percent sure."

"Zar, I am. I know I am."

"But you can't *not* go to the doctor. And you can't hide this. I mean, you're skinny. How do you figure you'll explain yourself when you're huge and look like you've swallowed a watermelon?"

"Maybe I'll be lucky and not gain any weight."

Zar tilts her head to the side. "Really? You're going with that, are you? Cause you and I both know, you're being a dumbass."

She's right; I am. I drop my head into my hands, and rub at my temples. "I'm going to have to tell them," I admit, knowing there's no other way.

"Well, yeah."

A few tears escape, falling to the table. I can barely see through the water in my eyes, and more tears keep coming. "Maybe I can run away," I say.

"I'm going to smack the stupid out of you if you say shit like that again. Look at me, Andy," Zar commands. I can't. I'm too embarrassed, and ashamed. "Look at me," her voice low, but damn strong. Taking several deep breaths, I let the natural sounds of the cafeteria take over. So many people talking and laughing. Someone shouting. Someone swearing. Normal stuff. This has an unusual calming effect on me.

When I'm finally calm, I look at Zar. "I won't run away," I say in answer to her unasked question.

Her shoulders relax, and she offers me a warm smile. Her beautiful white straight teeth, beaming behind her thick lips. Zar is so beautiful with her unruly hair, and dark chocolate brown features. She's simply stunning.

"Your parents love you, Andy. But you have to know, this will shock them. You can't expect them to be all sunshine, unicorns, and rainbows. They're going to react badly. Anyone would if their fifteen-year-old daughter told them she's been doing the nasty and now she's pregnant."

She brings a smile to my lips. "Doing the nasty?"

"Intercourse. Inter-course. In-ter-course." She breaks down the word, saying it with full, slow pronunciation.

"You can stop now."

"Whatever happens, they love you. And you have to remember this will be more of a shock to them than it was for you."

"Stop being logical. But, I know you're right. This will be a huge shock."

There's a long pause, neither of us saying anything. Zar stands, comes over to my side, and hugs me. "It'll be okay," she whispers, breaking the tense silence.

"Hey, what's going on?" Alex's voice booms, he sounds worried.

Quickly, I wipe my eyes before looking up at him. He sits on the other side of me, and wraps his arms around me, essentially pushing Zar out of the way. "Hey," Zar snaps.

She makes me smile. "It's okay," I say, pleading with my eyes to not say anything.

"I gotta go to the bathroom." Standing, she slings her bag over her shoulder, and moves away from us. Not before looking back at me, and giving me a small head nod.

"What's wrong, beautiful? Why the tears?"

I shake my head. A lump is forming in my throat. This isn't the place to tell Alex. Not here, and not like this. So many emotions are bubbling away inside. I know I'm going to have to tell him, and the right thing to do is to tell him before my parents. But I know he's going to freak out, and likely storm off. I've gotta make sure it's in an environment where he can yell and scream, and it won't be overeard by everyone. I know it's selfish. I'm only thinking of myself. But I'm scared.

"Just, emotional," I finally reply.

"That time of the month, huh?" For a guy, he's pretty intuitive.

"Something like that." I don't want to lie to him, but the cafeteria is definitely not the right place to say, 'Hey, Alex. You're going to be a dad.' Come to think of it, no place is the right place. All I know is that it's got to be somewhere far away from other people.

"I'll get you a candy bar. I know how much you like Butterfingers. Want one?"

I shake my head. I'd rather have a banana with ketchup. But even I know that combination is weird. "I'm okay." I lean in and hug him tighter. "I'll be okay," I say again on a long sigh.

CHAPTER
6

I 'VE BEEN DREADING this moment.

Sitting at the dinner table, Mom and Dad are talking about a client who came out of his house in his underwear. His very tight, very small, underwear. Mom's laughing as Dad recounts the story of the client. He was sipping his coffee, (in his tight underwear), while standing there talking with Dad. He then lifted his leg to rest it on the top step of his stairs, and Dad said he could see hair. It was enough for Dad to high-tail it out of there. Mom's laughing as Dad tells the story detail by detail. But me, well I'm barely listening.

My hands are sweating, and I feel sick to my stomach. I don't want to tell them. But if I don't, I know they'll somehow find out by accident, and I don't want that to happen. The very least they deserve is to hear it from me.

Mom laughs at something Dad says, and she looks over to me. I smile, pretending I'm not fighting a civil war inside my head.

"You okay?" Mom asks. "You've been unusually quiet."

I let out a breath. But my heart is bouncing like it's on a trampoline. "I um…" I rub my sweaty palms down my pants.

Dad lowers his fork, and looks to me. "What is it, bear?"

Clearing my throat, I look past them, unable to meet their eyes. "Um, there's um… ahhh, there's ahhh, um, there's something, I um, kinda…" I let out another breath.

"As long as you're not doing drugs, having an affair with a teacher, or pregnant, then there's nothing you can say that'll shock or disappoint us," Mom says.

Dad chuckles. "Really, Laura? Having an affair with a teacher?" Dad laughs again.

Mom joins in on the laughing.

I don't.

Because one of their guesses is right.

They both look at me. I'm not finding anything they've said funny. Tears well in my eyes. Dad stops smiling. Mom follows.

"Andy?" Dad asks in a small voice. "You're not having an affair with a teacher, are you?"

Goosebumps appear on my arms, and my body temperature chills to ice. "No, I'm not having an affair with a teacher," I say in a tiny voice.

"And you're not doing drugs?" Mom says in a whisper.

I shake my head. But I can't keep looking at them. I'm too embarrassed.

"Andy?" Dad says in an incredibly controlled voice. "Are you pregnant?"

I can't bring myself to confirm or deny. I lower my head even more, and just let my silence answer the question. My tears speak louder than words.

"Oh my God," Mom says. I look up to see her covering her mouth with her hand.

"What the…" Dad adds, staring at me in disbelief, his mouth hanging open.

Silence enshrouds the three of us. The air becomes thick with tension and my body freezes, tensely waiting for their reaction. I know whatever they're going to say and do is justified.

More tears fall as I wait for them to react.

"Andy..." Mom's voice cracks when she says my name. I still can't lift my head to look at them. "Look at me." I shake my head. "Look at me!" her voice is stern, yet not angry.

I take several breaths, swallow the lump down, and look up at my parents.

I see it, right there in their faces. They're extremely disappointed in me.

"You're pregnant?" Dad asks calmly.

I look down again. "Look at me," Mom says. I lift my head. Tears fill my eyes so full I can only just make out their shapes. "You're pregnant?" Mom asks, her voice hardly above a whisper.

I swallow again, but this time, find my voice. It's small and barely audible. "Yes."

Dad stands so forcefully from his chair that it shoots back and falls to the ground. The loud thud makes me jump in my seat. "You're pregnant?" he yells. "Pregnant? As in you're going to have a... a... a.... *baby?*" he spits the last word like it's venom coming out of his mouth.

"Robert, calm down," Mom says.

"Calm? Calm? How the hell can I calm down when my fifteen-year-old-daughter is knocked-up by God knows who? Do you know what people are going to say? Do you realize that our... this child is having a damn child? Do you realize this will ruin her life? This bastard child is going to destroy her."

I take a sharp breath in. The words Dad's spewing are hurtful. "Robert," Mom snaps again. "Sit down so we can calmly discuss this and decide what we're going to do."

Dad keeps pacing, back and forth. He runs his hand through his hair many times, while huffing in disbelief, and possibly frustration.

Finally, he lifts the fallen chair, and sits opposite me. His eyes are hard as he stares into mine. I can barely keep eye contact. Shame fills every part of me.

"First, who's the father?" Dad asks.

I look up, hurt that he thinks I'm someone who bed hops. "Dad, don't make me out to be some kind of girl who sleeps around. And even if I was, which I'm not..." I struggle with my words. Opting to shrug and shake my head. "But it wouldn't matter even if I was."

"Robert." Mom places her hand on his arm. This seems to calm Dad further. He lets out a deep sigh, but I can tell by his tense jaw and narrowed eyes, he's still angry. Or possible embarrassed.

"So, it's Alex's?" Dad asks.

I nod.

"Why didn't you tell me you were sexually active?" Mom asks, hurt. "I would have put you on the pill. Taught you about condoms. Helped you make decisions that wouldn't have led us to this." Mom pointedly looks toward my stomach. Hanging my head again, I look at my feet. Mom sighs deeply. "But no use in complaining now about what *could* have happened. We have to deal with what *has* happened."

"Well, she has to get rid of it. It'll ruin her life," Dad says. He's talking about me like I'm not in the room. "I'll find a place to get it aborted."

I cringe. It's not like I haven't thought about it myself, but the way Dad's talking, he's so *cold*. Maybe even heartless.

"Robert, we have to think about this calmly. You can't just say she's going to have an abortion. We have to think with a clear head, and not with an emotional one."

Dad turns to look at Mom. "How can you not be emotional about this? Our daughter, a mere child, is pregnant by her stupid boyfriend, who didn't have the sense to wrap his dick! God knows if he gave her anything else, like an infection."

Mom sits back in her chair, her eyes glassing over as she thinks about Dad's words.

"We were each other's firsts," I say quietly, although I know it doesn't really make much of a difference.

"Young, dumb and full of…"

"Robert!" Mom snaps again.

"Young, dumb and full of what?" I ask.

"It doesn't matter," Mom answers. She turns to Dad. "Enough, until we get our thoughts in order. That's enough from you."

Dad huffs, but nods, agreeing with Mom.

More silence fills the room. I've stopped crying, and my heartrate isn't racing anymore. "I'm sorry," I finally say.

"'Sorry' isn't going to help. What we have to do first is decide what the next step is. I'll make an appointment with our doctor, and we'll see what's happening." Mom again looks at my stomach. "Maybe you've just missed your period." She looks at me, hopeful.

I shake my head. "I'm pregnant. I've taken some pregnancy tests."

"Well, then. We have to make a list of options." Mom is really calm. Too calm. "There's abortion, and adoption."

The only two options jars me. "I can also keep it."

"Don't be ridiculous," Dad snaps. "You're a child. And if you keep this child, it'll destroy your entire life. What kind of education do you think you'll be able to get? What type of job do you think you'll find with a baby in tow? Who will hire you? Not only will no one hire you, but also think about the minimum-wage jobs you might be able to get. You want to flip burgers for the rest of your life? Living on welfare and food stamps? Is that your grand plan?" Dad's voice is rising slowly.

"I don't have to do this on my own."

"You think Alex is going to stick around? That boy is working on a scholarship. The moment you tell him you're pregnant, he's going to dump you and move on to someone else. That's what boys do," Dad says.

"You didn't."

"We'd been married for eight years before we had you, Andy. And we weren't fifteen," Dad tone is angry.

"Let's just relax. We're not going to be able to move forward if all we're doing is arguing with one another," Mom says.

She's right. We need to make a plan for moving forward.

"You're right," Dad concedes.

"First, we'll go the doctor and see how far along you are. Then, we'll decide from there what the next step is. If it's safe, then you'll get an abortion. If it's not, we'll um, ship you upstate to your Uncle where you can stay until you have the baby, and then we'll put it up for adoption."

I shake my head again. "Am I an embarrassment?"

", you're not exactly a blessing at this point," Mom says.

My heart tears in two. Standing, shaking with fury, I leave them and head into my room. Crying, but still angry, I take my backpack, empty what's in it, and start stuffing some clothes into it.

I can't believe they're saying these things. I know being pregnant at fifteen isn't ideal, but it's also nothing to be ashamed of, is it? Well, I suppose it is. I just don't know. This is just too much. But the one thing I know for sure is that my parents don't want me. They don't want anything to do with me. It's obvious by the hurtful, cold things they're saying.

Heading into the bathroom, I grab my toothbrush, and comb, and jam them into my bag. I sling it over my shoulder, and move quickly down the hallway toward the front door. Mom and Dad are talking in the living room, and don't see me leaving.

Quietly as possible, I open the front door, and head down the street. It's dark out. The moon is just rising over the horizon, outshining the few stars in the sky.

With tears in my eyes, and my soul in agony, I walk toward Zar's house. She doesn't live too far from me, just ten or so minutes. I pick up my pace, wanting to reach her sooner rather than later.

The night air is cool, not cold. Sadness fuels me, keeping me warm. When I get to Zar's, I sit on the curb, and send her a message. *Can I stay at yours tonight please?*

Immediately I get a reply. *Yeah, want one of my brothers to pick you up?*

I'm sitting out front.

I don't get another reply. Not even thirty seconds pass before I hear the front door open. "Girl," I hear Zar's voice before I see her. Standing, I turn to face her. She sees me, and instantly knows. "Oh man." Her shoulders slink down. "You told them."

"I did," I say as I burst into tears again.

"They threw you out? I never expected your parents to throw you out. I thought they'd be angry, but to chuck you out?" She steps in for a hug. "That's cruel, man."

"They didn't throw me out. They don't know I've left."

Zar pushes back, and tilts her head to the side. "They didn't throw you out? And you left? What happened?"

"Zar, whatcha you doing out there with Andy? Hi Andy," Miss Dixon says. Zar's mom has always said I can call her Miss Dixon, or Momma D, I call her whatever comes to me at the time.

"Hi Miss Dixon. Would you mind if I stayed tonight?" I ask.

"'Course, sugar. You know you're always welcome here."

Miss Dixon is like Zar. She's confident, and loud, and has the most amazing full-body shape I've ever seen. But I think the most wonderful part is the way she carries herself with complete confidence. She's so sure of herself. And she doesn't take any crap from anyone. Including Mister Dixon, who she kicked out when she discovered he was more involved with the dog walker then just taking the dog to be walked.

"Thank you." Zar drapes her arm around my shoulders, and we both walk into her home. Miss Dixon is standing at the door, in her dressing gown and slippers. She looks at me, and I notice her eye twitches. "Thank you for letting me stay tonight," I say again.

"Come into the kitchen, sugar. I think you need a cup of my hot apple cider." She looks me over, from head to toe. "With ginger. Ginger will settle your stomach."

"There's nothing wrong with my stomach."

"Sugar, you may be able to fool others, but you can't fool me. How far along are you? About six, seven weeks?"

Zar and I stop as we enter the kitchen. "I'm not… I ahhh." I don't want to lie. Momma D is kind enough to allow me to stay here tonight, and I don't think I should repay her with a lie. "I don't know how far I am."

"Seems you got yourself in a right mess. Babies having babies." She goes about preparing the apple cider, and turns fast on her heels to face Zar. "You come home like this one, and I will kick your ass into next week. Only after I kick your ass will we get through it."

"I won't, Momma," Zar replies. Her voice terrified.

"Now, this baby. The papa is that boy of yours, yes? Alex?"

I nod my head. "How do you know?"

"Momma has a way of knowing things."

Miss Dixon brings over the cider and places one in front of me, one in front of Zar, and then retrieves her own. "What are you going to do? Your parents know." It's not a question, more like a statement. "And obviously, they're not too happy about it, considering you're here. But sugar, you gotta sort it out with them. You can stay here until you do, but this is something that the family has to come together for. Support one another."

"They said I was a disappointment." I lift the cider, and sip. I've never been a fan of cider, but this has a strange, calming effect on me.

"Andy, they're not really disappointed. They're just shocked. Give them a chance to think about it with a clear mind. Right now, all they can think about is you and Alex having sex. No parent wants to know their fifteen-year-old is doing that. And most parents would hope their fifteen-year-old would talk to them."

"It's just…"

"No, sugar. You don't get a choice in telling them how they feel. You sprung this on them, and you want them to react by throwing you a party? Let your parents get over the shock first, then you can talk about it with them. Can't run from this one. Because, in a few very short months, you won't be on your own any more. You'll have someone who's going to need you more than you know."

I sip on my cider, and let Miss Dixon's words play around in my head. Her reaction is much calmer than I thought it would be. I was absolutely convinced people would react differently.

But then again, Miss Dixon has never been *ordinary* people.

Her reaction to her son being bisexual should've proven her open-minded ways to me.

Mom and Dad are usually open-minded too. They just need some time to adjust.

"Are you going to answer your phone?" Zar asks, bringing me back from the brink of anxiety.

I hadn't even heard it ringing. Taking my phone out of my jeans pocket, I see *Mom* splayed across the screen. I huff, knowing she's going to yell at me. "Hello," I say.

"Where are you? We came to your room and you were gone? Are you okay? Tell us where you are so we can come get you."

"I'm okay, Mom. I'm at Zar's."

"She's at Zar's," Mom relays to Dad with a sigh. "Why did you leave?"

"You told me I'm a disappointment. I thought it'd be better if I left. Let you and Dad calm down before we talk about me being pregnant."

Mom exhales a long, drawn out sigh. "I'm sorry, Andy. It wasn't anything your father or I were prepared for. Saying what we did was uncalled for, and I'm sorry." Tonight's a highly emotional night. Another tear rolls down my cheek. "We'll come and get you, okay?"

I look at Miss Dixon, and I know she knows what Mom's saying. "Okay, thank you."

Mom hangs up, and I put my phone away. "You going home, sugar?"

"I am." Picking the cup up, I finish the cider. "Thank you for allowing me to stay, but I think I should go home."

"I think that's the best idea," Zar says. "Talk to them. They're probably calmer now. And judging by the fact they called to see where you were, that should be enough to tell you they actually do care. About you, and about the baby."

She has a point, they wouldn't have called if they didn't.

There's a knock on the door, and it's only logical to assume it's my parents.

Miss Dixon leaves the kitchen, and goes to the front door, leaving Zar and me alone. "It'll work out. It always does. And just remember, you have me. I'll help when I can."

"I haven't decided what I want to do yet."

She steps in and hugs me. "My offer stands regardless of what you're going to do. I'm here for you, Andy. This decision isn't something that can be rushed. Because whichever way you decide, it's something *you* have to live with for the rest of your life."

"I know," I say acknowledging the huge gravity of the situation. "See you tomorrow at school." I give her a kiss on the cheek. "Thank you for being you." Letting go, I pick my backpack up, and make my way out to find Dad standing at the door talking to Miss Dixon. "Thank you." I give Miss Dixon a hug.

"Anytime, sugar," she whispers.

Dad takes my backpack, and we head out to the car in silence. I know Dad's angry, probably about everything. I can't flee or push him away. We need to talk about it and come to some kind of agreement.

Dad drives home in silence, which I'm thankful is only a few minutes away. I don't think I could take this stillness for too long. I feel so isolated, but I have to keep reminding myself that my parents want what's best for me.

Pulling into the driveway, I lean back and grab my back pack before I make my way up the front garden path and into the house.

Mom is pacing around the family room while chewing on her nails. The moment she sees me, she runs over and embraces me. "Don't ever do that again," she manages to whisper through her tears.

"I'm sorry," I say, still hugging her.

Dad comes in, and shuts the front door. Mom and I are hugging, and I feel Dad's warm and protective arms wrap around us both.

We stand entwined like that for a long time. No one is addressing the elephant — or pregnant teenage girl — in the room. I have to do it. I can't hide from this. "We need to talk," I say.

Dad pulls away first, then Mom. "Yes, we do. And we've both calmed down." Mom walks over to the sofa, and sits. Dad beside her, me opposite the both of them.

"At least now it doesn't feel like a hostile takeover."

Mom sighs, and clasps Dad's hand. "We're calmer now. When we came to your room and found you missing…" Mom clutches at her chest. "It was like the entire world stopped. For us, the most important thing is that you're happy, healthy, and safe. And we failed miserably at that tonight."

Man, that makes me feel so bad. "You didn't. I'm sorry. I knew I had to tell you, and I didn't want to hide it from you. It's not fair of me to do that to you. And besides, I doubt I'd be able to hide it for too long, unless I ran away."

"You did the right thing by coming to us," Dad says. "But we were shocked. We had no idea you were…" He swallows hard before he continues. "…sexually active. It's not something either of us expected to happen so early."

"Most important thing is your safety," Mom cuts in. "Have you thought about what this baby will mean?"

"I've done nothing else *but* think about this baby. It's been killing me keeping this a secret from you both."

"You don't have to go through this on your own. We *are* here for you, even though I know our reactions weren't favorable," Mom continues. "There are many options." She takes a deep breath. "There's adoption, and abortion, and also keeping the baby."

My parents' calmness, places me into an easier frame of mind too. "I don't think I want to abort." I really don't deserve this support from them, but I'm grateful for it.

Mom's brows fly up in surprise. "Then that leaves adoption, or keeping it."

"I don't want her to give the baby up for adoption. It's still our grandchild," Dad says. This nearly floors me. Dad was the one I thought who'd be the most adamant about *not* keeping it.

Mom purses her lips together. She wants to say something, but is holding back. She straightens her shoulders, and chews on her bottom lip. "Say it, Mom." She shakes her head. "Please, just say what you want to. This is the time for honesty."

"This baby will ruin you, Andy. You can't prepare for being a parent. And think about it, when your friends go to prom, you'll be stuck home with a baby. When your friends go to college, you'll be stuck home with a baby. When your friends want to go out for the night, guess what, you'll be stuck home with a baby. Your entire life will change. Forget about sleeping, and your body being your body. For the next few months, all you'll be is a human incubator. Then, you'll be a food supply. And you'll have no time to be a kid, because you'll be looking after this baby. And let's not even think about school. Who's going to look after the baby while you're at school?"

I look down at the carpet, and just stare. "You don't want me to keep this baby, Mom?"

"No, I don't," she answers candidly, "but I love you. And I would do anything for you, except let you dump this baby on me, and continue to live your life as if you didn't have a baby. Children are a lifelong responsibility, Andy. *Lifelong.*"

Standing, I go and sit beside Mom, wedging her between Dad and myself. I throw my arms around her. "I know you're scared, Mom. I'm absolutely terrified. Am I prepared to be a mother? Hell no. Do I have any idea what being a mother is about? Again, no. I'm even more scared than you, one hundred percent. Because all these things you're feeling, I'm feeling them too, plus more. But you know what? This is a bump in the road. A bump, where the direction of my future will change forever. Will this make me a bad mom because I'm young? Hopefully not. Because if you have enough love in your heart to support me, then those tough days won't be so unbearable. I have no idea what I'm doing. But with love and support from you and Dad, we may just get through it and on the other side, your heart may grow enough to include this baby."

Mom cries into my shoulder as she hugs me. "This is a terrible idea."

"I know. But this is the hand fate has dealt me."

"We can alter the future."

"Yes, we can. And so am I, by keeping this baby. I know I'm young, and I can only imagine what people will say once they find out. But, I don't care what others say. Do you?"

"Right now, you want to keep the baby. But it may be different in a few months, Andy. People will treat you differently. They'll look down at you. They'll call you horrible names," Dad says.

"As long as those people aren't you, they can say whatever they want. Most people have known me since I was born. I'm not a trouble-maker, I don't do drugs, drink or party, or do anything else I'm not supposed to do." I think about my words. "Well, except for this." I look down at my stomach. "If they've got a perfect past, they can judge me, but if they've got even one blemish on their record, then they're hypocrites."

"You may be feeling mature right now, but the world is about to turn on its axis," Mom says.

"Then I guess I'd better hang on."

"Laura, she's our baby, and she's *having* a baby. Is it ideal? Of course not. But we have to stick together if we want our family to stay a family. I won't run the risk of losing Andy, or you. We're a family unit. And soon, we'll be adding to it." I can see Dad's not happy about the situation. I wouldn't be either if my fifteen-year-old daughter told she was pregnant, I guess.

CHAPTER 7

"HEY, WHAT HAPPENED? You didn't text me when you got home. I was up all night, worried," Zar says the moment she sees me coming into school.

"Well, we've made a decision about what we're going to do."

Zar claps her hands together with great enthusiasm. "Tell me!"

"I'm keeping it," I say in a low voice while looking around to make sure no one can hear. "And you know what? I slept like a baby. Best night's sleep I've had since I found out."

"Oh my God!" she squeals. "Really?"

"I don't know why you're so excited. You don't have to push a watermelon out of a hole the size of a lime."

Zar crinkles her nose and steps back. "OMG, TMI! But I have an idea. Now, don't say no until you've heard it."

Oh no, what crazy idea has she come up with? "No," I say straight off the bat.

"Just listen. When you tell Alex, if he reacts in a non-favorable way, then I'm coming to all your baby appointments."

"I think my parents will want to do that."

"Good, that means they can give me a ride."

"I'm thinking that you're not going to take no for an answer."

"I'm going to be baby Zar's best aunt in the world."

"Baby Zar?" I question as I open my locker, stick my bag in and take out my laptop and text book.

"Yep, it's a girl. And you're going to call her Zar. After me. Cause, well let's face it, I *am* awesome."

"It might be a boy."

"Girl," she counters quickly. "Are you going to find out?"

"Yeah, of course. I think. I don't know. Maybe? Crap, I haven't thought about it."

"Then baby Zar it is."

"I have to tell Alex first. How do you think he'll react?"

Zar lifts her shoulders in a shrug. "I'd like to say he'll be *so* happy. But hey, he's a guy with his whole future ahead of him. He might react well, but historically, seventeen-year-old guys usually run."

A lump forms at the base of my gut. This is a fear of mine. I still have to face him and tell him. But not here. "I'll tell him after school today. It's the only thing I can do. Mom's booking me into the doctor to see how far along I am, and if the baby is healthy and okay. Zar, I'm terrified."

"And so you should be. This is the most frightening, most beautiful thing you're ever going to do in your life."

"Great. That makes me feel *so* much better," I say sarcastically. "Any other words of wisdom?"

"Andy, this won't be easy. But it'll be worth it. Especially if you don't breed an asshole, and have a decent kid. Now, seeing as *her* name will be Zar, I can't see how you'll go wrong."

There's no use in arguing with Zar. I'll let her have her moments and think this baby is a girl and her name will be Zar. But something tells me this baby is a boy.

I've spent the day avoiding Alex. He knows something's wrong, because he's been sending messages asking what's wrong.

At lunch, I said I had an assignment due, so I went to the library to work on it. He came to find me. I had to get rid of him because I didn't trust myself to say nothing about the baby while at school. And school isn't the right place to tell him.

> *Hey, you've been avoiding me. What's happening?*
> Another message from him.

> **Can we walk home from school together?**

> *Are you going to break up with me? Did I do something wrong?*

I feel even worse. I've been pushing him away, and I haven't stopped to think how this would make him feel. I've been too self-absorbed in my own feelings and haven't thought of him.

> **No, nothing like that. Talk after school.**

> *Are you okay? You've been different.*

> **In class. Talk later. X**

> *X*

My hands are shaking from my nervous energy bubbling inside. In under an hour, I'll be telling Alex I'm pregnant. I'm of two minds about telling him. If I don't tell him, then I can change schools, have the baby, and not screw up his life like I'm screwing up mine. But he has a right to know. He did help create the baby.

I'm too jittery to concentrate in biology. I know there's a quiz coming up, but I'm struggling, only thinking about Alex and what his reaction will be.

I think this is the only time in my school life, where I want the clock hands to slow to a stop. But nope, they're speeding ahead like I'm part of time travel.

The bell sounds for the last class, and I sit, rooted to the spot, unable to stand and leave.

"Andy, are you okay?" my biology teacher asks.

"Yes," I reply without thinking about the question she asked. I'm terrified about what's going to happen next.

"Are you sure? You look pale. Do you want me to call your parents?" I shake my head. She walks to me, and places her hand to my forehead. "Are you sure you're okay?" She sits beside me, and waits for my answer.

"Sorry. I'm um, just dreading something that's about to happen."

"If you're in trouble, I can help." She straightens her shoulders, concerned.

"Oh no. Nothing like that. I'm just nervous." I try to lift my voice so she's not concerned.

"Are you sure? I can walk you out, if you like. Wait with you until you call your parents."

I can't have her hanging around. The news of my pregnancy will spread within weeks once it gets out there. I don't want my teachers judging me already. "I'm okay. I'll be fine." Standing, I pick up my laptop, and turn to leave. But not before turning to the teacher and saying, "Thank you." Rushing out of the classroom, I nearly run to my locker to get my backpack. Not sure why I'm in such a hurry. My guts are twisting with dread, apprehension coursing throughout me. I feel like I'm going to be sick, but I know it's just my nerves because I'm about to tell Alex.

"Hey, beautiful." His voice sends chills down my spine. Today, it's not because I'm excited to see him, but because I'm absolutely terrified.

"Hi," I say, my voice coming out unusually high.

He glares at me, but smirks. "That's a sound I haven't heard before." He leans down to give me a kiss. "And I've heard lots of your sounds," he whispers seductively.

Oh no. This makes me feels even worse. My mouth dries, as my hands shake. I sling my backpack around my shoulders, and shove my hands into my jean pockets; hopeful he doesn't see them trembling.

I start to walk away from the school. Alex is beside me, not talking. He stands nearly a head taller than me, and I can see out of my peripheral vision that he keeps looking down at me before turning to look where he's walking. "Thanks for walking me home today," I say.

"What's wrong?"

I can't bear to look at him. I turn to make sure no one is behind us to hear. "Um, so there is a reason I've been avoiding you."

"You're breaking up with me?" His voice is incredulous and full of pain.

"Well, no. But you'll probably break up with me after what I'm about to tell you."

"Have you been seeing someone else?"

"Oh, no, nothing like that." Our walk slows to almost a stroll. "It's um…" God, how do I tell him? "Um, well, um, you see." I can feel my heart beating so fast in my chest.

"What is it? Are you moving away?"

I stop walking, close my eyes, and blurt, "I'm pregnant." Silence. I'm too afraid to open my eyes. But I do. Because I have to face this. Alex has also stopped walking. His mouth is gaping open, and his shoulders are slumped forward. He's blinking at me rapidly. He's obviously trying to compute what I've just said. I step closer toward him, he steps backward. I move away. "I'm pregnant," I say again.

"I…" He's pointing to me, then him, then back to me. "I…"

"Yes, Alex. You're the father," I answer the question that must be burning on his lips.

"I…" He's still pointing. "I'm um, I'm… a… Whoa." He sits down heavily on the curb, draws his knees up to his chest and hold his head in hands.

I don't dare try to go to him. But I do sit, a distance away. He needs a moment to comprehend it all.

"You're pregnant?" he says, still not looking at me.

"I am."

I can see his chest heaving quickly back and forth. "Pregnant." he says again, less a question this time.

"Are you okay?" I ask.

He swings his head to the side, then jumps to his feet so fast. "Okay? You've been acting so weird, and I had no idea why." He paces back and forth, running his hands through his hair. "You're pregnant and you ask me if I'm okay? There's nothing okay about this. I... I..., do you have any idea what this is going to do to me? I'll have to drop out of school to support... *it*," he spits out the last word with such bitterness. "And you're sitting there all calm and cool, like it's nothing to you. You've ruined my life, Andy! I hope you're happy with yourself. I won't marry you. And really, how do I know that's *my* baby?"

I spring to my feet in less than a second. "Tell me what you heard come out of my mouth? Was it, *Hey Alex, I secretly became pregnant to trap you?* Or did you hear, *Hey Alex, thought it would be fun if we had a child at the age of fifteen and seventeen?* Because I didn't say either of those. I didn't ask you for a God damned thing. I was telling you because it's the right thing to do. You are under no obligation to hang around. But I suggest if you don't want this to happen again with the next girl you stick your dick into then wrap it up. Maybe even twice." I pick my bag up, turn, and leave. I don't look back. He has me fuming with his reaction.

"Andy!" he calls after me.

My arms tense with anger. My shoulders hurt from being so uptight. I expected he would react badly, but I didn't think he'd be reacting *this* badly. I stick my middle finger up at him as I walk away. I can't deal with him right now. I know this will probably be most people's reactions when they find out. But I don't care about *most people*, I care about him.

Taking my phone out, I dial Zar's number. "Ugh. How did it go?" she asks knowing I was going to tell Alex after school.

"Well, let's just say Alex and I are no longer dating."

"Oh no. I'm sorry."

"Don't be. His reaction is enough to tell me he no longer wants to see me."

"So he didn't say you were over?"

"No, not in those words."

"Then, just give him some time. You know, being pregnant at fifteen doesn't just involve you and your family. There's Alex and his too. This is something you've known about for a while, and you've only just told him. Give him time."

"Yeah, I know. And I've given him the option to not be involved. It's not fair to him to demand that he stick around."

"And that's bullshit right there. Part of that baby came from him. That's fine if he doesn't want to stick around, but he's got to take responsibility for this too. You both had consensual sex. Neither forced the other, which means you're both responsible."

"I suppose," I sigh into the phone. My rage has settled now, I'm more thinking about it more as a whole, as opposed to this one incident.

"No *I suppose* about it. You're both responsible regardless of wherever your relationship is going to end up."

"Let's face it, Zar. What are the chances that two high school kids will be together in the future? Not many survive that long."

"You don't have to survive a relationship. You just have to be on the same page. Anyway, what would I know?" She chuckles. "I'm a fifteen-year old virgin, and I'm keeping my legs crossed until I'm forty," she adds sarcastically.

"Really? Forty?" I challenge.

"Well, maybe not forty. But my momma will whoop my ass if I come home pregnant before I finish college. So, nope, not going there. And if I do, I'll be on every birth control method available to me."

"I'm nearly home. I'll talk to you later. Mom's taking to me the doctor."

"Okay. Let me know how it all goes."

"I will. Hey, thank you."

"Baby Zar needs someone normal in her life. I'm the normal."

"Dork."

"Hussy," she replies. Chuckling to myself, I hang up as I get to my front garden.

Mom's car is in the driveway, Dad must still be at work. I take a deep breath, because now reality is going to sink in. We'll be going to the doctor, and the onslaught of questioning looks are about to start.

Awesome.

CHAPTER
8

THE RESULTS CAME back today, and I'm definitely pregnant. *So* pregnant. The doctor has referred us to an OBGYN, so Mom is organizing that. The doctor thinks I'm nine weeks pregnant.

I *know* I'm nine weeks pregnant, because that's the first-time Alex and I had sex.

"Can you help with dinner?" Mom asks.

"What do you need?" I make sure I'm available for her. She's not happy about this whole situation, but she's supporting me, and that's the most I could ask for.

"There's lettuce, tomatoes, cucumbers, and peppers in the fridge. Can you make a salad while I cook the meat?"

"Sure thing." I go to the fridge and take out the ingredients. My stomach rumbles, and I catch a glimpse of the bananas sitting on the breakfast counter. I peel a banana, get the ketchup, and drown it before inhaling it. I see Mom's perplexed stare. "What?"

"Did you just eat a banana soaking in ketchup?"

"Yeah, it's so good."

She dry-retches. "Ketchup and banana… interesting. Not a combination I'd ever think would work. Mind you, when I was pregnant with you, it was grilled cheese. Everywhere I went, all I wanted was grilled cheese."

"I love grilled cheese."

"That's all I wanted. Then I had you, and I never again craved grilled cheese like I did while I was pregnant."

"Funny, hey?"

"I've made the appointment with the OBGYN. She's a woman, seems quite nice. I explained your delicate situation, and she's happy to see you."

"Delicate situation? That I'm fifteen or pregnant?"

"Both."

"When's the appointment?"

"We'll see her in three weeks."

Mom starts cooking the meat, and I can barely hold onto the contents of my stomach. The smell is off. Like the meat is rancid. Running to the bathroom, I make it in just enough time to throw up in the toilet. Mom is only steps behind me. "Go away," I say, not wanting Mom to see me like this.

"I'm your mother, I've seen you in worse shape. Now, let me help." She holds my hair back, while I continue to throw up. And just as quickly as it came on, the nausea has disappeared. "Better?"

"It comes on so suddenly. I get a waft of something that doesn't agree with him, and that's it. I need to throw up."

"It's called morning sickness. But, here's a little secret, it doesn't happen just in the morning."

"Miss Dixon made me warm apple cider with ginger and some other spices. That made me feel better. I'll see if I can get some more from her, or the very least, her recipe."

I brush my teeth, getting rid of that awful taste in my mouth, before heading back out to the kitchen. The meat smell is lingering, and I'm doing my best not to throw up again.

"Your father should be home soon."

"Okay." I breathe through my mouth, trying to get that rotten smell out of my nose.

The doorbell rings, and I walk over to see who it is. I open the door, and there's Alex standing behind his Mom and Dad. "You did this to trick my son into marrying you," his mother attacks before I even have a chance to grasp what's happening. "You know he's going to do something great with his life, and you want to latch onto him. You're no good for him. You're worthless."

"That's enough, Mary," Mr. Wulff says to his wife.

"Emil, this girl is nothing but trouble. She'll bring our son down."

"We talked about this," he says calmly.

"What's going on?" My Mom appears next to me. "Emil, Mary, would you like to come in?"

"Your daughter is a slut!" Mary says.

"You've been a frequent guest in my home, Mary. But if you speak like that about my daughter again, I'll throw your ass out so fast you won't know what hit you," Mom warns through a tight, clenched jaw. "Now, if you want to talk like civilized adults, you're welcome to enter. If not, get out and don't show your face here again."

Mary looks shocked. She drops her gaze for a split second, before lifting them again to look at my mother. She avoids eye contact with me. "I'm sorry," she mumbles to Mom.

"Would you like a drink? A coffee, or a tea?" Mom offers.

"I'd like a water," Mr. Wulff says.

"I'd like one too," Mrs. Wulff echoes.

"Andy, why don't you and Alex go to the kitchen and get some water?"

"She's not going anywhere with my son," Mrs. Wulff says getting defensive again.

"Why? What are you worried about? Her getting pregnant?" Mom asks sarcastically.

I can't help but smile. But I look down, not wanting them to see me smiling. It's not a funny situation, but there's nothing anyone can do about the past. It's done now.

"Andy, Alex." Mom gestures with her head.

Alex and I go to the kitchen. I lean against the kitchen counter, looking down at my feet. "I'm sorry, Alex. I didn't want this to happen. I didn't think it *could* happen. But it has."

"I know and I'm sorry for what I said to you."

"Is that why you weren't at school today?"

"Mom… she's not taking it well." He looks out toward the family room. "She was up all night crying."

I push off from the counter, and come to stand beside him. "I know this isn't ideal. It's definitely not what I wanted. I never even thought of kids. And I really don't expect you to marry me or anything, because I think that's old-fashioned. I just want you to be involved in his life."

"It's a boy?" he asks with what resembles amazement.

"I don't know yet. I just have a feeling." I smile weakly. "I get it. Really, I do. This is a lot to take in. I'm going to be a mom before I turn sixteen. This is going to turn my life upside down."

"I said some really horrible things. When I went home, I told my parents. I was listening to them fighting and screaming, and Mom crying. I stopped thinking about me, and started thinking about you. I'm not the one who's carrying *him*. I'm not the one who has to go through all of this. I don't want you to go through it on your own. That's not fair."

"Andy," Mom calls. That's my cue to come out with the waters. I pour cold water into two glasses, and take them out to Alex's parents. His mom is *not* happy with me, and doesn't even say thank you when I give her the water. Alex's dad does. "We've been talking," Mom starts.

"If you're going to keep it, then we want a paternity test," his mom blurts.

"I've asked you for nothing. I know this is Alex's baby, because he was my first and only."

"A girl like you…"

"Mary. Stop it right now," Mr. Wulff demands. She lowers her gaze, though her thin, pursed lips are busting to say more hurtful things. "Andy, we only learned of this yesterday. And truthfully, we're still in shock. We're trying to understand, what you want to get out of this."

I look at him, tilting my head to the side as if to say… huh? "Well, let me think out loud for a moment, if that's okay with you?" I ask. Mr. Wulff nods his head. "What I want to *get* out of it. Hmmm, so I'll be a sixteen-year-old mother, who'll be forced to re-evaluate my entire life plan, because now it's not just me anymore. It's me plus one." I point to my stomach. "I'll be up through the night looking after him, I'll be the one with sore nipples trying to feed him. I'll be the one who'll be at the doctor with him. I'll be the one who's putting her life on hold to raise him. Mr. Wulff, with all due respect, I want nothing from you. Alex is welcome to be as big a part of this baby's life as he wants. I'm hoping he wants, but I refuse to bully him, or force him to do anything. I love this baby. And I'm hoping, in time, you'll love this baby too."

"Mom, Dad, Andy didn't get pregnant on purpose." I look to Alex, who gives me a small smile. "This wasn't intentional."

"Why aren't you on birth control?" his mom asks.

"Why is it only my daughter's responsibility? Why couldn't Alex have used a condom?" Mom retaliates.

"My son is innocent. She probably persuaded him."

"Mom, she didn't. We already spoke about this."

"She should be on birth control. Because God knows how many more illegitimate children she'll give birth to."

"Enough!" barks Mr. Wulff. "This is bordering on bullying, Mary."

"If we can't talk about this like adults, then leave," Mom says firmly.

"Look." I stand and pace in front of them, gathering all their attention. "This is scary for me too, Mrs. Wulff. I'm only fifteen. I don't know why you insist on shaming me. Maybe it's the only way you can cope. This isn't going to be fun. This definitely isn't going to be easy."

"Then you should adopt it out, or get rid of it," she adds.

I worry my bottom lip between my teeth. "Should you have done that with Alex?" I say hitting her hard.

"How dare you speak to me like that," she nearly screams.

"If I have no right to speak to you like that, then what makes you think you can talk to me in the same way?"

She narrows her brows, and opens her mouth to say something, then stops. It takes a long few seconds before she says, "You're right. I apologize."

"This is a new future for me. If you want to have something to do with your grandchild, I'm prepared to include you. If you don't, then I'm prepared to cut you out of it too."

Mrs. Wulff grabs at her chest. "You don't want us to be included?"

"That's not what she's saying, Mary," Mr. Wulff answers. "I think out of all of us, she's being the most mature one. This isn't an optimal situation for any of us. But let's make it work, because despite the fact they're both so young, she's still carrying our grandchild."

"But..."

"No. We do what we need to in order to make this work." Mr. Wulff turns toward me. "We'd like to be as involved as we can be."

Mrs. Wulff doesn't look so pleased, but she too nods her head. "I'll try not to be so..."

"Judgmental?" I finish her sentence. With shame, she nods her head. "I have an OBGYN appointment in three weeks. You're welcome to attend it."

Mr. Wulff stands, comes over to me and gives me a hug. "Thank you, we'll be there. Just let Alex know the time, date, and address, and we'll be there."

This is awkward. I was expecting more anger from Mr. Wulff, but it seems he's the one with the level head. "Thank you."

"We should be going. Alex, Emil." Mrs. Wulff stands.

"Can I stay for a while?" Alex asks. Mrs. Wulff's jaw flexes. I know she wants to say no, but instead, she nods her head. "I'll walk home later."

"I'll come back to pick you up," his mom insists. She gives me one final glare, and leaves. Mr. Wulff offers me a glimmer of kindness when he smiles.

This is going to be a hard and very long seven months. Especially if I'm met with so much hostility from Alex's mom. Hopefully, she'll come around soon.

"Can we talk?" Alex asks.

I look to Mom, who gives us a head nod. "How about we sit outside for a bit?" I don't want Mom thinking we're in my room doing the dirty. Alex and I head to the back, where we sit at the outdoor table. "You okay?" I ask.

"You know, I'm freaked out. It's not what I wanted."

I chuckle. "You think it's something *I* want?"

"That's not what I mean, Andy. I mean... I never expected this to happen."

"If you insert part A into part B, sometimes part C happens." I look down to my stomach.

Alex breaks into a smile. "I understand the dynamics." His smile is quickly replaced with heartfelt worry. "I don't know what it takes to be a good dad for this baby."

"Just follow in the steps of your parents. Your mom, although she hates me, is still a good mom. She's protective, that's all. And your dad, he's kind and compassionate and understanding."

"How did we get ourselves in this mess?"

"When part A is inserted into part B…"

He smiles again. "You're a dork."

"Yep, I am. But now, I'm a pregnant dork." The mood changes between us again. It becomes more intense. "Alex, you don't have to stick around. I'm giving you a way out. If you don't want to be part of this, you don't have to."

"No, we're both responsible. But in saying that, I have to get my head on right before I can commit to you."

"I don't want you to do something you don't want. How about, for now, we just take a break?"

"You're breaking up with me?" he asks, hurt.

"Not breaking up, just letting this…" I rub my hand on my stomach. "…catch up with this." I tap my temple.

"I don't want to see anyone else, and I don't want you to be seeing anyone else either."

"Yes, because I'm such a catch. Hey, I'm fifteen and pregnant, wanna go out?" I say sarcastically.

"You're adorable. Even though you're pregnant."

"Ha! I'm not sure how to take that. It's kind of an insult met with a backhanded compliment."

"You know what I mean."

Shrugging, I give him a small smile.

I have no idea what the future holds for Alex and me. Whatever it is, I know he's not a bad person, and hopefully he'll be in our son's life forever.

CHAPTER
9

"I TALKED TO my parents, and they said you can come to the OBGYN if you like. It's next week. But the appointment is on Monday at eleven, which means you're going to have to miss school," I say to Zar.

"I'll ask Mom, but I don't think she'll let me take the day off school." She picks at her lunch, and I eat my banana. Which, incidentally, has become a staple for me. Bananas and ketchup washed down with apple and ginger cider.

"I'm nervous about it. I've been thinking, what if I'm pregnant with twins, or triplets?"

"Girl, then you're screwed. I mean, you're *really* screwed. Fifteen with triplet newborns. Whoa, I wouldn't wish that on my own worst enemy. Anyway, you haven't started showing yet, so I doubt you've got more than one in there." She nibbles on her lunch.

"Chances are low. Twins don't run in my family. And I don't think they run in Alex's either."

"How's it going with you two?"

I turn my head, and shrug my shoulders. "We're not… I don't know. It's just kinda weird now. We talk, but it's different. It's more strained. I feel like I'm doing something wrong all the time. And I feel guilty he's involved. I gave him the option to just, you know leave."

"You did what?" Zar nearly yells, causing a few of our friends to turn and look at us.

So far, no one knows about my condition. But I don't expect it's going to stay a secret for long. "It's what I thought was fair."

"Fair for him? Giving him the easy way out? No way. He's involved. We've already talked about this. He was there when you both did the deed. Neither of you had to do it, but you both chose to. Now, you're both responsible."

"That's all well and good in the make-believe world, or a book, or a movie, but here in reality, the chances he's going to stick around are quite slim. And I don't want to force anyone to be in my son's life if they don't want to be there."

Zar shakes her head. "You girl, are one dumb-ass. Besides for obviously getting yourself into this position to start with. But no, you don't give him a choice. If he walks out, then that's on him, you don't give him the option to leave. He stays, and he looks after baby Zar too. None of this bullshit again, Andy."

"I know. I just feel so bad."

"You'll be feeling something else when you're pushing her out," she adds with sass.

"It's a boy."

"It's not, it's a girl."

"I have a feeling, it's a boy. I have psychic abilities."

Zar glares at me, with her chin tilted down. "You mean psycho!"

"He hasn't been sitting with us. Have you noticed that?"

"Yeah, I have. Thought maybe you had a fight or something."

I turn to look for him, and he's not even here. Alex has been avoiding me, but I do understand. Jessica, Bek, and Angie walk over to sit with us. "Hey," Angie says as she sits beside me. "What's happening?"

"Nothing," I answer. "Just talking."

"Where's Alex? Are you two still together?" Jessica asks.

"It's kinda complicated. We're not *not* together. We're just kinda taking a break."

"Is everything alright?" Bek asks, looking concerned.

Jessica, Bek, and Angie are really nice. We're not best of friends, but we hang out from time to time and get along well.

Then, there's Blair and Ruby, who are sisters. Those two have a posse of girls who hang around with them, and they're nothing but horrible bitches. They make everyone's lives a living hell. But because their parents come from money, they think they can say and do whatever they want.

"Yeah, everything's fine. Just stuff." I add in a casual shoulder shrug.

"If you want to talk," Bek says with a smile. She's sweet. She always has been.

"Thanks." I smile, dreading what she's going to say once she finds out. Actually, I'm dreading what everyone is going to say. I guess, I won't have to wait for long.

"Hey." Out of nowhere, Alex appears, leans down and gives me a soft, gentle kiss on the cheek. It's strained between us, but this is the first time since we talked that he's trying. "How are you?" He looks at the girls sitting at the table with me, silently asking if they know. I slightly shake my head.

"I'm okay. You?"

"Getting there." He stands awkwardly for a moment, flagged by Hunter and Finn. I look to Zar who's giving Hunter googly eyes.

"Hey, Alex," Blair flirts as she walks past with Ruby.

"Ugh," Zar grumbles. "One day, I'm going to punch that girl in the face."

"It's not worth it. You'll get suspended and your mom will be mad."

Alex looks at Blair and gives her an awkward head nod. It's a cross between 'I don't want to talk to you' and 'why are you talking to me.' "I can't stand her," Alex says.

"She's been trying to ride your stick for ages," Hunter blurts.

I look to him. His face reddens and his eyes widen as he catches me glaring at him. "I'm sorry."

"It's not like I don't know, but really? I'm sitting right here."

"Sorry, Andy," he sheepishly replies.

Blair and Ruby sit at their regular table, Blair keeps turning to look at Alex. I'm about two seconds away from ripping her a new one, but I decide against it. It's not good for me, or my boy.

"I've got practice. So I'll catch you later?" Alex asks.

"No, you don't," Hunter reveals. "We don't have practice 'til tomorrow." He sees the look of disbelief on Alex's face, then adds quickly, "Oh yeah, I remember. Coach called an extra practice."

"You suck at lying," Zar says. "Like really bad."

"Sorry." He ducks his head.

"Walk you home?" Alex asks. I nod then he gives me another kiss on the cheek before he leaves.

Bek leans in, making sure no one can hear. Zar is staring at Hunter's butt as he and Alex leave, and Jessica and Angie are talking between themselves. "You sure you're okay?"

Should I tell her? Bek is really nice, and I don't think she'll say anything, but I don't want to risk it either. People will find out, it's really only a matter of time. And the fact that Alex and I are avoiding each other, people might start talking. I really should tell her. No, not yet. This internal battle is only the beginning. Finally, I choose not to share it with her yet. "Yeah, you know." I end it there, not wanting to dwell on anymore.

"Okay." She smiles at me. But I can tell, she knows there's more to this than I'm letting on.

The lunch bell rings. Zar and I stand, and make our way to our next class. "That Blair," she grumbles again. "I tell ya, I don't like her at all."

"Don't worry about it."

"The fact she flirts with Alex in front of you, makes me want to hit her."

"Honestly, don't worry about. I've never worried about it before."

"She ain't taking him from you."

"It isn't taking if he willingly goes."

"If he goes to her, I'm smacking him harder than I'm smacking her." Zar holds her hands up in surrender. "You can't help stupid, but you can certainly fight hormones."

And right at that moment, Blair, and Ruby walk together, in the opposite direction. "Hi Andy," Blair says with a wicked smirk plastered on her face. I give her a head nod. What is it with these two? "Have you seen Alex?"

My blood's boiling with anger. "Yeah, I did," I lie. "He's coming over to my house after school, do you want me to give him a message?"

Ruby giggles behind her hand. They want to get a reaction out of me. "Oh no, I'll catch up with him later."

"I'll tell him you're looking for him." I keep walking, ignoring her and her bitchy sister.

"Bye Andy," Ruby calls.

"Is it bad that I want to flick them the bird?" Zar asks. "But I really want to wipe that stupid smile off their faces."

"Just ignore them. In the grand scheme of things, they're nothing to me."

"Oh, snap. Andy's all grown up now." Zar snaps her fingers with sass.

Chuckling, I roll my eyes as we walk to class.

"Blair is hitting on me hard. I tell you she thinks she's the be-all and end-all. She just loves herself so much," Alex says as we walk home together.

I chuckle at what he thinks of her. "She's not exactly hiding how she feels about you."

"She even told me she wouldn't say anything to you if I wanted to have a little fun with her. Nearly made my balls shrivel up."

I burst into laughter. "She's that bad?"

"I have no idea how many guys at school have been through her. I hate that she thinks she can do this."

"No need to shame her for liking sex."

"Oh, I'm not. I'm shaming her for being shameless with me. I mean, she knows we're dating, but she still keeps trying."

"Are we?"

"Are we what?"

"Are we still dating?"

Alex slows and kicks a pebble. It flitters along the road ahead of us. He doesn't answer the question. The silence between us is painful. I want to say something, but at the same time, I don't want to make his mind up for him. He has to decide for himself. "Yeah, we are."

"Then why have you been avoiding me? I know I said we should cool it, but it feels arctic between us."

"Because this is weird," he replies with a gesture between us.

"Weird? As in how?"

"One minute we're dating, the next I'm going to be a father. I wasn't prepared for it. I get it, you weren't either, but it's just weird. Kids never even crossed my mind."

"Yeah, I get it. It's intense, and a lot to handle. Thankfully we have seven months to get a grip with it and deal with the situation."

"You know what's heaps strange?"

"What?"

"In fifteen years, you'll be thirty with a fifteen-year-old. And I'll be thirty-two with a fifteen-year-old. How bizarre."

My eye twitches when he breaks it down so bluntly. "He better not be a parent at our age. I'll kick his damn ass."

"Ha! Ironic, right?"

"No!" I nearly yell at him. "Okay, yes, it is. But he better not." We keep walking home. "How are your parents coping?"

"Mom is beside herself. She's so angry and upset. One minute she's yelling, the next she's crying. I've never seen her in a temper like this. But Dad, he's chill. A bit too chill. I think he's compensating for Mom's mood swings. She keeps saying I'm too young, and how you'll ru..." he stops talking, catching himself before he finishes.

"Ruin your life?" Alex turns his head, not wanting to look at me. "Thought so."

"She's not coping. I'm hoping she'll be okay though."

"Are you coming to the OBGYN next week?"

"I'll definitely be there. Not sure about Mom yet though. Dad too, he'll be there."

"Right." I purse my lips together. I suppose finding happiness will be something they'll struggle with. I guess I will, too. We round the corner to my house, and I look to see neither of my parents are home. But I'm tired, and don't want to invite Alex in. I'm still not really sure where we stand. Only time will tell. "Thanks for walking me home." We both stop outside my home, and Alex looks to me, waiting for me to invite him in. "I'm going to lie down for a bit until Mom and Dad get home. I'm working tomorrow, maybe we can hang out after work?"

His jaw flexes, and I can see, this is obviously a problem for him. "My Mom wants me to break up with you."

My brows fly up, and I worry my bottom lip between my teeth. "Of course, she does," I mumble under my breath but still loud enough for him to hear. "I'm sorry, I shouldn't be nasty. I think I'd react the same way."

"I'm not going to though."

I love how Alex is willing to stand up to his mom, but in reality, he's still her son, and I'm still the fifteen-year-old girl who's pregnant. "I gotta go. I'll see you Monday, right?" I don't bring up hanging out with him tomorrow again. It's best if we take some time.

"At the OBGYN. Yep."

I give him a hug, but even that is awkward now. "Bye." I reach up and give him a kiss on the cheek.

This has been a weird day.

CHAPTER
10

"Y OUR SHIFT DOESN'T start until 10 today. What brings you in so early?" Clarence asks as I arrive for my day at CCC's.

"Mom had some errands to run, so I had to come in with her."

Clarence smiles at me, her eyes traveling the length of my body. "You look different today, Andy."

"Do I?" Instantly I freeze on the spot, hoping I'm not showing yet. Which is dumb, because I know I'm not. "I haven't really been sleeping well."

"Really? But your skin looks so… like you've had a facelift. It's so radiant."

I gulp. I've been reading a lot about pregnant women, and one of the most common things people say is how they look like they're glowing. "I ah, I'm not, ah, okay." Smiling, I see there's two tables yet to be cleaned. I hurry to clean them, opting to exit this conversation as fast as possible before I slip up and tell her. Or worse, she figures it out.

"You okay? You're acting a bit peculiar."

"I'm fine," I call from the front. A customer comes in, and I find instant relief that I don't have to be subjected to Clarence's line of questioning anymore. I'm going to tell her, just not yet.

When I finish with this customer, another two come in. The busy time of the day is starting, and this gives me the opportunity to focus on them, and not myself.

The café is getting busier, and Clarence is buzzing behind the counter. Arthur comes in at the right time, and helps by clearing the tables.

It takes a few hours for the rush to calm, and by that time I'm ravenous. I want to eat everything Clarence has in the store. Thankfully, I brought bananas and a container of ketchup. "Clarence, I'm a bit hungry. Do you mind if I go out back for a moment and have a quick bite?"

"I'll look after the front. You go eat. Cake?" she offers.

Cake really isn't going to cut it. My craving is for bananas with ketchup and apple cider. "Not at the moment."

"You sick, child?" Clarence asks, surprised by reaction. I don't think I've ever turned down cake, not from Clarence.

"I'm just a bit turned off cake. I don't know what's wrong with me."

"Hmm," she grumbles and narrows her eyes at me. "You better not be getting sick."

"I'm not," I reassure her. *Trust me, I'm not.*

"Then, go eat. Come back when you're ready."

Sneaking out the back, I grab my bananas and my container with ketchup. I peel my first banana then dunk it in the ketchup.

Just as I take a bite, Clarence walks in and stops. She looks at the clear container with something red in one hand, and the banana in my other. My mouth chewing frantically. "Are you eating a banana with jam?" She comes closer, the smell of the ketchup catching her by surprise. "Ketchup?" She quizzically tilts her head, not quite understanding my choices.

"Yeah, it's a banana and ketchup." Now I'm freaking out. I

can imagine the look on my face, because I can feel myself frowning with worry.

"Banana and ketchup?" I swallow hard, but nod. "Together?" I nod again, remaining quiet. "Why would someone do such a thing? That poor banana. Ruining it with ketchup." She shakes her head, like she's trying to dislodge an offensive image. "I've only ever seen such bizarre things when women are…" she stops talking. Looks up, her mouth wide open.

I cringe, and let out a long breath.

Here's where she's going to ask if I'm pregnant. And here's where I'm not going to lie and say no.

I wait with agonizing pain in my heart, because I'm hoping she doesn't think badly of me.

"Andy…" she draws out my name. Tears well up in my eyes as I lower my head, unable to look at her. "Oh Andy." She rushes over to me, and hugs me tight. "You're so young," she whispers. Arthur walks in and sees us embracing. "Nothing to see here, Arthur. Nothing to see," she snaps at him as she shoos him back to the front of the café.

I snicker. "Yeah, I know."

She lets go of me, and backs away. "Do your parents know?" I nod my head. "And Alex?" I nod again. "And his parents?" I crinkle my mouth, but nod. "Oh, like that is it?"

"His mom isn't taking it well."

"I wouldn't be taking it well either. But, these things do happen, and we have to keep moving forward. What are your plans for the future?"

"I'm keeping it."

"Whoa," Clarence says as she steps back further and leans against the counter. "You're going to have to develop a thick skin, my dear. Because the moment everyone finds out, you'll be open for a lot of scrutiny and criticism. But I hope that some will show kindness toward you, too."

"You're optimistic. I'm not. All I've gotten so far is

judgement. Well, except from you and Zar. Well…" I look away thinking, "Even Zar was a bit judgmental."

"Don't confuse judgment and shock. People will say things when they're shocked, but quickly apologize for it once they realize what they've said. Being judgmental though, that can be toxic."

"I know I'm young, and I know I have no idea what I'm doing. What I'm definitely sure of is that I can't do this on my own."

"Lucky you have your parents, and Arthur and me. We'll help with whatever we can."

"Thank you." My stomach rumbles, reminding me to eat my banana.

"I interrupted your food. Do you want some cake?"

"I've been craving bananas with ketchup."

"Stand up, let me take a good look at you." I stand, and Clarence holds out my arms wide. She casts a wary eye over my body. "It's a girl," she says with confidence.

"I'm convinced it's a boy."

"Mother knows best, but I think you're wrong. I think it's a girl."

I shake my head. "I think *you're* wrong." She gives me a hug. "Thank you," I whisper.

"You work here for as long as you can, then when you're ready, you can come back." Clarence is so beautiful and sweet. "But for now, I have to get back to work, and you need to eat."

Clarence walks out to the front, and continues with the orders Arthur's been taking. I eat my bananas with ketchup. Three bananas, and ketchup.

"Cake?" Clarence asks again. It's toward the end of the day, and we've been fairly consistent even after the lunch rush.

"You know, I really wouldn't mind some."

"Red velvet or chocolate and orange?"

"Actually, the chocolate and orange." I've been eyeing it since I got in to work.

"One piece of… no, make it two pieces of chocolate and orange cake coming right up. Why don't you finish with the dishwasher, and wipe down the tables? I'll get the cake ready for you."

Stacking the last of the dishes into the dishwasher, I get the cleaning products and go out to wipe the tables. Clarence goes back into the store room and I'm left out the front on my own. Arthur left to get more strawberries for Clarence's strawberry jam from a farm that's about an hour away.

"Oh my God!" the voice is a high-pitched shriek. And attached to Blair. "I didn't know you worked here." She looks around the small café, her face drawn into a look of disgust.

"Hi Blair. Hi Ruby." I give Ruby a small courteous nod.

"Hi Candy," Ruby says then looks down at her phone.

"Andy," I correct, but know she's saying it to irritate me. She knows my name.

"Whatever. Make me a coffee. Decaf soy latte, extra shot and cream," Ruby says. Soy *and* cream? Really? Defeats the purpose, doesn't it?

"And I'll have a non-fat Frappuccino with extra whipped cream and chocolate sauce." Non-fat with extra whipped cream and chocolate sauce? Are they serious?

Pretentious much? "We're not Starbucks. We don't have that. I can make you a coffee, or a tea if you prefer. But we do have really good shakes."

"Ewww, a shake? That's just pure fat."

"What's cream and chocolate sauce?" I blurt before thinking.

Ruby straightens her back, while Blair's face morphs into a mask of rage. "Excuse me, are you talking back to me? The customer is always right!" Ruby yells. Blair stands closer to her, making sure she knows she has her back.

Holding my hands up in surrender, I bite my tongue, choosing to ignore their outburst. "My apologies," I say.

"You *should* apologize! And I think you should comp us for being such a bitch," Blair says.

"I beg your pardon. You don't talk to my employees that way. I heard the entire thing, and you are nasty. Get out of my café," Clarence says as she comes to stand beside me.

"It's okay," I say in a low voice.

"Get out, and don't come back. Because I will find your parents, and I'll tell them what horrible, petty little children they have."

Blair's mouth falls open, her eyes wide. Ruby clenches her jaw but opts to remain quiet. Clarence crosses her arms on her chest and stands her ground, refusing to budge until they leave.

Both Blair and Ruby leave the store. When they walk past the front window, they stick their middle finger up at us.

"If they were my kids, they'd have their booty whipped red." Clarence turns and rubs my tummy. "We have to make sure you're protected, little one."

I smile at Clarence. "They're from my school. Blair, the one on the left, she's been flirting with Alex. I can handle them. They're pretty easy to ignore."

"Girls can be so horrible. Mind you, boys can be just as bad. Anyway, I got your cake." She pointedly looks over to counter, and there's one huge slice of chocolate and orange cake. It's bigger than two pieces put together.

"Yum," I say as I pick it up.

Armed with my container of cake, Clarence sends me home. Alex is outside waiting for me. Clarence sees him before I leave, and calls him in. Alex looks puzzled, but comes into the now closed café. "Hi Clarence," he says as he enters.

"You, my boy, are going to be a father." Alex looks at me,

shocked that I told her. "She didn't say anything; I guessed. I'm hoping that regardless of what the future holds for both of you, you'll be there for this baby."

Alex visibly swallows hard. He peers down at his feet, before lifting his head and nodding. "I will be, ma'am."

"Good. Do you know she's craving bananas with ketchup? Keep her well supplied with those."

"Clarence," I murmur. "It's okay."

"The boy can at least keep a steady supply of those for you."

I know she means well. "I'll see you next week."

"Good luck on Monday," she says, knowing about the doctor's appointment I told her about earlier in a quiet moment.

"Thank you." I hold up the container of cake. Alex and I leave. "I'm sorry. She did guess. She saw me eating my banana, and saw the ketchup and put it together."

"She was bound to find out sooner or later." He opens the passenger door of his Dad's car for me, and waits until I'm in before closing the door and jogging around to the driver's side.

He gets in, starts the car, but we sit stationary for a moment. "You okay?" I ask.

"It's kind of surreal to me."

"Yep, I know the feeling. It's like I'm walking on eggshells, waiting for something to happen."

"Like what?"

"Like everyone finding out, and I don't know…" I'm frustrated. I know everyone *will* find out, it's inevitable. "I just don't know," I express again. Alex pulls out on the street, and drives toward my house. I don't want to go home yet. "Can we go somewhere?"

"Like where?"

"How about we head toward the lake? I just don't want to go home yet."

"Um, yeah, sure."

I send a text to Mom. *Going to be a bit late, heading out to the lake with Alex. Won't be long. Just need to talk with him.*

Be home by seven.

"Mom wants me home by seven."

"Yeah, my mom will probably freak out. But it's okay. I'll let her know where I am when we get to the lake."

The drive out isn't long, maybe around fifteen minutes. "It's so pretty out here," I say as I stare at the rolling green meadows and the tall trees lining the highway. "Peaceful." I take my hair out of the ponytail, and redo it, putting in a messy topknot.

"It is."

The tension between us is mounting. But Alex is trying, and for that, I have to give him credit. We arrive at the lake and Alex parks the car. Getting out, he takes my hand in his, and we walk toward the body of water. Sitting on one of the many benches, I look out at the calm, still water. "Alex."

"Yeah."

I take a breath in. "I'm sorry."

"Why?"

"I didn't mean for this to happen. I didn't want to trap you or try to get you to stay with me. It really was, for the lack of a better word, an accident."

"I know. What I said to you, I didn't mean it."

"It's okay, I know you were shocked. Hell, so was I."

"I can't imagine what it's like for you. You kept it a secret, not saying anything to anyone. You don't have to keep things from me. I'm so sorry, Andy. I reacted really badly."

I look to him, smiling. "It's okay. You're here now, and that's all that matters."

"Can I say, I'm actually looking forward to Monday. I'm not sure Mom will be coming." He grimaces. Judging by her reaction, I don't think his mom wants anything to do with our baby. "She's coming around, slowly," he says, trying to sound positive.

"That's great," I say. But I don't believe him. "Both my parents will be there on Monday too. Zar wants to come, but her mom said she can't miss out on school."

"I go to bed every night, and it takes me ages to fall asleep. I'm still in shock."

"You and me both. But the fact is, this is happening." I notice Alex looking at my stomach. "What?"

"When will you start to…?" He makes a ball like motion around his stomach.

"When will I start showing? I have no idea. I reckon once it's bigger than a pea."

"It's the size of a pea?"

"Probably smaller. I don't know. We'll find out on Monday."

"What if we're having twins?"

I start laughing. "I've been worried about that too, but I doubt it. Twins don't run in my family."

Alex turns to me, his face pale and his eyes filled with fear. "What if we're having triplets?" He gags, like he's about to throw up. "Oh my God." Letting go of my hand, he grips his head, and bends at the waist. Breathing frantically, I can't help but laugh at him. "I'm not sure I could do twins, or triplets. I'm barely coping with the idea of just one."

"You have to stop freaking out." I rub my hand on his back. "I really don't think there's more than one in here."

"How do you know?"

"I have a feeling. Like I have a feeling it's a boy."

He turns his head, the rapid breathing easing to something more sedate. "You think it's a boy?"

"Yeah, I told you before."

"Did you? Anyway, a boy?"

"Yeah."

"What's his name going to be? I like Alex Wulff Junior. Has a nice sound to it."

"Well, no. Whatever his first name is going to be, his last name will be Price."

"But he's my son. He should have my name."

"I tell you what. You carry him, you birth him, and you breast feed him, and he can have your last name."

"That's impossible. I can't do that."

"And I won't give him your surname. I'm carrying him for nine months, and he'll have my last name."

"But the right thing to do is to give him his father's last name."

Standing, I'm becoming frustrated with him. "I'm sorry, but no. If we were married and I took on your last name, then yes, I'd be happy to give him your name. And this is not a gimmick to get us married, because we're way too young for that. We're way too young for this too." I rub my stomach. "But it's done now."

"He should have my name." Alex is adamant.

"Great. So we've decided he'll have my name."

"No, that's not us deciding. He should have mine."

"That's not going to happen, Alex. I'm going to be the one who's up with him when he's sick. When he's crying at three in the morning. Me, not you. He's going to have my last name, not yours."

"This isn't right, Andy." He shakes his head. His red face tells me how bitter he is. But this is something I'm not going to cave on. "He should take my name."

"I'm not even going to apologize for this. The answer is no. He'll be a Price; my decision is final."

"I can't believe you," he grumbles.

"Okay, give me your reasoning as to why he should be a Wulff and not a Price."

"Because it's tradition. It's what's supposed to happen."

"Tradition went out when our parents got married. The

world is changing, and you better keep up. This little guy, he's a Price. And if he wants to take your name on when he's legally old enough to do so, he can. But he'll be a Price."

"What about, if he's a Wulff-Price?"

I think about it for a few seconds. "It's not offensive. I'm not saying yes, but I am saying I'll consider a hyphened surname."

"I can live with that, I suppose."

It's a reasonable request. I sit down next to Alex, both of us staring out at the water. "I don't want us to fight about everything, Alex. We have to find a way to be on the same page. To do what's best for our son, rather than what's best for us."

"Like him taking my last name," he grumbles.

"Like how we're going to bring him up. And how we're going to make sure he has everything he needs, so he doesn't end up being a statistic."

"I'll get a job," he says quickly. "I've been thinking about dropping out of school, and finding a job."

"That is the dumbest thing I've ever heard, Alex. What are you going to do? Do you think you'll be happy flipping burgers for the rest of your life? You have to go to college and study chemistry. It's what you love. And I don't want you resenting me or our son."

"I would never resent you," he quickly says.

"Yeah? Tell me, how do you think you'll feel watching your dreams slip away because you have to be here, working a job where there's no opportunity for you. You can't drop out of school."

"Well it's my choice, and if I want to, I'll drop out."

I can't sit back and let him do this. It's not fair on him. "You won't be able to give our son everything he needs if you drop out now."

"It's my damn life, Andy. And I'll be dropping out of high school," he says with finality.

It pains me, absolutely makes my heart hurt with grief. But I can't let him do it, or he'll have a life of misery. Gathering all my strength, I stand and walk toward the car. "Take me home," I say. "We're done." Tears spring to my eyes. I'm being the bad person again. I got pregnant, and now I'm refusing to let him throw his life away. "You and I are done."

"Wait, Andy." He catches up to me as I walk to the car. Grabbing me by the upper arm, he swings me around to look at him. "Why are you doing this?"

"I won't let you throw your life away just because we made one mistake. I won't let you keep making mistake after mistake. This is going to affect everyone. You leaving school isn't a smart thing to do. You love chemistry, and now you want to give it up?"

"To support you and our son."

"But you won't be supporting us. Can't you see? If our son has a mother and father who are both high-school drop-outs, what chance does he have?"

Alex steps back, his lips in a tight, thin line. "You're worried," he finally says.

"Of course, I'm worried. I'm worried for him." I nod toward my stomach. "For you." I point to Alex. "And for myself. I never, in a million years, thought I'd be fifteen and pregnant. Sixteen with a baby. But this is forcing me to grow up fast, and look at what I can give him. Not what I can do for myself. Because it's not about me anymore. It's about him. And making *his* life worth living."

Alex takes a step closer to me. I counter with a step backward. The more distance between us, the better. "You'd be willing to break up with me because you're worried about his and my future?"

"I want the best in life for all of us. But, yes. I don't want you ruining the chances you have because we had unprotected sex."

"This is the first time I've heard you referring to our son as a mistake."

"He's not a mistake. What we did was. We should've been more careful. Both of us were stupid for thinking the withdrawal method was sufficient. But, him." I rub my hand over my stomach. "He's not a mistake. He's going to be anything but a mistake."

Alex smiles and we continue toward the car. "Okay, I won't leave school."

"Good."

"No more talk of breaking up. Though, it would make my mom happy."

Pained, I let out a small sigh. No more talk of breaking up. We'll just see how everything goes. We're *so* damned young.

CHAPTER
11

A LEX'S MOM AND dad, Alex, my parents, and I are all sitting in the doctor's office waiting room.

The room has pictures of babies on the wall. So many of them. The room is light and airy, with themes of baby pink and pale blue everywhere. In one corner, there's a small bookshelf, lined with children's books. And beside it, there's a children's table with blank sheets of paper and colored pencils.

There's only us, and another woman in the waiting room. She's heavily pregnant and looks uncomfortable. I can't help but think how I'll feel when I'm at that stage in the pregnancy.

She looks at me and smiles. But her eyes quickly take in the army of people I have with me. I can see she's trying to process who's actually pregnant.

Surprising even me is the fact Alex's mom is here. She is young looking, and it quite easily could be her having another child.

The pregnant woman is still studying us.

"Andy, Doctor Morgan is ready for you," the receptionist says as he waits for me to follow him into the doctor's office.

Standing first, I grab onto Mom's hand. "You're coming with me, aren't you?"

"Of course." Mom stands. Then the rest of my entourage stands too. "We'll go in first, then I'll come get you," Mom says to everyone else. "Robert." She gestures for Dad to come in with us.

"I want to be there too," Alex's mom says as she stands.

"I'm sorry, Mary, but not yet. I'll come to get you when we're ready," Mom says, standing her ground.

Alex's mom sits again. She rolls her eyes and grumbles something beneath her breath. The heavily pregnant woman is trying not to watch, but she looks like she's enthralled by the drama now. She's probably also blinded by the fact it's me who's pregnant, and not Alex's mom.

My parents and I head into an office that's fairly warm and friendly. An older woman sits behind this big, beautiful, wooden desk. I can tell, this is a desk that's probably been in her family for many generations. It has gorgeous carvings in the wood edges, and is the richest of browns. The top of her desk is strewn with many papers. A lot in piles, some, loosely shuffled into make-shift stacks.

She looks up, and sees my parents, then me.

Looking down at her paperwork, she reads it before looking up again. "You're Andy?" I nod my head. "And you're fifteen?" I nod again. "You'll be sixteen in nine months?" I nod again.

The impending question is burning in my mind.

"The father of the baby?" her voice is cold, stern.

"He's sitting out in the waiting room with his parents," I answer.

"How old is he?"

"Seventeen."

"Bring him in."

When I go out to the waiting room. Alex sees me, and stands immediately, followed by his parents. "She wants to see you," I say.

Alex looks over his shoulder at his dad, obviously needing his support. "We'll come in too."

I lead them into her office and they stand behind where I sit. She's scribbling something on a piece of paper. "You're the father?" she asks Alex in her no-nonsense tone.

"Yes, ma'am," he replies with a shaky voice.

"Were you trying to get pregnant?" Dr Morgan asks sharply.

"No!" Alex and I both reply quickly.

"No, ma'am," Alex says. "We were just dumb. We should've used protection. But we didn't. I withdrew before I..." Alex is obviously uncomfortable talking about it. His cheeks pinken, and he lowers his head.

"Before you ejaculated. Well, now you know that method is near useless," Doctor Morgan says. "I'm satisfied. You can leave." She looks back down at her paper.

"Mom, Dad," Alex says and indicates for them to leave.

Again, his mom looks less than impressed. I'm not even sure why she wants to be here. They leave, but not before his mom huffs a few times.

"Now, first day of your last period?"

"I can tell you the day I got pregnant, because it was the first-time Alex and I had sex."

"First time, hey?" I nod. "First time and pregnant."

"I know." My shoulders sink. I feel so bad. She's making me feel bad about myself. "I already feel like a failure. And I'm terrified. So there's not much you can say to make me feel worse."

"I'm not here to baby you, Andy. I'm here to help you through the next few months. You'll be judged and ridiculed and who knows what else by everyone around you. You're going to have to develop a thick skin. But my job is to make sure you and that baby are both safe throughout the entire pregnancy, and after. Now, when did you have sex?"

I give her the date, and she types it into her laptop that's sitting open beside the paperwork. "I think I'm nine weeks and four days pregnant."

"You are." Mom squeezes my hand. Doctor Morgan gives me my due date according to when I got pregnant. "We'll do an ultrasound to make sure everything's okay. But first, being fifteen and pregnant is going to be challenging. First, I'll need to see you more often then I normally would anyone else. I'll be sending you for more blood tests than I normally would. The risks you're facing are high blood pressure, anemia, and one of the biggest risks is that the baby's head will be bigger that your pelvis. Meaning we might be looking at doing a caesarean."

I feel my forehead crinkling. "Caesarean? Where you make an incision?"

"If it's needed, yes, that's what we'll be doing."

"Will that likely happen?" Mom asks.

"Because of Andy's age, it's a possibility. She's not fully grown yet. And the other high risk is a pre-term birth. So, I'll be monitoring for all of this, and making sure Andy and the baby are doing well."

The more Doctor Morgan talks, the more I'm becoming horrified. But interestingly, the more I understand about the risks just because of my age. "Will the baby be okay?" I finally ask as my mind clears.

"Both you and the baby should be fine. We will have to keep a close eye on you."

Worry suffocates me. Worry for me, for my son, and for my parents. "It'll be okay," Mom says, reassuring me.

"I'm going to ask a hard question here, Doc," Dad says, speaking for the first time since we've been in here.

"Which is?"

"Is my daughter at risk of dying because of her age? If that's a risk, we're not going to go ahead with this pregnancy."

"Dad?" I whisper.

"I'm not losing you." His shoulders are back in a rigid line, but I know this is tearing him apart. "I'm not living a day on this earth without the people I love. And you bury us, we don't bury you."

My heart hurts. "Dad." Tears well in my eyes, but they don't break through.

"The only real risk is if you didn't seek medical advice. You're here now, and I'll be keeping a close eye on every stage of Andy's pregnancy. Which is why I'll be seeing you every month until you're seven months. Then every two weeks until you're eight months, and every week after that until you have the baby."

"No risk?" Dad asks again, wanting reassurance.

"There's always risk. But with today's technology and medical advancements, the risk is lesser."

Dad seems satisfied with Doctor Morgan's reply. "Okay." Dad nods.

"Now, I've got a small ultrasound machine here. I'd like to have a look at the baby, see how it's doing. Would you like Alex and his family in here with you?" She looks to me, asking my opinion.

I nod. "Can I go get them?"

"They're not going to be able to see from out there. Before you do, jump on the scales so we can make a note of your weight."

I stand, take my shoes off and get on the scales. "Hundred and fourteen," I read the numbers flashing at me.

"Good. You know you'll put weight on?"

"Yes, with the number of bananas and ketchup I've been eating."

Doctor Morgan smiles. This is the first time I've seen her looking anything but severe. "Go get the others."

I head out to the waiting room and call for Alex to come in. Alex and his parents follow me.

"Andy, up on the exam table." Doctor Morgan points to it. "Undo your jeans, and slide them down a bit." I do. "This is a gel. It's cold and will feel disgusting."

I'm liking Doctor Morgan more and more. She doesn't sugar-coat anything. She squirts some gel onto my stomach, then places a T-looking device on my stomach and presses hard.

The room fills with a sound I've never heard before. "What's that?" I ask, startled.

"What you're hearing is your baby's heartbeat. And if you look here, on the monitor." She taps with her free hand, "You'll see the baby."

The sound of something humming fast, mixed with the picture of a blob on the screen, fills my entire body with an emotion I don't think I've ever experienced in my life.

My arms break out in goosebumps and an icy chill runs through my body. "Is that my baby?" I ask in a whisper as I stare at the blob.

"See that thing pulsating on the screen?"

"Yeah." All of us crane to get a better look.

"That's your baby's heart."

I watch closely as the pulsing dot on the screen matches the amazing sound filling the room.

"Oh my," Mom whispers.

"Wow," Alex's mom echoes.

"Your baby is the size of a cherry."

"There's only one in there?" I ask, petrified, yet overwhelmingly excited too.

"All I can see at this stage is one." She lifts the device from my stomach, turns off the monitor, then gives me a few tissues to wipe the gel from my stomach. "You'll have to have another ultrasound at twelve weeks. Call and make an appointment. Then I'll see you again after that ultra-sound. I'm writing out a prescription for a particular type of prenatal vitamin I want you to take. And I want you to increase your iron intake. Before your next appointment with me, you need to have a blood test. Here's the referral for it."

I take the slip of paper, and fold it. "Want me to take it?" Mom asks.

I nod, feeling quite overwhelmed by everything.

"I'll see you after you get the ultrasound, and blood test. Just remember to take your vitamin every day." Doctor Morgan stands, and heads for the door.

"That's it?" I ask.

"For now, that's it. Study up on what you can't eat. Soft cheeses, raw meats, deli meats. There are a few things. Keep your water intake up, and what was it you enjoy eating? Bananas and jelly?"

"Ketchup," I correct.

"Enjoy them. Eat as many of those as you want." She holds the door open, and finally offers me a smile. It's small, and cold, but I think that's how she'd be with all her patients.

"Thank you," I say as I walk out.

My parents, Alex, and his parents all follow me out.

Mom goes ahead to pay, and I hang back with Dad. "That sound was amazing. It was so fast."

"The fact it looks just like a blob blows my mind," he adds.

Alex's mom still appears to be angry. She's huddled with her husband, talking softly between themselves. Alex is in limbo. Unsure of where to go. It's obvious he wants to be with me, but at the same time, he doesn't want to upset his mom. "Just go," I whisper to him.

"Right, I want lunch because I'm hungry. You?" Mom asks looking at me.

"I could eat."

"I'm talking about something more than bananas."

Dad chuckles from beside me. "Yeah. I'm hungry," I say

again. Looking over to Alex, I lift my brows, silently asking if they're coming.

"I'm not hungry," Alex's mom says, looking down her nose at me.

"I'm hungry, Mary," Alex's dad says.

"So am I," Alex responds.

His mom doesn't look happy. She really doesn't want to be here, and I have no idea why she came. But when she was listening to my baby's heartbeat, and looking at him on the screen, I could swear I saw tears in her eyes.

"Fine." She turns, flicking her long, dark hair, and walking out of the waiting room.

"Cheesecake Factory?" Mom asks. I nod, Dad nods, Alex, and Alex's dad nod too. The only person who's not here to agree — or in her case, probably disagree – is Alex's mom.

"The one on the Parkway?" Alex's dad asks.

"Yeah, we'll meet you there," Dad responds.

We leave in our respective cars, and I can't get the sound of my baby's heartbeat out of my mind. Mom and Dad are talking in the front, but I'm zoned out. Completely in awe of everything I saw and heard in Doctor Morgan's office.

My eyes drift closed, and I'm barely able to stay awake. The constant, fast beat still drums in my ears. That's something I'm never going to forget.

"Andy."

Startling, I jump in my seat. "Yeah, I'm okay," I say as I blink the sleep away while trying to focus on where we are.

"You were snoring," Dad says.

"No I wasn't. I wasn't asleep." But I know I was.

"Come on, Sleeping Beauty. We're here. And by looks of things, Alex, Emil, and Mary are already here. This should be interesting," Mom's tone says a lot about what she thinks of Mary.

Following behind my parents, we head into the Cheesecake Factory. Alex and his family are waiting for us. His mom looks even less impressed when she sees us enter.

"Hey," Alex says as he comes to stand beside me.

"This is awkward," I whisper.

"Mom's been making mine and Dad's lives a living hell. I think she's going to do the same here."

We're shown to a table that can seat all of us. Alex's mom sits on the end, refusing to talk to any of us. How long can she hold onto this grudge? By looks of things, a long time.

The waiter comes and takes our order. I'm ravenous, so I order the spaghetti and meatballs. Alex orders the everything flatbread pizza. Instantly, I get food envy, and vow to have a piece of his when it comes. "I'm going to try your pizza," I whisper to him, not really giving him a chance to say no.

"And I'm going to have one of your meatballs."

I shake my head, smiling. "Sorry, I'm eating for two, which means I get to share your food, but you get to share mine only if I don't want any more."

"That's not fair."

"No, no it's not."

He smiles, and gives me a small wink.

When the waiter gets to Alex's mom, she pores over the menu, before giving me a sideways glimpse. "Edamame," she says, closes her menu and hands it back to the waiter.

"Would you like anything else?"

"No." She's so short in her response, it makes me question what her motives are.

Alex's dad orders a steak. And with his order, the waiter leaves.

The conversation around the table is strained at best. Alex's mom is refusing to contribute to any of it. Instead, she looks around at the other diners, down at her nails, pulls her phone out of her bag and seems to be more interested in it than what we're all talking about.

It's painfully obvious she doesn't want to be here with us. Or maybe it's just me.

Either way, she's making me feel uncomfortable.

"When we had the boys, the technology wasn't like it is now," Alex's dad says. "Listening to the heartbeat. That was unbelievable. I mean, it's just... I can't even tell you. Thank you for allowing us into the room to listen to it." He looks to me and gives me a small, appreciative nod.

"Hmmm," Alex's mom huffs.

We turn to look at her, and she rolls her eyes, twisting away from us.

She's making me more frustrated than uncomfortable now. And judging by the tension around the table, I'm not the only one annoyed by her behavior.

The waiter begins to bring our meals out, mine being one of the first. I can't wait. It smells so good, and looks so delicious piled high in a bowl. Picking up my fork, I start eating. My stomach rumbles with appreciation the moment I've taken a bite.

"Hmmm," Alex's mom sniggers again.

I ignore her, choosing to eat my lunch.

Alex's pizza comes, and my eyes grow so big. "Wow, that looks good," I say.

"Doesn't it?" His dad echoes.

"Have a piece," Alex offers me.

I finish eating one of my meatballs, and pick up a piece of pizza.

"Ugh," his mom grumbles even louder.

"Do you have a problem?" I finally snap. I know I shouldn't, but I can't help myself.

"Excuse me?" She furrows her brows at me, as she picks up

an edamame, opens it and pops the bean in her mouth.

"You've been huffing and puffing the entire time we've been here."

"You're eating my son's lunch. Is that what you're going to do once the baby comes? Offload it to him all the time, robbing him of his time, so you can go out with your friends?"

"Mary, enough," Alex's dad says in a low voice.

She looks at him, rolls her eyes, then picks up another edamame.

I try to change direction of where this is going. It's no use coming at her head-on, because she has a clear animosity toward me. She thinks I'm going to ruin her son's life. We need to find common ground, because although I'm not a fan of hers, she still *is* my son's grandmother. "What did you think of the ultrasound?" I ask her directly. I need something to go in my favor here.

She shrugs, nonchalantly and focuses on her edamame.

"The heartbeat blew my mind. I couldn't believe how fast it was. Did you know a baby's heartbeat is that fast?"

"It's an embryo. That's it," she snaps.

"And soon that embryo will be your grandson."

Something visible happens to her. While she's staring down at her half-eaten plate of edamame, her features transform from hard and cold, to softer. Her eyes tell us all exactly what she's thinking.

I gave what's growing in my stomach a title. Grandson. And that must've hit a nerve.

"You think it's a boy?" she asks.

"I know it's a boy," I reply.

"I knew both of mine were boys too, from the moment I found out we were expecting."

Out of the corner of my eye, I notice Mom's expression. She's noticeably shocked by Mary's reaction.

Although there's a lot of hostility in his mom, I think she might, eventually, come around.

I damned well hope so.

CHAPTER
12

I'M ACTUALLY REALLY looking forward to school today. After hearing my baby's heartbeat yesterday, and seeing him on the monitor, I feel like a different person. I've got newfound confidence and happiness.

"Andy!" Zar yells my name. She hurries toward me, appearing to be on a mission. "I'm so sorry." Her apology strikes me hard.

"What have you got to be sorry about?"

Zar's eyes grow wide. Her mouth falls open. "Shit," she says. Taking me by my upper arm, she leads me into the female bathroom closest to us. "You don't know what's happening?"

"Why would I know?" Nervously, I rub my hands together.

"It's all over social media."

"What is?" I take my phone out of my pocket, but don't even have a chance to look when the bathroom door opens and two senior girls walk in. They stop walking when they see me, and immediately break into a giggle. Narrowing my eyes at them, I have no idea what's happening.

"That's her," I hear one say to another.

"OMG!" the other says.

My high school is small, but it's still big enough for me not to know everyone's name. They both backtrack, but not without laughing behind their covered mouths.

Turning to Zar, I can see the pained look on her face. Oh crap. They know. How do they know though? "How?" I ask.

My heart's beating fast, and I feel a wave of nausea hit me.

Luckily, there's a wall behind me so I lean against it. "Zar?" I reach to grab her.

"It's okay," she says, wrapping her arm under my arms to help hold me up.

"How?" I ask. My body shakes with fear. Everyone is going to know. Or worse, everyone already knows. This is a small town, this'll spread like wildfire on a hot, dry day.

"Blair saw Clarence rubbing your stomach. She's been telling people you're pregnant."

I think back to when I saw Blair, and the only time was when I was at work. Oh, God! She was there, giving me grief with her sister. When Clarence threw them out, she rubbed my stomach. Oh. My. God. "I am pregnant, Zar."

"I know that, and you know that, but Blair is just trying to cause shit. She's been telling people how you're pregnant and she overheard you saying it was someone who you had a fling with."

"Fling? Really?" My anger heats, because she's spreading lies. "And people believe her?"

Zar shrugs. "Apparently so."

Ugh. "Well." I hate Blair. "If they want to believe her, then so be it."

"Are you going to tell anyone?"

"No need. I'm sure everyone will hear about it by the end of the day."

"Everyone already knows."

"Screw 'em," I say. Looking in the mirror, I can see the redness in my face. Turning the faucet on, I splash water on my face, trying to calm my irritation. "They can say and think whatever they want."

"You're stronger than I am," Zar says. She leans in, and gives me a hug.

Walking out of the bathroom, it's either paranoia, or it's actually happening. Everyone seems to be staring at me. "Is everyone staring?" I whisper to Zar.

"Yeah, most people."

Holding my head high, with my shoulders back, I stroll through the sea of glares and ocean of whispers. Some are even pointing. Zar and I head to her locker and then to mine.

Out of the corner of my eye, I see someone walking toward me. Turning, I roll my eyes as I see Blair and Ruby carrying a gift.

"Hi Andy," Blair screeches. The mere sound of her nasally voice makes my skin crawl.

"What do you want?" I ask.

She looks around, and notices people staring, waiting for something to happen. "Hey," Alex says from behind me. He leans in and gives me a kiss on the cheek. "What's going on, Blair?" his tone changes, becomes harder and more forceful.

The gift Blair is holding has baby footprints in various hues of pinks. "This is for Andy. I just wanted to be the first to congratulate her on the news."

"News?" Alex asks, his tone hard and flat.

"Yes, didn't she tell you? She's expecting a baby."

"You enjoy causing trouble, don't you, Blair?" I say loudly enough for everyone to hear.

Blair holds out the gift, and I look at it like it's poison. "Us?" Ruby asks feigning hurt.

"Is this because Clarence threw you out of her store after you were being a horrible bitch?" I ask loudly, making sure everyone who's gathering knows exactly why Blair and Ruby have done this, shifting their focus from me to them. Blair's features change rapidly. "Or is this because you're both narcissistic cows who have to be the center of attention all the time?"

Ruby's face changes color, reflecting her namesake. "We know it's not Alex's," she says as she snatches the gift out of Blair's hand and thrusts it into mine.

"Congratulations to you both. You've successfully made yourselves look like fools." I chuckle, as do most people standing around waiting to see where this confrontation is going to go. "Oh, and by the way." I rip the paper off the gift and find it's a box of condoms. Smiling, I can't help but find this amusing. "I was going to insult your intelligence, but it's no use, because I know you have none."

"Oh my God!" Zar says laughing.

"Did she just call you dumb?" Ruby whispers to Blair.

"No, I don't think so." Blair's perplexed look speaks volumes.

I throw the box of condoms to Blair. "I know you're a bit slow, so let me clear this up for you. Yeah, I called you *both* dumb." I shrug. "Bye, idiots." Walking past them, I can't help but notice the shocked, furious look in their eyes.

The moment I'm away from them, I turn to Zar and let out the air I've been holding in.

"I'll give you one thing," Zar says.

"What?"

"You are quick on your feet. I think I would've crumpled."

"Doubt it."

"I thought you told them," Alex says standing to my side. "I was going to blow it, but noticed you were angry. I looked at Zar, and she shook her head. Why are they like that?"

"Because Blair wants to ride your..." Zar blurts and quickly flicks her gaze to his crotch area.

"Zar," I say, feeling sick at the image she's planted in my head.

"She's not going to!"

"I know," I say. Letting out a sigh, it hits me hard. "Everyone's going to find out soon."

"No reason to tell anyone now, though," Alex says.

The bell sounds, and we all walk to class. Alex goes toward his, and Zar and I walk together to English. "God, those two just annoy the hell out of me," I say.

"Want me to beat them up?" Zar throws a punch into her palm. "I'll so drop them. Put them on their asses. Take down — Zar style."

She makes me laugh. Zar is sassy, and smart, but she's so tiny I doubt she'd do well in a fight. "They're really not worth it."

"Hey," Bek says as she walks in behind me to class.

"Hey." She looks like she wants to say something, but also doesn't know how to. "Just say it, Bek."

She sits beside me, on the opposite side of Zar. "They're nasty. Both of them. They've been saying really horrible things about you."

"Of course, they have."

"I don't believe them." Though by her delivery, she wants me to confirm or deny their heartless gossip.

"If you want to believe them, you can. If you don't, then don't."

"Huh?" Bek says. I can tell she's still thinking. She leans in close, making sure no one can hear us. "If you actually are pregnant, then I don't believe it's anyone else's but Alex's. You wouldn't do that. Not to him."

I'm carefully constructing my response. "Alex means too much to me to treat him so badly." Bek smiles, seemingly happy with my answer.

Sitting in the cafeteria, I make sure I eat normal food, because I feel like everyone's watching me.

Blair and Ruby in particular.

"Why do I feel like their eyes are boring into me?" I ask Zar.

She looks around and smiles. "Because they are."

Turning, I look at them, and stick my middle finger up. Blair glares at me, but turns so her back is to me.

"She's ruthless," Alex says as he sits beside me.

"Don't tell me... Blair?"

"I don't know what the hell it is with her. But she's been carrying on all day. It feels like she's been going out of her way to be where I am. Even Finn told her to back off."

"She's unbelievable," Zar says.

"What's her game?" I ask, genuinely perplexed by her suddenly bizarre behavior.

"Once she has her sights set on someone, and she doesn't let up until she gets them. She's like a dog with a bone," Alex replies.

"She's never caused me any kind of trouble in the past. But now she's turned into this demonic, sex-crazed nutcase."

"I'm the new flavor." Alex's face speaks a million words, his flat tone, even more.

"Most guys would jump at the opportunity," I say.

"I'm not most guys."

"No, no you're not." I lean into him, and give him a small kiss on the cheek.

"Ugh. You two are gross. Get a room," Zar's sarcastic tone makes us both chuckle.

Hunter joins us at our table, and Zar's fun personality changes the moment she sees him sit. "Hi Zar," he says.

"Hi," she squeaks in return. She clears her throat, then says in a calm and collective voice, "Hey," she says, adding in a cool head nod.

She looks like she has a crick in her neck. "You okay, Zar?" I ask. She kicks me under the table. "Why'd you kick me?"

"I didn't kick you." Her jaw tightens in irritation.

"So, I'm thinking of seeing the new Marvel movie," Hunter says to all of us. But I think he's trying to see if Zar's interested.

"You love Marvel, don't you Zar?" I say.

"Yeah, Iron Man's my favorite character. Then Spider Man."

"I thought you'd be a Thor fan," Hunter says to Zar.

She ducks her head down, then pulls her hair behind her ear. Oh nice one, Zar. You're trying to flirt with Hunter. "I like Thor, but not like I love Iron Man and Spider Man."

"Have you seen the new Marvel movie yet?" He turns so he's talking to her directly instead of all of us.

"Not yet."

"Want to see it?"

This time it's me who kicks her under the table. She gives me a bug-eyed glare with a *stay out of this* look. "Like all of us?" she asks.

No Zar! Why'd you ask that? Ugh.

"Yeah, um, yeah sure. Saturday?" Hunter looks hurt. His shoulders drop and he averts his eyes. He's not sitting as tall. "You in?" he asks Alex.

"Um, yeah, I think I can."

"No, you can't. You and I have something on," I say.

"What?"

I tilt my head, trying to give him *the look*. "That thing."

"Oh crap. Do we? Okay. Sorry, Hunt. No way can I make it."

"It looks like it's just you two." I look at him, then Zar.

"We can get a group of people together if you want," Hunter asks Zar. Man, they're each as bad as the other.

"Ah, if you want," Zar replies.

I feel like bashing my head on the table. They're dancing around each other, and it's painful to watch. "I'm okay with just the two of us. Unless you're not."

Bash.

"Yeah, I'm good. I mean, I'm fine. I mean, yeah, that's good." Zar stumbles over her words.

Seriously? It's like someone's pulling my fingernails off, one by one.

"Saturday night? I can come by and pick you up if that's convenient for you." Hunter is so sweet. He's trying so hard to make it a date, and she's fumbling.

Just say yes!

"Yeah? Thanks. I've gotta ask my Mom. Can I let you know tomorrow?"

Phew, finally.

"Yeah. Cool. Maybe we can catch a bite before the movie?"

Zar smiles wide. And finally, Hunter doesn't look like he's sitting on a cushion made of nails.

"Yeah, I'd like that." They keep talking, easily switching between topics. They're engrossed with each other, and don't even see me leaning into Alex. "That was painful."

"Tell me about it," Alex says. "What stuff do we have to do on Saturday? Is it baby related?"

I smack my forehead with the palm of my hand. "For someone smart, you're a dumbass."

Alex stares at me. His brain ticking over quite fast. It dawns on him in about thirty seconds. "Ohhh."

"I'm working, but we can do something after work if you like?"

"Yeah, I'd like that.

Sitting back, I watch as Hunter and Zar keep talking. I do notice a few people still looking at me. But I choose to ignore it. There's going to be loads more whispers and stares to come. Especially when they all find out for sure.

CHAPTER
13

THIS WEEK AT school has been infuriating, but also fun.

I'm still getting looks from most people. Blair in particular seems to have a vendetta against me. Not sure why. Well, other than the fact she wants Alex, and I'm standing in her way.

Thankfully, today's Friday, which means I only have to put up with her sneering stares, and nasty comments for the rest of the day, then I get two days Blair-free.

"So, you and Hunter?" I say to Zar as we sit at our usual seat for lunch.

"Yeah, about that." Zar looks away, avoiding me. "It's probably best if I... you know." She lifts one shoulder in a non-committal gesture.

All week I had a feeling she was going to cancel on Hunter. "What are you scared of?" I ask as I peel my banana.

"You're going to turn into a monkey." She pointedly looks at what I'm holding.

"Deflecting, huh? Nice."

Zar bites on her inner cheek, holding in a smile. She knows *I* know what she's doing. "Anyway."

"You've been avoiding him, haven't you?"

"No!"

"Hi Zar," Hunter says from beside me, as if he's popped out of the ground. "Hey, Andy."

"Why don't you join us, Hunter?" I ask. Zar kicks me under the table. She likes doing that. Hunter moves to sit beside me, but I stop him fast. "Alex will be here soon."

I hear Zar groan from the opposite side.

"Sure." Hunter smiles widely. Only too happy to sit beside Zar. He shifts pretty easily, moving next to Zar. "Do you like pizza?" he asks.

"Yeah, why?"

"What about pizza before the movie?"

"Before I answer that question, you have to answer one of *my* questions first."

"Which is?"

"Pineapple. Does it belong on pizza?"

Zar hates pineapple on pizza. He'd better answer this right, or I can see she's going to lose it with him.

"Hell, yeah it belongs."

Crash and burn, buddy. Crash and burn.

I wait for her response. She's going to rip him a new one, and he won't even know what hit him. Poor guy. I really should have warned him. I brace for impact. The Zar impact.

This is going to be brutal.

"Then you can order two pizzas. One for you with pineapple, and one for me without it. And, you're paying. And just an FYI for you, pineapple doesn't belong on pizza."

I stare at Zar, shocked. "What just happened?" I ask, still

perplexed by her tame and calm response.

"I don't have to have pineapple. Have you tried pineapple on pizza though?"

"Hold up a moment, Hunter." I hold my hand up, stopping him. "Why didn't you tear him limb from limb?"

Zar's eyes widen. "Who, me? Don't know what you're talking about." She looks sideways toward Hunter. "I'm not a fan of pineapple on pizza, but I'm not going to stop anyone else from eating it."

"Aha," I tease. Suddenly an aroma drifts by nose, causing my stomach to stir. "Crap, not now." I look to Zar, silently pleading with her.

She stops smiling, her brows drawing in together. "What's wrong?"

Standing, I put my hand to my mouth. "Shit," I cry.

Zar looks panicked. She stands as quickly I did, and she leaps over her seat.

As I dash toward the bathroom, I catch a glimpse of Blair. She's smiling as she watches me. Her mouth is pursed into a smug, tight line. She taps Ruby on the shoulder, and gestures with a head flick toward me.

"I thought you were over the food poisoning," Zar asks keeping up with me. She's loud enough for everyone to hear.

"Told you she's pregnant," Blair says as we pass her.

Rolling my eyes, I don't have the time or the energy to argue with her. I'm focused on the fact, I'm about to vomit in front of everyone.

The moment I'm in the bathroom, I lean over a toilet and vomit. My stomach settles, for all of three seconds before I vomit again.

"Are you okay?" Zar asks from the other side of the bathroom door.

"I think so." And I vomit again. "No." My forehead covers in a sheen of sweat. Something's wrong. I can feel it. I've vomited with morning –or should I say — all-day sickness, but only once and then I feel better. My entire body screams in pain. Everything hurts, as my stomach feels like it's contracting.

While I'm vomiting again, alarms scream in my head. Something isn't right. I can't stop this vomiting.

"See, told you Ruby, she's pregnant," I hear Blair's irritating voice say.

"We already knew it. Now everyone else will too," Ruby shrills back. She sounds like a budgie squawking.

"She's not pregnant you idiot, she has food poisoning. How dumb can you be?" Zar spits at them.

"She's so pregnant," Blair insists.

"Turn that off. What weirdo comes into the girls' bathroom recording with her phone?"

Fabulous. Blair or Ruby are recording me vomiting.

"I'm going to prove to everyone that she's pregnant," Blair says with no conscience at all. "And I bet Alex doesn't even know. The moment I show him this, he's going to dump her ass, and I'll be ready for him."

"You really are a total idiot," Zar repeats. "Good idea, go show him. Just leave."

"I'm uploading this to social media." Blair giggles.

She's so damn horrible, and all because she wants to destroy me so she can get to Alex.

"Do whatever you think is right," I yell from the bathroom between bouts of vomiting.

"Oh, we will," Ruby answers for her, then adds in a laugh.

"Bye, girls," Blair says in a high-pitched, saccharine voice.

I hear the door close, and throw up, again. "Are we on our own? I ask Zar.

"Yeah. I'm up against the door so no one can come in."

"I think something's wrong."

"Crap. I'll go tell a teacher."

"No!" I yell, too loudly.

"I can't leave you here. And lunch will be done soon. You can't stay on the floor of the bathroom."

"Shit," I grumble knowing my bag and phone are back at the table we were sitting at.

"What's wrong?" Zar's tone changes to more worried.

"I left my bag at the table, and my phone is in my bag. I need to call Mom."

"I'll run back and get our stuff. Will you be okay in here?" Finally, I'm feeling slightly better. I flush the toilet, and open the door to the stall. "You look so pale, and crappy."

I wash my hands, then splash water on my face. "I feel so bad." And then the twisting feeling in my stomach starts again. "Oh no!" Turning, I only just make it to the toilet as I vomit. My hands are shaking, and I feel sweat rolling down my back. "I can't do this again." *Vomit.*

"Where's Andy?" I hear Alex calling.

"I'm here."

"You can't come in. This is the girls' bathroom."

"I don't care." Then I hear a knock on the door. "Andy, what's happening? Are you okay?"

Vomit.

Tears erupt, cascading down my cheeks as I continue to vomit. I don't even know where all this food is coming from. "I'm scared," I finally admit.

"Open the door, Andy."

"No, I'm vomiting. I look terrible."

"Open the door!"

"No."

"Open it, or I'll break it down." His serious tone tells me he'll definitely break the door down if I don't open it.

"I'll go get our stuff," Zar says.

I lean over and open the door. Alex sees me sitting on the floor, tears pouring down my cheeks. "I'm sorry," I say.

He kneels in the cubicle beside me, holding me in his arms. But I push him away, and vomit again. The contents are just liquid now, more like water coming up. "You don't have anything to be sorry about."

"I don't know what's wrong with me."

"We have to tell a teacher," he says.

"No! We can't."

"We have to. There may be something happening..." He points to my stomach.

"No." Though that's what I'm worried about too. "Okay," I concede. "But no teacher, I have to call Mom."

Alex takes his phone out of his pocket, and is already dialing Mom. "Mrs. Price, it's Alex." He listens and smiles. "I'm fine, but Andy isn't. She's been throwing up." I hold my hand out to take his phone. "Hang on." He passes me the phone.

"Mom," I say, then vomit again. "I don't know what's wrong. I keep throwing up. I haven't been able to stop."

"Are you bleeding?" she asks. I look down to my crotch and shake my head. "Andy?"

"No, I'm not. But, Mom, I can't stop vomiting."

"I'll be there in a few minutes. Get to the office, and I'll come get you."

"Bring a bucket." Mom hangs up, and I hand the phone back to Alex. "Mom's coming to get me."

"I'll come with you," Alex says.

"I've got your bag," Zar says busting into the bathroom. She looks to me, and to Alex. "What's happening? Are you okay?"

"Mom's coming to get me."

"I'll come with you," she says.

"No, I'm going," Alex says.

"We'll both go."

The bell sounds, and I know it's the end of lunch. "I've got to get to the office. But I'll wait for a bit, until no one is around. Especially Blair and Ruby."

"I'll go wait for your mom." Alex stands and heads out of the bathroom.

"I don't have a good feeling about this," I say to Zar, still hovering over the toilet. My stomach keeps contracting. While the frequency of my nausea is intense, it's now just dry heaves.

Zar hears me throwing up, and comes into the stall, rubbing my back. "Nothing's coming out," she says.

"I know. But it won't stop."

"I wonder what's going on?"

My body is completely drained. "I'm so tired," I say as I try to close my eyes for a few moments between the bouts of vomiting.

"Blair and Ruby are causing so many problems."

"To tell you the truth, Zar, at this stage, I really don't care. I'm too exhausted to worry about them."

"Right, sorry," she says in a small voice.

"Sorry, I didn't mean to snap. I'm just saying, they're nothing but pains in my ass. If it's not this, it would be something else. You know how Blair can get."

"I wonder why she's adamant about Alex now. She's never done this to you before."

"No idea." I shrug. Then gag. Again.

"Sweetheart?" Mom bursts into the bathroom, followed closely by Alex and Ms. Dawson our principal. "Are you okay?"

"Mom." I look over my shoulder, but have to turn back quickly when the urge to vomit hits me again.

"What's happening?" Ms. Dawson asks.

"I told you, she ate something," Alex says, trying to convince Ms. Dawson.

Ms. Dawson is fairly young, especially considering she's a principal too. But, she's not an idiot. She cocks an eyebrow, and I know she thinks there's more going on than just food poisoning. Maybe Blair's gotten to her, too.

"She was sick last night, and I told her not to come to school today," Mom confirms.

"Food poisoning." Ms. Dawson asks in a deadpan voice.

"Come on, sweetheart, let's get you up." Mom hooks her arm under mine, and helps me up. "I'm taking her home."

"Of course," Ms. Dawson replies. She's suspicious.

Mom supports me while we walk out, my stomach contracting and spasming with every movement. "Bucket?"

Alex's hand shoots out with the bucket. I stop my slow walk, and attempt to vomit, but nothing comes up.

Embarrassed, I look around and notice there's a handful of students left in the hallway. I'm super ashamed. People are watching me leave the school with my Mom, Alex, Zar and principal Dawson all following. This is definitely going to fuel the gossip. How humiliating.

I'm going to come back to school on Monday, and all the things Blair and Ruby have been spouting, will be circulating in overdrive.

"I've got it from here," Mom says to Alex, Zar and Ms. Dawson.

"I'm coming with you," Alex says.

"Me too," Zar interjects.

"We'll let you know what happens." Mom keeps walking. She's just essentially told them they're not coming.

"Mrs. Price?" Alex's voice is pained. "Please, let me come."

"After school, Alex." She turns to give him a stern 'no' look.

I look back, Alex's shoulders have slumped forward, and he's stopped walking. "Mom," I plead.

"I'm taking you to the hospital," she says in a low voice. "He can come after school. If he comes with us, people are going to start wondering why I allowed it, and they may start putting things together."

She has a valid point. "I hate to tell you, but Blair and Ruby have already figured it out and are trying to break us up. Blair thinks I've had sex with someone else, and now I'm pregnant." But stomach seizes again. "Bucket!" We stop walking, and Mom shoves the bucket under my chin. I try to vomit.

"This is a joke." I finally say after trying again, but nothing coming out. "My stomach is convulsing, but nothing is coming out. What's wrong with me?"

We continue on to the car. Mom unlocks it with the fob, helps me in, and places the bucket on my lap. She opens the trunk of the car, and swings my bag in before sliding into the driver's seat. "I don't know, but I'm taking you to the hospital."

"I don't want to go."

"I don't give a rat's ass if you want to go. Something's not right, and we have to find out what it is."

"They'll judge me."

"Get used to it. Because you're going to have to face judgement for the rest of your life."

A surge of tears fall on their own. "I can't do this," I say. "I can't be a mom. I don't want to be judged."

"Snap out of it, Andy. You made a choice to have this baby. If you want to change your mind, now's the only opportunity you'll get. After this, there's no more chances; it will be too late. You either accept it and become a mother, or we find alternate arrangements. Abortion or adoption."

I stop crying, and turn to mom. "I..." I look at her, unable to comprehend what she's proposing. "I don't want to do either." I'm shocked she's so casual about this. "And I can't believe you'd say this. How can you? How can you say something so horrible about my baby?"

She gives me a small smile. "See, you *can* do this, because the alternative isn't an option. Is it?"

I furrow my brows. "You were trying to make me see?" I ask.

"This isn't going to be an easy life, Andy. But you were going to fight me for what I said. Which means you're going to protect this baby, no matter what. And your father and I will be there to support you."

My stomach contracts, and another spasm of dry heaves overtakes me. I'm going through the motions. Absolutely nothing but bitter bile comes up. "What's wrong with me, Mom? Is my baby okay?" My voice is high and shaky.

"We're nearly at the hospital." Mom speeds up, and gets us to the hospital within moments.

The doctor opens the curtain and walks in. He's an older man with thin, graying hair, and a large hook nose. His face is weathered, his demeanor harsh. Automatically, I don't like him.

"Who do we have here?" he asks as he peers over his paperwork at me. "Oh, you're pregnant." He lifts a furry eyebrow. Here comes the judgement. "How old are you?" He looks down, referring to his paperwork, and looking up at me. "Fifteen?" He adds in a headshake.

"We're not here for your judgement," Mom says. "We're here because she hasn't stopped vomiting."

The doctor's attitude changes. It's almost like he can't be bothered treating me. "What's happening?" he asks, bored.

"I haven't stopped vomiting. I've been like this since about one."

"Any bleeding?"

"Nothing. Is my baby okay?"

He sneers and rolls his eyes. He really doesn't like me. "I suspect it's *hyperemesis gravidarum.* I'll run some tests. Give you something for the vomiting and rehydrate you." He pinches my skin on the back of my hand, and nods to himself. "Yep, you're dehydrated."

"What's *hyperemesis gravidarum?* Is that dangerous? Will we be okay?"

He lets out an annoyed sigh. "Basically, it's extreme morning sickness."

"Do you have a problem with my daughter? Because judging by your obvious eye rolls, your lack of civility, and your dismissive attitude, I have serious reservations about your ability to treat her. And if you can't treat her with compassion, I have zero faith in you. Perhaps I'll go speak with the head of the hospital and have another doctor treat her."

The doctor's jaw clenches as he stands taller, straightens his shoulders, and looks around to see who else heard Mom ripping into him. "I can assure you, Mrs. Price, my personal feelings have nothing to do with my professional conduct," he bites back.

Mom drops my hand, and takes a step closer to him.

Oh crap. She's pissed.

"Your personal feelings seem to be overpowering your professional conduct. You're clouded by your prejudice toward my daughter. I refuse to let you continue treating her. Either get another doctor, or I'll go see the hospital administration. Lawsuits can be quite expensive, could ruin peoples' reputations, don't you think?"

The doctor's mouth flattens. This is a battle of wills, but Mom brought up the possibility of a lawsuit, and I doubt he'll want that.

"Andy, I apologize for my behavior. Mrs. Price, I extend my sincere apologies." I look to Mom for guidance. She gives him a curt nod, and steps back beside me again. I nod too, and offer him a kind smile. It's more than he's given me. "I'll order an ultrasound to make sure everything's okay. But I do suspect this is a severe case of morning sickness. You've had no bleeding?"

"Nothing."

"You're very dehydrated. We'll keep you in here for the night, get some fluids into you, and give you an injection to stop the vomiting. Have you experienced diarrhea too?"

"No, just the vomiting." I haven't stopped vomiting since I've been here. Except, I'm feeling weaker.

He shakes his head. "Okay, let's give you something to stop the vomiting, then get an ultrasound done. That'll show us how the baby is."

"Can this hurt the baby?" I ask, worried.

"No. It's uncomfortable for you, but the baby is well protected. It won't know you're going through this. Have you seen an OBGYN yet?"

"Yes. Tracey Morgan," Mom responds.

"She's an excellent doctor. Has she started you on vitamins?"

"Yes, I've started."

"Good. I suggest you call her on Monday and tell her what's happened here. She may want you to have extra B-6 vitamin. Or she may want to see you again." Although the doctor's attitude isn't as hard, his tone is still clipped. I imagine this is because he doesn't like getting told off.

"Thank you," I say.

He steps away without saying anything, his focus on the paperwork he's writing. A nurse comes in, and he talks to her about what he wants. He turns before he leaves. "I'll come back once I have the test results. You'll be moved into a private room."

"Thank you," I say again. Mom says nothing, and gives him a nod. I look at her, and she gives me a smirk. "That was a battle of who's most stubborn."

"He was being an ass."

I laugh. "Yeah, he was. I also expect this is going to be my new normal."

"I hate to say it, Andy, but yes. I think you're right."

The nurse arrives with a wheelchair, and smiles. "Hi Andy. I'm here to take you for an ultrasound."

"Can I bring my bucket?" I ask.

"I'll give you something else, something we can throw out." She hands me a plastic bowl-shaped basin.

I hop into the chair, and she wheels me away to get an ultrasound. Mom follows. I hope everything's okay. I'll find out soon.

CHAPTER
14

"READY TO GO home?" Dad asks as he waits for me to pack the rest of my things.

"Yeah, I am. Is Mom not coming?"

"No, she has some work in the office she had to finish, so it's just you and me, kid."

"I called Clarence and told her I was in the hospital. I felt bad that I couldn't work yesterday."

"I bet Clarence was more concerned for you and the baby then she was about you going into work."

"I know." I sit on the hospital bed, still feeling terrible that I let Clarence down. "I don't want her to think this was something I did on purpose. I still feel terrible."

"Bear," Dad says as he sits beside me on the bed, "you've been working for Clarence for over a year now. How many times have you let her down?"

"Only when I'm sick. Even then, I felt terrible."

"How good would it look to customers if you're there

sneezing over their food and drinks? Or in this case, running out to the back so you can vomit?"

Hmmm, he has a point. "Not good at all."

"And what did Clarence say to you?"

"That she's glad the baby and I are okay. And she'll see me next Saturday."

"So why are you beating yourself up over something you couldn't control?"

I shrug. "I suppose it's more than letting Clarence down. I don't want to let anyone down."

"As long as you do the right thing, you're not letting anyone down. You have to stop being so hard on yourself."

"I'm not being hard on myself."

Dad gives me a sideways glance, tilting his head to the side. "Really? You're not worried about what everyone is thinking? What people will say when they find out you're pregnant? What you could've done differently to avoided being in this position to start with?"

I lower my head, chewing on the inside of my cheek, thinking hard about what Dad's said. "I suppose I am," I concede.

"You can't make people like you, Andy. And you can't make people change their opinions of you. Their opinion is really none of your business. Regardless of how accurate, or stupid, or smart their opinion is. You can't control anyone but yourself and how you see yourself. Letting other people dictate how you feel, well..." He pauses and takes a breath. "That's as useless as tits on a bull."

I look at Dad and scrunch my nose. "Tits on a bull? I've never heard that before." Then I get the instant mental picture, of a bull with boobs. I can't help it. I laugh. "What size would they be if bulls did have tits?" Dad chuckles. "Would they be like *man boobs*, Dad? Like what you have?" I tease.

Dad stands, and puffs his chest out. "I'll have you know, I have a rockin' body, and your mother loves it."

I cover my ears with my hands, and start singing, "Lalalalalala." I look at Dad, and he's laughing too. "Please, never say those words again." Mom loving Dad's body. Parent sex…yuck. "I don't want to know."

"Look at it this way, I know you've had sex." Dad returns the gesture toward my stomach.

"Well played, Dad, well played." Standing, I pack the rest of my overnight bag.

"How are you feeling?"

"Once they gave me the injection to stop the vomiting, and Doctor Morgan came to see me, I feel okay. She put my mind at ease, and told me this is a lot more common than people think. It effects up to two percent of pregnant women. That blew my mind. I'd never heard of it before."

"I had no idea what it was either until she explained it. You have to keep up with your fluid intake, because it can happen again."

I scrunch my nose. "Yay," I say sarcastically. Looking around the room, I make sure I haven't left anything behind. "Okay, I think I'm ready to go."

"Mom will be home when she's finished at the office. Better to get it done today when no one else is there to distract her. So, what do you want for lunch?"

"Banana and ketchup. I've been craving it. I haven't had it in two days." Dad crinkles his mouth in disgust. "You don't have to eat it."

"Thankfully. Anything else? Like real food?"

"Bananas are real food."

"Not when they're dripping with ketchup."

We walk out of the room. Dad taking my bag, slinging it over his shoulder. I thank the nurses who've been looking after me before I leave. "I could eat. As long as I can have my bananas and ketchup when I get home, I'm good to have anything. What do you want?"

"How about Olive Garden? I feel like chicken parmigiana. What about you?"

"Yeah, I could go for something. Maybe some pasta. I could eat some ravioli. Yum." My stomach agrees. "But as long as we have bananas at home," I double check with Dad.

"Mom bought five pounds yesterday. She even got more ketchup."

"I'm so hungry," Dad says after we've ordered and are waiting for our food.

"Me too."

"You look like you've lost weight."

"I have, but only a couple of pounds. Doctor Morgan said that's normal. Especially considering I spent most of Friday and some of yesterday throwing up."

Dad takes a sip of water. "You know, we haven't really talked about this since you told us about the pregnancy. I know we've talked, but not just me and you."

Disappointment washes over me. "I'm sorry, Dad. I'm sorry for letting you down."

"You didn't let me down, Andy. You made a bad choice in a moment where it could've been avoided. But this baby is going to be here much quicker than you know. And as much as I really don't want to be a grandfather at the age of forty-one, it's happening. Nothing is going to stop that now. So we all have to learn how not only to live with it, but embrace it."

"I'm a disappointment," I whisper, my eyes downcast.

"Not to me."

"You're not disappointed that I'm pregnant at fifteen?"

Dad sighs. I can tell he wants to say something, but he's thinking about it carefully. "Like I said before, this isn't what I would call ideal. But it's not a death sentence either. It's a path you've embarked on, and everything will be different for the rest of your life. For the rest of *all* our lives. Yours, the baby's, your mother's, and mine. Not to mention Alex and his family. It will be what you make of it. If you want to spend the rest of your life living in the past, all you're going to achieve is a lifetime of misery and regret. And I, for one, refuse to torture myself that way. Once this baby is here, he'll need all of us if he's going to have a great life." I smile. This is the first-time Dad has referred to my baby as a boy. "What?"

"You didn't say *it,* you said *he.*"

"You're convinced he's a *he,* and not a she, so of course I'm going to call him *him.*"

Dad warms my heart. I've always known he's a good guy, but this just proves how wonderful he actually is. "This is going to be tough."

"Yep. Hard as hell. You have no idea what you're in for."

"What was I like as a baby?" Maybe I can gauge how my son will be.

"Pain in the butt. First six weeks was absolute hell for your mother and me. More your mom than me. She was the one who was breastfeeding, but I'd still get up with her to support her. She was a walking zombie." He shakes his head, remembering the memory. "We had no idea what we were doing as parents, completely winging it."

"Really? But you have it so together."

"Yeah, we do now. But a baby, whoa, kiddo, that's another whole level of insanity."

"Was I that bad?"

"Nah, you were worse!" He laughs, and guilt pours through me. "Don't feel bad," he says, obviously knowing how I'm feeling. "You're gonna be in the same boat too. Only difference is, we intend to be hands-on grandparents."

"What about Grandma and Grandpa? Nan and Pop?" I'm referring to both sets of my grandparents.

"They were good; they helped us out as much as they could. But we were adamant we wanted to do it on our own. Your mom and I had been married for a few years, had a good business going. But you know how the saying goes?"

"Saying?" I try to think of every saying I know. "What saying?"

"It takes a village to raise a child." Dad chuckles again. "I really wish I'd listened to my parents when they wanted to help more with you."

"But it gets better, right?"

"Oh yeah. Of course. But don't expect it to be better for at least the first two years. First, it's the constant crying, and you have no idea *why* the baby is crying. Then, when you finally figure out which are the hungry cries, the wet diaper cries, or the tired cries, the baby is sick for the first time. We freaked out and took you to the hospital. Luckily, we weren't neurotic parents. We were pretty chill. But lack of sleep can send the sanest of people nuts."

"The more you tell me, the more I'm freaking out." Am I ready for this?

"Ha! You know what you have? You have us. We're not going to raise him, that's your job. But we'll be there to help with whatever we can."

"I'm having doubts."

"About the baby?"

"No. About me."

Dad sips his water again. "Good. So you should. Because whatever you think you're prepared for, you *cannot* prepare for this. No amount of reading or people telling you what it's going to be like can get you ready for what you're going to go through. Plan to not sleep for at least a year."

"A year?"

"At least." I feel my grimace. Dad's having a chuckle again, obviously proud of himself. "But you know what?" I shake my head. "I wouldn't change it for all the money in the world. Not one single moment. And you'll feel the same. You'll struggle, and you'll feel like giving up. You'll doubt yourself, and you'll lose all your confidence. But once you work it out, then life becomes a bit more..." He scratches his chin, trying to think.

"Easier?"

"Ha! Nope, doesn't get easier. It just gets *better*."

"Dad, you're really scaring me."

"Good." He slaps his hand on the table, causing the water to ripple in his glass. "If you're not terrified, then you're in for one helluva shock when my grandson makes his appearance."

I'm conflicted. Frightened, but happy how Dad said his *grandson*. The waiter approaches and places our meals down in front of us. Dad's already into his, while I push my pasta around on the plate. It looks good, but I'm also thinking about what my son will mean to me in a few short months.

"Not hungry?" Dad eyes my meal, while still inhaling his.

"Yeah, I am." I eat a small amount, but my mind is somewhere else.

"Kiddo, look." Dad places his fork on the plate, and gazes up at me. "This is life-altering. I don't want to scare you, but reality is, you're only fifteen. You'll be a sixteen-year-old mother. Think of it this way. You can't legally drink or smoke but you'll have a baby you're responsible for."

"Jeez, when you put it like that." I lower my own fork, and sit on my hands. Fear bubbling deep inside my gut.

"You're frightened?"

"Well, yeah. I don't want to screw him up."

"And that right there," he points to me, "is why I know you'll make a good parent. Because you're thinking of him, and not just you. Being a parent is about sacrifice, and discipline and love. And once you hold him in your arms, nothing will be able to come between you and him."

"Dad." He makes me feel better, and terrified all in the same breath.

"Just like nothing will come between you, and me. Including a baby. So instead of thinking of him as a burden, I've accepted him as an extension of you. You'll find everything changes."

"I'm scared."

"So were we when we had you. We still are. Each stage of your life comes with challenges."

"What do you mean?" I pick up my fork and start eating, my appetite returning with ferociousness.

"Being fifteen comes with its own tests. But now, being fifteen and pregnant… well, I hate to think what you're going to go through. And you know what?"

"What?" I ask.

"Imagine these poor kids, who are like you, whose parents aren't supportive. Or worse still, throw them out of their home."

I think about what Dad's said. Being thrown out for being pregnant would be hard. I'm thankful I have them in my life, and even more thankful of how supportive they are being. But I really can't stop thinking about others who are like me. "Can you imagine, being alone?"

"Being alone isn't bad by itself. But being lonely is heartbreaking. Especially if you're so young and with a child." Dad shakes his head, sadness filling him. "My heart goes out to them."

There's a heaviness in my soul. My own heart is fractured by the thought of how many girls are pregnant at my age. "Do you think this is a common thing?" I look down at my stomach, indicating my pregnancy.

"With girls your age?" Dad asks.

"Yeah. It feels like I don't…" I pause, unable to clearly communicate what's going on in my mind. "I mean, I kinda feel…" Yeah, that's not working for me.

"What do you feel?" Dad pushes.

"I don't know how to say it. Because it's not exactly what I mean."

"Just try your best to describe it." He sips on his water.

I think about it more, then take a breath. "Before I told you and Mom, it kinda felt like I was the only person in the world who could know how I was feeling."

Dad chuckles. "Let me tell you, bear. You're not the first fifteen-year-old to get pregnant, and you certainly won't be the last."

A smile tugs at my lips. "I suppose you're right."

"Suppose?" Dad arches his brows. "Your father is smart." He taps his temple.

"You're alright," I say with a lighter tone.

"Alright? Huh. Don't think so. I'm awesome."

I shake my head and finish eating. Dad's pretty cool.

CHAPTER
15

"YOU'RE *THE* HOT topic," Zar says when she sees me at school.

"Why?" We walk toward my locker so I can put my backpack into it.

"Two words." She holds her first finger up. "Blair." Then holds her second finger up. "Ruby."

"Ugh. Are they still prattling on about me being pregnant?" I look around to make sure no one can hear me.

"What else?"

"Hey, where were you? I've been trying to call you?" Alex says.

"I'm so sorry. Friday and Saturday was a blur. I was discharged yesterday, and I've basically been in bed since I've been home. I was going to call last night, but I was out of it."

Alex frowns at me. His lips purse together, and his brows draw in. "Whatever," he huffs, turns and leaves.

"What's wrong with him?" I ask Zar.

She tilts her head to the side. "Really? You're seriously asking?"

"What?" I shove my backpack in my locker. I turn to find her still glaring at me. "What?"

Zar's frustration is obvious. But I have no idea why. "You can't be that clueless."

"If you tell me, then I'll know."

She leans in close to me. "You're carrying his child too, Andy. We care about you, including me. And you couldn't call us and let us know if you were okay? We tried calling, and you didn't respond to me or him. We had no idea what was happening. If you were okay, if the baby's okay. Both of us are worried for you, and the baby."

My shoulders sink, and I lower my head in shame. "I didn't think," I say. "I'm sorry. I should've kept you both in the loop of what was happening."

"Yeah, you should have. We've got your back, and it feels like you don't have ours."

"I'm so sorry," I whisper, truly ashamed of myself. "I honestly didn't think."

"Obviously."

I look up at Zar. She's so annoyed at me. "I'm sorry. I'll try not to be selfish."

"Good, because next time, I'll kick your ass." She smiles. I give her a hug, grateful for her friendship. "You need to apologize to Alex. He's been worried. He even called the hospital to find out how you were, but because he's not family, they wouldn't tell him anything."

I clutch my hand to my chest. That's why he's upset with me. "Really? He should've…"

"He did, and you didn't answer his calls or his text."

"I have to find him and apologize."

"Yeah, you do."

I pull my phone out of my pocket, and send him a text. *I was an ass—I'm sorry.*

I see he's read it, but doesn't respond. As we walk to our first class, Derek, one of the seniors walks up beside me. "Hey," he says, smiling.

"Hey." I give him the side eye and turn to look at Zar. She lifts one side of her upper lip, and her shoulders at the same time.

Derek's cute, and most of the females in school lust after him. Except me and Zar, and maybe only a few other girls. "So, how are you?" he asks as he falls in beside us.

"Good."

"I was thinking, would you like to go out on Friday?"

"What?" I ask, completely startled. We've never really talked, and I've been with Alex for a long time.

"Do you wanna go out on Friday?" He lightly touches my arm. "A movie, maybe dinner." He gently strokes the length of my arm. It makes me recoil in revulsion.

Creep.

"Are you for real?" I pull my arm away from his disturbing touch. "What do you want?" I nearly shout at him.

"I just heard you're up for partying. Blair..."

"Blair's an idiot, and she wants to screw my boyfriend. If you want to take anyone out for a movie and dinner, take her. I heard she likes to open her legs for anyone." I storm off, angry at him, and even angrier at Blair.

I shouldn't have said anything nasty about Blair, but, man, she's damn cruel.

"So that's a no?" Derek calls from behind me.

"That's a hell no!" I shout without turning back to see him. "Can you believe Blair and him?" I ask Zar.

"He's a dick. She's no better."

I see Blair walking ahead with her sister. I charge toward her, and push her so hard she stumbles forward. "What the f..." She turns to see who's pushed her. She smirks when she sees it's me.

"Stay out of my way. Don't talk to me, don't look at me. And the next time you try to pimp me out, I'll have to tell your parents about what you did during summer vacation." I'm completely clutching at straws here, making it up. But judging by Ruby's shocked look, and the way Blair's eyes widen, I've hit a nerve. "Leave me alone. Both of you. Or I will tell them." Turning, I walk away, still fuming.

"What did she do last summer?" Zar whispers. "And why haven't you told me before now?"

I keep walking. When I round the corner, I look over my shoulder to see Blair and Ruby in a deep huddle. "I have no idea what she did. I was bullshitting, making it up."

"Oh my God, you sure?" Zar's as surprised as me.

"Honestly, I have no idea. I just want them to leave me alone."

Zar steps backward, and pokes her head around to see them. "Now, *this* is exciting. You should see them. Blair's pointing at Ruby and Ruby's looking down. You know what this means?" I nod. "Something interesting's happened. Oh, I want to know what." Zar claps her hands together and appears to be enjoying this way too much.

"As long as she leaves me alone, I don't give a crap about what she did." I notice Jessica and Angie walk past. "Hey," I say to them. They both turn, give me a strained smile, and keep walking. It's then I observe how many more people are looking at me, then turning away when they see me. "Is this because of Blair?" I circle my finger, indicating everyone.

"Friday, when your mom came to get you, Blair was shooting her mouth off. She was relentless. Anybody who'd listen, she was telling them you're pregnant."

"She's horrible," I say, shaking my head.

"Unfortunately, people are listening."

I let out a sigh. "Everyone will find out anyway, sooner or later. I'm not going to tell anyone, but I'm not going to deny it either. People can believe whatever they want."

"Problem is, she's telling everyone you screw around."

"Which is why Derek wanted to take me out." His crude pass makes sense now.

"You'll probably get a few more propositions." I roll my eyes. *Idiots.*

I look at my phone again, to see if Alex has replied. He hasn't. My shoulders slump, and I feel even worse than I did before. "I have to make this right."

Zar knows exactly what I mean. "Yeah, you do."

"I'll talk to him at lunch."

"I think you should," Zar agrees.

"Am I a bad person?"

"Nah, more like self-absorbed. But then again, with everything happening with you." Her eyes dart away, then back to meet mine. "It's really no wonder."

"You have to stop making excuses for me."

Zar shrugs. "Okay then, you're an ass who doesn't care about anyone but herself. Better?"

"I can always count on you," I sigh, smiling.

"Yep," she cheerfully chirps. "I'll call it as I see it. No use in lying."

The bell sounds, and we walk toward class.

"Hey, can we talk?" I ask Alex as he arrives in the cafeteria and lines up to get food for lunch.

He shrugs, still not happy with me.

I stand beside him, the awkward silence playing havoc in my mind. Is he angry enough to break up with me? Is he upset and now doesn't want anything to do with me and the baby? Is he ever going to talk to me again? Is he believing the stupid rumors Blair and Ruby have been spreading, that I'm an easy score?

We shuffle forward. He looks at me then turns away. This is killing me.

My stomach is flipping, and my hands are sweating. Can't he talk to me? Say something? Something to put my mind at ease. Just… anything.

What if he really hates me?

He picks out what he wants for lunch, and heads over to the furthest table. One where no one is sitting at. My heart is racing, and the blood in my veins feels like it's icy. Panic darkens my heart as my stomach flips, then flops, then flips again.

He sits on the chair, I sit opposite him.

"You hurt me," he says coldly. "A lot." He picks at his food. Not really eating it, but not wanting to look at me either. "What you did…" He shakes his head. "It wasn't right, Andy."

I'm embarrassed, and totally ashamed. "I know."

"To lock me out like that. I didn't hear from you all weekend. I get that you were sick, and you needed to rest. But I had no idea what was happening."

"I'm sorry," I say, hanging my head with regret. "I didn't think. And I don't want to make an excuse. I was wrong."

"Yeah, you were."

"The baby's fine. He's doing well. Doctor Morgan came to see me. She told me the baby is completely oblivious to what was happening to me."

"What *did* happen to you?" He looks up at me, flicking his food back on the tray.

"It's got some long technical name I can't remember. Basically, it's extreme morning sickness. It doesn't happen often, but it's not unheard of either."

"And it can't hurt you or the baby?"

"Not our son, and it's more a pain than anything for me. It makes me sick to the point where I can't stop vomiting and I have to go to the hospital for them to treat me for dehydration and to give me something to stop the vomiting."

"Don't push my away like that, okay?" He narrows his eyes, pleading for me to not shut him out.

"I won't. I'm…" I take a breath, trying to express myself. "It's like my brain is foggy. I'm not thinking properly. I'm sorry I hurt you. I promise, I won't do it again."

"Okay." He doesn't look convinced. I'll have to prove it to him.

"He's doing well. All I want to do is eat bananas and ketchup."

"Will it happen again?"

I shrug. "Maybe, maybe not. The doctor says it's a real possibility."

Alex lets out a heavy sigh. "How are you today?"

"Heaps better. I stopped vomiting on Saturday, but they kept me in for observation. Doctor Morgan came by," I say again. "They did an ultrasound to make sure he's okay, and he is. And they wanted to make sure the vomiting had stopped before I was discharged."

"Mom's not happy."

"Your mom isn't liking me very much because of…" I place my hand to my stomach. "I can imagine what she's thinking of me now."

"Dad was worried, she was angry."

I feel even worse. My heart sinking further. "I'll call them to apologize."

"Don't. Don't worry about it. It'll make things worse between Mom and you. Just leave it."

I'll follow Alex's advice and leave it alone. "Okay. I've got my next appointment with Doctor Morgan in two weeks, do you and your parents want to come?"

"Yeah. For sure."

Standing, I round the table, and give him a hug. Kissing him on the cheek, I whisper, "I'm sorry for being a jerk."

"Just don't be a jerk again, and we're all good." Alex pushes his chair out, swings in one fluid motion, and sits me on his knee.

"I promise, I won't."

He leans into me, nuzzling into my neck, and kissing me softly.

"Oh, how cute," comes Ruby's nasally, high pitched voice.

"Love-birds," Blair says, and adds her giggle.

"You sound like idiots. But hey." I lift my brows, smirking at them. Blair stops walking past to glare at me. I can't help it, I turn Alex's head, lean in, and give him a passionate kiss.

I hear Blair huff before she walks away.

"You enjoyed that." Alex beams, obviously pleased too.

"As much as you did."

"I enjoyed it for a different reason." He leans in again, kissing up my neck.

"Oh, I like that too." Closing my eyes, I lean into him. Loving how he's touching me.

"Get a room," Hunter says as he sits opposite us. "Why aren't we over there?" He points behind us to our regular table. "Zar's there, not here." Both Alex and I look at Hunter. "Not, that... you know. God no." The tips of his ears get pink, and it's funny to watch.

"So you're not into her?" I ask.

"Nah, nothing like that. I mean, everyone's over there and you two are here. Did something happen?"

"You sure you don't like Zar?" Alex asks, completely ignoring his concern as to why we're here.

"What? Yeah, nah. Not like that." He stands abruptly, grabs his lunch, and walks away.

I start to laugh. "He's so crushing on her."

"You have no idea how much."

"Really?" I ask. "Bad?"

"He's into her. But he's too gutless to ask her out."

"Why?" I look over to Hunter, he's now at our regular table, sitting at the furthest end from Zar. But the way he's positioned, he can see her clearly.

"Because he's got balls," he says as if that's supposed to make sense to me. I shrug, and add in a small shake of my head. "He wants them attached to his body."

"What are you talking about? He's already asked her out."

"She's like crazy and shit."

"Huh? She's not crazy... or shit," I add with a smile.

"She's kind of hardcore. And he's afraid if he screws it up, she'll destroy him and his balls."

I laugh, hard. "Are you kidding? Just tell him not to hurt her. Anyway, they were supposed to go to the movies. Oh man." I lightly slap my forehead, feeling even worse. "I forgot to ask her how it went."

"It didn't. She cancelled."

"Why?"

"Because she was worried about you. And she was waiting for you to call so she could come see you."

And there goes the shame climbing to a new high. I've been letting my best friend and my boyfriend down. I sigh, embarrassed and ashamed. "You're both too good to me."

"'Cause we love you."

"I know. I don't deserve it, not after what I've done."

"Don't be so hard on yourself. I know Zar's forgiven you, and so have I. And you promised not to do it again."

Sitting on Alex's lap, I know how much he loves me. This really could've driven a wedge between us. He could've used it as an excuse to say he doesn't want anything to do with us.

But he didn't. Instead, he's sticking by me.

And our son.

CHAPTER
16

I 'M SICK NEARLY every day.

I've only had two days where I haven't vomited. Nothing like what landed me in hospital, but constant morning, *all-day-sickness*. I hate it. I can barely keep anything down, the hot apple cider helps, but then there are times is feels like it does nothing.

Today's Saturday and I'm working at CCC's all day. She's been preparing her jam for the festival, and has been using the kitchen at CCC's to get it ready. She does this every year.

"I'm taking you to work today," Dad says as I walk into the kitchen to get my banana and ketchup. I nod my head, as I peel my banana. "Ugh. I have no idea how you can eat that." I look over to him, Dad's nose is scrunched with disgust.

"It's really good. You should try it."

"I will not try it." He squares his shoulders and puffs his chest out.

"Then don't make that face." I circle my finger around, implying the disgusting expression on his face. "Until you try it, you can't knock it." I dunk the last of my banana in my ketchup, and eat it.

"Fine, I'll try it. Hand it over." He points to one of many bananas sitting on the kitchen island. I push away from the opposite counter, grab a banana, and hand it to him. Then, place my bowl with the ketchup in it on the counter and push it over to him. "I can't believe I'm going to do this."

I can't help but smile as he dunks the banana. He's struggling to bring it to his mouth to even taste it. I'm smiling like an idiot watching Dad. "It's good," I try to encourage.

His hand shakes, and I keep smirking. "I don't think I can."

"Try it. You'll probably end up loving it."

"Fine. Here goes." He quickly shoves it into his mouth and chews. His face morphs from cringing to flat-out dry-retching. He runs over to the trash, flips the lid open with his foot, and spits into it. "You've got to be kidding me. That's the most revolting thing I've ever tasted."

Faking hurt, I clutch at my chest. "My heart is broken. Broken…" I fake whimper.

"There's no way I will ever put that in my mouth again." He points to the semi-chewed banana in the trash.

Laughing, I walk toward the bathroom, needing to pee. Again.

"Yuck." I hear the faucet running, and Dad washing his mouth out. "Be ready to go in about fifteen minutes," he shouts down the hallway.

"I'll be ready," I reply before closing the bathroom door.

"How are you, Andy?" Arthur asks when I walk into the kitchen. "You're looking particularly lovely today."

I adore Arthur, he's such a beautiful old man who'll do absolutely anything for Clarence. "Thank you. I'm feeling okay."

"In comparison to what happened last weekend?" He's referring to my hospital stay.

"Absolutely. That was hell."

"Clarence was so worried for you. Actually, I was too. But you seem… hmmm, what's the word? Glowing?"

"Glowing?" I smirk, looking down at my tummy.

"You do. You have a lovely glow about you." He walks over and gives me a small hug which catches me unaware. "I'm glad you and the baby are okay," he whispers.

"Andy!" Clarence nearly yells.

I break out of Arthur's hug, and turn to a new embrace from Clarence. "I was worried. But your momma, she kept me in the loop of what was happening." She hugs me tighter.

"Hi Clarence."

She steps back, and instantly I smell the sweet aroma of strawberry jam on her. Looking around, I can't see the jars, or the huge pots usually cooking on the range. "No jam?"

"Not today. I'm slightly worried." She furrows her brows.

"Why? Do you need help? You don't have to share the recipe, but I can do whatever you need me to."

She places her hands on either side of my face, leans in and kisses my cheek. "You're a sweet girl, Andy. Nothing like that. But I think I've got the ratios of something wrong. Or the strawberries aren't as good as they have been in previous years."

"I got them from, you know," Clarence says, not wanting to give away their secret location.

"I'm not doubting you. Maybe they used something on them that they normally don't. It's okay. I'll make it work."

Clarence steps back. I hear some people come in, and I look over my shoulder in the direction of the front. "My offer stands. But for now, I better get to work."

"No, Arthur can serve them. Go, Arthur," Clarence barks. Arthur has a huge smile on his face, but quickly goes to serve the people who've walked in.

"Have I done something wrong?" Worry flits inside my tummy. My son and butterflies both dancing merrily.

"What? No, why would you say that?"

"Because I'm supposed to be out there." I hook my thumb over my shoulder.

"Dear girl. Arthur and I bought something for you. And I wanted to give it to you."

"Oh." Immediate relief takes over. "I thought I was in trouble."

"Just wait here." Clarence disappears out the side door leading to a small store room. She comes back pushing a stroller. Inside the stroller are two boxes of Huggies diapers, and several other smaller packs of various things.

Clasping my hand to my mouth, I tear up. "What did you do?" I ask.

"I know this will be a hard time, and Arthur and I wanted to make it a little bit easier for you. It's not much, just a little something to let you know we're with you." I lower my hand, still crying. "Aw, Andy, we did this because we love you."

"I don't know what to say." The stroller is new, it still has some tags hanging off it. It's sleek and sturdy, and looks so perfect. "Thank you," I whisper. I throw my arms around her, hugging her closely.

"You're welcome."

"Oh no, I knew this was going to happen," Arthur says as he walks in and catches me crying, and us hugging.

"Arthur, thank you." I open my arm, accepting him into our embrace.

"You're welcome."

"I really didn't expect anything. Thank you so much. This means so much to me."

"Well, I know we're all emotional, but we have work to do. And I need to work out why my jam is all wrong. Andy, go." Clarence points out the front.

I take one last look at my new stroller, and smile. I place both my hands over my chest, and whisper, "Thank you."

Clarence and Arthur both look so proud, and happy.

Heading out to the front, I serve a customer who's waiting. Nothing, and I mean absolutely nothing can knock me off my perch today.

"You ready?" Mom asks as she sips on the coffee I made her.

"Laura, I didn't realize you'd arrived already," Clarence says when she walks out to the front and sees Mom.

"I've only been here a few moments." She takes another sip. "Andy makes a good coffee."

"That she does."

"Mom, guess what?" I say, jumping out of my skin with utter excitement.

"What? Is everything okay?" Mom's smiling, watching me become more and more excited.

"Everything's so good. Look." I hold my hands out, both palms pointed toward Mom. "Don't move. Just wait." I run out into the kitchen where my new stroller is.

"Where is that girl going?" I hear Mom ask.

"She's excited," Clarence replies.

"I can tell."

Pushing the stroller out, I show Mom. Mom places her mug down on the counter, and takes a few steps around the side. Her mouth opens in shock. "What is this?" she says, stepping closer.

"Clarence and Arthur bought this for my baby," I say, still so happy and grateful.

"Clarence. I'm…" Mom shakes her head. Tears welling in her eyes. "I don't know what to say."

Clarence flicks her hand at Mom. "There's nothing you need or have to say. We love Andy," Clarence drapes her arm over my shoulders and hugs me to her body, "like she's our own."

"This is so generous," Mom says. "Please, let me pay you."

"You'll do no such thing. This is a gift, from us to Andy and the baby."

"You're so kind. Thank you." Mom smiles at Clarence. But I can see the tears about to fall. This really is a beautiful moment.

Neither Mom nor I expected anything like this.

"Don't go crying. I don't need that kind of drama in here," Clarence says, making Mom and me laugh. "Andy, finish cleaning the coffee machine, and you can go." Clarence turns, and leaves without saying anything else, disappearing into the kitchen.

I know she's getting choked up over our obvious over-emotional ways. She doesn't want to show us how we're affecting her.

"Andy, this is so sweet of Clarence and Arthur."

"I know. I couldn't say thank you enough."

"How beautiful." Mom smiles still looking at the stroller. "And diapers. And wipes. Wow, I'm speechless."

"I know. I'm really thankful. I thought Clarence was going to be angry at me for being sick last weekend. Instead, she and Arthur gave me this."

"They're really good people. They didn't have to buy you anything."

"I know," I say agreeing with Mom. "I better finish cleaning the coffee machine."

"I'll wait." Mom walks back to where she left her mug, picks it up and continues drinking it, all the while she keeps looking at the stroller. "That's a really good stroller. I was looking at it recently."

"You were looking at strollers?"

"Yeah, I've been looking at things on-line. Just gauging prices, and what you'll need."

This shouldn't surprise me, but it does. Mom was adamant at the start that I should explore other options, so to hear her saying she's looking at baby things, really shocks me. "Why would you be looking?"

"Like I said, I was looking at things you'll need."

"Mom, you don't have to buy everything. I've got some money saved from working here. I can buy things."

"This is my first grandchild, your father and I will be buying things for him and for you."

I smile to myself while I continue cleaning the coffee machine.

I'm truly blessed to have these amazing people supporting me.

Being fifteen is hard. But being fifteen and pregnant, is the hardest thing I'll ever have to do in my life. But, I'm so lucky, because I think I've got the best people in the world around me.

CHAPTER 17

"**S**HE'S KILLING MY head," Alex says when I get in the car for him to give me a ride to school.

"Who's killing your head?" I ask.

Before he takes off, he takes his phone out of his pocket, scrolls through it and hands it to me. "Check *her* out."

And just by the way he grumbles the word *'her'* I know who he's talking about. Looking at the messages, I can't believe how desperate Blair is turning out to be. "I don't get why she's so adamant to get to you," I say.

"Oh, right. Thanks," Alex says, hurt.

"I don't mean it that way. I mean, why is she so persistent? Doesn't she get it?" The messages are teasing and some are even down-right explicit. "Whoa," I murmur reading one venomous message about me. What I notice is it's all one sided. Alex only responds once, to tell her to stop messaging him. "What made her finally stop, I wonder?"

"I blocked her. Look at that last message. I had enough by that stage. She wasn't getting the hint, so I blocked her ass."

I scroll to the bottom, where there's a message about what she wants to do to him, with Hunter, Finn, and Elliot watching. "Wow." My eyes bulge at the overly detailed description.

"I'm thinking I might need to go to her parents. Cause this is full-on."

"That's an understatement," I whisper and look out the window at the scenery toward school. "I don't know what to do. I have no idea why she has this fixation on you. Not saying you're not worth it," I quickly add in case I upset Alex. "But she knows you don't want her."

Doubt climbs inside my mind. Does he want her? Has he told her something to make her think she's got a chance? Is it because I'm pregnant?

Worry is clouding my every thought. Frowning, I feel myself move closer to the door. My mind is playing havoc with me, convincing me Alex no longer wants me, and now wants Blair.

"You okay?" Alex asks.

"Huh?" I mumble, my own anxious mind not wanting to let go of thoughts of Blair and Alex together.

"Are you okay?"

I'm struggling. Should I say something? Tell him it's okay if he doesn't want me but wants her? Should I pretend to be fine with it?

"Andy, what's happening? Is it the baby?" Alex asks as he pulls into a car space at school and immediately turns toward me.

"No, it's not him."

"Then what?" Another car pulls up beside us. The passenger and driver are both seniors, Taylor and Justin who are dating. They link hands and walk away. "Andy!"

"Is something going on between you and Blair? I mean, it's okay if it is. I get it." Lowering my head, I wring my hands together, nervously.

"Okay? You'd be okay if Blair and I were dating?" the tone in

Alex's voice tells me he's not exactly thrilled by my question or maybe my response.

"I'm just trying to say, I'd understand if you were seeing her." I refuse to make eye contact. Mostly because, I'm upset. I can barely keep my voice from cracking.

"You think because of these messages, and her attempts to try to make me leave you, that I want to go? I don't. I'm not interested in her. There's nothing Blair can offer that would make me look her way."

"She's not pregnant." The words hurt as they leave me.

"Which means she's not carrying *my* child. I told you, Andy, I don't want her."

I look over to him, and motion with a weak smile. "Are you sure?"

"Positive." He leans over and gives me a small peck on the cheek. "I love you," he says.

"I love you."

He pulls away, opens his door, and waits for me to join him by the front of the car. "Mom isn't going to come to the next appointment," he says in a small voice. I think he was waiting to break the news to me.

"I figured she wouldn't want to."

"I'll try to talk her into it."

"Please, don't. I don't want her there if she doesn't want to be. It's okay."

"Okay, I won't bring it up to her again. But dad's coming, for sure." I let out a small chuckle. "What's funny?"

"Mom wasn't particularly invested when I first told my parents, but Dad seemed okay. And your dad appears to be okay with it too. Why is it the dads are more accepting than the moms? Mom is fine now, though, but it took some time."

"Parents are weird. What do you think we're going to be like?"

I shrug my shoulders. "I just don't want to screw up."

We walk into the main building, and head toward my locker. "Hey guys," Bek says as she approaches us. She looks really nervous.

"Hey, Bek. How was your weekend?" I ask.

Alex gives me a quick kiss before turning to leave. "Um, I think you better stay," Bek says.

"What's happening?" Alex looks at me, and I shrug. Then he turns to Bek.

"There's something going around, and I think you both should know."

"What now?" Alex asks, sounding exasperated.

I move closer to him, having no idea what Blair's cooked up now. I know it's her; it has to be. She's the only one causing all this unnecessary drama.

Bek purses her lips together. She pulls her phone out of her pocket, scrolls through it and hands it to Alex but so we can both see it.

There's a picture of me pushing the stroller out in front of Clarence's cafe, with Mom standing beside it. The look on my face says it all.

"Right," Alex whispers.

"Don't tell me, Blair?" I ask, already knowing it's her.

"Ruby," she corrects.

"If it's not one, it's the other," Alex says. He hands Bek back her phone.

Bek hesitantly places it back in her pocket. "So, it's true?"

Before Alex denies it, I nod my head. "Please, don't say anything though. I'm not ready for everyone to know."

"I promise, I won't." She smiles. She steps forward and gives me a hug. "Congratulations," she whispers and tightens her embrace. "You're keeping it, right?"

"Yeah." Funny how everyone who knows asks me the same

question. If I was twenty-five, no one would utter those words.

She steps back, and quickly scans my body. "I'm happy for you. For both of you," she says as she turns to Alex. Stepping back, she ducks her head down and hurries away.

"She's going to tell everyone," Alex warns.

"I honestly don't think she will. Bek isn't like Blair and Ruby."

"If you trust her, okay. I gotta go to my locker. See you at lunch?"

"Yeah."

He takes off in the direction of his locker, and I stay at mine, getting my stuff ready. Zar is nowhere to be seen. Grabbing my phone, I send her a quick text. *You coming to school?*

She replies within seconds. **On my way. Crazy morning. By crazy I mean I slept in and didn't want to wake up.**

Laughing, I close my locker and start walking to class.

Instantly a heaviness settles in my stomach.

Great, my first class for Monday, and Zar isn't here yet.

"Why'd you even bother coming today?" I ask Zar as we walk to the cafeteria.

She holds up a finger and says, "Mom."

"Ah." I totally understanding.

"I hear Ruby's causing problems. Although, I doubt it's Ruby who's behind it. She's not really that smart. It would be Blair. Actually, come to think of it, neither are too bright. Devious, but not bright."

"I really don't know what to do about them any more," I say earnestly. "It's all petty shit."

"Tell me about it. But I think you have to tell your parents about them."

"It really is crap. Blair's hell-bent on having Alex. I honestly think it's just the chase. If she actually gets him, she'll probably drop him and move onto someone else within a week."

"A week? Gee, that's being generous." Zar laughs. "She's still trying to spread rumors about you. She's adamant you're pregnant."

"Well," I murmur, both of us knowing I *am* pregnant.

"Did you see that picture of you?"

"Yeah, Bek showed me this morning. She asked me if it's true. I told her."

"Why would you do that?"

"I trust her. And if she does tell anyone, well, then I'll stop trusting her."

"That's pretty black-or-white, isn't it? She'll either keep your secret or betray you."

"I wouldn't say betray. Because let's face it, everyone's going to find out sooner or later. I'd rather they find out when I'm ready to tell them."

"I suppose." Zar throws her hands up.

We sit at our usual table, and I know everyone's talking about me. Truth be told, I don't care anymore. They can say whatever they want. "Why haven't you and Hunter gone on a date yet?"

"What?" Zar averts her eyes, and she presses her lips into a thin line.

"Zar?" I question. This response isn't anything I would've expected from her. Her shoulders have tensed, and she avoiding looking at me. "Zar!"

"What?" she replies, still not looking at me.

"Oh my God. Have you two gone out on a date?" Her huge smile tells me they have. "Why didn't you tell me?"

Zar finally meets my eyes. "You have so much going on. I thought it might... I don't know." She's lost for words.

"You're not embarrassed to tell me, are you?"

"God, no. I really like him. But I don't want to jump ahead of myself either. Maybe it was just a one-off date. You know, maybe he doesn't like me the way I like him."

"When did it happen?"

"Saturday. We went for pizza, and a movie. And he ate his pizza with pineapple." She balks and shakes her head. "Who has pineapple on a pizza?"

"Don't ask me. I eat bananas dipped in ketchup."

"Yuck." Zar sticks her tongue out. "Anyway, I think it went okay, considering."

"Did you kiss?"

"No!" Zar snaps. "I was sitting there watching the movie, and all I could think about was kissing him. My hands were sweating, my heart was going crazy. I don't even remember the movie." She beams.

I laugh. "And you didn't hold hands, I'm guessing?"

"Did you not hear what I said? My hands were sweating. He bought popcorn, and I had some. Got stuck in my throat and then I went into a coughing fit. Everyone turned around to see who was coughing so loud they couldn't hear the movie. Then I got up to go to the bathroom, and slipped on the last step. Fell on my butt. Now I have a bruised butt, and a bruised ego. So yeah, considering all of that, I think it went well."

"Oh Zar, that sounds painful."

"My butt is still hurting, so yeah, I agree with you."

"Have you heard from Hunter since?"

Zar's shoulder slink down. "Nope."

"Oh," I say slowly. "Is he here today?" I look around, expecting to see him with Alex and the other guys who are standing in line for food. He's not there. "He might not be here."

"Or he's avoiding me."

"Did you send him a message?"

"No! I'm a freaking lady, Andy. I'm not chasing him. He wants me, he can chase me."

"Maybe he thinks you're not interested in him, and he's

avoiding you so he doesn't get hurt."

"What? That's not what's happening."

"You're not going to know if you don't send him a message."

"Nope, he can come to me."

"Ha!" I huff, rolling my eyes.

"What's that supposed to mean?" Zar snaps.

"It means, you might miss out on possibly the best thing that could happen to you, because you're too stubborn and scared to send him a message."

"I'm not scared."

"Says the girl who's terrified."

"No, I'm not!"

"Aha. As long as you believe it, that's all that matters."

"I'm not. Look." She lifts her phone, unlocks it, sends Hunter a message then places her phone down again. "See, message sent." I smile cheekily. It dawns on her within a few seconds. "Oh my God. You goaded me into doing that."

"I didn't do anything." I peel my banana, and eat it.

"Eat your stupid banana, with your stupid ketchup," Zar sulks, playfully. "I can't believe you bullied me into doing that."

"I didn't bully you. You just don't like being called scared."

"Shut up." She bites into her wrap, giving me the stink eye.

"Hey," Hunter says standing beside Zar. Zar has her mouth full when she looks up to Hunter.

"Hey," she says with a mouthful of food.

Hunter draws his brows together, and forces a smile.

Zar chews so fast as she lowers her head, totally embarrassed. How funny, and cute. They're so digging each other, but neither are game enough to say anything.

"Can I sit?" Hunter asks.

"Sure thing," I reply for us both, considering Zar is still chewing.

Hunter sits beside Zar. And when she finishes, she smiles at Hunter. She also has something green stuck between her front two teeth. "How are you?" she asks.

Hunter and I can't help but look at her teeth. They're so white against her dark chocolate skin, but that green thing sticks out pretty badly.

"Zar," I get her attention. She snaps her head around, giving me more stink-eye. I motion to her teeth.

"What?" I indicate she has something in her teeth again, without actually saying it aloud. "You have got to be kidding me," she mumbles angrily, then tries to pick it out.

It's all quite funny. One comedic episode after the other. She looks at me, and smiles, I shake my head. She's made it worse.

"Excuse me," she says as she leaps up, and heads to the bathroom.

Hunter can't control his smile. I look at him, he looks at me, and we both start laughing. "Poor Zar," I say.

"She gets so awkward around me. I love it. It's so cute."

"I heard about your date."

"I felt so bad for her. I just wanted to wrap her in my arms and hug her. But she was super on-edge, and I didn't know what to do. But this, this just tops it all off."

"Did you have a good time?"

"The best. When she's not stressing out, she's so much fun to be around. She was giving me shit about having pizza with pineapple. I know that's a conversation that can divide people, but man, I had no idea she hated it that much. Then she went all quiet on me again."

"She likes you," I admit to him.

The tips of his ears get pink, as a wide smile lights up his face. "I like her too. A lot."

"Tell her. I think she's feeling like you don't like her."

"Did she say something?" he asks.

Man, why did I have to bring it up? I've got Zar's back, but the fact is, they like each other, they're both scared to say anything. "Look, Hunter." I lean forward, so I can drop my voice and no one hears me. "She likes you, you like her. No need to make anything complicated."

"Ha. Yeah, well, if I knew she liked me for sure, then I'd definitely go for it."

"Jeez, what do you want? I'm telling you, she likes you."

Alex sits beside me, and looks at Hunter, then me. "What's going on? Seems a bit tense."

"I'm trying to tell Hunter how Zar likes him and to go for it. Tell her how he feels. But he needs confirmation that she does actually like him."

"Confirmation? Like what? Ask her out, don't be a pussy, man." Alex scrunches up a piece of blank paper laying on the table, and throws it at Hunter.

Zar's walking toward us. Her eyes widen when she sees Hunter. She fans herself, as if to say he's hot. I can't help but laugh. At that very moment, Hunter sees me looking at Zar, and turns to see who I'm looking at.

Zar's caught fanning herself.

She stops walking, and the smile on her face disappears. Her arm drops beside her body, and her mouth opens to a near perfect O.

She stares at me, then Hunter. Straightening her shoulders and holding her head high, she continues walking toward us. *Go girl!*

Sitting down next to Hunter, she leans over to him, and kisses him.

"Whoa!" Alex and I echo together.

The kiss is long, and passionate and quite sexy.

I have a giant smile on my face, and Alex is sitting beside me, with his mouth gaping open. Neither of us look away, although we probably should. *Been there, done that.*

Zar pulls away from the kiss, turns back and keeps eating her lunch. The pride rolling off her is undeniable.

Hunter is left speechless, and he's looking at her.

He opens his mouth.

Then closes it.

Then opens it again, lifts his hand in gesture, then lowers it again.

"I kissed you," Zar says.

"I know," he responds, still shocked.

"Got a problem with that?" She doesn't turn to look at him, instead she keeps eating her lunch.

The silence between them is tense. He's not responding. I can see Zar's confidence is quickly dwindling. She's waiting for him to say he loved the kiss, or hated it. *Something.* Her eyes redden.

My heart slowly breaks for Zar. The longer she sits without a response from Hunter, the more she's struggling to hold in the tears.

I watch as her jaw quivers.

Hunter's still staring at her.

I feel like kicking him under the table.

But suddenly, he leans over to her, cups her face in his hands, and moves in to kiss her the way she kissed him.

"Aw," I whisper, placing my hand to my heart.

He pulls back from the kiss, both are staring into each other's eyes. It feels like such an intimate and personal moment. "That's what I think," he replies quietly.

About time these two found their groove.

Looking down at my food, I internally high-five Zar. I'm proud of her for taking a risk. Obviously, Hunter's impressed.

"Oh joy, another hot one gone," Blair's annoying voice scratches through me.

The hair on my arms lift when I hear her talk. "Do you have

anything of interest to say? No? Good, go away," I say before anyone has a chance of saying anything to her. I look back down at my food, ignoring her.

"I just find it interesting that you've been caught with a stroller, and you're still insisting you're not pregnant. Is it because Alex isn't the father?"

I look up, smile, and say, "Oh, I didn't realize you were still here. I thought it was an annoying sound, but I didn't realize that annoying sound was you."

Blair's jaw tightens, her eyes enlarge and her lip curls into a snarl. "Bitch!" she screams at me as she throws herself at me.

She lands a slap to my face, and knocks me off the seat. Falling backward, I hit my head on the floor. Before I know it, Blair's sitting on my stomach. She lifts her hand, makes it into a fist, and slams it into my face.

I hold my hands up in self-defense, but my first thought is that I can't let her hurt my baby. She's pulled off me by someone, and I hear someone yell, *"She's pregnant."* I'm not sure who's said the words aloud.

Blair stumbles back, a look of satisfaction crossing her face. "I knew it!" she proudly admits. "I knew it. You're pregnant. It's not even Alex's, is it? You slut," she spits toward me. She steps closer to Alex, trying to console him. But he pushes her away, and comes to help me up. "Alex, darling," she says, shuffling closer.

"You're the biggest idiot I know," he says.

"But, sweetheart."

I look around the cafeteria. We've amassed a huge crowd of people. Miss Haines and Miss Foster both quickly enter, assessing what's happening.

"I'm not interested in you, Blair. I've never been interested in you. Leave me alone."

Blair isn't happy with his response. She looks around, noticing the number of people gathering. "What does she have that I don't? She's a pregnant slut, I'm not."

I go to step forward, but Alex steps in front of me, shielding me with his body. "What does she have that you don't?" he asks. She nods her head, and crosses her arms in front of her body. "My heart."

"Whatever." She flips her hand at him dismissively. "She's screwing around. I would *never* do that to you. I've loved you since the beginning of the year, I'll love you forever."

"Bunny-boiler much?" Zar says loudly.

I look to Zar, she shrugs as if to say… what?

"Not that it's any of your business, but she doesn't screw around."

I place my hand on Alex's arm, and step out from behind him. Everyone's watching. A few people are whispering. But pretty much, all eyes are on us.

"What's going on?" Miss Haines asks as she stands between us.

"Blair attacked Andy," someone says. I don't catch who.

"Why?" Miss Haines looks to Blair, then me. "Why?" she asks again. I look down not saying anything, Blair does the same thing. "Right, everyone, back to your own business. You three, with me." She points to me, Blair, and Alex.

We fall into line behind her. Alex and I are holding hands, and Blair is behind us. I can feel her eyes boring into my back. I know Blair's angry, and she'd love to try and hurt me again.

We go into a vacant classroom. Miss Haines is waiting for us to enter before she closes the door. "Now, what's going on?" she asks, looking to us.

Blair says nothing, so I decide, I better tell her. "Blair's been hell-bent on getting into Alex's pants. She's tried her hardest to get everyone to believe that I'm pregnant, and how the baby isn't Alex's. Today, she was mouthing off, and I told her she was annoying and to leave us alone. She lunged at me, slapping, and nearly punching me."

"That's not true. All I was doing was walking past her, and she tried to trip me. I've never said anything about you being pregnant. Are you pregnant?" she asks innocently.

Miss Haines looks to me, then puts her hand up to stop this topic.

"Miss Haines, can I show you something?" Alex says.

"Please do."

Alex lifts his phone, and goes to the string of messages Blair has been sending him. "She's the problem, Miss Haines. Look." He thrusts the phone into Miss Haines's hands, and steps back, giving her room.

Her eyes are glued to the phone.

Blair's reaction is priceless. "You did this, Blair," I say to her.

"He's too good for you. You're nothing but a slut who can't keep her legs closed. He deserves someone like me."

"Enough!" Miss Haines barks at Blair. "Stop speaking like that. Now, why are you doing this?"

"He shouldn't be with her."

"He'll be with whomever he wants to be. You've got to stop this." Miss Haines turns to me. "How long has this been going on for?"

"Weeks," I answer.

"Actually," Alex interrupts. The pained look on his face tells me he's been hiding something from me.

The hair on the back of my neck stands to attention. What's he not been telling me? "Actually?" I ask, crossing my arms in front of my chest.

"It's been happening for months. At first I tried nicely to tell her that it wasn't going to happen. But she's really adamant. I blocked her on social media, and my phone. I don't want anything to do with her or her horrible sister."

"She's been doing this for months?" I ask. Alex nods his head. "Why didn't you tell me earlier?"

He looks down at his feet. "I thought she'd leave me alone."

"Obviously not," I answer.

"Obviously not," Alex echoes.

"Blair, I do believe a conversation with your parents is warranted. From here on in, don't talk to either Alex or Andy. I have to involve your parents."

"That's not fair. What about her?" She points a skinny finger at me. "She's pregnant and she's not in trouble? You're such an idiot, Alex. I could've given you whatever you wanted."

"That's enough from you, Blair! What has gotten into you?" Miss Haines asks. "Go straight to the office. Wait for me outside Ms. Dawson's office. I have to involve the principal too."

"She shouldn't be here. It's not safe for someone who's pregnant," Blair blurts, tears running down her cheeks. She's desperately trying to get me out of this school. Maybe this is her way of getting rid of me, so she can get close with Alex.

"Out!" Miss Haines says, extending her hand, and pointing out of the classroom.

Blair narrows her eyes, as she stomps out of the room. She looks over her shoulder at me, and flips me the bird then quickly slams the door as she leaves.

Miss Haines lets out a deep breath. "Well." She shakes her head. "What's happening?" She looks to me, then Alex.

"Exactly what we've said. She hasn't been at all shy about trying to split us up," Alex says.

Miss Haines scrunches her mouth. "Are you pregnant?" she asks.

The question is tough. Hard for me to say yes aloud, but I've been asked by a teacher. It's not something I was expecting I had to tell the school yet, but I suppose I'm an idiot for thinking Blair was going to let up.

I should've known.

In hindsight, I should've predicted this was going to happen.

"I am," I say.

Miss Haines doesn't look surprised. Perhaps she is, but she's hiding it. "And… um…" Her gaze switches between Alex and myself. "You're the father?" It's not exactly a question, but it's not a statement either. It's somewhere in between.

"Yes, I am."

"Do both your parents know?" Miss Haines is uncomfortable.

"Yeah," we answer in unison.

Miss Haines lets out a long breath. I think she's relieved she's not discovering this and has to be the one to tell our parents. "How far along are you?"

"I'm nearly eleven weeks."

Miss Haines looks lost in what she has to say. I don't think she's dealt with a student being pregnant before. Discomfort is evident on her face. She's shuffling from foot to foot, and avoids looking at us. "I'm going to go deal with Blair. Then I'll have to talk with Ms. Dawson."

"Okay," both Alex and I say.

"For now, just…"

"We know. Don't say anything to anyone," I say.

"Yeah, I think that's best until I talk to Ms. Dawson."

Alex and I link our fingers together, and wait for Miss Haines to give us more instructions. "Can we go?" Alex asks.

"Of course."

Alex and I walk out of the classroom, leaving Miss Haines behind.

"That was weird," I say. "I think she has no idea how to deal with me."

"I think you're right. At least Blair's going to leave us alone."

"For now," I add.

"Yeah, for now."

We walk back into the cafeteria, and the moment we do, all eyes are on us. Whispers can be heard from all around the room.

"Ignore them," Alex says as he squeezes my hand tighter.

"Oh my God. What happened?" Zar asks the moment we sit. "Tell me, she's being thrown out of school? Tell me Miss Haines smacked her down. Tell me Miss Haines yelled and screamed at her." Zar eagerly looks to us.

"Nothing like that," I reply.

"No, nothing so dramatic. But. Miss Haines is going to talk to her parents," Alex says. He looks over to Hunter, who's talking with Trey, filling him in on everything he missed. "And we told her, about…" Alex discreetly nods his head toward me.

Zar's eyes widen, "What did she say?"

"Nothing she really could say," I answer. "She's going to talk to Ms. Dawson."

"Is that all?" Zar leans forward, wanting more juicy gossip. But there really isn't much to say.

"She looked really uncomfortable. Almost like she didn't know what to say," I add. "What's been happening here?"

"Everyone's talking about it. It's spreading like crazy that you're… you know. Out of everything that happened, that's the biggest thing."

Turning, I notice the looks everyone's giving me.

They're whispering behind their hands, some laughing, some turning away in disgust.

"So everyone knows, then?" I question, more for confirmation than anything else.

"I'm pretty sure everyone will know really soon," Zar says.

"It's okay. We'll get through it." Alex embraces me, reassuringly.

Looking to Zar, she smiles. But her smile doesn't reach her eyes. Actually, she appears to be worried.

I don't know. I'm not as confident as Alex. I think everything's about to change.

CHAPTER
18

"I'M DRIVING YOU to school today," Mom says as she rushes into the kitchen, pours herself a coffee, then rushes back out again.

"Why?" I call.

Mom emerges from the hallway, mug still in hand, one shoe on, and one shoe off. "The school called. They want to talk to me."

"To you? Is it about what happened with Blair?" curiously, I ask.

"Ugh, don't even get me started." Mom rolls her eyes, then leaves again. "They haven't said why they want to talk to me," she yells from her room.

Eating my banana and ketchup, I can only imagine why the school wants to speak to Mom. It's most likely about what happened on Monday with Blair. School yesterday was unusually quiet. Lots of people whispering, but no one came out and asked me directly if the rumors are true. Weird.

"I think it's because of Blair."

"More than likely." She emerges again, this time both shoes on, mug still in hand, and her hair swept into a low ponytail. She walks over to the sink, rinses her mug, then looks to the microwave for the time. "Crap, we're going to be late. How long before you're done eating your banana and ketchup?" Scrunching her nose, she pokes her tongue out in disgust.

"You should try it," I say. I quickly fix my hair, wrapping it into a messy topknot.

"Your father told me how delicious it was. No, thanks," she says sarcastically. "When will you be ready?"

"I'll go brush my teeth, then we can go."

"Okay, hurry up."

Rushing off, I brush my teeth, slip my feet into my shoes, grab my backpack and head out to the kitchen. Mom gets her car keys, and I feel the impending niggle of vomit starting. "Wait!" I yell as I dash off to the bathroom, and throw up everything I just ate.

"You okay?" Mom asks. Though, as I'm progressing with my pregnancy, she's less concerned about the morning sickness. Only when I don't stop, which has only happened once.

Kneeling in front of the toilet, I vomit again. My stomach settles immediately. "Yeah. Just need to brush my teeth again," I say to Mom, who's now inside the bathroom, leaning against the wall.

Mom helps me up, and I go to brush my teeth. When I'm done, I head back out, grab my bag from where I dropped it and wait for Mom so we can get to school.

"You okay?" she asks.

"Yeah. Morning sickness." I scrunch my nose.

"Hopefully it settles within the next week or two. It usually disappears after the first trimester."

"I'm sick of vomiting. Not knowing when it's going to strike. Worst, is not knowing once it starts if it's going to stop."

Mom shrugs her shoulders as she locks the house, and we

walk to her car. "Have you thought of names yet?" Mom asks. Her tone is cautious, like she doesn't really want to ask.

"Not really. I know it's a boy."

"As you've said many times. But you haven't thought of any names?"

"I need to think about it. I'm not sure."

"What if it's a girl?"

"*He's* not."

Mom reverses out of the driveway, then starts toward school. "He may be a she. You have to think about names for both."

I chuckle. "I don't have to think about names for a girl, I know it's a boy. I can feel it right here." I place my hand over my stomach.

"Gut feelings. I know them, and I'm a firm believer of listening to them, and not ignoring them."

"See, you get it."

Mom laughs and takes in a deep breath. "I get it, but until my grandbaby is born, that's the only time we're going to know if it's a boy or girl."

No use in arguing with Mom. I know it's a boy, and that's all that matters. Now, I have to think of a name.

"Mrs. Price, I'm glad you could come in today," Ms. Dawson says as she closes the door to her office. "How are you, Andy?"

"I'm okay," I reply, wary of her careful tone.

Ms. Dawson isn't very old, maybe the same age as Mom. She's tall though, and has short, blonde hair that frames her heart-shaped face and hides her wider forehead. Her eyes are an intense dark brown, and anyone who looks into them knows Ms. Dawson means what she says. I like that about Ms. Dawson, because you always know where you stand with her. She's a woman of her word.

Ms. Dawson walks around her desk, and sits. There are high stacks of papers on her desk, but they're all sorted into organized piles in trays. "I've called you in to talk about…"

"Blair," I say, finishing her sentence.

Ms. Dawson crumples her mouth, before shaking her head. "No, not Blair. Although I did hear about that, and we've contacted her parents about her behavior. She's being reprimanded. But the problem here, is you, Andy."

"Me? Why am I the problem? I haven't done anything to Blair. She's gone crazy for Alex and has done nothing but antagonize me, and continuously flirt with him, even though he's blocked her from all his social media accounts, and her phone number from his phone," I say in one long breath.

"Andy, that's not what I brought you in here for. It's because you told Miss Haines you're pregnant."

"Me being pregnant is a problem?" I ask in a small voice.

"What does this have to do with us being here?" Mom cuts to the points.

"It has to do with what services we can provide to your daughter."

"What does that even mean?" Mom snaps.

"You *are* pregnant, Andy?" Ms. Dawson asks.

"Yes, I am." I feel myself slinking back in my seat, like I'm in trouble and I want the seat to swallow me up.

"How far along are you?"

"What are you getting at?" Mom says, more forcefully. "She's pregnant. Until the twelve-week ultrasound, we had no intention of letting you know. It's none of your business."

"Actually, it's very much my business. I need to make sure every one of my students is in a safe, supportive environment conducive to learning." She takes a breath, turns to me and smiles. Though I have a feeling the smile is about to come with a huge *but*. "But…" And here it is. "Andy being pregnant is causing problems with the student body, and it doesn't set the proper example for the younger students. And after Blair attacked you, it's clear we can't offer you a safe learning environment. I'm sorry, but you'll need to find an alternative. There's a high school in one of the neighboring suburbs that offers night classes for girls who are in the same position as you. They teach more things to do with…"

"Wait just a second!" Mom nearly screeches. "Are you telling me you're throwing my daughter out of school just because she's pregnant?'

"I'm saying this isn't the right place for her while she's expecting. Anything can happen, and in her condition, it's not safe."

"Condition?" I stand and begin to pace behind Mom's chair. "Are you kidding me, Ms. Dawson? I'm not a difficult student. I've never caused you any concern. Why would you do this? If Blair hadn't caused all these problems, you wouldn't have even known about me and the baby."

"Regardless of how I know, the fact is, I *do* know. And we can't have you attend classes here, not until after you've had the baby."

"This is ridiculous. You can't stop my daughter from coming here."

Ms. Dawson looks down at her knitted hands. "Actually, I can. It's in the school district's rules. The moment a pregnancy is confirmed, we can no longer offer the education required to that student. In this case, Andy." She signals toward me. "I have nothing against you. You're a fantastic student, but this is about safety for everyone."

"What happens now?" I ask.

"You'll have to clean your locker out." Ms. Dawson does look like she's hating every moment of this conversation. "Andy, you're incredibly bright, and all your teachers like you, you have an amazing future."

"Not without an education," I say.

"Andy," Mom says, standing. "It's for the best."

I draw in my brows, surprised by Mom's quick reversal of emotion. "Mom?"

"Andy, we'll find a way. Ms. Dawson, thank you for your time."

"Good luck. Please, keep in touch, Andy. Once you have the baby, you're welcome to return."

"A year behind everyone else." I feel all the breath leave my lungs as I drop my head, and walk out of her office.

What a damn mess.

I *never* thought I'd be kicked out of school.

"It'll be okay," Mom says as we walk toward my locker. Thankfully, everyone's in class, and no one is here to see the humiliating way I'm leaving school.

"Okay? I'm fifteen, pregnant and been kicked out of school. What can be okay about this?" I'm angry. Angry at Ms. Dawson. Angry at Blair. But mostly, angry at myself.

"We'll find a way to make this work."

"I'm not going to a school where they teach you how to change a diaper, or feed your baby. I need an education, not that."

"Andy, stop," Mom says as I walk toward my locker. My anger feels like it's growing by the second. "Stop!"

I huff, and turn to look at Mom. "This is shit!"

"Watch your language." Mom points at me. She's not a fan of cussing. "I know you're frustrated, and so am I. But Ms. Dawson makes a good point. This isn't somewhere for you while you're pregnant. We'll figure this out."

"I'm angry at that stupid cow, Blair. If it wasn't for her, we wouldn't be in this position."

"Yes, we would. It just would've taken another month, maybe two, maybe even three. But here we are." She casually points to me. "And here you are, fifteen and pregnant." The hard lines on Mom's face tell me she's serious. "We'll deal with it. That's what life is, Andy. A series of unpredictable events. The only thing you know for sure is that you don't know when or what things will happen."

"And death," I say as I open my locker, and begin to empty it.

"Well, that's not morbid," Mom replies sarcastically.

"It's true. It's the only thing we're really guaranteed of." There's not much in my locker, so when it's empty I get a sick feeling in my stomach.

"Yeah, you're right. Death is guaranteed, but so is a beautiful life if you want it. And your beautiful life will include a baby."

I'm somewhat distracted by Mom's words. But the emptiness of my locker makes me emotional. This is the most horrible of feelings. "I feel so empty," I say, unable to hold my emotions back.

"Why? Because of school?" I nod. "This is a temporary setback, not a permanent end to your education."

"I feel like such a disappointment." I hug Mom. My heart is pounding rapidly as I beat myself up over the immense failure I've become.

Mom hugs me, her hands gently rubbing my back. "It feels like it's hard."

"I don't know if this is the right decision." Pulling away, I wipe my face. "We should go, before anyone sees and more rumors start."

"They won't be rumors," Mom adds.

"I suppose not. Everyone's going to be asking why I'm not at school." I shrug, and let out a deep sigh.

"Are you really worried about what everyone thinks of you? 'Cause if you are, then you may be right, Andy. You may not be cut out for this. If rumors are going to worry you, then..." Mom lifts her shoulders as we walk to the car. Her tone says it all though. "Truthfully, I think you're emotional. So many hormones are going haywire in your body, and your mind is going crazy with all these feelings."

"Yes!" I nearly yell, too loud. "I feel angry, and sad, but happy. And like I'm on the verge of tears nearly all day."

Mom laughs. "Oh baby, I can tell you some stories." She chuckles again, and this piques my interest. "Actually, it's best if you ask your father."

"I think I will," I say as I get into Mom's car. She starts the car, and gently eases out of the parking spot, and onto the street.

I look out the window, and start crying again. This hormone crap is getting on my last nerve. When will it end?

CHAPTER
19

"I CALLED CLARENCE today," I say to Mom and Dad as we sit for dinner.

"Why?" Dad asks.

"I asked her if she can give me hours during the week." I peel my banana.

"Huh." Mom sits in her regular spot while Dad brings over the pot of stew I made for dinner. The smell of the meat made me gag a few times but thankfully, I didn't throw up.

"What did she say?" dad asks.

"She said she can give me another day of work. So, I'll be working there Thursdays and Saturdays."

"I need help in the office. You can work Fridays with me," Mom says.

"Are you offering me a job?"

"No, not offering. Telling. I need help, and instead of me interviewing someone to help me, you can do it."

"Do I get paid?" I ask, cheekily.

"Yes. You get paid in the form of free accommodation, food on the table, endless supply of bananas and ketchup." She eyes my bowl of ketchup as she ladles her dinner into her bowl.

"Thanks," I mumble. Though, I'm really grateful for the help.

"Are you going to eat anything other than that?" Dad asks.

"Yeah." I finish eating my banana, then scoop some of the stew into my bowl. Lifting my cutlery to my mouth, I eat a bit of dinner. Nothing tastes as good as my ketchup-drenched bananas, though. I'm struggling to finish what's in my bowl, obsessing over my bananas. "Dad."

"Yeah." Dad continues to shovel food in his mouth. "Mom said I should ask you about her hormones."

Dad starts choking. Mom turns and gives him a filthy look. Clearly, she's not impressed. He finally manages to get what's in his mouth down, then he lifts his glass and takes a sip of water, avoiding Mom's filthy looks. "Your mother has never been hormonal," he says.

"Now you're just being an idiot," Mom chastises him.

I'm trying to hide my smile, but I can't. Dad looks at me, almost pleading, and turns his gaze to Mom. "I don't know what answer to give here. I have the love of my life sitting next to me, and my pregnant fifteen-year-old daughter sitting opposite me. I feel like this is a trick question." Dad breathes out, then adds. "Is this my last meal? Am I going to die tonight? Is my will in order, darling?"

"Everything goes to me anyway, so just answer the damn question."

Dad groans. "I'm going to die," he says in a low voice, but loud enough for us to hear. "Your mother can be somewhat hormonal sometimes." He looks down at his food, then yelps, "Ouch! What did I do? I'm answering Andy's question that you told me to answer."

"She means when I was pregnant," Mom says through a tight, clenched jaw.

"Oh, yeah she was bad. But she's not now. She doesn't have mood swings now. Not at all."

I'm still laughing. Dad's trying to make it better, but the more he talks about Mom now, the angrier she's getting. "So she had hormones when she was pregnant?"

"Hormones! Before we found out she was pregnant, she was yelling at me for everything."

"No, I wasn't," Mom corrects him.

"Then you tell Andy what you were like." Dad picks his fork up, and resumes eating. "I'm glad there'll be another boy in this house. Who am I kidding? I'll still be outnumbered," Dad mumbles.

"Alright, alright, I'll be quiet. Tell Andy how I was."

"You sure?"

"Tell her before I change my mind."

Dad places his cutlery down, then takes a breath. "She was horrible. There was this instance where she came home from buying groceries and I was in the family room, with the TV on. Beside me, on the floor was a bowl with my nearly finished lunch. I was asleep because I'd been working nearly twenty-hour days to get some projects completed."

Mom starts laughing.

"Oh no," I say.

Dad looks to Mom and shakes his head. "I did hear her come in, but must've gone back to sleep. Your mother didn't like that. Nor did she like that I had a bowl on the floor. She picked up the bowl, and tipped it over my head."

I gasp. "You didn't, did you?" I turn to ask Mom. She nods. "Why?"

"Because she was filled with crazy-ass hormones. But, that was only the beginning of it."

"There's more?" This worries me.

"More?" Dad groans. "I'd love to say no, but that would be a lie."

"Mom?" I nearly shriek.

"I couldn't help it. I felt like I was a mess, all the time. My head couldn't cope, and I'd get angry, then I'd burst into tears. Then five minutes later, I'd find something funny and start laughing."

"One time, she was unstacking the dishwasher, and a plate was slightly dirty, she kicked the dishwasher and was yelling at it. It was crazy. I honestly thought she'd gone mad. I know when your mother's getting her period, unfortunately like I know when you're getting yours. That's when I know it's wise to stay at work longer, or to get out of the house."

"Hey, I don't get hormonal," I argue.

"Yeah, okay, let's go with that," Dad responds. "Honestly, I'm thankful you're having a boy."

"We don't know that for sure yet," Mom says.

"I know, Mom. I know this little guy, is in fact, *a guy*." I rub my tummy. "I wonder when I'm going to pop out?"

"Your boobs have gotten bigger."

"Oh man," Dad groans. "I don't want to hear about my daughter's breasts." He shivers, disgusted.

"They have," Mom says.

"No. Nope, I don't want to hear it. I'm not comfortable in hearing this. If you two want to talk about..." He makes a circular motion around his chest, "Then I'll leave. Just don't."

"Does that mean you won't be in the delivery room with me?"

"What? No. I can't unsee... that."

"Weren't you with Mom? Helping her?"

"That was different. I've seen your mother's... look, stop." Dad stands, still shaking his head. His shoulders are high and tense, and the pained look on his face is enough to tell me not to talk about this. "I'm going to be there for you and the baby, but I *won't* be in the delivery room. I'll wait outside. It's not something I feel like I need to be inside the room for."

"You're being a moron," Mom says.

"I'm not, Laura. I can't see my only daughter in that position."

"Naked?"

"In pain. I can't do it. I felt hopeless and helpless when you were in labor with Andy, and I don't think I can do that again."

"Dad, are you scared?"

"Scared? Are you kidding, I'm terrified. Doctor Morgan is a fantastic doctor, and she'll be in there with you. But I don't think this is something I can go through with. I'm sorry." Dad takes his bowl, places it in the sink, then disappears out of the kitchen.

I look to Mom. Her lips are pushed together. "Will you be there?"

"Hell, yes I'm going to be there. I'm going to be there every step of the way."

My shoulders sink as I think about Dad. "I want Dad too."

"You have to respect his wishes."

"I'm not disappointed, I just thought he'd be there."

"He'll be there. But until you have the baby, he'll stay outside."

I suppose if Dad can't be in there with me, then so be it. He'll be close by, and I'm really grateful for that. Suddenly, that damn feeling quickly escalates, and I run to the bathroom to vomit.

Kneeling on the floor, I vomit what feels like everything from inside my stomach.

"You okay?" Dad asks from the other side of the door.

I vomit again. "I thought it was easing." And again.

"Andy?" he calls, his voice concerned.

"I'll be okay." Standing, I walk over to brush my teeth. But that familiar feeling is gnarling at my stomach. Rapidly rising to the back of my throat. "Not again," I say as I lunge for the toilet and vomit.

Oh no. I think I might be getting another one of those attacks, which may land me back in hospital.

"Andy?" Dad's more concerned. "Open the door."

I vomit again. The contents are becoming less and less, but the vomiting isn't easing. "No," I cry, as I relentlessly keep vomiting.

"Andy." Dad tries the handle, and finds it open. "What's happening?" he asks, and immediately looks my body over. "Are you bleeding? Is everything okay?"

I try to respond, but my stomach twists, and contracts, and I double over in pain, before vomiting.

"Laura!" Dad calls.

I hear the soft padding of Mom's house shoes coming down the hallway. "What's...?"

"What do we do?" Dad asks.

This vomiting is cruel and never-ending. It's also painful, because it feels like my stomach is spasming and contracting. This feels so much worse than the first time it happened.

"We have to call Doctor Morgan." Mom kneels beside me, rubbing her hand gently on my back. "Are you okay?"

I've gone from happy and vibrant, to totally exhausted in a matter of only a few moments. It's like all my energy has been sucked out of me. I vomit again, this time only bringing up a yellow-colored liquid. "Everything hurts," I say as I clutch onto my stomach.

"I'm going to call Doctor Morgan, okay?" she asks. I nod my head, weakness taking over my entire body. "Keep an eye on her."

"I will."

Mom's footsteps become more urgent as she scurries down the hallway. The vomiting doesn't give me a chance to hear what she's saying, though I do know she's talking to Doctor Morgan faintly.

"Hey, kid. You doing okay?" Dad sits on the cold, hard bathroom floor beside me.

"I feel like crap."

"I bet you do."

I hold a finger up, then lean over the toilet, and vomit. "I can't believe how quickly this has come on." I spit into the toilet, hoping for this to finish. Of course, the rumble in my stomach, and the illness rushing up through my throat, tells me I should get myself settled on the bathroom floor.

"Doctor Morgan said to take you straight to the hospital."

"I don't want to move," I whine. "I'm tired." I vomit.

"I'll help you up," Dad says, springing to his feet.

"Wait." I bring myself up to my knees, ready to stand, but my body protests, and I vomit consecutively, moment after moment.

Dad steps back, and waits. I can hear Mom pacing, worried. "I'll get a bucket." Mom rushes out of the bathroom.

"Dad," I grumble between being sick.

"What is it, bear?"

"I'm sorry."

"Nah, no need to apologize. Now, can you get up?" I nod my head. Pushing up off the floor, I don't dare leave the bathroom, because I know I'm going to be sick, again. This vomiting crap is getting old.

"Here, I have the bucket. Take her to the car, I'm going to pack an overnight bag with clothes for us."

"I need my phone, and my charger too please."

"I'll grab those. Anything else?" I shake my head. "I'll be out in a few moments. Get her in the car."

"You okay to walk?"

I smile toward Dad. I know if I say I can't walk, he'll pick me up and carry me to the car. "I can walk. Just slowly." It feels like my stomach is doing all kinds of crazy acrobatics. But it's painful.

"What sort of pain is it?"

"Like it's cramping, but just before I vomit, it twists."

"I wish I could take your pain away," Dad says, supporting me as we get closer to the car. "I hate seeing you in pain."

"No one tells you how much this hurts."

"Ha! You've only got a little while to go. It'll go away once you have my grandson."

Dad's words make me smile, although my stomach is still doing that weird twisty thing. "I'm going to vomit." Dad looks around, totally freaking out. There's nothing for me to vomit into, so he cups his hands together and offers them to me. I refuse to vomit on my Dad, so I grip his shoulder, double over, and throw up on the lawn.

Pulling myself up straight, I hang onto Dad, because I can feel how weak I actually am. This has taken everything out of me. "You okay?"

"Yeah."

"You're all white and pasty. You've got dark rings under your eyes too. Amazing how something so small, can cause so many problems. But as long as you'll be okay, and he'll be okay, that's all that matters."

Shuffling forward, we make it to the car. Dad opens the back door, and I try to climb in. I feel depleted of all energy. "I feel so numb. I want to lay down and sleep for an eternity."

"Good luck with that, especially after Junior comes along."

"Junior?" I question.

"It's presumptuous of me to call him Robert, so I've nicknamed him, Junior."

Dad brings another smile to me. "Junior, huh?"

"Robert sounds good too. Baby Robert. Sounds good, yeah?" the question is rhetorical.

"Okay, I've packed an overnight bag for Andy, and some clothes for me too, in case I'm staying. Let's go." Mom shuts the door, puts her seatbelt on, and turns to look at me. "You're looking terrible."

"Thanks," I say, but know what she means.

"No, really, you are. Doctor Morgan will meet us down there. Andy, you've got huge bags under your eyes. They're awfully dark. Does she look worse to you this time?" Dad quickly turns to look at me. "Don't take your eyes off the road. What are you doing?" This is Mom, in panic mode. "Well, don't you think she looks terrible? I hope she's okay. I hope the baby's okay."

"Mom, calm down," I try to soothe Mom's frantic behavior. "It's the same as it was last time. That long name Doctor Morgan called it. Extreme morning sickness, I'll be okay once they give me some fluids and something to stop the vomiting."

"Hmmm." I see Mom reach for Dad's hand. This is another one of her signs. When she's extremely worried, she looks to Dad for comfort. "I hope so," she says in a tiny voice. So small, it barely reaches my ears.

Within a few more moments, we reach the hospital. Dad stops the car near the emergency room entrance, and Mom goes ahead in to find Doctor Morgan.

"Are you okay?" Dad asks.

"I think Mom's in a worse state than me. At least she gave me the bucket." I hold onto it, hoping I won't have to use it.

"Your Mom is worried, that's all."

"I know."

The next few events happen fairly fast. Doctor Morgan has already booked me a room, and I'm rushed into it, where a young nurse is waiting with Doctor Morgan. "You look dehydrated," Doctor Morgan says in her normal no-nonsense tone. "Cannula, and saline bag," she says to the nurse.

The nurse looks so young. She doesn't look like she's old enough to be a nurse, but she is. She nods, and leaves the room quietly.

"We'll get an ultrasound done, but first, we'll get some fluids into you."

I look around the room, trying to find my bucket. "Bucket." I point to it where it lies beside Dad's feet.

Doctor Morgan reaches over to the side of the bed, and hands me a small plastic basin, same as the other doctor did the first time. "Use this."

I vomit. But by now, I'm completely worn out and empty of everything, so it becomes a series of dry heaves.

"We'll give you something to stop the vomiting too. You'll be here overnight. We'll check all your vitals, make sure you're okay. When's your next appointment with me?"

"She's supposed to have her ultrasound at the end of this week, and her appointment with you is next Monday."

"I'll see you again tomorrow morning. I'll go write up your medical plan for tonight, and I'll see you in the morning." Doctor Morgan leaves the room. This is just the person she is. She doesn't mess around. She gets the job done. I can imagine people couldn't warm up to her bedside manner, but I like her. I think she's straightforward, and efficient.

Mom and Dad are talking about the appointments when the young nurse comes back into the room. "Hi," she says shyly to me.

"Hi," I reply and offer her a weak smile.

"We're going out to ask Doctor Morgan something, and we'll be back in a few moments. You okay?"

I nod. "Your parents seem really loving," the young nurse says.

"They are. And truthfully, I'm not sure if I could get through this without them."

"That's really sweet. Can you make a fist please?" She ties a tourniquet around my arm. "Doctor Morgan is an exceptional doctor. She'll look after you, and the baby."

"Have you worked with her for long?"

The nurse smiles. "She was my doctor when I had Jayden."

"But you're so young," I blurt, then quickly place my hand to my mouth. "I'm sorry. I shouldn't have said that."

"That's okay," she says. "Slight pinch." She pushes the needle into my arm.

"I'm sorry," I say again. "It's hypocritical of me to say that. Can I ask how old you are?"

"I'm twenty-four."

"Wow," she looks much younger than twenty-four. I thought she was eighteen or nineteen.

"I get that a lot. But you're right, I was young when I had him. I was pregnant at sixteen, and had him the day after my seventeenth birthday."

"Wow," I say again. "You look so young now, so I can only imagine how old you looked at sixteen."

"I looked like I was twelve. Good genes, but it made for some interesting stares, and a lot of judgement."

"From whom?"

"Everyone. I'd be out walking Jayden in the stroller and I would get a lot of stares, and whispers. Sometimes, parents would cross the road with their toddlers just so they didn't have to acknowledge me."

I chuckle. "It's not like pregnancy is contagious."

"I know." She too laughs. When she finishes setting the IV up, she moves beside the bed. "How are you finding things?"

"Well, I got kicked out of school because I'm pregnant."

She scrunches her nose. "And the kids, at school? I assume they all know."

"No, just my best friend and my boyfriend knew for sure. Mind you, there is this one girl, she's a bitch. She's guessed, but I haven't confirmed it."

"I think you being out of school is confirmation enough."

"Can I ask you a question?" I feel comfortable around her.

She nods. "How did Jayden's father react when you told him you were pregnant?"

"Well." She checks the line going into my arm. "He took his wallet out, threw fifty dollars on the table and told me to '*take care of it.*'" She uses air quotes when she repeats what he said.

"Ouch. I'm assuming you didn't want to do that?" Her face screws. "I'm sorry, I'm asking questions that really aren't my business."

"I didn't know what to do. I was petrified and didn't know how to tell my mom. Dad left when I was eight, and never wanted to be part of my life. I was so terrified, I didn't say anything. I hid it beneath oversized sweaters. It wasn't until my water broke that anyone knew what was happening."

"But Doctor Morgan, I know we've had appointments with her. How did you afford those? How did you see her without your mom knowing?"

"Doctor Morgan is a blessing. She saved me. I came into hospital with serious complications and thankfully, she was in here visiting a patient when I was brought in. Both Jayden and I could've died. She saved us."

"Wow," I whisper, enthralled by this retelling of her own birth story.

"If it wasn't for her, I wouldn't be here. Neither would Jayden. But we became, for the lack of a better word, friends. But we're not friends, if that makes sense. She's more like my mentor. She took me under her wing."

"That's fantastic," I say.

"What's fantastic is having your parents here. Family support is important when you're pregnant at a young age. I should know."

"How did your mom respond when she found out?"

"It was a struggle for her. But she stepped up and supported me."

"At least you had her. But his dad, what a loser." I shake my head, upset for her.

"Jayden doesn't have a father listed on his birth certificate."

"Wow." I watch as she fusses over me, not wanting to look me in eye. "You're courageous," I say to her.

"You learn to be. Because once you have your baby, nothing else in this world matters. And you'll do everything in your power to do right by that baby."

I smile. "Hey, I haven't been sick."

"That's because of what Doctor Morgan said to give you. It stops the vomiting."

"Thank you… ahhh," I pause and wait for her name.

"Vivian."

"Thank you, Vivian, I appreciate your help."

"My shift doesn't end until six a.m., so I'll come and check on you again."

Mom and Dad walk in as Vivian walks out. "You're already looking so much better. You have color in your cheeks," Dad says.

"I can't believe how much better I'm feeling."

"I'll be staying with you tonight, and tomorrow Dad will come and get us."

"You can go." I look around the room. "There's really no use in staying considering I'm already feeling okay. And there's only an uncomfortable chair to sleep on. I don't want you staying on that."

"I'll be fine," Mom persists.

"No, Mom, please. Go home, and come back tomorrow morning. Anyway, I'm going to message Zar and Alex, let them know I'm in here."

Dad looks at his phone clock. "It's late, Andy. I don't think you should disturb them."

"Both of them were angry at me the last time for not letting them know what was going on. I promised them I wouldn't do it again."

Dad sighs. "Fine. A promise is a promise."

"Hand me my phone, please?" I reach toward my overnight bag.

"Do you want us to stay for a while?" Mom asks.

"No, just go. Have a good night's sleep, and come back tomorrow. Is that okay?"

Mom slides her arm around Dad's waist and hugs him. "I'm not sure about this, Andy."

"Mom, if anything happens to me, I promise I'll call. But really, I'm in the best place possible."

"She's right; she'll be fine."

"And just like that, she no longer needs us." I can see Mom's eyes becoming red, as she tries hard to hold in the tears.

"I'll always need you. Both of you." I smile to her and Dad. "But it doesn't make sense for you to stay when there's nothing you can do for me."

Mom exhales loudly, and Dad hugs her tighter. "We'll be back in the morning."

"I love you," I say to them. They're both hesitant, not really wanting to leave. "Honestly, it's okay," I try to reassure them.

"You'll be okay?" Mom asks, again.

"Perfect. I'm already feeling better. I haven't vomited."

"And you'll be okay to go for a shower and to the bathroom?"

"I'll have a shower in the morning once the line is out."

"I can stay to help, in case."

"Please, I'll be fine."

Dad breaks away from Mom, comes over and gives me a hug, and a gentle kiss on the forehead. "If anything happens, call us immediately. Okay, kiddo?"

"Absolutely."

"Doesn't matter what time."

"I will."

Mom slowly shuffles forward, and she too hugs and kisses me. "I'll be back first thing."

"Don't rush, Mom. Because I'm sure Doctor Morgan will want to see me before I can go."

"Okay." Mom nods, but I know she won't be able to sleep tonight and she'll be here the moment she can in the morning. "Love you."

Dad takes Mom's hand, and they both hesitantly leave the room. I keep looking toward the door, half expecting Mom to return.

I wait a few moments, just in case.

When I know Mom won't return, I open the message app on my phone, and start a conversation among Alex, Zar and myself. *I'm back in hospital with extreme vomiting. I'm okay, and so is the baby.*

I barely finish sending it when Alex replies with; *I'll be there soon.*

Zar's response isn't too far behind Alex's. *Hayden's bringing me.*

You don't have to. I'm okay.

I hate putting them out like this.

I'm coming. Alex replies.

So am I. Zar says.

Doesn't seem like I'm going to change their minds, so I tell them my room number. I figure it's no use in trying to argue with them. Both are strong-headed. Whatever they want to do, they do. Especially Zar.

I lay back, closing my eyes, and fighting to stay awake. But the vomiting has really drained me. Although I feel better, I'm still worn out by it all. I can feel myself slipping into sleep. My eyes are heavy, and my breathing has changed. It's slower, and more even.

"Hey," I hear a voice rousing me from my sleep.

Alex stands inside the door, staring at me. "Hey." I smile. Alex's brows are drawn in together, with his shoulders high with tense. "I look worse than I feel," I say. I pat the side of the bed, inviting him over.

Alex slowly walks forward, his eyes looking at the line going into my arm. "Are you okay?" he asks. Standing beside the bed, he's staring at me, unsure of what to do.

"Here." I move my hips over, and pat the bed beside me.

"I… will I hurt you?"

"No, not at all. I'm already feeling better."

"Is our baby…?" He can't bring himself to finish the sentence.

"He's fine. He's protected in here." I place my hand to my stomach. "Want to feel?" I ask.

"Can you feel him?" Alex's eyes light up. Suddenly not so terrified of seeing me like this.

"Not yet. But you never know. I think he knows you're here."

Alex moves toward me, and sits on the bed. He gently places his hand on my stomach. "I was terrified," he says. "The moment I saw that message come through, I started panicking. I knew I had to get here to make sure you're okay."

Smiling, I sit up further in bed, lean over and kiss him on the lips. "I love you," I say.

"I love you too."

"Drama queen!" Zar announces loudly. "It's all about you, isn't it?" she says cheekily. Hayden follows closely behind my best friend.

"I told you not to come."

"And I told you I was coming. Too bad. Suck it up." Hayden chuckles from behind her.

"Hey," I say to Hayden.

Alex stands and goes over to Hayden, shaking his hand. "Thanks for bringing her."

"Like I had much of a choice," Hayden grumbles.

"I'm so sorry," I say, feeling terrible.

"Don't be. If it wasn't me, it would've been Ma."

"What's happening? Are you okay? Is mister okay?" She pointedly looks to my stomach.

"Yeah. He's fine. Protected in his little bubble. I started vomiting, and couldn't stop."

"Will this happen again?" Zar asks as she sits on the bed where Alex was.

Shrugging, I can only answer as honestly as I know. "Who knows. When it comes on, it just puts me on my ass. I can barely stand, let alone anything else."

"I remember," Zar says. "But he's okay?' she asks again.

"Yep. This is something that can happen to anyone who's pregnant."

Zar screws her mouth up. "Nope, not for me."

"What?" I ask.

"Pregnancy."

"That's because Ma would kill you if you came home pregnant," Hayden says.

"She ain't getting grandbabies from you!" Zar bites back.

"Just because I'm bisexual, doesn't mean I can't have children."

"You need to impregnate a woman. And you don't like putting your junk anywhere near a woman's area."

"I like both men's and women's areas," he sasses. "Ewww. The fact you called my penis 'junk' is grossing me out. Can you not think about where I put my penis?"

"Do I have to separate you two?" Alex says as he steps forward. "This is a hospital."

"I'm telling Ma," Hayden says as he backs away.

"What? That she's not getting grandbabies from you? Or that you stick your…"

"Stop it!" Hayden says, raising his voice.

This is quickly escalating. I know they love each other, but man, they came here to fight? "Perhaps you should go home to finish this," I suggest.

Zar exhales, hangs her head down before looking to me. "Sorry. Anyway, how are you feeling?"

"Better. It's the same thing that happened last time. I started vomiting, and couldn't stop. I'm hoping this is the last time this happens."

"They say after the first trimester; the nausea and vomiting should settle down. And you're nearly there. Your twelve-week ultrasound is this week. Fingers crossed."

"How do you know all this stuff?"

"My best friend has become a human incubator, so I've been researching." Zar smiles proudly.

"Human incubator?" Alex roars with laughter, a little too loud.

"Shhh. It's late." I can't help but laugh too. That was funny.

"It's true. She's merely a host body for an alien who's taking over and makes her sick."

"Don't forget the emotions. A plethora of emotions," I add.

"Plethora? What are you? Like thirty?" Hayden asks from the chair he's sitting in. "I don't even think Ma says *plethora*."

"If I could, I'd throw something at you," I say with humor.

"Yeah, yeah. Whatever." He flicks his hand dismissively at me.

"Anyway. What's been happening at school?" I ask.

"Ugh. School," Zar says. Alex echoes her complaint.

"Why? What's happening?" I ask. "I know I've been gone only a few days. But, what's happening?"

"Two words. And both those words are names." Zar holds up two fingers, waiting for me to guess. I roll my eyes, dreading what she's going to say. "Yep, Blair and Ruby. Blair's heaps worse than Ruby. She's been trying to hang out with us at lunch. We came into the cafeteria, and she was sitting where we usually sit. She saw me approaching, and smiled so wide at me. Should've heard her, Andy." Zar tries to flick her hair, mocking Blair and how she is with her long, blonde locks. "Oh hi, Zar, I hope you don't mind, but can I sit with you guys?" she adds in a fake giggle. "It was sickening."

"What happened?" I ask, interested.

"Hunter and Alex walked over," Zar smiles when she says Hunter's name. Dead giveaway on how much she likes him. "Her eyes lit up the moment she saw Alex."

"Oh no," I say, my gut churning with anxiety. I almost don't want to ask, but I have to know what happened. "And?"

Zar starts to laugh. "Alex stopped beside her, looked her up and down, and said to me, 'Let's change seats, these are filthy.'"

"Oh no! You didn't?" I say to Alex.

"She irritates me. Her attitude is shit."

"And she's a bunny boiler," Zar adds.

Hayden laughs. "Bunny boiler," he repeats. "Funny as."

"What's with bunny boiler? I've heard you say it before," Alex asks.

"I can't believe you don't know the movie. Watch it. *Fatal Attraction*. It's an old movie, but man, it's great," Hayden answers.

I look around the room, and know Alex and Zar are here because they want to be. It warms my heart knowing they'll be here for me, and my son. "Thank you," I say feeling sentimental.

"What for?" Zar questions.

"For being here. You didn't have to come, but you did. So, thank you."

Alex, Zar, and Hayden all smile. "Yep, we're all sentimental and shit," Zar says making us all laugh.

It does bring tears to my eyes. Without them, I don't know where I'd be.

CHAPTER 20

"**Z**AR CAN'T MAKE it. But Alex is meeting us there," I say to Mom and Dad as we get ready for my first, official ultrasound.

"He knows the time?" Mom asks in a panic as she rushes around the house, trying to get all her things ready.

"Yes, Mom," I say, sitting on the sofa, waiting for her. I turn to Dad, who shakes his head and lets out a loud puff of air. "Why is she panicking?"

"She's nervous."

"I gathered that. But why?"

Dad shrugs, then looks back down at his phone.

Mom appears, frazzled. She's wearing two different shoes. I have no idea how she's managed to do that. "Mom."

I pointedly look down at her feet. Mom's eyes follow the direction of mine, and she mumbles, "Damn it," before racing back to her bedroom to change. She appears within a minute, looks down at her feet to check, then raises her head. "I'm good."

"Why are you so nervous?" I ask, standing from the sofa, and making my way over to her.

"I don't actually know. I've been like this since last night. I barely slept, tossing, and turning all night. I don't know what's wrong with me."

"You're worried, obviously."

"Well, of course I'm worried. This ultrasound will show if our grandbaby is healthy."

I've been researching the importance of this ultrasound, and I've prepared myself for it. I just don't want to freak out, because if I do, I'll be putting myself under stress. I know stress is bad for both my son and my parents. And I don't want to do that, not to my son, and definitely not to my parents. "I know, Mom. I'm positive he's just perfect in here." I rub at my stomach.

"Come on, we're going to be late," Dad hollers, now standing by the front door.

Mom and I walk out the door. Dad's already heading to the car. Mom locks the house, and together we head to the car. Mom's jittery, which is making my anxiety levels escalate.

"You ladies ready?" Dad asks when we're in the car.

"Yeah," both Mom and I reply in unison.

I send a text to Alex on the ride over. ***We'll be there soon.***

His reply is fast. *Here already, I'll wait outside for you.*

I feel a goofy smile tug up at my lips. ***Love you.***

Love you too.

Looking out the window, I watch as we quickly approach the hospital. The ultrasound is in one of the outer buildings of the hospital. The moment we drive in, I see Alex and his dad standing outside.

Dad parks the car, and the three of us walk up to the building.

Dad shakes Emil's hand, and Mom leans in to give him a friendly kiss on the cheek, which he reciprocates. "I'm sorry, Mary couldn't make it," Emil says. His tone indicates it's not that she *couldn't* make it, she didn't *want* to make the appointment.

It doesn't upset me, but I look to Alex who lowers his chin, looking down at his feet.

We all know what Emil meant, and none of us are surprised.

"Okay, let's do this," I say.

Nerves quickly take me over. So much is happening inside my mind. I want to run away, but I'm also excited too. I can't wait to see my little boy, but what if he has some kind of disability? Will I be able to care for him if he does?

What if he has a life-threatening disability?

What if, he has something so wrong with him, that I'm forced with having to make the decision of termination?

Could I do it?

My heart beats fast, as my stomach churns with worry. I'm not sure I can do this.

"What's wrong? Your hand is clammy."

"Nothing," I say to Alex as I pull my hand away to wipe it down my pants.

"No, something's wrong," he adamantly persists.

"Andy?" Mom says, stopping us from walking any further. "What is it?"

I want to tell her, but I can't. I have to not say anything. I don't want to worry her. "Nothing, just nervous," I say, this time managing a false smile.

My head is screaming at me. The more I try to quiet my fright, the more scenarios develop in my head, and they're getting progressively darker. My absolute worst fear is to learn something risky is happening to my son.

"I think we need to discuss baby names," Alex says, bringing this conversation up again. I give him a sideways look. "I know, I know. Wulff-Price."

"I haven't agreed to that yet. I said I'd consider it."

"What's this? The baby isn't taking our name?" Emil asks as we enter the elevator to go up to the floor we need to go. "He has to have Wulff as a surname."

"I'll think about it. But he'll be a Price. If anything, I'm considering Wulff-Price."

Emil crinkles his brows, obviously not impressed that his grandson won't be taking his name. "I don't agree with this, Andy."

"I think it's a lovely gesture on Andy's behalf," Mom says. "The kids aren't married, and even if they were, it doesn't mean she has to take on your surname. If she hyphenates our grandson's name to Wulff-Price, then it's a considerate choice she's making."

"The child should have our surname," Emil persists, shaking his head.

"Dad," Alex sighs. "Stop," he whispers.

"It's not right," Emil argues. He looks to me, his eyes fierce. "You have to give him our surname. It's the way things are. Babies should have their father's surname."

"The best I might be able to offer is a hyphenated surname."

"It's not right," he says again, this time straightening his shoulders and looking ahead of him.

"I mean no disrespect, Mr. Wulff, but Mrs. Wulff refuses to have anything to do with this. I have no faith that will change once he arrives. Why should I honor her, and not my own parents who've been here for me from the moment I told them I was pregnant? Why do they not deserve the same, if not more, recognition?"

Mr. Wulff says nothing. He holds his head higher, but I know he's thinking about what I've said.

"Thank you," Alex says. I shrug, unsure why he's thanking me. "For hyphenating."

I've backed myself into a corner, but I suppose, it's the only fair thing to do. Unless Alex decides to abandon us once our son is born. I doubt it though, if Alex was going to ditch us, he would've done it already. "You're welcome," I say and give him a smile.

The elevator doors ping open to a foyer that's light and airy. The walls are painted a light green, and the furniture is wooden, but with a dark stain on it. It's pretty in here. Calming. It doesn't feel like it's part of the hospital.

Mom walks ahead and tells the lady at reception who we are and what we're having done. The lady lifts her head to look at me. I walk over to Mom, leaving the others to sit on one of three sofas. "Hey," I say to Mom and smile to the lady.

The woman looks at me, then down at her notes. "You're Andy?" she asks in a curt, blunt voice.

"I am."

She narrows her eyes as she looks to the computer screen. "Oh," she says. She's seen my age. There's undeniable censure etched on her face. She disapproves of someone so young coming in here for a pregnancy ultrasound. "Take a seat, we won't be long."

I grab onto Mom's hand, and gently tug on her arm. "I can't believe her," Mom says, looking over her shoulder at the woman.

"Don't worry about it," I reply. "People are going to be judgy for the rest of my life now."

"They have no right."

"Can't help ignorance."

"No, you can't," Mom replies.

"What's happening?" Dad asks as he moves to sit beside Mom.

"Ignorant receptionist," Mom whispers. Though I gather by the loud tone of her whispering, she wants the receptionist to hear.

"Mom, it's not worth it."

"You're right, it's not." Mom's throwing some pretty filthy looks in the direction of the receptionist, making me smile.

The receptionist ignores us, but Mom is like a dog with a bone. She keeps gazing over to her. "Mom," I say trying to gain her focus.

"What?" She turns, but I can see she's still fuming.

"Do you think it'll be weird if I start bringing ketchup with me everywhere I go? And bananas?"

Mom shakes her head, before bringing her hand up to rub her forehead. "I know people will look at you like you're a freak."

"Suppose I am." I shrug.

"Don't suppose, you *are!*"

"Andy?" a different woman calls me. Standing, Mom grabs my hand and we walk toward the lady. "Hi, Andy?" She looks to me, smiling.

"Yeah. This is my Mom. She can come in too, right?"

"Sure." She looks over my shoulder to Alex, Dad, and Alex's dad. "Would they like to join us too?"

"Is that okay?" I ask eagerly.

"Of course. The room isn't huge, but if they don't mind standing to the side, then, they're more than welcome." She smiles again.

There's no judgement in her eyes. She doesn't look at me like the first lady did. Immediately, I feel at ease with her. "Thank you." Turning, I gesture with my head for them all to come in.

We all follow the lady into a room. She wasn't kidding when she said it was small. Mom stands to the right of a small examination table. "I need you to lie down, please," the lady instructs me.

I hop up on the table, where Mom is to my right, Dad is at the top and Alex and Emil stand at the foot of the bed. Both look really uncomfortable in being in here. They're fidgeting, and looking around the room, not sure where to look.

"I need you to pull your shorts down to just above your pubic bone," the lady says. I do as she instructs, and Emil clears his throat and looks away. "Now, I'm going to put some gel on you. It's cold. Sorry," she apologizes. She squeezes the gel on my lower stomach, and she's right. It's really cold. "How much water have you had this morning?"

"At least six cups, and I want to pee."

"Sorry. This is going to be uncomfortable, because I need to press firmly. But we usually get a better picture if your bladder is full."

"Great," I grumble. She presses quite forcefully on my lower stomach, and my bladder responds. "Yep, I have to pee."

She lets out a small chuckle. The room fills with the sound of my baby boy's heartbeat. "Can you hear that?"

A huge smile creases my face. Emotionally, my eyes fill with tears. "That's his heart."

"It is."

Mom squeezes my hand. I look over to her, and see she's completely enthralled with Junior on the screen.

"He looks so beautiful," Alex says.

"You already know the gender?" the lady asks, perplexed.

"I don't need you to confirm. I just know he's a boy," I answer.

She nods her head, and looks at the screen again. "Can you see this?" She points to the screen. "This is your baby's arm. It looks like he's relaxing."

"It is a boy?" I squeal.

"He's not in the right position for me to confirm. I still need to do some measurements to confirm how far along you are, and the fetus's age."

"Baby," I correct.

"The baby," she says. The room is quiet, with the steady, fast thrum of his heart. "He's a good size. Here. From this point, to this point is where we measure." She indicates on the screen with the cursor where we should be looking. I hear someone moving, and see Alex and his dad move closer to get a better look. "At this stage, you're twelve weeks and two days pregnant, judging by the measurements of your baby. He's two-point-seven inches from head to rump. See?" She points again. "And he weighs about point seventy-five ounces. His head accounts for about a third of this."

"He has a big head?" I ask. This doesn't sound healthy.

"He does, which is normal. I'm just checking for Down's syndrome now. We check the thickness of the skin on the back of the neck." She does some more measurements. "Looks good. A full report will go to your OBGYN."

"Doctor Morgan's appointment is in two days," Mom says.

"We're almost finished here. Would you like to take a photo home?"

"Yes!" we all say in unison.

The lady looks to us, and smiles. "I'll print a few then."

Within seconds, she's wiped the goo off my stomach, and tells me I can get up. Emil turns to face the door, while Mom lets go of my hand so I can stand.

"Wow," Alex says, excitedly. "I don't think that's something I'll be able to get used to." He points to the monitor. "Just... wow."

"I know. Mind-blowing, right?" I ask.

"That's our baby." He hugs me and kisses the top of my head. "Our baby," he whispers.

"Here are your images." The lady hands me a long, thin strip of paper with various black and white images of our baby.

I tear off the bottom one, and hand it to Emil. "For me?" he asks, surprised.

"For you and Mary." I try to offer him a smile, knowing Mary won't respond well to the offer. But, it is what it is.

"Thank you." He takes his wallet out of his back pocket, and slides it into the small clear window, covering an earlier photo of Alex. I can see he's genuinely moved by what he's seen. I hope Mary can put her dislike for me aside, and get to know her grandson.

I hug Emil. I think he needs it. "You're welcome." It takes him a few seconds, but he returns my embrace.

Pulling away, I turn to Mom. "I need to get to work."

"So do we," Dad says.

"Although eventful, you need to get to school. And I need to get to work," Emil says to Alex. He turns to me and adds, "Thank you for inviting us to come with you today, Andy." His smile is natural, and honest.

"I can let you know when the next one is," I offer.

"I'd appreciate that." He turns to Alex. "Let's go."

Alex comes in for one more hug, and kisses me on the cheek. "Want to go for a drive tonight?"

I immediately turn to Mom, silently asking for her approval. She nods. "Sure. Around what time?"

"I'll text you."

"Okay."

We all walk out, a little happier knowing my little man is all safe and cozy in his home.

CHAPTER
21

"**I** FEEL LIKE a sloth," I say to Alex as I slowly set the table for dinner. Alex has been coming around a lot more, wanting to be with me as I progress with our baby.

"You look beautiful," he replies.

Dad pops his head up from his tablet, shakes his head and rolls his eyes. "You think I look ugly?" I playfully torment.

Dad tilts his head to the side as he lifts his brows. "No," he grumbles. Dad likes Alex so I know he's teasing.

Alex looks down at his hands, knowing Dad was balking at what he said.

"My stomach has definitely popped. Look." I pull my t-shirt tight across my stomach, revealing my baby bump starting to protrude.

Dad looks around Alex's body, wanting to see for himself. I stand so both Dad and Alex can see, and pull my t-shirt tight again. "Huh," Dad mutters. "So you are."

"Your grandson is cooking away quite nicely," I say,

dropping my t-shirt and rubbing at my belly.

"Andy, get a move on," Mom barks from the kitchen.

"Sorry, Mom." Hurriedly I go back to setting the table, although I feel like I'm moving so slow.

"I'll help," Alex offers. "You go sit. I can do it." Alex heads into the kitchen and takes the cutlery from the drawer. I've already set the plates, so he finishes by setting the cutlery and the glasses.

"Dinner's ready," Mom announces from the kitchen.

Dad stands and goes in to help, I feel like I'm waddling over to the dining table. I feel guilty that Alex is finishing setting the table, while I stare. Dad carries a large bowl in one hand, and his other has a plate with garlic bread. Mom steps behind him, carrying a large, deep dish.

"This looks fantastic, Mrs. Price."

Mom smiles at Alex. "Thank you." She places the dish on the table, and takes off the oven mitts, turning to throw them on the kitchen counter.

"Yum. What is it?" I ask.

"Lasagna, salad and garlic bread."

My stomach churns. Baby boy doesn't want lasagna, salad, and garlic bread. But Mom's gone to so much effort I have to try and eat it.

I sink into my seat, feeling like I'm going to be sick. Mom, Dad, and Alex all dive into the food. I sit back, waiting for them to finish so I can attempt to eat. I scoop a small piece of lasagna onto my plate, and stare at it. Mom, Dad, and Alex are eating and talking, while I stare at the food.

"Don't you like it?" Mom asks.

"Yeah, I love your lasagna." I place some on my fork, and bring it to my mouth. I'm trying my hardest not to gag, but I can't do it. I look at Mom and see the hurt in her eyes. Her shoulders slump as she dips her head, avoiding eye contact with me. "I'm sorry, Mom."

"It's okay." She lifts her head, but the fake smile can't replace the true hurt etched deep into her face. "Banana?" she asks as she stands, and walks over to the fruit bowl overflowing with bananas. She grabs two, then heads over to the fridge to get the ketchup. She brings them over to me. "Here you go, sweetheart."

My heart is breaking. I know Mom spent time in the kitchen making this beautiful meal, and I can't even eat it. "I'm sorry," I say again, the guilt consuming me. Bursting into tears, I stand and run toward my bedroom.

"What's going on?" Mom asks as she enters my room seconds after I do.

"I don't know," I reply. "I feel terrible that I can't eat what you've made."

Mom sits on my bed beside me, and smiles. "I know what's wrong." I look at her, questioning. "Hormones."

I turn away, and think about it. She's right. I can go from happy to sappy in two-point-three seconds. "My head is a mess. Especially about food. I want to eat something other than bananas and ketchup, but I can't."

"It's okay." Mom places her arm around my shoulders and drags me in for a hug. She kisses my head and says, "There's no rule book with pregnancy. No one ever warns you of the emotional turmoil you'll go through. Your body is learning to cope with someone who's growing inside of you. Life is never easy, and although pregnancy can be beautiful, it can also be brutal."

"Brutal, ha!"

"It's probably worse for you because you're young. You don't have the life experience someone older has, so for you these feelings and emotions are all so foreign."

"Just tell me this, Mom."

"What?"

"It does settle down, right?" I ask, hopeful.

"Yep." She stands and faces me. "In about eighteen years." Smiling she heads out of my room. "Come have your banana and ketchup." Mom holds her hand out to me, waiting for me to take it.

"Ugh. Eighteen years," I grumble as I stand.

"At least. Could be more."

"Could be less?"

Mom chuckles louder. "If that brings comfort to you, then let's go with that."

Great. So basically, I'm going to be an emotional wreck forever. Something to look forward to.

I follow Mom out to the dining room, and sit, feeling completely embarrassed by my sudden attack of tears. "You okay?" Alex asks quietly.

"Being a girl is hard sometimes."

"I really wouldn't know."

"Alex, I suggest in times like these, you simply stay quiet," Dad says. I look at Dad. His eyes are lowered, looking at his food. "She's staring, isn't she?"

"Yes, I am."

"See. Don't ever make eye contact."

I start laughing. "You're a dork, Dad." I can see Dad's cheeks fill out like he's smiling. "Sorry. Just emotional. I have a lifetime of being emotional to look forward to."

"Excellent," Alex mumbles under his breath.

"Say nothing, Alex," Dad says.

Suddenly, I feel something weird happening to my stomach. "Ugh," I grunt as I place my hand to my stomach.

"What's wrong?" Mom looks worried.

"It's weird. It's like I'm nervous for some reason. You know when you get butterflies in your stomach? That's what it's like." I look to Mom, Dad, and Alex. Alex shrugs, having no idea what I'm talking about. Mom's smiling and looks like she's about to jump out of her skin. Dad's smirking and nodding his head proudly. "What?" I ask.

"That's the baby moving," Mom says.

"Huh?" Alex's hand immediately flies to my stomach. "I can't feel anything."

"You're not going to be able to yet," Mom says. "But Andy can, which means that in a few weeks, we will too." She claps her hands together, excitedly.

"Oh my God. He's moving?" I ask, nearly breathless. Tears are welling up in my eyes, and I'm getting choked up on all these emotions flooding through my body. "I'm such a mess." I wipe at my eyes, totally embarrassed and overwhelmed. "What's wrong with me?"

"Nothing at all." Alex wraps his arms around me, bringing me in closer for a hug. "You're perfect," he whispers.

"I'm crying, and now I don't even know why I'm crying. I should be happy."

He pulls on me, sliding me off my chair and onto his lap. Gently he soothes my hair, while continuously peppering soft kisses on my cheek. "It's okay," he proceeds to say.

Leaning my head against his, I take a few deep breaths calming myself. This is crazy. *I'm* crazy. Once calmed, I lift my head, and look around at my family. "I'm so sorry."

"Don't be," Mom says.

"These emotions are nuts. I went from happy to sad in a nano-second. How's that even possible?"

"Because you're knocked-up," Dad says in a sarcastic *'duh'* tone. Mom hits Dad on the shoulder. "What? Pregnant women are nut cases." Mom gives Dad a look, one that says, *'I dare you to keep talking.'* "What?"

I can't help it. I burst into laughter. This time, I'm laughing so hard, I have laughter tears rolling down my cheeks. "You're so clueless," I say between the gales of laughter.

Dad shrugs his shoulders.

Settling back into my seat, I pick my banana up and dip it in ketchup.

Man, this whole being pregnant thing is so bizarre. I have no idea what my hormones are going to do from one moment to the next. Let's hope they settle down after my little man is here.

CHAPTER 22

Gestation Twenty-Eight Weeks

I'M HUGE, AND uncomfortable, and I've put on over forty pounds. The vomiting hasn't stopped, and I've been admitted into hospital a total of five times for extreme morning sickness.

Each time is the same as the last.

My boobs feel so big, and I have stretch marks everywhere. And let's not even mention the pressure on my pelvis.

"I think it's impossible to get any larger," I complain to Zar who's brought over her momma's hot apple cider and is pouring it into a mug for me.

"You look so good. Stop complaining."

"I can't sleep on my stomach anymore."

"Because you have a human growing inside of you."

"And I feel like I'm waddling."

"Penguins can do it. Why can't you?"

"And I can't see my feet."

"I'm sure the abominable snowman can't either."

I'm about to complain about something else, when I stop in

mid-thought. "The abominable snowman?"

"Yeah, you know. A yeti."

I crinkle my mouth, confused, but amused too. "You're weird."

"Says the fifteen-year-old pregnant chick," Zar teases.

She makes me laugh. "What's happening at school?" I ask.

"Nothing really. Except, Blair and Ruby now have boyfriends."

"Yeah, Alex told me Blair's left him alone."

"How are you doing? Still getting filthy looks from people?"

"Ha, yes! Filthy is an understatement. The way people look at me. I almost want to tell them to go screw themselves. Should see them coming into work, and eyeing me over, like I'm some kind of feral animal who's got an untreatable disease." I shake my head, annoyed by the judgement I've been experiencing. But I push past it, and try to focus on anything but them. "Anyway, I have to go down to the mall, want to come?"

"When?"

"Now? I can ask Dad to take us."

"Sure. I'll just text Mom to let her know." She pulls her phone out of her pocket and sends her mom a quick text asking if it's okay.

"Dad." I go to find him, but he's not in the house. "Dad?" I call louder as I head out to the back garden. He's outside, soaking up some sun on the deck while playing a game on his phone. "Dad?"

"Hey, bear. What's up?"

"Can you take Zar and me to the mall? I need to get some stuff."

"Whatcha getting?"

"Well..." I pause, not really wanting to tell Dad, but I suppose I shouldn't be ashamed. "I need new bras. My old ones are too tight."

Dad turns his head to look at me. "You need bras?" his voice cracks while his cheeks grow pink. "Yeah, give me a few minutes."

"Thanks." I head back inside to drink my apple cider. "This is so good." I drink it quickly, and instantly regret it because it goes straight through me. "Ugh," I grumble as I leave the kitchen.

"What's wrong?" Zar calls after me.

"Bathroom. Again!"

I hear her laughing as I waddle down the hallway to the bathroom.

"Target has maternity and nursing bras, and so does J.C Penney. Can we go there?" I ask Zar.

"Yeah, I don't need anything, so wherever you wanna go is good with me."

"I'm hungry," I say as I reach into my bag and get a banana.

"You just ate at home."

"I didn't put on forty pounds by not eating."

"Oh my God! How appalling. She's just a child," I hear someone gasp.

I don't know why that remark made me look around, it had something to do with the revulsion in the tone. I look to my left, then to my right, where I see two fairly old ladies sitting at a bench seat, staring at me. They're both just glaring at me.

I look around, to see if it's me they're actually looking at, or someone else.

"What's their problem?" Zar asks.

I exhale, drooping my shoulders. I should be used to these types of comments, but I'm not. I still look around me to see who these nasty people are talking about. "Let's go," I say as I grab onto Zar's arm and try to waddle away as fast as possible. My hunger is now gone, and I throw the remainder of my banana into the closest trash can.

"Couldn't keep her legs closed," I hear one say to the other.

"They're getting younger and younger," the other replies.

Tears well in my eyes. I'm barely choking back the whimper wanting to burst through. "Can we get out of here?' I ask Zar as quietly as possible.

The two women keep their assault up on me. Looking at me, shaking their heads and tsking as I walk away.

"Nah, this is bullshit. You shouldn't be made to feel so bad." Zar drops my arm and turns to walk toward them. "How dare you," she says to the two women. "You have no idea about her age, or even why she's pregnant. You sit there, all old and waiting to die, thinking you know better."

"Zar, leave it alone. They're like every other judgmental person in the world," I say as I try to get her away.

"You mean ignorant, and narrow-minded?" Zar corrects me.

"How dare you speak to your elders like this!" one of the women scolds Zar.

Zar places a hand to her hip, and shakes her head. "Funny, isn't it? You demand respect from us younger people, but you refuse to give it. Hypocritical much?" Zar lets out a chuckle. "What a shame you're so closed-minded." With that, Zar doesn't give either of the women an opportunity to respond.

"You shouldn't speak to us like that," one of the ladies says to our retreating backs.

"Leave it alone," I say turning to Zar, trying to pull her away. But as I turn to her, I can see the frustration on her face. She stops, wanting to go back, but I pull on her arm, refusing to allow those women to rob us of any more of our time or energy today. "It's really not worth the argument, because if it was, we'd be arguing with every second person."

"I don't know how you do it. They infuriated me." She grips onto my arm tighter. Her shoulders are high, and her jaw is gritting tight. "I can't believe them."

"This is what happens when you're pregnant at my age."

"But they have no right…"

"No, they don't. But it doesn't stop people judging. It's human nature. Attack what you don't know, and refuse to listen to reason."

"You can't really believe that."

"I never used to, but since I've popped and now look pregnant, people have been, generally, quite horrible toward me."

Zar exhales. "How sad people are like that."

I shrug. "I suppose people only see the exterior and make a judgement. They have no idea why or how, and are either too afraid to ask, or don't want to ask because they won't like the answer. Or maybe they suspect the answer won't agree with their assumptions."

"What do you mean?"

I shrug again. "Seeing someone at my age pregnant might mean that I'm easy, you know, like a party girl. Or, it could mean something more sinister."

Zar lowers her head slightly. "How sad if people see that in you."

"I've got to remember, it's not me personally they're judging, it's the situation. They don't know me, they have no idea about my life. People see what they want to see, and most people don't want to listen. Look at those two back there, they had it in their minds that I'm a terrible person because I'm young and pregnant. They weren't willing to listen, because their ego was wounded once you took a stand against them."

"You could've said something to them."

"Why?"

"To make them see."

"Again, why? They're of no importance to me. Their opinion of me is not anything I can control."

"But they were being vocal about you."

"Yeah, they were. But it shows *their* ignorance, not mine. I've decided on a new rule I'm going to live by."

"What's the rule?"

"It's the five-five-five rule." Zar looks at me questioning. "Will it matter in five weeks, five months or five years. If the answer is no, then I have to let it go."

"Huh!" She starts giggling to herself. "Well then, I'll start living by the Triple S rule."

"Triple S?"

"Yep. Are they stupid, skanky and special? If they are, then it doesn't matter." She draws the double o sound of "stoopid."

I pause walking for a second, letting her Triple S rule sink in. Holding my stomach, I start laughing. "Stupid? Skanky? Special?"

"Yep. If people want to be one of the three S's, then screw 'em, I don't want anything to do with them."

"I really don't know what I'd do without you."

She flicks her hand at me dismissively. "You'll never have to find out." She slings her arm around my shoulder and tries to hug me. But it's awkward, because I'm so round. We kinda stumble. "Well, that didn't go quite like I thought. I was hoping to hug you, but instead, you hip bumped me and nearly knocked my ass over."

"If only we lived in a movie, or a book. They always have flawless hair, and walk perfectly in the stupidest of high heels, and are impeccably beautiful. You honestly don't see someone like me."

"Like you?"

"Yeah. Messy top knot, boobs hurting, stomach so big it has its own zip code. An emotional mess. And not to mention fifteen and pregnant. I'm not exactly a great role model for anyone my age."

"It's not always like that in movies and books, but usually, yeah. But then again, who'd want to watch a movie or read a book based on a fifteen-year-old pregnant hussy and her ultra-cool best friend?" She points to me, then to herself.

"Ultra-cool?" I lift my brows. "Really?"

"I'm so cool I should be arctic."

Walking into Target, I can't help but laugh. "You're so fringe."

"You're so pregnant," she playfully snaps back.

"I love you, Zar." I'm so happy she's my best friend.

"So you should."

We head to the maternity section of Target, and the first thing I see is a pair of maternity yoga pants. "Yes, these look so comfortable." Picking them up, I see how the stomach is made from an elastic type of material, meaning they'll be able to expand as my little man gets bigger.

"You know, I've never looked at maternity clothes before. Never had a reason to." Zar picks up a bra. "It says it's a nursing bra. How does it work?"

"Here." I take it out of her hands, and unclip the small clip above the cup.

"So your boob flops out to feed the baby? Huh, right." She screws her mouth up, repulsed.

"Yeah."

"Are you going to breast feed in public?"

"I've seen how some women put a cloth over themselves and do it discreetly. I could do that, but I'm not sure I'm comfortable enough to feed in public. Besides, what if he doesn't want to latch on? Then I'll have to bottle feed."

"I've been reading up on breast versus bottle."

"Have you?" I ask.

"Well, duh. My best friend is having a baby. I want to be able to help with whatever I can. Except the feeding thing." She gestures towards her breast. "Obviously if you're breast feeding, I can't do that."

"So you'll look after him?"

"If I can, I will."

"Clean his dirty diaper?"

Zar crinkles her nose. "Yeah, I'll do that too. Under protest, but I'll still do it."

"This looks really comfortable. I'm definitely getting a couple of these."

"What are they?"

"Seamless sleep bras. Feel how soft they are." I thrust them into Zar's hands. "See."

"Get them."

"I will. Oh, and I need one of these too."

"A support belt?" Zar asks.

"Yeah. As he gets bigger, he's sitting lower, dragging my stomach down. It's really uncomfortable. Hopefully this will help."

"Oh my God. Andy. It's seventy dollars."

"Yeah, I know. There are other ones that are cheaper, but this one looks more comfortable than the rest. The others look a bit restrictive, and I don't want that. My back is sore," I complain. "Can we buy these, and sit? I'm a bit tired too."

"Do you want to go home?" Zar's concerned. "Is that baby okay?"

"He's fine. I'm just a little tired. I could sit for a bit."

"Are you sure?" Zar fusses.

"I'll pay for these few things, then we'll head out and grab a drink. Is that okay?"

"Anything you need."

Taking the belly support and three identical bras to the cashier, I wait in line behind a few people. A little girl in front of me turns, sees my protruding stomach and smiles. "Have you got a baby in your belly?" she asks.

"I do." I return her smile.

Her father turns to see who his daughter is talking to. The moment his gaze lands on me, the smile in his eyes disappear and they widen as he pulls his daughter behind him. "Daddy says a man puts a seed into a woman's belly. Is that how you got your baby?"

"Shhh, Savannah," her father scolds. He doesn't want her talking to me.

"Here we go again," Zar says loudly. "I can't believe in today's day and age people are so cruel and judgmental."

"It is what it is," I reply.

"I think it's a baby girl," the little girl says.

"Do you?" I ask, still smiling at her.

"Savannah! I told you, look away."

"Yep. I think it's a little girl, and I think you should name her Savannah."

"Savannah!" her dad croaks.

"I think that's such a pretty name," I say.

She gives me a huge smile; her two front teeth are missing. Her bangs hang low, and her pretty blue eyes light up her entire face. "Thank you."

We shuffle forward, and it's their turn to be served. Her father maneuvers Savannah so he's between me and her. Peeking out from behind him, she waves as they leave. Her father turns, rolls his eyes, grabs her hand, and hurries out of the store.

"Hi," says the girl serving us.

Giving her my things, she scans them all, and tells me the tally. Handing over my card, I scan it and wait to see it's approved. But that man is really playing on my mind. I'm used to people looking at me and giving me snide remarks or looks. But he wanted to make sure his daughter wasn't even *looking* at me.

That's quite upsetting.

Am I really the type of monster that parents need to protect their kids from?

Am I on the same level as murderers, rapists, and pedophiles? He couldn't get out of the store fast enough. He was trying to shelter Savannah, so she couldn't talk to me.

This hurts my heart so much.

It hurts me to my very soul.

Of all the bad in the world, do people really consider me dangerous?

A tear falls from my eye, and I quickly wipe it away, hoping Zar doesn't see it.

Thankfully, she doesn't.

I just need a few moments to regroup, and push past this.

Damn hormones.

And society.

CHAPTER
23

"EVERY TIME I see you, you get bigger, sugar," Clarence says when I find her in the kitchen making her secret recipe strawberry jam. She won her fifteenth ribbon for the best strawberry jam in Black Pine.

"I feel it," I puff while leaning against the wall. "Why more strawberry jam?"

"I've sold out of my first batch and have a wait-list of people wanting to buy some. I have to make more. Arthur's gone to get me more strawberries because this definitely isn't enough for the customers waiting." She stirs two huge pots on the range. "Before I know it, you won't be able to help me."

"I'm going to be here until the moment I can't."

Clarence turns, smiling at me. "I know you will, sugar. But let's face it, you're thirty weeks now, and getting bigger and bigger."

"I know." I exhale, feeling terrible, knowing I won't be here in a few weeks. "Before I open, have you turned the coffee machine on?"

"She's all warmed up and ready to go."

I walk out to the front, check all the sugar packet containers, wipe down the tables and make sure all the lights are on before turning the closed sign around to open.

Before long we begin getting a steady stream of the usual morning customers wanting their coffees on their way to work. I know a lot of the regulars, and how they like their coffees. Most are kind, and some have given me small gifts for the baby. Of course, there are the ones who look at me like I have two heads, but they're few and far between, thankfully.

"Josie, your coffee's ready," I say to one of our regulars.

"Thanks, Andy. I'll see you tomorrow?" she asks on the way out.

"I'm here all week." Clarence needs me more than the original two days a week.

"Bye."

I've got a few moments of quiet, and I head out to the kitchen to see if Clarence needs me. "Doing okay?" I ask.

"I'm okay. You doing alright on your own?"

"It's steady today, mostly the regulars."

"Hello?" someone calls from the front.

When I reach the counter, I stare at her for a second, immediately recognizing her. "Vivian, right?"

"Yeah. Um…" She points at me thinking where she's seen me. "Oh yeah, how silly. You're Doctor Morgan's patient. I've seen you at the hospital so many times. Andy, right? Sorry, I obviously need my caffeine today."

"I don't usually see you in here."

"Oh no, but this will be my regular stop from now on. It's between where I live and the hospital, so it's convenient. I used to be a regular at another coffee store across town, until I discovered the strawberry jam at the Black Pine Festival. And the lady, Clarence, is so lovely. And besides, the other place…"

She scrunches her nose and shakes her head in disgust. I want to ask what's made her have that reaction, but I choose not to. "I found a hair in my sandwich."

"Ewww." I crinkle my nose.

"And it certainly didn't belong to me."

I dry retch, revolted by the thought. "Gross," I whisper. "Anyway, what can I get for you?"

"Black, no sugar. And as big as they come, please. Intravenously if possible," she jokes.

"That bad a morning?" I ask.

"Jayden's been sick. And I've been up all night, checking on him. Stat with that coffee too please, Andy."

As I make her coffee, I ask her, "Is he okay?"

"Yeah, he'll be fine. I'm just an overprotective parent."

"I think I'll be like that too. I mean, I'm totally in love with this little man." I gently rub my protruding belly.

"Oh, I didn't know you knew the sex. Congratulations." She takes the coffee I'm offering.

"Every time I have a scan, his legs are crossed, but I just know, you know?"

Turning to Vivian, she's smiling at me. "It's a mother's instinct. But, it doesn't always work out that way."

"I know there's a possibility, but I honestly believe over ninety-nine percent, that this little peanut is a boy."

"Well, only time will tell. Thank you for the coffee. I'll see you tomorrow?"

"You will."

Vivian leaves with her coffee, and I continue with the next customers.

Lying on my bed, I'm listening to music as I feel my little man kicking away happily.

"Amazing, isn't it?" I ask him. "You're in my tummy, kicking around and I can feel you. Can you feel me?"

The song playing in the background is slow and soft. "You know what else? You're so loved out here. Your grandparents can't wait to meet you." I smile as I run my hand across my stomach. A gentle kick comes in response to my words. Truthfully, I know his kicks aren't because I'm speaking to him, but I can wish and hope he's trying to communicate with me too. "Your Auntie Zar is as crazy as they come, but I know she's going to love you like you're her own." Another delicate kick. "I wonder what you're thinking."

I sigh, thinking about life. "This world is crazy, and scary and can be brutal and horror-filled. But there's so much beauty to it too. Random acts of kindness happen every day. From big, to small. From famous people fighting for our environment, to someone buying a homeless person a meal. These things make our world. And you'll get to be a part of it. A huge part where you can do and be anything you want."

There's a knock on my door, then Mom opens it. "You okay?" she asks.

"Yeah, just talking to this little guy." I rub at my tummy.

Mom sits on the side of my bed, and I scoot back so she can lay down too. She positions herself so we're face to face. "Do you know, not even fifty years ago, if a young unwed woman or girl became pregnant, the parents would generally send her to a home to see out her pregnancy, then they'd give the baby up for adoption?"

"Why?"

"Being pregnant at such a young age, or even being unwed and pregnant was seen as sinful."

"Ha," I chuckle. "Because that's the worst thing in the world, right? Being young, or not married?"

"Back then, it was considered disgraceful. It would bring shame to the family."

"Are you ashamed of me?"

"What? No." She huffs, and screws her mouth up, like she wants to say more. "I wasn't exactly thrilled with the notion of you being pregnant so young. It's not where I thought your life would go."

"It isn't exactly what I had in mind, either."

"And having a baby at such a young age, it could be disastrous."

"Oh," I say. My tone is sad, as is what Mom's saying.

"But the most amazing thing is, you have us here. We're going to help you, Andy. We're going to help you and this baby as much as we can. We want you both to be happy, safe, and healthy. And your father and I will be here for you, through whatever happens." She places her hand on my stomach. My little man kicks. "Wow," she whispers and smiles. "Bringing a baby into this world is wonderful," she says, "and damn hard. You'll have so many emotions and feelings. But just know we're here for you."

"Thank you, Mom." I'm already an emotional mess, it can't possibly get worse.

"We have to finish the nursery. I know Clarence bought you so many things, but we really need to hurry up and get things done before this little one makes his entrance into the world."

"I don't think I want to paint the nursery blue," I say.

"You don't have to. We can choose any color you want. Pink, green, purple, yellow… whatever."

"Do you think Dad would mind if we choose something other than blue?"

Mom smiles. "Have we not proven to you over and over again, that we only want you happy, healthy and safe? The color of the nursery is inconsequential. We just need to make sure you and the baby are both happy, healthy and…"

"And safe," I finish. "I know." I exhale. "I don't want to disappoint anyone."

"You won't. Just be the best version of you. Anything less is a waste of everyone's time."

"Huh," I grumble. "That's so true." Mom has spoken a truth I've never really thought about before. Why don't we live the best version of ourselves every day? "Huh," I huff again.

"Andy?" Mom says.

"Yeah, what?"

"Did you hear what I said?" I shake my head. "What were you thinking?"

"I'm thinking about what you said. Being the best versions of ourselves. Those are words I think everyone needs to live by."

"We all have flaws, sweetie. But if we can live our best life, and be the best we can be, then life would be so much easier for all of us."

"So true. Anyway, what were you saying?"

"I asked if you wanted to go baby shopping on Wednesday. I'm not going into work 'til after your ultrasound, so we can go and buy some furniture too."

"Is Dad coming? Alex can't because he needs to finish his college applications. Actually, he wanted to come, but I insisted he finish his applications. Deadline is the end of the week. He did say if he gets them done he'll be there. I think he'll bust his ass to get done so he can be at the ultrasound. If not, he wants us to get him a copy of the sonogram."

"That boy is persistent, I'll give him that. Your father and I thought he'd bail the moment you told him you're pregnant."

"He's not like that, Mom."

She smiles. "The thing I know is regardless of how things turn out, he'll be a good father to the baby. I think he'll honor you both."

"What do you mean by *how things turn out?*"

"The future is not given. Only the past is certain. Who knows what'll happen with you both?"

"But we love each other."

"And you're both incredibly young. Feelings change. People change. Just be true to yourself, regardless."

"By others, you mean Alex?"

"By others I mean Alex," Mom confirms.

I want to be adamant and tell her that Alex and I are strong. As strong as steel. But she's right, people *do* and *can* change. Maybe though, maybe it won't be him who'll change. Maybe it'll be me.

CHAPTER 24

"MORNING ARTHUR," I say as I enter CCC.

"Morning, sweet pea. How's that baby of yours doing? I see you're looking very healthy." He smiles.

I'm not sure how to take his last remark. Is he saying I'm looking fat, or... Snap out of it, Andy. His intentions are good. Arthur has a beautiful, caring soul. "Thank you. Is Clarence in the kitchen?"

"She's making her chocolate and orange flourless cake. Got a special order for three."

"Why didn't she call me to come help?"

Arthur shrugs his shoulders but continues wiping the tables down.

"Clarence?" I say as I enter the kitchen. She's fussing around like a headless chicken. "Why didn't you call me, I could've helped you."

"Don't be silly. I'm okay." She flicks her hand at me.

"Do you think you can make a banana cake?" I ask.

"No. I don't *think* I can make it, I *know* I can." She adds a smile to her sass. "Matter of fact, my granddaddy passed down a beautiful banana cake recipe. Hmmm." She places a finger to her chin and scrunches her brows. "I haven't made it in such a long time." She looks behind me, then shouts, "Arthur. I need some bananas. But I want them black and at death's door. You know the type I'm talking about."

"You making the banana cake?" he eagerly asks.

"I sure am."

"Yippee, woman! I've been wanting you to make this for such a long time. I stopped asking when you kept telling me you'd do it next week and next week never came. How many pounds of bananas?'

"Ten should do it."

"Woman, I could kiss you right now." His eyes widen with excitement. A huge smile brightens his face. "You know what?" he walks up to her, takes her by the waist, dips her and plants a kiss right on her mouth.

I'm smiling like a goof, so happy to see them so in love after many, many years of marriage. "Aww," I gush over them.

"Let me up, old man." Clarence smacks him playfully on the shoulder.

"Who you calling old?" he replies as he lifts her. "I'm going to get you those bananas. I'll be back soon." He reaches for his cap, places it on his head and dances out to the front.

We hear the door close and Clarence shakes her head. "He always told me he fell in love with me because of my banana cake."

"I could see how excited he was when you asked for the bananas."

"He once told me if he's ever on death row, he'd ask for my banana cake as his last meal. I told him, if he's ever on death row, I'd kill him myself for getting there." I can't help but smile. "Sugar, it's time we open."

"The coffee machine is on?" I ask but quickly check it before Clarence has a chance to respond.

"It's on!" she says as she scurries to the door to flip the closed sign around.

It doesn't take long before our usual morning customers start coming in, waiting for their usual orders.

Some order muffins, or a slice of cake with their coffees. Everyone's different, but everyone is so nice to me. "Morning, Andy," Frank says as he steps forward.

"How are you today, Frank?" I ask as I begin his coffee order. Frank doesn't reply, which is unusual for him because generally he's really chatty and happy. I look over, and notice him staring at my stomach. "Everything okay?"

"Andy, my darling, are you..." He leans in, and quickly looks around. "Are you pregnant or...?" he doesn't finish the sentence.

I chuckle, because I know he wants to ask me if I'm fat or pregnant. What's so surprising is this is the first time he's noticing. "I'm pregnant, Frank. Thirty weeks."

He's hand flies to his chest. "Little lady, I had no idea. Hand on my heart, I never looked at you below the face, I honestly didn't know."

"Maybe you missed the memo, because a lot of people know about this." I rub my stomach, highlighting my baby.

"Do you know if it's a boy or girl?"

"He's a boy."

"Congratulations. You're an awful sweet girl, so I'm thinking this baby will be lucky to have you as his momma." Frank speaks like he's from the country, but he's such a sweet man. He owns the local mechanic shop, and everyone takes their cars to him because he's so genuine and lovely. "I'm thinking Imma need a muffin today too. Don't tell Doris, because she'd yell at me. *Watch your cholesterol; watch your sugar,* that's all she ever yells at me. I think life is too short, and if I want a muffin, I think I should eat a muffin."

"Your secret is safe with me," I say as I hand him his coffee, then go over to the display case and take out one of Clarence's muffins.

"I'll see you next time." He offers me a smile as he leaves.

"Was that Frank?" Clarence asks as she comes out from the kitchen.

"It was. Do you know he had no idea I was pregnant?"

"Frank's a good man, Andy. He only looks in a person's eyes when he's talking to them, and never listens to small town gossip. Shoot, I wanted to catch him to ask him to take a look at our car. I'll catch him tomorrow."

The store gets busy, then quiet, then busy again. This is how it flows normally. The lunch rush is usually quite frantic, but Clarence, Arthur and I can handle it. Today is no different.

"Hi there, can I help you?" I ask two older women who I've never seen before. One's wearing a one of those old-fashioned hats with netting that covers part of her face. She has a face full of make-up, her lips as red as a candy apple. The other woman is somewhat more modest. She's not wearing a hat, and isn't made-up to look like she's about to attend a special event.

The one with that hat looks straight to my stomach, and raises her brows. "We'll have two coffees, cream and sugar. And two slices of key lime pie," she says shortly. "And we'll be sitting right over there." She turns and points to one of the tables looking out of the large front window. She pays for their order without any further words.

Bizarre.

"Clarence," I call.

"Sorry, I was cleaning up out back."

"Can you make their coffees please?" I ask.

"Sure thing."

Clarence sets to making the two ladies' coffees, and I plate their key lime pies. I step out from the behind the counter, taking the pies to them. "Here you go. I'll be back in a moment with your coffees."

"Hmmm," groans hat lady.

I'm not sure what I've done for her to be so dismissive. But anyway, it is what it is. Walking over, I get the two coffees and take them back to them. "Ladies," I say with a smile as I give them their coffees.

"Are you pregnant?" hat lady asks.

"I am."

"How old are you, child?"

Right. This is about me being pregnant. I muster a smile, and reply. "I'm fifteen."

"Do I take it you're unwed?"

Aha. What bothers her more? My age or my marital status? "No, ma'am, I'm not married." I smile again, although now it's more forced. "Enjoy your pie." I step away, but her hand darts out to grab mine before I can leave. "Is there anything else I can get for you?"

"Having sexual intercourse with a boy before you've been wed is frowned upon in God's eyes."

"So is gun violence in our schools, but it seems to continue," I snap back.

"You'll be giving this child to a good home? To a woman who's married but is having difficulty getting pregnant." She's not asking, she's *telling*.

"No."

"But you're just a mere child yourself. You can't give this child what it needs," she continues.

"Do you know my personal situation?"

"I'm assuming this baby is from an unruly act of unkindness toward you." She smiles, but I can see the hatred inside her eyes.

"No, it isn't." I refuse to tell her anything else. "Enjoy your pie."

"You won't be able to provide. You must do the right thing and surrender this little life. Give him to a home where love, food, and education will be the only focus. Let me pray for you to choose the right thing to do."

The longer I stand here, the angrier I'm getting. "With all due respect, ma'am, you have no idea about my life. You don't know what kind of support I have. If you don't mind, I'd prefer for you to keep your opinion to yourself."

"How rude," she snaps. The other woman says nothing. She lowers her head, and drinks her coffee, stopping for a nibble of her pie. "God won't save you if you don't do the right thing. Being so young means you need saving. Especially someone in your condition." Her eyes travel to my stomach, then back up again.

"Someone in my condition?"

"Yes. You owe it to women who can't have children to give them yours. It's what you should do. For the Lord guards the path of the righteous, but the wicked will perish."

"You're telling me if I don't give my baby away, I'll be damned?"

"The Lord can save you, if you do the right thing."

"And doing the right thing is giving my baby away?"

"Yes. You need to be saved."

"There is neither Jew nor Gentile, neither slave nor free, nor is there male and female, for you are all one in Christ Jesus," Arthur says from behind me. I turn to see him standing with a box of bananas in his arms. He places them down on a free table. "The Lord is about acceptance and forgiveness, but all I see and hear here is ostentatious, archaic hypocrisy. Ladies, we here are not God-fearing people, but God-loving people who have the decency to be kind and accepting."

I swallow back the lump in my throat. Arthur has the most beautiful soul. This gives me the strength not to cry in front of them. Instead, I straighten my shoulders and smile. "Ma'am, as a woman you should be lifting another woman up, and not attempting to tear her down. Haven't we *all* had enough of that?"

She looks forward to her friend. Neither say anything, her friend not even able to make eye contact with me. They sip on their coffee, quietly.

"Have a good day," Arthur says, lifting the box of bananas. "Andy, I need your help."

"Enjoy your pie." Yeah, your humble pie.

Arthur goes into the kitchen. I move to where Clarence is making a coffee. "What was that about?" she asks.

"Nothing but ugly words," I say.

"Are you okay? I can throw them out, tell them not to come back again."

"I doubt they'll be returning in a hurry."

"Ignorant old farts," Arthur says from the kitchen loud enough for everyone to hear.

With that, both women stand, and head out. Their pies are half-eaten, but at least they've finished their coffees.

"Arthur!" Clarence snaps.

"Well, they are."

I can't help but snicker. They didn't like what we had to say, but were keen to tell me how I'm a terrible person for being pregnant. I clean their table and find a ten-dollar tip, and below the tip is a card to the church she obviously thinks I should attend. "I'll take this, but I have the perfect place for it." I take it over to the trash. "Clarence, they left a ten-dollar tip."

"Good, so they should." She goes to inspect the bananas Arthur has bought. "Damn nervy to come in here preaching to my staff. Who does she think she is?" Clarence mumbles angrily. "How dare she think she's above us? Who gave her the right to come in here judging us? No one, that's who."

"Just make me my banana cake and put those women in the past," Arthur says in an easy tone.

"It's okay, Clarence. I was getting upset, but then…" I shrug my shoulders. "I don't know, Arthur said what he said, and suddenly I found my words and my courage."

Clarence leaves the bananas and comes to give me a hug. "You, my girl, are one strong person."

Strong isn't the word I'd use to describe me. But I'll take it.

CHAPTER 25

T HE WOMAN AT the counter of the ultrasound lab isn't as judgmental as she was the first time we came here. Actually, she's quite nice. "Hello there," she says with a huge smile when I walk over to her. "How are you doing today?"

"I'm okay. I haven't been feeling as sick as I have been in the past."

"Still loving your bananas with ketchup?" Her nose twitches, but she holds in the repulsion most people exhibit when they see me eating it.

"More than you know. I think I'll never touch a banana again in my life when this little man comes out."

She smiles. "Your mom with you today?" She looks behind me and doesn't see Mom.

"She's parking the car."

"Anyone else coming?"

"Just Mom today."

"Okay, we'll wait 'til she's here before I take you in."

"Oh," I say as I get a swift kick to my side. "Ouch, that one hurt."

"Wait 'til he's sitting on your pubic bone. Once, my youngest sat in a position where she blocked my bladder. And let me tell you, I really needed to go."

"That would be torture."

"It was. Didn't last long, only a few moments. But man, oh man, I've never been so uncomfortable in my life." She smiles while reminiscing, and I smile with her. "Here's your mom."

"You okay?" I ask Mom who's looking red and flushed in the cheeks. Mom's distracted, and isn't even hearing me. "Mom," I say again, concerned.

"Yes, sweetheart?" she replies forcing a smile to her mouth. But her eyes look worried. Her face is red, and her brows are crinkled.

"What's wrong?" I chew on my nails, worried. "What's happening?"

"Nothing, nothing," her voice trembles. Something's happening, but I don't know what. "Are they ready for you?"

"Not yet." Mom and I walk over to two available chairs, and sit. Mom's fidgeting, looking at her phone every few seconds. "Mom!" I snap at her. "What is going on?"

"No, nothing. I'm sorry. Just, um…" She puts her phone in her bag. "Nothing, it's okay." She forces another smile, and now I know something is really wrong.

"What is it?" I ask, stressed and frustrated she's not telling me.

"Andy?" Before Mom can answer, I'm called in for my scan.

Mom and I stand, but I'm not letting this go. I need to know why Mom seems so distracted. I head in and Mom follows, as I turn to check on her, I notice she's left her handbag behind. "Mom?" I look at her bag, then to her.

"Oh man. I'm sorry. I'd lose my head if it wasn't screwed on." She tries to make light of the situation, but it's obvious something is troubling her.

The lady takes us into a small room with an examination table and the usual bulky machine. I know Alex can't come because he's still filling out his applications, so it's just Mom and me.

"How are you today, Andy?" the lady asks. She's an older woman who's scanned me before. She's so nice.

"I'm good. Stupid banana and ketchup cravings aren't going away. But, I haven't been feeling sick lately, either. So that's a good thing."

"Not feeling sick is a good thing." She's such a nice woman. "You're looking well. You have that beautiful pregnant woman's glow."

"Aww, thank you." I waddle toward the bed. "The usual?" I ask like I'm a pro at this.

"You know it. Pull your top up, and your pants down. You know the drill. Ready?" I position myself on the table, and wait for the gel. "You know it's cold."

"Yeah, I don't mind. Can I ask, I know he's a boy, but if you can see, will you confirm, please?"

"You positive you want to know?" Mom asks.

"It's a boy, Mom. But he's always got his legs crossed, so it would be nice to definitely know for sure."

"Well..." The lady looks at the screen. "No such luck today, Andy. See." She points out the screen. "Can't see a single thing down there. Mind you, look, he's sucking his thumb." As clear as an image on the TV, we can see him lying on his back, sucking his thumb.

"Aw! Wow. Look at that, Mom," I say.

"I'll take some measurements, make sure the growth is how it's supposed to be. Check a couple of things."

"When will he turn?"

"According to the measurements, you're thirty weeks and three days."

"Yeah, that's right."

"The baby could turn any time from now, but usually it's later, around the thirty-six plus weeks."

"Will I feel it?"

"You'll feel movement, but you may have no idea the baby is getting ready to make its entrance into the world. When do you see your doctor? It's Doctor Morgan, isn't it?"

"That's right. I have an appointment with her next week."

"I'll send the report over to her."

"Everything okay?" Mom asks.

"Everything looks perfect. Okay, I'm done. Here's a few tissues to clean the gel off." I clean myself up, and redress. "Here's a keepsake for yourself." She hands me a sonogram of my son. My perfect, beautiful boy. I can't help but laugh, because he's sucking his thumb. I ask her for another copy for Alex. "I'll meet you out in the front.. Mom says tensely.

She exits the room, leaving the door open for Mom and me. Mom's unusually quiet, which drives it into me, that she's certainly concerned about something. "I need to pee," I say to Mom.

"I'll pay and meet you out in the reception room."

I waddle to the bathroom.

The car ride home is strange. We're supposed to go to the store to buy the final things for the nursery, but Mom's so distracted and quiet that I think she's forgotten.

Mom pulls up along the house, not turning the car off. "Here." She reaches for her wallet, takes out fifty dollars and hands it to me. "Can you ask Zar or Alex to come for dinner. I won't be home for a while."

She said 'I won't be home' not 'we.' "I'm not getting out of this car until you tell me what's happening. You're acting weird, Mom. You're distracted and quiet." I look at her offered money, and shake my hand. "I'm not taking it."

Mom's eyes begin to tear. Suddenly, she starts crying, and drops her head into her hands, burying her face so I can't see. "Your father," I hear her whisper through small gasps of air. "He's in the hospital."

A blanket of ice is thrown over me. My skin chills as my heart jumps into the base of my throat. "What happened?"

"He was in an accident."

"Is he…" the words get stuck, I can barely think.

"He's in the hospital."

"Will he be…"

"I have to go, Andy."

"I'm coming with you." I secure my seatbelt.

"Andy, this isn't good for you, or the baby."

Turning to Mom, with my heart pounding in my chest I burst into tears. "I'll worry more if I'm at home by myself."

"I didn't want to tell you, not until I know how he is."

"Let's not waste a moment sitting here, Mom. Can we go?" I continue sobbing but refuse to get out of the car.

Mom takes a deep breath, then looks forward. "Okay," she whispers.

The drive to the hospital is filled with tension and questions. "What happened?" I ask again.

"I don't know exactly. But the hospital contacted me while I was finding a parking spot. They said he'd been admitted via ambulance and to get there as fast as I could."

"Mom, you should've just gone."

"We're here now." By some luck, there's a car reversing out of a spot as we pull in. Mom parks, and we try to rush into the hospital. It's harder for me, but I still manage.

We head to reception, where Mom gives Dad's name, and we're instructed as to the waiting area for the operating rooms.

Mom and I stand for a brief moment in time, staring at each

other. "Operating rooms?" we both say. "Mom, what's happening?" I ask trying to wrap my head around it all.

"I don't know," Mom replies, just as worried as I am.

We find our way to the waiting room and Mom asks for Dad. The man sitting at the desk says a doctor will be out soon to talk to us. "Try not to worry," he says. His eyes fall on my large bump, and he narrows his brows.

Now's not the time to be judgmental, buddy.

Try not to worry?! Are you kidding me?

"Please, is there anything you can tell us?" I forge forward and beg shamelessly.

Mom's gone into a panic, and is frantically pacing back and forth.

"I'm sorry, there's nothing I can report. But the doctor will be out to talk to you."

I rub my hand on my stomach, trying to ease a tightening above my hip bone. "Are you okay?" Mom asks.

"I'll be fine. I just need to know what's happening." My baby kicks me, hard. "Argh," I wince in pain. "Not now, buddy, not now," I whisper to him.

"Are you having contractions?" Mom stares at me.

The man at reception, stands. He walks over to me. "Are you okay? I can get a doctor to come look at you."

"I'm fine." And as if on cue, I get another severe kick and tightening in unison. "Ohhh," I grumble.

"I'm calling a doctor," he says and rushes back over to his desk.

Frustration is quickly overtaking every other emotion. "I just want to know what's happening with my father!" I shout aggressively.

"You have to calm down," the man says as he's on the phone.

"For God's sake!" Another huge kick, and more tightening, but this time, it's more under my stomach. "Ohhh, shit."

"Describe the pain," Mom says.

"Like damn period pain." I want to double over, but with my stomach the size it is, it's impossible. "Across the front, and across my back."

Mom starts rubbing my lower back into a circular motion. "Here?"

"Oh, yeah," I groan with appreciation.

"Andy?" I hear a woman calling. Turning, I see Doctor Morgan walking toward me. "You're not due yet. What's happening?"

"Dad's in there." I point at the door to the operating room. "And no one will tell us what's happening." Another tightening. Gritting my teeth, I let out a long moan. "And I've got pains."

"Describe the pain."

How is she here so quick? She was probably seeing a patient.

I take several deep breaths, trying to fight through the tightening, and the ache. "It comes and goes."

"How long have you been like this?"

"Only since we got here. I don't know, ten minutes or so."

"Okay, let's get you into a room."

"But my Dad."

Doctor Morgan pulls out her phone, and dials a number. "Patient Andy Price. Get her records, and find out what you can about her father. His name is…" She looks to me for his name.

"Robert Price," Mom answers.

"Robert Price. We'll be in delivery room eighteen."

"Delivery room?" I say.

"Get me a wheelchair," Doctor Morgan yells to someone over her shoulder.

"Delivery room?" I say again.

"Is she in labor?" Mom asks.

"I have to examine her, but it looks and sounds like she is."

"But she's only thirty weeks."

"I know," Doctor Morgan replies grimly. The man brings a wheelchair over to us, and Doctor Morgan thanks him. "I need you in the chair, Andy," she instructs with a no-nonsense tone.

Sitting in the chair, the tightness increases again. "Whoa," I moan as I rub the bottom part of my stomach. Doctor Morgan moves fast through the hospital. Whipping through the corridors like she's on a mission. Mom is only steps behind us. "Mom." I reach for her hand.

"It'll be okay."

"Stay with Dad. I'll be okay."

"I'm finding out what's happening with your father. But we need to focus on you," Doctor Morgan says. We reach the maternity suites, and Doctor Morgan is met by Vivian and a male nurse. "Andy, I need to go wash my hands so I can examine you. I need you up on the bed, underwear off."

"Okay." She darts off quite quickly leaving me with Vivian and the male nurse. "Um," I say looking at the male nurse, then Vivian.

Instantly, she recognizes my skepticism. "James is the best, most qualified neonatal nurse in the hospital."

James turns his head and smiles. "Hi there, Andy," he says. His smile and easiness immediately calms me.

"Hi." The pain in my back and my lower stomach is intense. "Holy crap!"

"I need you to strip your lower half," James says. "I can help." He steps forward and begins to squat.

"I'm here for that," Mom says, standing in front of me. She leans down, and I use her shoulders to steady myself while she helps me strip. "You okay?" Mom asks.

All my modesty is out the window. The pain is so intense, that I don't give a damn about who's seeing me naked. "Oh, it hurts," I say as I lean against the bed.

"Okay, let's see what's happening," Doctor Morgan says as she enters the room. "I need you on the bed."

Slowly I climb up between the pain and what feels like my little man kicking.

"You're doing well," James says in a soothing voice as he smiles.

"I'm going to place your legs in the stirrups so I can get better access."

Now that's a sentence I never thought I'd hear. "Okay." Doctor Morgan lifts my left leg into a stirrup, then my right. I'm wide open. And by wide open, I mean *wide* open. Yep, no modesty here. "I'm going to do an internal, to see what's happening. It's uncomfortable, but it has to be done." She slides her hand inside me. Doctor Morgan pushes her hand further in, and I close my eyes trying to not focus on the pain of the stretching. "I'm sorry, but I have to do this."

"It's okay." But it's awkward and uncomfortable.

"Okay," she says once she takes her hand out. She walks over to the trash and takes her latex gloves off. "You're dilated. You're in early labor."

"What does this mean?" I ask. James lowers my legs from the stirrups, and I don't even care that he's got an unobstructed view of my vagina. So be it.

"What's going to happen?" Mom asks worried.

"You're at one centimeter. Which, thankfully means we can stop the labor from progressing any further. It's too early to give birth. You'll have to stay here for at least three days so we can monitor you both. But, for now, I'm going to give you something called terbutaline, which should stop the labor. James?" She turns to James. "Point two-five milligrams and again in half an hour." He nods in acknowledgement before disappearing out of the room.

"What does that do? What's going to happen?" Mom asks.

"There's a risk in premature labor. Coupled with Andy's age, we want to avoid this as much as we can. James is going to administer the medication, and we'll have her on heart monitors, and checking the baby for the next three days. In case the medication doesn't stop the labor, we'll also be giving Andy a steroid injection."

"Steroids?" I ask.

"Yes, it's to help the baby with his lungs. Being born at thirty weeks means the lungs aren't as developed as we'd want them to be. As a precautionary measure, we'll be giving you a steroid injection. We'd rather be safe, and give you both the best possible chance." Doctor Morgan is clear, and to the point. "What we want is to keep this baby in there for as long as possible. The longer the baby stays, the better it'll be for both of you." She turns to Vivian, and starts instructing her on what she has to do. "Every day matters."

Another contraction hits hard. The pain travelling from the top of my head, to the tips of my toes. "I can't do this," I say through the intense, excruciating pain.

"Yes, you can," Mom says grabbing onto my hand as I fight through the agony.

The contraction subsides, and not even a moment later, James is in the room. "Okay. Now, I need to give you this, but I have to find a vein. Let me look at your arms." I hold out my left arm, and James takes it, pressing around my elbow. "Let me look at the other one." He walks around to the other side of the bed, taking my arm, and pressing. "Yeah, this one's better. Make a fist, then relax. Do it a few times." As I do this, he gets the needle ready, then wipes at my arm. "Okay, little sting." He pushes the needle in. "You okay?" he asks.

"Yeah, I am." Slowly he injects the stuff into my arm. When he finishes, he takes the needle out, takes his gloves off and leaves the room. "Momma," I say looking to Mom. I'm worried. I'm worried for Dad, for me, and for my son. "I can't have him yet."

"This should stop labor," Mom says.

"Okay, we're going to put these on you. But first, I'd like you to change into a hospital gown," Vivian says as she drags a monitor behind her.

"What is it?"

"We need to monitor your heart, and the baby's too. Just to make sure you're both okay." Vivian is usually so bubbly, but she can easily switch into serious. I like this about her.

"Andy, Laura, I've just received news on Robert," Doctor Morgan says.

I eagerly listen as Vivian places a clamp onto my finger, then a thick black belt around my waist.

"Is he okay? What's happening?" My anxiety spikes again. This is insane.

"Where is he?" Mom asks, letting go of my hand and stepping forward.

"He's in surgery. There was a witness who said Robert got out of his car, and was rounding the vehicle. Another car plowed into his car, not even a foot away from him. I've spoken with the surgeons, and they said he was thrown quite a way because of the speed the other car was doing. He broke a rib, which punctured his lung. They had to do a chest drain."

"Oh shit," Mom says, clutching at her chest. Her face pales, drained of all the blood.

"A chest drain sounds horrible, but it's not too bad."

"Thank God," I whisper.

"Why's he in surgery then?"

"He also broke both his legs, so they're operating on them."

"I thought you were going to say something much worse," I say. I look to Doctor Morgan; her wrinkled forehead tells me there *is* more. "What else?"

"Robert's in an induced coma because he also has swelling on the brain."

Mom stumbles back, reaching for something, anything to stabilize her. She collapses on the bed. "When can I see him?" she asks in an almost non-existent voice.

"He's not out of surgery yet. When he is, I've asked them to let me know." Doctor Morgan turns to me. "No contractions."

My mind had been racing as I've been taking in all the information Doctor Morgan is giving us about Dad, I didn't even notice that the contractions have stopped. "Oh." I look down at my stomach, not sure what I'm expecting to see.

Doctor Morgan walks over to the machine monitoring me. She reads it, and nods her head. "I still want another point two-five," she instructs James.

He nods, smiles, and leaves the room.

"Are you hungry, or thirsty?" Vivian asks. I shake my head. "Would you like something?" she asks Mom.

Mom's barely got any color back in her face. Her eyes are watering, and she's staring at the floor. "Mom." She hardly moves. Her eyes are fixed on a spot. Other than her chest rapidly moving up and down, she's not moving. Not even fluttering her eyelids. "Mom," I say again, louder.

She rapidly blinks before turning her head to look at me. "I'm..." And she bursts into tears. She buries her face into her hands, covering herself so I don't see the tears.

"Mom, Dad will be okay." I reach forward, cradle Mom in my arms, and try to move her to lay down on the bed with me. Holding her in my arms, I let Mom cry.

Her sobs are tearing my heart apart.

"He's the love of my life, he can't die."

"He's not going to."

"I can't even think what'll happen if..." She can't bring herself to say the word, and neither can I.

"He'll be okay, Mom." I hug her tighter. But my tummy is too big, and I have a monitor strapped to it too.

"I've never known love like the one I have with your father."

The more she sobs, the more my soul grieves for a possibility I hope doesn't occur. "Mom, Dad's strong. He's a fighter, you know this."

"I can't lose him." There's not a lot I can say with words. Nothing will ease her fear. Instead, I remain quiet, and hold her as tight as I can.

I hold her because I need her to know, we're in this together. All of us. Mom, Dad, me, and my son.

"Thank you," she whispers.

CHAPTER
26

MOM'S ASLEEP IN the chair in the room. I can't find a comfortable position at all. Being thirty weeks pregnant means I definitely can't sleep on my stomach. And I need a pillow between my legs when I lay on my side. And lying on my back puts a lot of pressure on my lower back. So basically, I get an hour or so of light sleep, before I wake and need to pee, or move.

Vivian walks in to check the monitor and sees me sitting up in bed, playing a game on my phone.

"You okay?" she asks. "Do you need anything?"

"Just to know how Dad is."

"There's been no word other than what Doctor Morgan told you. He came out of surgery, and he's in an induced coma. They've got to wait for the swelling to go down before they know any more."

"I feel so helpless being stuck in here."

"There isn't anything you could do for your dad even if you weren't stuck in here."

"I know."

"And you have to take it easy."

"I know," I agree again. "But I feel useless."

"Why's that?" Vivian sits on the side of the bed and reaches for my hand. She places two fingers on my wrist to check my pulse.

"I'm thinking that it's because of me Dad's in this position."

"Now, that's crazy. Were you driving the car that hit him?"

"Well, no. But…" I take a deep breath and lower my eyes. "So many thoughts are going around in my head. If I wasn't pregnant, then maybe Dad wouldn't have been where he was, maybe the accident wouldn't have happened."

"You think because you're pregnant, that caused your father to be involved in the accident?"

I lift my head, and nod. "A big part of me feels guilty."

"You weren't driving the car though."

She drops my hand once she has my pulse. I rake my hands through my hair, feeling guilty, and confused. But mostly emotional. "I feel responsible."

"You're overwhelmed, and that's okay. You're also thirty weeks pregnant, so you're probably super hormonal and scared of what's going to happen. But you are in no way at all responsible for what happened with your dad. You have no control over anyone but yourself."

"I know," I sigh. "It's stupid that I'm feeling like this. But I have so many emotions going around in my head. I'm a damn mess."

"A lot has happened."

"I read so many stories online of people saying pregnancy is wonderful and the best time of a woman's life."

Vivian lightly chuckles. "Pregnancy is different for everyone. Some people can breeze through it, some people have horrible times. But one thing is for sure, these emotions send us all crazy, at least once through the pregnancy. The real test of these emotions is after you have the baby."

"I've been reading up on post-partum depression."

"Yeah, it's a real thing. I suffered with it. Badly. I don't know if you remember me telling you, but I had complications with Jayden."

"I do," I respond. "You told me when I first met you."

"Yeah, I didn't cope well when I had him. I'd go to the mall with him, and think if I jumped off the top level that everything would be okay."

"Oh my God!" My mouth falls open, and I quickly cover it in shock.

"It got really bad. I drove him to the fire department, and sat in the car trying to get the courage to take him in and leave him. I was desperate. And my mind was a mess. I wasn't sleeping, and Jayden would cry. I thought of hurting myself so many times." She looks away from me as a tear rolls down her cheek.

A huge lump sits in my throat. I don't know what to say to her. There are no words I can say to ease her, none at all. Instead, I reach for her hand, and give her a gentle squeeze.

"My days were filled with self-hatred. And resentment toward Jayden. It was bad."

"How did you get through it?"

"Doctor Morgan." She smiles, though it's not a smile of genuine happiness, more like of real admiration for Doctor Morgan. "She saved my life, and Jayden's. She recognized the signs of post-partum depression and not only got me help, but prescribed antidepressants. It made a world of difference."

"Are you still on antidepressants?" I ask.

"No, I only needed them for about ten months."

"I hope I won't need them."

Vivian stands and smiles. "I've learned a few things while I've been working for Doctor Morgan. And the biggest thing is this. If you need them, take them. The only people who'll judge you for taking them are people who don't matter. Like I say to anyone who's not coping for any reason, you have to do what's right for you."

"I think I have to stop being so hard on myself. I feel like I'm letting everyone down."

"The people who love you will understand. And that's all that matters."

"Thank you, Vivian. I really appreciate it."

"I'm going home soon, but I'll be back tomorrow."

"Okay. I'll try and get some sleep."

"Good idea. Do you need anything before I leave?"

"I'm fine."

Vivian walks out of the room, and I turn to look at Mom. I start giggling at her. She's got her head tilted to the side, with drool coming out of her mouth. She moves her lower half, and when she does, she lets out a huge, long fart.

I laugh a bit harder.

Mom's snoring, drooling and farting.

And I know just how lucky I am. Because I've captured a moment of Mom's pure vulnerability.

CHAPTER
27

T HE BRIGHTNESS MAKES my eyes open and drags me out of my sleep. Mom's not in the chair she fell asleep in, and the room is unusually quiet.

Trying to sit up in bed, I'm hit with the urge to pee. And of course, my stomach grumbles at that very moment too.

"Settle down, I'll get you some food." I rub my tummy, trying to calm my little man down.

Once finished in the bathroom, I open the door to find Mom standing just inside the room. "Oh, there you are," she says and comes toward me. "I bought you bananas and ketchup." She holds out a brown paper bag toward me.

"Life saver." I reach and get the paper bag. Opening it, I see four bananas and a bottle of ketchup. "Yum."

"Good morning, Andy. How did you sleep?" James asks.

"I only slept for a bit."

"I need to take your vitals." I settle on the bed, peel the banana, and open the ketchup, squirting some on the banana.

"Interesting choice of food." He jerks his chin indicating the banana and ketchup.

"It's pretty much the only thing I want to eat. And my best friend's mom's hot apple cider. Speaking of which, I better message Zar and Alex." With everything that's happened, I've completely forgotten to let them know what's happening. "Any news on Dad?" I ask both Mom and James.

Mom smiles, and lets out a deep sigh. She looks happy. "He's in recovery and is doing really well. The doctor I spoke with said they've already seen signs of the swelling reducing. They're hoping to wake him within a day or two."

"The body is an amazing thing. It has the ability to heal itself when it's at its worst. It never stops shocking me," James says as he checks my vitals.

I stare at him just thinking about what he's said. "He's right," Mom says.

"Yeah, he is."

"I'm always right," James adds with sass. "Just ask Doctor Morgan."

"What are you asking me?"

James's face reddens, and he lowers his eyes. "I wasn't saying anything."

"Oh, yes he was," I say playfully. "He was saying how he's always right and we should ask you."

Doctor Morgan slowly turns her head, and gives him a look I can only describe as something between, *we'll talk about this later* and *you're going to suffer*. You can tell though, it's just friendly banter between them.

"I think I'll just leave now. Oh look, another patient needs me." He hands Doctor Morgan a file with my notes and readings.

Doctor Morgan takes the file, and watches as he leaves. The moment he's out of the door, she smiles. "I love making him suffer." She reads over the notes. "The contractions have stopped which is good. But I'm going to do an internal to make sure dilation has stopped." She closes the door, and draws the curtain around the bed. "I need you to remove your panties." I do what she asks, then get up on the bed. "Make a fist with both your hands, and place them under your bottom." I do. "I'm just putting gloves on. Can you spread as far as you can?" It's not really a request, more like a demand. "Okay, you ready?"

"Yeah." Not really. It's not exactly a pleasant feeling.

"Okay, good."

The best thing is she's quick. Thankfully. "Am I okay? Is everything okay with my baby?" I stand and put my panties back on.

"Yes, to both questions. But it's still really important you stay here for at least a few more days. Any kind of exertion could result in a resumption of early labor. We'll keep monitoring you here, and if it's okay after a few days, you'll be able to go home."

"Do you want me on bed rest then?"

"God, no. Contrary to what most people think, bed rest isn't the ideal thing. I just need you to take it easy. Don't do anything too exhausting."

"Ah, okay. Can I still work?"

"You can, but you have to take it easy. It's more about the stress of things. Like with your father. Your pregnancy was progressing beautifully until you heard what happened. I need the stress to calm down. Speaking of which, good news with Robert too. I just came from his room, and the doctors are really happy with his progress."

"I know," Mom says, a smile spreading across her tired, weary face. "I'm looking forward to this entire experience being over and done with."

"It'll be okay, Mom," I reassure her.

"I know it will be. One day at a time."

"Okay, I'll leave you two now, and I'll see you later tonight." Doctor Morgan pointedly looks to me.

"Thank you," I say to her retreating back.

Mom lets out a huge breath, then sits on the side of the bed. "I'm sorry," she says to me.

"What for?"

"I feel like yesterday, I wasn't there for you."

"Mom, no. These last twelve hours have been…" I search for the right word. And I say the only one that makes sense of it all, "A clusterfuck."

"Andy!" Mom scolds me. "You know I don't like such vulgar language." She nods her head, "But you're right, it has been a clusterfuck."

"Mom!" It's my turn to be shocked.

"They have. But when I saw your father, I just got a good feeling. I know this is going to be hard, but we'll get through it. We're strong, and as long as we stick together, we'll be okay."

"I know we will be."

"Just remember, Andy. These next few months are going to be incredibly stressful, as long as we keep the communication open, and realize we're going to get irritated with each other at some point, but we're a family. We're there for each other."

"I know, Mom." I give her a hug. "I need to call Alex and Zar to let them know what's happening with me, and Dad."

"I think you better do that. Zar is such a great friend to you. And Alex is a good kid."

"Can I tell you something, Mom?"

"What?"

"I'm kinda scared that Alex and I won't last."

Mom's quiet for a little bit. I can tell she's thinking. "It's likely you won't. You're both still so young, and you're both bound to change as you grow older. But nothing's carved in stone. You may last, after all."

"I know, but I don't know."

Mom chuckles. "That was a clear response."

I laugh out loud too. "I mean, what happens if we don't?"

"Then you work through it. You try to stay on good terms, for your child's sake."

"What if he doesn't want anything to do with him?" I place my free hand on my stomach.

"You can't control what Alex does or says. All you can do is be the best mom possible to my grandbaby. And, I'll be the best nanny possible to my grandbaby. And let me tell you, Dad is super excited too. He can't wait to teach him how to throw a ball, and how to play Monopoly."

"Monopoly?" I question.

"Your Dad's just so excited. Everyone he meets, he tells them he's gonna be a granddaddy."

This brings the biggest smile to my face, because it makes me so happy that my parents have got my back. "I think I want Zar to be this little man's godmother."

"I think that's a smart idea." Mom leans over, and gives me a kiss. "I'm going to go get a coffee, and check in on your father. That should give you enough time to call Zar and Alex. Do you want anything from the cafeteria?"

"Nah, I should be okay. I have my bananas, and ketchup. If Zar comes, I'll ask her for some apple cider."

"I shouldn't be too long. If you need me, call me. I have my phone on." Mom stands and walks out of the room.

Leaning over, I get my phone from the side table next to the bed. I look at my phone and see so many unanswered messages and calls from him. Dialing Alex's number, I wait for no more than two rings before he picks up. "Andy, are you okay? I didn't hear from you yesterday. Is everything alright? The baby? You?" The barrage of questions makes my heart beat quickly with guilt.

"I'm so sorry, Alex. I meant to call you yesterday, but I couldn't."

"I came to your house to see you, but no one was home."

"Dad was in an accident."

"Shit," he says. "What happened? Is he okay?"

"He's in an induced coma. But..."

He cuts me off the moment I say *but*. "But what? Are you okay? The baby?"

"I'm in the hospital too."

"What the hell? Why?"

"I went into early labor."

"What?" he screeches. "I'm on my way."

"I'm okay, Alex."

"I don't care, I'm on my way. I have to be there with you. Does Zar know?"

"No, not yet."

"I'll pick her up on the way over. Tell her I'm on my way."

"It's not that bad."

"Bullshit, Andy. If you went into labor, we both need to be there."

"Alex," I try to stop him.

"Just call her." He hangs up on me before I get a chance to respond. He's worried, and I can understand that. If the roles were reversed, I would've wanted to know when it all happened so I could be there, supporting Alex.

I stare at my phone for a moment before I dial Zar's number. "Where have you been?" she snaps.

"I'm sorry." I close my eyes and rub my hand over my temple. "Dad was in an accident, and..."

"Is he okay? Are you okay? Where are you? I'm coming now."

"I thought you'd say that. Alex is on his way to your house to pick you up."

"Okay, we'll be there soon." She doesn't even say goodbye, she hangs up and I'm left sitting on the bed with a dead phone. Great.

Sitting in the room, my bladder decides to join the party again, needing me to get up and go pee.

As I close the door, I hear James calling me. "Andy, are you in the bathroom?"

"Yeah, I shouldn't be too long." I finish in the bathroom, and when I open the door, James is ready by the bed to check my vitals. "Again? You only did it a little while ago."

"Yep. Again."

I sit on the bed, and give him my right arm so he can check my blood pressure with that stupid, restrictive cuff they put on. "The whole peeing thing is driving me nuts."

"Wanna know what's funny?"

"What?"

"When you have the baby, you'll be able to go for hours without peeing because there's going to be so much room in there."

"Huh. I never thought of that."

"No baby pushing up against your bladder."

"Can I ask a question?"

He holds a finger up while he listens to my heart. "Yeah, what?" He lowers the stethoscope from his ears.

"Do you see a lot of girls my age in this condition?" I gesture to my stomach.

"That's a hard one, Andy. I see women of all ages, sizes, and backgrounds who are pregnant."

"So there are a lot of girls like me then?"

He chuckles. "I used to live in a different state, and the hospital I worked in had a high rate of teenage pregnancies. It's not so high here, but mind you, it's not low either."

"I wonder why it was higher there than here?" I ask, curious.

"Different place." He shrugs his shoulders. But I have a feeling there's more to it than he wants to talk about. "Do you know there's a support group the hospital runs here for younger mothers?"

"No, I didn't." This piques my interest. Maybe I can go to it and try to, I don't know, bond with others who are like me. "What day or night is on? And time?"

"I'll get some…"

"Oh my God! What is going on?" Zar shrieks when she sees me.

"I'll get some information for you." James smiles, and steps away, quietly leaving the room which has quickly become quite crowded.

"Are you okay? What's happening?" Alex asks. His cheeks are red, and his shoulders are high with tension.

"Sit." I offer the only chair to Zar, and half the bed to Alex. Both sit, and both look at me, eager to learn why I'm in here again. "Dad was in a car accident."

"Oh shit," Alex says.

"What?" Zar asks. "Is he okay?"

"Apparently, he got out of the car, and someone hit his while he was walking around it. He's in an induced coma because he has swelling on the brain. He broke a rib that punctured his lung, and both his legs are broken. He's stable though."

"And what about you? Why are you here? Vomiting again?" Zar asks.

"Afraid not. I went into labor when Mom told me about Dad."

"What the hell?" Alex stands and steps forward. Both his hands raised up, as if he's not really sure if he should touch me or not. "The baby?" He looks around the room, then to my stomach.

"It was pure luck that Doctor Morgan was here. She's stopped the labor, because it's too early for me to have him."

"What? Huh? I don't get it," Zar says.

"The stress of what happened to Dad made my body react by going into early labor. But this little guy isn't ready yet. Doctor Morgan stopped the labor from progressing, which is good. And she gave me a steroid injection to help with his lungs, in case they couldn't stop labor."

"What happens now?" Alex asks.

"I have to take it easy. Try to minimize stress. But I should be able to go home in a day or two."

"But you're okay?" Alex asks.

"Yeah, and so is our little man."

"And what's happening with your dad?" Zar questions.

"He's in this hospital too. Mom's gone to get a coffee, and see Dad. She'll be back later."

"Oh, I forgot. Here." Zar leans over and takes an insulated drinking flask out of her bag. "Mom sent warm apple cider."

"Yum." My body instantly craves it. "It's like you have a connection to this baby. The moment you said *warm apple cider*, my body started begging for it. Speaking of which, gimme." I hold out my hands, wiggling my fingers at Zar.

"Hey, kids," Mom says as she walks in.

"Hey, Mrs. Price," both Zar and Alex say almost simultaneously.

Mom's carrying a coffee cup from the cafeteria. She looks much chirpier than she did when she left. "Did you find out anything about Dad?"

"The swelling is coming down fast. They're going to try to wake him tonight. The doctors feel really confident with how he's doing."

"Wow, thank God," I say.

"Here you go," Zar moves so Mom can sit.

"No, no. I'm just dropping off my bag, then I'm going back to Robert. How long will you two be here, so I can give you some time?"

"Maybe we can have lunch here?" Alex asks.

"I'm not sure if I can go. I'll ask James." I press the buzzer and wait for James.

"Who's James?" Zar asks.

"He's a neonatal nurse. He's really good. Oh, you should meet Vivian. She's so nice."

"Who's Vivian?" Zar asks again.

"She works for Doctor Morgan. She's really so nice. Everyone has been fantastic."

"You okay, Andy?" James stands just inside the door.

"Can I go to the cafeteria or do I have to stay here?"

"Let me check with Doctor Morgan, and I'll let you know." James goes to leave, but turns back. "Everything else okay?"

"Yeah, I'm hoping I can go for a walk down to the cafeteria, that's all."

"Let me check."

"He's cute," Zar says when he leaves the room.

"And what about Hunter?" I ask.

A smile graces Zar's pretty face. She lowers her head so I can't see the smirk. "What about Hunter?"

"Come on, spill the beans."

"I really don't want to hear this," Alex says. "He's one of my best friends."

"Yeah, well, too bad." Zar points a finger at Alex. "He's good. Like really good. He's such a good kisser."

"Oh man," Alex whines. "Really? Do I have to hear this stuff?"

"And Mom likes him." Zar gives Alex a look to say, *shut up and suck it up.* "And did I tell you he's a good kisser?"

"Ugh," Alex mumbles.

"Hey, if you don't like it, then go for a walk or something. Me and my girl have things to catch up on."

Alex rolls his eyes and looks away.

"It's going well then?" I ask.

"So good. It took Hayden a bit to adjust to him. First night

Hunter came over for dinner, Hayden told him he and my brother will hurt him if he hurts me."

"Oh no."

"Yeah, but Momma told him if he does to me what Alex and you did, she'll castrate him."

"Hey," Alex protests.

I burst into laughter. "What did Hunter say?"

"He looked at Momma, and with a straight face told her, 'No, ma'am, my penis isn't going anywhere near your daughter's vagina.'"

"He did not?" I say.

"Yep. Made it even more awkward. Momma's face changed about a thousand different expressions. Hunter got scared."

Alex laughs but says nothing.

"No way."

"It was so bad. He tried to recover from that. But once the words penis and vagina are said out loud, there's no turning back."

Talk about embarrassing.

"I talked to Doctor Morgan, and she said you can go to the cafeteria," James pops his head in to say.

"Awesome. Thank you." I grab my phone and send Mom a text telling her we're heading down to the cafeteria. "Wait, can you hand me Mom's bag? I'll put it in the drawer so no one takes it." Zar passes Mom's bag, and I slide it into the bottom drawer. "I'm actually hungry."

"I'm starving," Alex says.

"Yeah, me too."

"Wow," I say as we move along the corridor to the elevator. "Feel this." I grab Alex's hand, and place it on the side of my stomach. "Can you feel that?" He nods his head. "He's kicking."

"Wow. That's amazing." He keeps his hand there for another few seconds.

The elevator arrives, and the three of us get in. "Check this out." I lift my t-shirt on the side, and Zar and Alex watch as a something protrudes, and moves. "I think he's stretching."

"It's like an alien," Zar blurts. "It's weirdly fascinating to watch. So bizarre though."

I lower my t-shirt when we arrive on the cafeteria floor. We walk in, and find seats. It's not really busy, but there are a few people in here. I get looks from some people, and I have to push past it and ignore them.

"What do you want? I'll get it," Alex offers.

"Actually. I want some fries." Yes, fries. Yum. "A lot of them. Two servings, and ketchup. Oh, I think I want mustard too."

"Two servings of fries, ketchup and mustard. Anything else?"

"Oh yeah. A chocolate milk too."

"What happened to the god-awful banana and ketchup?" Zar asks.

"I still want that, but I want fries and chocolate milk. I don't know." I throw my arms up in defeat. I have no idea why this little man is changing his mind.

"Thank God, cause for a while there I thought you were going to start to look like a banana with the amount you were eating," Zar says.

Alex shakes his head. "Do you want anything, Zar?" he offers.

"Yeah, I'll have a chicken sandwich."

"Do you want a soda or anything?"

"Just a water, please."

"Okay, I'll be back." Alex leaves and I watch as he walks away.

"You know, I'm kinda amazed he's stuck around."

"Why? He loves you."

"I know, but I'm fat and pregnant at fifteen. What can he

possibly love about this?" I wave my hand over my stomach and body. "Why is he sticking around?" The tears well in my eyes, and I'm on the verge of crying.

"Wow. You've gone from normal to an emotional mess in a matter of seconds."

"It's the hormones, I swear. My brain is acting like a flea, hopping around all over the place."

"Hey, guess what I found out about Blair?" Zar leans over to tell me. "She's doing what you and Alex have been. You know, find the sausage. Hide the pickle. Nailing in the screw driver. Banging. Putting his P in her V." I stare at her in disbelief. "Humping. Hooking up."

"I swear to God, Zar. You have to stop." I'm laughing so hard I'm sure I'm going to pee any moment.

"But I have more."

"Find the sausage?"

"Yeah. I should keep listing them."

"No! I'm getting a very clear picture as to what she and her boyfriend are doing."

"She's telling everyone he took her V card."

"Honestly, I really don't want to know." I shudder at the mental picture of Blair having sex. "Yuck." A shiver runs up my spine.

"Horizontal mambo," Zar says.

"Enough!"

"Mountain biking," Zar mumbles.

"Mountain biking?" I ask. Zar stares at me for a second as I figure it out. "You have way too much time on your hands to come up with all these terms for having sex."

"I googled them. Some I already knew, but some just made me laugh."

I tilt my head to the side. "Way too much time."

Alex returns with a tray filled with food. He places the fries in front of me, and I dunk them between the ketchup and the mustard. I can't believe how much I'm loving them. I inhale them, regardless of the fact that they're hot.

"Slow down, asbestos mouth," Zar says. "You'll give yourself indigestion."

"Asbestos mouth?"

"How can you eat them so fast? I'd burn my mouth if I was eating like that."

"I'm hungry," I snap.

"Really? No one's gonna steal them from you. You can slow down."

"Tell *him* to slow down." I point to my stomach.

Zar clicks her tongue against the roof of her mouth, before eye rolling her eyes and smirking. "Sure, blame the baby," she says playfully.

"The one thing I've learned is to never say anything about a female eating," Alex says while watching Zar and me jokingly spar.

"Oh, you think because I'm eating these fries that I eat too much?" I give Zar a sly wink.

"What? No. I mean I um… Well, I mean… Shit, why did I say anything?" Alex lowers his head, refusing to make eye contact with either Zar or myself.

"Now we're fat, are we?" Zar plays along.

"No! Oh my God, no, I mean…"

"Are you calling your pregnant girlfriend *fat*?" I keep eating my fires, enjoying every single one I'm shoveling into my mouth.

"You know what? I'm going to sit here and say nothing."

Zar and I look at each other. Poor Alex, we've given him enough grief. Both Zar and I burst into laughter. Alex looks up and sees us laughing. "Right then, that's it." He stands in an over-dramatic way, straightens his shoulders, and lifts his chin.

"If you can't respect me, then I'm going to buy a muffin." He takes a few steps away then turns back smiling. "Do either of you want one?"

"I'm good," I say.

"Yep. Blueberry. Get me the biggest one, need it for my hips." Zar slaps her side, emphasizing her robust body.

Alex looks up to the ceiling, places his hands together and says, "Please Lord, give me strength when I'm around those two."

This of course, makes us laugh.

CHAPTER
28

"WHAT TIME'S THE appointment?" Dad asks Mom as she fusses over him, bringing him his breakfast.

"We have to be out of the house by ten." She sits opposite me, and brings her coffee mug to her mouth.

"It's good having you home, Dad."

"I couldn't stand another day in there. I just feel so…" He looks down at his legs, both in casts. "Useless," he sighs.

Dad's been home for a little over two weeks and Mom and I are trying to keep his spirits up. "Don't feel like that," I say. "It was an accident. A terrible, inconvenient accident. That's all it was."

"I've gone from providing and being there for the most important people in my world, to this." He gestures at the wheelchair he's in. Dad lowers his chin, frustrated at his inability to do anything; Mom and I have to do everything for him. Mom even helps him bathe.

I peel another banana, trying to think of what I can say and do to help him. "Dad, we're a family. We stick together. I'm pretty sure you said those same words to me when I told you about Junior." I rub my expanding stomach.

"That's different. You and your mother have to rely on me. I'm the man of the house."

"Pffft," Mom snorts.

"What?"

"Since when have we been conventional? And to top it off, what's with all this 'man of the house' crap?"

"It's just that I…"

"No!" Mom snaps. "No, Robert. You were allowed to feel like shit while you were in the hospital. You were allowed to feel like shit until they told you that you're going to make a full recovery. But now…" She waves her finger at him. "Now, you get the best opportunity ever to make a recovery with your wife, daughter and soon-to-be grandson by your side. You have to stop feeling sorry for yourself, and look at what you have around you and be thankful."

"I'm sorry," Dad mumbles.

"No need to be sorry, Dad. Just think, in only five weeks, you're going to meet this guy too."

"I hope I'm out of the casts."

"And even if you're not, you're still going to hold him," I say with a smile.

"Just so we're on the same page, I'm going to re-confirm, I'm not going into the delivery room with you. I don't think I can handle seeing your… you know."

"Vagina?" Mom says.

"Yeah, not gonna happen. I already told you both, I can't be there."

"Dad, if it makes you feel any better, I don't want you there either. But I have no idea why you're so hung up about seeing me give birth." I shrug, questioning.

"I don't feel comfortable. I'll be there, waiting, but as your father, I don't need to see any of that. And before you say it, it has nothing to do with your age. It has to do with me, and my respect for you. But the biggest thing is, like I've said before, the fact I can't handle seeing you in pain."

"What if I want you to be there though?"

Dad looks at me with a half-turned up smirk. "If you wanted me there, then I'd overcome what's going on up here." He taps his temple. "And I'd be there. But that's only if you really insisted."

"Ugh, this conversation is getting old. You're not going in. Blah, blah, blah, blah." Mom makes a mouth with her right hand, opening and closing the mouth when she says 'blah, blah, blah, blah.' "Here's the thing, Andy. We're preparing for you to have a natural birth, but anything can happen."

"I know, but I really want to try going natural. I've been reading about recovery, and women recover quicker when they have a vaginal birth."

"Yep, this is true. But you have to consider that anything can happen."

"Doctor Morgan said she's happy with how my pregnancy is going. As long as I don't get too stressed, I should be able to go to forty weeks."

"Sweetheart, I know this is what you want. But…"

"No! He can't come out like he tried before. I'm thirty-five weeks and even though the chances are much better of survival, it gets greater as the days go on, so he has to *stay* in here," I say, beginning to get angry.

"Andy, you have to calm down," Dad says.

I catch myself … "Oh my God," I whisper, looking down at the banana peel on the table. "I'm… um… I'm going for a shower. I'm sorry." I leave before Mom or Dad can say anything. I feel like such a fool. They need me to be strong, what with Dad's accident and everything. The last thing they want is for me becoming an emotional nutcase who cries every three-point-six seconds.

Ugh.

What the hell is wrong with me? Why am I acting like such a damned lunatic?

I take myself to the bathroom, and sit on the edge of the bath staring down at the tiles. "What an idiot," I say to myself. "What is wrong with you? You'd think you'd get a hold on these damn emotions by now."

I shake my head at myself. Frustrated and angry.

"Get yourself together." My little boy kicks, as if he's agreeing with me. "I know, I know," I say to him as I rub the side of my stomach where he's kicking.

He's right, I have to pull myself together. I have to push past whatever the hell is going on up in my head, and just focus on what's important, which is me *not* being an emotional mess.

"So, Alex and I have no idea what we're going to call you."

Stripping my clothes off, I turn the water on and wait for it to come up to temperature before stepping in, and letting the water run down my back. I don't want to wet my hair, because I want to straighten it.

"I'd like to call you Robert Junior, but Alex isn't fond of that. And your Daddy wants to call you Alex Junior, which I'm not fond of. You know, we argued over whose last name you should have. It's going to be mine, or hyphenated."

He kicks, and this makes me smile. "Oh, so you want it hyphenated, do you?" And right on cue, he kicks again.

"Well then, Price-Wulff it is. Or maybe Wulff-Price? I don't know, but what about your first name?"

There's a knock on the door, then seconds pass and Mom says through the door, "Andy, we have to leave soon. I think it's best if you come with us."

"I'm tired, Mom. Can I stay home?"

"I'm opening the door." She doesn't give me a chance to dispute it, before she swings the door open, steps forward and leans against the jamb.

"Are you right there?" I ask, sarcastically.

"I've seen it all before." She flicks her hand dismissively at me. "And besides, who do you think is going to be in the delivery room with you? Who cares if I see you naked."

"Still…" I grumble under my breath. "I don't want to come to Dad's appointment. Can't I stay here?"

"Ordinarily I'd say yes. But with the scare we had when labor started five weeks ago, I don't feel comfortable with you staying here on your own. If something like that happens again, I need to be here, so I can get you to the hospital."

I hate it when Mom makes logical sense. "You have a point."

"Can you hurry up please?"

"Okay. Do I have time to straighten my hair?"

Mom looks at her watch, then back up to me. "Do you think you can be ready in twenty minutes?"

"Um, yeah, I think I can."

"Then yes, you have time to straighten your hair. But you don't really need to. Just throw it up in a messy bun."

"It's always in a messy top-knot, Mom. I want to feel a bit better about myself."

"You'd better hurry up." Mom steps back, and closes the door.

"I hate it when you do that," I groan. Finishing my shower in record time, I quickly get changed, and go into my room. I turn the hair straightener on, and go into the linen cupboard to get a towel so I can lay it on my desk to keep the straightening iron from burning the desk.

"Are you ready yet?" Mom asks as I'm straightening my hair.

"You told me I had twenty minutes." I look at the alarm clock sitting beside my bed. "I still have three minutes left."

Mum groans, and rolls her eyes. "Hurry up. We have to go." Mom turns to leave. I can hear her stomping down the hallway. Her quickened footsteps and huffing, tells me I'd better be quick because she's in a rush.

"One more minute." I quickly finish straightening my hair, before looking at the time again. "I'm done," I yell as I grab my phone and head out to the family room.

The front door is open, and Mom's pushing Dad outside to the car. It takes a few moments for Dad to get into the car, seeing as how his legs are in casts. I watch them and feel helpless. I can't do anything. All I can do is stand out of their way.

My own stomach moves as my little man stretches inside of me, taking my thoughts away from how incompetent I feel. "You'll be here soon," I say as I rub my stomach. He kicks.

"What are you smiling at?" Dad asks.

"He's moving."

"I've always wondered what that would feel like."

Mom takes the wheelchair around to the trunk, then slides it in. "Lucky we have such a large car."

I get in the front, with Dad kind of stretched out on the back seat. Unlocking my phone, I send Alex a message. *On the way with my parents to Dad appointment. Our son is going crazy.*

The three little dots on the screen tell me he's replying. *Is he kicking?*

> *So much! I'm getting more and more excited to meet him.*
>
> **Me too. We need to pick a name. I still like Alex.**
>
> *Nope.*
>
> **What about Emil?**
>
> *If we're not naming him Robert, then we're not naming him Emil.*
>
> **We have to pick a name. We can't not name him.**
>
> *What if you pick ten names, and I'll pick ten names and we'll compromise. We have to see what goes with Price-Wulff.*

We're hyphenating? I'd much rather Wulff, but I'll take the hyphenation.

You pick ten, and I'll pick ten, and we'll narrow them down. It's the only way I can see us picking a name.

I completely ignore what he's said about my son taking only his surname. I don't agree with it. We're in the twenty-first century, not the nineteenth.

Let's go to iHop tonight. Just you and me.

A small smile creeps onto my face. Alex makes me happy. "Hey, Mom. Can I go out tonight with Alex?"

"Where to?" Mom asks, concerned. "The only reason I'm asking is because, you can go into labor at any moment."

"I still have five more weeks."

"Doctor Morgan had to stop pre-term labor, Andy," Dad says.

My shoulders sink. I know, but I just want to get out for a bit, I'm going stir crazy at home all the time. "It's just to iHop. We won't be too long. And I promise, if anything happens, I'll call right away."

I'm asking my parents. I'll let you know when they tell me.

Okay. I've gotta go, class. Either way, I'll see you tonight. I'll come by after dinner if you can't.

Okay. Love you.

Love you too.

"Dad and I will discuss it, and let you know. Let's just focus on Dad's appointment for now."

"That's fair," I say. But secretly I'm disappointed they haven't said yes. But then again, I get it. They want to make sure the baby and I are both safe.

We arrive at the hospital, and again my own insecurities push forward. I've gotta get over this. I can't help it. I wish I could, and I wish Mom didn't have to do everything when it comes to Dad.

Ugh.

Stupid head. Stupid emotions. Stupid everything.

"Can you carry my bag?" Mom asks as she locks the car with the key-fob.

"Sure." I hold my hand out, taking her bag.

"You have to stop this," Mom says.

"Stop what?"

"I can read you like an open book. You're beating yourself up because you can't help."

How does she know? Am I really that obvious? "No, I'm not." *Yeah, I am.*

"Honey, don't even try to outsmart your mother. She's the smartest person I know. And she *knows* things," Dad says from the wheelchair Mom's pushing.

No use in pretending. "I feel useless. You're doing everything, and I can't even help with Dad."

"Ha! How do you think I feel then? I'm stuck sitting, not being able to move. Watching you and your mother do everything while I sit around, waiting for my legs to get better."

"Both of you are idiots," Mom says with a serious tone. "We're family. We look out for each other. A peak can't exist without a valley on either side. We might be in a valley at the moment, but soon, we'll be standing at the top. All together."

"See, she's a smart woman. It's why I never argue."

Mom makes me feel better. So does Dad.

"I'm sorry. I'm in this screwed up headspace, and I'm struggling with it."

"Hormones," Mom says. "Damn hormones."

"I know. And I try to push past them, but for whatever reason, I get stuck and get caught up in this cycle."

"Normal," Dad replies. "So normal."

"Other than carrying your bag, can I do anything else?"

"Wanna give me your legs?" Dad says and quickly adds in a sniff. Whenever Dad says something he finds funny, he adds a sniff at the end of it.

"And there's the sniff," I say.

"Fine, I'll just shut up and say nothing." Sniff.

I can't help but chuckle.

We get inside, and Mom leaves us in the lobby so she can find out where Dad has to go.

"You know what, kiddo?" I shake my head. "We're all going to be okay. This…" He gestures to his legs. "It's just temporary. It's nothing more than a bump in the road."

This takes me back to when I first told my parents about being pregnant. And I'm pretty sure, that's the exact words I used too. "Funny, hey?"

"What's funny?"

"I think you're right. This moment in time is exactly that. How boring would life be if we didn't have some kind of excitement in it? Given, you being in the accident isn't exactly what I'm talking about, considering you could've died."

"Could've died, shmouldve died!" Dad waves his hand dismissively at me. "Here's a hot tip for you. Have you ever seen me and Superman in the room together?"

"What?" What is Dad going on about?

"See. You haven't because, come here." He motions for me to come closer. I move in for him to say what he wants. "I'm Batman," he says in a low, hoarse whisper.

"You just asked if I'd seen you and Superman together, and now you're saying you're Batman."

He looks around, cautiously. "Never know who's listening. Had to throw them off the scent." Sniff.

"You're such a dork." I lean back.

"Just saying. Shhh. It's a secret." He brings his finger up to his lips.

"What are you two talking about?" Mom asks.

"Dad's a dork."

"I think we can trust her with my little secret," Dad says to Mom.

"That you're a dork? She's pretty smart, she figured it out herself."

"Yes, make sure no one hears of my real identity." Dad looks around again. Sniff.

"That you're the Flash? Why can't you be a Marvel character? Say The Hulk? Or Tony Stark."

"Everyone knows who they are. But I'll say hello to Iron Man next time I see him."

"And here I was worried about my mental health. I think we have to get Dad checked out for his."

Dad laughs. Mom does too.

We walk down the corridor toward where Dad's appointment is, and I say, "Thank you, Dad. You make me feel better."

"Kiddo, you make me feel alive every damn day."

Aw, I want to hug him, but that's nearly impossible as Mom's pushing him in the chair. I'll reserve it for when we get home.

CHAPTER
29

"DO YOU WANT lunch before we head home?" Mom asks Dad and me.

"I'm not really that hungry, but I could eat a banana."

"You're going to give birth to a monkey," Dad grumbles from the back seat. "Maybe that can be his name. Monkey." *Sniff.*

"Really, Dad?" I turn to give him the stink eye. But I can't while seeing him spread out on the backseat. "I have to say, I'm relieved everything's healing the way it's supposed to."

"You and me both, kiddo."

"I might stop and get a coffee from Clarence. And a piece of her orange and chocolate flourless cake." Mom moves her hand off the wheel to tap her mouth briefly. "Actually, I'm going to get two. And, I'm not sharing it with either of you."

She pulls up in front of CCC's, and I unclick my seatbelt. "I'll come with you." Looking through the window, I can see Clarence and Arthur both inside. "Do you want anything, Dad?"

"I'm good."

Mom and I head in, and the moment Clarence sees me, her eyes light up and a huge smile brightens her face. "Andy, my beautiful girl! How are you?" She comes out from behind the counter to hug me. Then she hugs my Mom. "Laura, you're looking well. How's Robert doing? Is he okay?" her tone darkens when she asks about Dad.

"He's in the car. Both legs are in casts, so it's a bit difficult for him to get around. But we just got the all clear for everything. It's now a waiting game. Waiting for his legs to heal."

"And for this one to have her baby." Clarence rubs my stomach. "Oh, I felt that. He's quite anxious to come out, isn't he?"

"He's been kicking me all day." I lean in and hug Clarence. "I miss working."

"We miss you too. Arthur!" Clarence calls loudly, but he doesn't respond. "Arthur!"

"Arthur clean the tables. Arthur, the customers are waiting. Arthur, go get me oranges. Arthur this, Arthur that." He walks out, and stops when he sees me. "It's your fault," he says with a smile. "Since you've been gone, it's Arthur, Arthur, Arthur. I need you back!"

"I miss you so much." I walk over to him, and give him a huge hug.

"We've been missing you too. You have to come back."

"I will, once I can."

"Don't listen to him. He's an old fart. You take as much time as you need, sugar." Clarence turns to Arthur. "Arthur, that table needs clearing."

"I'm a jack of all trades!" Arthur goes over to the unkempt table, and starts clearing it.

"And a damned master of none," Clarence bites back.

Arthur leaves the dirty plates and cups, walks over to Clarence, embraces her, and gives her a scorching kiss.

God, they're so cute! I want what they've got after so many years of marriage.

Arthur spins Clarence, turns without a word, and walks over to the table. "Thought that would shut you up."

"Before you two either kill each other, or have sex in front of us, can I get a latte to go, and two pieces of your orange and chocolate cake please."

"That man," Clarence playful grumbles. "You'll be the death of me, Arthur."

"Keep talking, my love."

"Do you want some banana cake, Andy?"

"I'm not feeling hungry. I wanted a banana in the car, but I'm not feeling it now."

"Thirsty? Want anything to drink?"

"I'm all good thank you."

"Here's your coffee, Laura. Let me get your cakes too." Clarence places two pieces in a container then hands them to Mom. Mom holds up her credit card, but Clarence flicks her hand.

"You have to take money, Clarence," Mom insists.

"Andy's like family, which means, you're like family."

"Please, take money. I can't expect you to give me free coffee and cake."

"I'm giving it to Andy." Clarence smiles.

"She'll charge you double next time," Arthur yells from the kitchen.

"We all need something good to happen from time to time. All I ask is you pay it forward for someone else when you can."

"Deal. I promise I'll pay it forward. Thank you." Mom lifts her coffee and drinks it. "Best coffee in town."

"Yes, it is," Clarence agrees.

"Bye." I walk behind the counter and give Clarence a hug, before heading into the kitchen where Arthur's stacking the dishwasher. "Bye." I give him a quick squeeze.

"You let us know if you need anything, okay?"

"I will, Arthur. Thank you."

"Andy, let's go," Mom calls.

I adore Clarence and Arthur. They're just genuinely good people. And the love they have for each other is heartwarming.

Getting in the car, I hold the cake while Mom sips on her latte, before putting it in the cup holder. She starts the car, looks over her shoulder, and starts pulling out slowly.

Quite suddenly, she stops. A fire engine zooms past us.

"I didn't even hear them," I say.

"I did, but not before I saw them."

"Did you get me cake?" Dad asks.

"You said you didn't want anything," Mom scolds him. "So we didn't get you anything. Clarence didn't charge me either."

"That's sweet of her."

We hear another siren, and I turn to see another fire engine hurtling past us. "What's going on?"

"Look, over there." Dad points to the left. "Big cloud of smoke. I hope everyone's alright."

"That's near us, isn't it?" I ask.

"Yeah, it is. I think we're more over toward the right." Mom points in the direction of our home.

Mom keeps driving. And yet a third fire engine, followed by an ambulance and police fly by us.

"This is scary," I say. "That fire looks close to us. I hope it's not someone we know."

The black clouds of smoke are getting bigger as we approach our neighborhood. It's got to be really close.

The sky is darkened under a thick blanket of charcoal fog. There's an eerie veil of heaviness sitting low, consuming everything it touches.

We turn into our street and see the angry, brilliant licks of red and orange.

"Mom," I say in a small voice.

"Shit," Mom responds.

Through the dimness of the smoke, we see extraordinary ruby flames billowing from our home. Police stop us before we can get there.

Mom stops the car, jumps out and begins running toward our home.

I'm right behind her. "Mom," I cry.

"You can't go down there," a police woman says as she stops us from heading to our flame-ridden home.

"That's our home!" Mom cries.

"Mom," I say again. But my eyes are glued to the inferno glowing ferociousness. "How?" And suddenly, it comes back to me. "My hair straightener! I must have forgotten to turn it off." I fall to my knees. Sickness consumes me. Guilt follows. "I did this."

Our house is engulfed in flames because of my own stupidity.

Fire crews are working like a perfect ballet, syncing together to get the fire extinguished.

"Mom," I say again.

"It's okay, Andy. It's okay," Mom tries to comfort me.

"It's not okay, I did this. I left the hair straightener on. It's all on me." I try to stand, but my pregnant stomach nearly tips me over. The police woman helps me up. "I'm so sorry," I cry into Mom's shoulder.

"It's okay."

I pull back, and stare at Mom. Looking down, I see a patch of water on the asphalt. "Mom."

Her eyes follow down my body. "Shit," she whispers.

And a contraction hits so hard, it nearly cripples me. "Oh my God!" I yell.

"How far along are you?" the police woman asks.

"She's thirty-five weeks," Mom responds. Mom grabs me around the waist, trying to support me through this ultra-full-on contraction.

"We need to get her to the hospital," the police woman says.

"Oh my God," I holler, as my stomach and lower back tighten with absolute agony.

"I'll… um, I… um. I'll," Mom's so flustered, she can barely speak.

"Mom, I'll go to the hospital. I'll be okay, you stay here. I'm so sorry. I did this." I look over to our house, crumbling second by second.

My heart is shattered.

My soul is weeping with my own stupid actions.

"I'm not leaving you."

"I've made a mess with everything, Mom. I'm so sorry." I burst into tears. And get hit with another monster contraction. "Shit," I say as I try to breathe through it.

"She needs to go to the hospital, now," the police woman says. "You can either follow me, or I'll take you. But you need to get there."

"I'll take her. We'll deal with this later." Mom points at our now-smouldering home. "You're most important right now."

"What's your name?" the police woman asks.

"I'm Andy."

"Andy, I'm Claire. I'd like for you to come with me. I can get you there faster."

"Mom?" I search for Mom.

"Go with her, and we'll be right behind." Mom's already jogging toward our car.

"Andy?" Claire helps me as I get in the police car. She's taken off so fast, that I have no idea where Mom and Dad are. "You doing okay?" Claire asks. She calls ahead to let the hospital know we're on our way. The conversation is short and to the point.

"Oh man. These contractions are a bitch," I say through gritted teeth.

"I believe you."

The contractions are coming one on top of the other. "Jesus."

"We're nearly there."

"Oh." I can't even double over in pain. My stomach is in the way.

"You doing okay?"

"Yeah," I squeak.

We pull up at the hospital, and as I'm getting out, one of the nurses is running toward the police car with a wheelchair.

It feels so surreal, like I'm in a movie. But I want to actually walk, regardless of the fact that these contractions are so heavy. "Can I walk?" I ask the nurse waiting for me.

"Doctor Morgan would prefer you be in a wheelchair," she replies.

"How?" I can't even finish the question, before another full-on contraction hits.

"I called her on the way," Mom says from beside me. I didn't realize she'd get here so fast.

"Where's Dad? You didn't leave him in the car, did you?"

"I'm getting a wheelchair."

"Jesus!" I groan, holding in the scream I want to let loose. "This shit hurts!"

"Yes, darling. You've gone into labor, that's what labor feels like," Mom responds.

I have to stop walking, and brace myself on the nurse as another contraction hits hard again. "Go get Dad, I'll be okay." I want to tell Mom I'm sorry I burned down her house. I want to tell her to leave me and go. I want to tell her I'm a crappy daughter for causing her so much stress. I want to tell her everything.

"I'm going. We'll find you." Mom dashes away.

I feel like I'm not making any progress. "Can I change my mind?" I ask the nurse.

"I was hoping you'd say that." She maneuvers the wheelchair so I can sit. And in a matter of minutes (and what feels like one long contraction), I'm in a birthing room.

"Andy, how are you?" Doctor Morgan asks as she enters the room.

"I think I'm having contractions."

Doctor Morgan stands in front of me, talking to Vivian and James but watching me too. "Looks like you are. You're thirty-five weeks. I'm going to try to stop it again."

Another contraction hits.

"Can you get up on the bed, Andy, or do you need help?"

The contraction subsides. "I can do it," I say, all puffed out.

Vivian helps me up from the wheelchair, takes my pants and underwear off, and helps me onto the bed. "You're doing really well," she says. "Squeeze my hand if you need to."

"Okay, Andy. I'm checking to see how dilated you are. I need you to spread your legs, makes fists with your hands, and pop them under your bottom. Can you do that? Or would you prefer the stirrups?"

I hated those things. "I can do it."

I do as Doctor Morgan asks. She pops on some gloves then approaches me. It's more uncomfortable than I remember it to be. And edging on the side of painful too.

Doctor Morgan also presses on my stomach, not hard enough for it to concern me, but it still feels weird.

"Alright," she says after a few seconds. "Your parents shouldn't be too far behind."

"Mom's getting Dad." The mother of all contractions hits. "Oh shit," I barely get out. Clutching the side of the bed, I roll with the contraction, just trying to get through it.

Doctor Morgan calls for James, and they both talk quietly.

Worry creeps through me.

"What's happening?" I ask.

"Andy!" Mom calls as she enters the room. "Doctor Morgan." Mom frantically looks over to the doctor.

The room is filled with calm, but my mind is the complete opposite. "What's happening?" I ask again.

Doctor Morgan steps forward, so she's close enough for me to hear. "Andy is in labor. She's dilated to seven centimeters, which means she'll be having this baby soon."

"What? No! I'm only thirty-five weeks."

"Yes, you are. But I'm not worried about you being thirty-five weeks. The lungs are working well, and the chance of survival is over ninety-nine percent."

I smile, relieved.

"But, the baby is breech. Which means, it's coming out feet first, not head first."

"This isn't good," I say. I've read enough about breech births to know things can go horribly wrong. "What do I have to do?" Another contraction hits again. And as soon as that one finishes, it's no more than a few seconds before another takes its place. This one, more painful than the last.

"I tried to turn the baby. I pressed on your stomach, so he comes out head first."

"How do we know if it's worked?" Mom asks.

"I'll do another internal in half an hour, and if it did, then we'll continue with a vaginal birth. If not, we'll have to perform a caesarean."

"I don't want a caesarean," I whisper. But I have to do what's right for my son. "But I will if I have to."

"If you feel like pushing, you need to let Vivian know."

"I'll try not to," I say.

"It doesn't work like that, Andy. The body will take over, and you'll push because the body wants to. You'll have virtually no control over it."

Great. Sounds so pleasant… not.

"Call me when you need me," Doctor Morgan instructs James. "I'll be in my office, Andy. If you need anything, let James or Vivian know."

"Okay," I say.

James and Doctor Morgan both leave. Then Vivian says, "I'll come in and check on you in a few minutes, okay?" I nod my head, and smile. Vivian's always been so kind to me.

"Mom?" I reach for her hand.

"Sweetheart, it's okay. We're going to meet this precious little boy soon."

"I'm so sorry. I'm sorry for burning our home down."

"The house is nothing more than a thing. We'll rebuild. And you have nothing to be sorry for."

Another contraction. "Argh!" I yell, this one being even more intense than the one before. From the top of my head, to my toes curling, this is a powerful contraction. "I need to change position." Mom helps me up, and I find relief with me semi-bending over the bed. A contraction hits, and although it's unbearable, it's not as bad as the ones I've been having. "Mom, I need you to call Alex and Zar. Let them know what's happening."

"I'll go out and let your father know what's happening, and call them. I'll be back in a minute. I'll get the young one to come in and stay with you."

"Young one? You mean Vivian?"

"Yes, I like her. She's very quiet, but quite good at looking after you."

"Yeah, I like her too."

"I'll get her. But I won't be long, okay?" I nod. "If you need me…"

"Mom, just go." Mom takes her phone out of her bag, and hesitates. Hovering in the doorway for too long. "Please, go. I'll be okay."

Mom's eyes narrow as a pained expression etches its way on her face. She's torn between if she should go, and needing to go. "I'll…"

"Just go!" I yell at her as a contraction hits. Lowering my head on the readjusted pillow, I breathe through the pain and swivel my hips. The circular movement of my hips helps me cope through the pain.

"How you doing, Andy?" Vivian asks.

"I'm finding a lot of relief when I do this." I show her my hips moving. "It actually helps so much."

"You do what you need to in order to get through the pain. We can offer you drugs too, if you need or want them."

"I'm doing okay for now. But I can't believe how draining these contractions are." Another hits, and I slowly move my hips in a clockwise direction to get the relief.

"They can be exhausting. But just wait until you're holding your little baby in your arms. You'll know it was all worth it."

The contractions are so forceful now, each more painful than the one before.

"Okay, I called Alex's mom and told her, and I told Zar's mom. They're all on their way."

"Even Alex's mom?" I ask.

Vivian slinks away quietly, leaving Mom and me in the room.

"She sounded happy," Mom says. "Which surprised the hell out of me."

"And Dad?"

"Dad's outside in the waiting room. He's not going anywhere."

I let out a laugh. "It's not that he can even if he wanted to."

"This is true."

Mom rubs my lowers back, and it feels like I'm on a cloud floating in heaven. "Wow. That feels so nice," I say, my voice mellowing out. "Oh crap." Another contraction.

"Breathe through it. Focus on how nice the massage feels."

I want to yell at her, and tell her all I can focus on is the pain. But I know she's just trying to distract me, to keep me from losing my shit. "I'm trying."

"It'll all be over so soon. We'll be holding our beautiful little boy in our arms before you know it."

"Can you rub on the left?" Mom finds the spot, and I groan in appreciation. "Oh yeah, there." The contraction eases. "That feels so nice. Move around a bit now." Mom changes spots, not spending too long on one area. But when the contraction hits again, Mom starts massaging the spot on the left of my lower back, and it makes the pain almost tolerable. "I need to go to the toilet."

"Nope. Let me call Vivian." Mom hits the buzzer, and within seconds, Vivian comes in. "She needs to go to the toilet."

"Andy, I'm going to call Doctor Morgan. Don't go to the bathroom."

"But I have to. I feel like I need to poo." A contraction hits again, this time, making me really need to go to the bathroom. "I don't think I can hold it in."

"Vivian's gone to call Doctor Morgan."

"Why do I need to go to the bathroom now?" I ask Mom.

"Your body is getting ready to push."

This makes me both happy, and terrified at the same time. The last nearly nine months comes down to these moments. These extreme, life-altering moments.

What if I turn out to be a terrible mother?

What if I end up screwing my child up?

What if I don't love him?

There are so many worries, and doubts all crawling through me. I don't think I can do this. I burst into tears. Chaos is rippling through me, causing me to be so unsure about everything.

"It's okay," Mom says in a gentle, smooth voice. She leans over and whispers, "You can do this."

"Okay, let's see what's going on with you, Andy," Doctor Morgan announces as she calmly enters the room. "On the bed."

"But this is comfortable," I whine.

"Doctor Morgan won't get on the floor," Vivian says to me quietly. "She's a phenomenal doctor, but getting on the floor is not her thing," she says in a *'if you know what's good for you, just do what you're told'* voice.

Vivian has a way of making me feel lighter. The heaviness in my head is overshadowed by Vivian's words.

I move to get up on the bed.

"I'm putting your legs in stirrups this time." There's no negotiating with Doctor Morgan. She slings my legs in the stirrups, puts gloves on and starts her thing. "You're at nine centimeters. The baby is still breech. He hasn't turned."

A contraction hits, and now I understand. "I'm pushing," I yell as this contraction comes on. My body takes over. I can't control anything happening.

"Get me a stool," Doctor Morgan yells over her shoulder. She sits on the swiveling stool, and with her head down, she's doing whatever the hell she's doing down there.

"Andy, I need you to try not to push." She looks over her shoulder, and asks Vivian for certain things. I think it's a surgical kit, but I have no idea.

Within seconds, Vivian is assisting Doctor Morgan. Bringing out surgical tools still sheathed in their sterile, plastic wrapping.

"Crap," I yell through the pain. "I need to push."

"Try not to," Doctor Morgan instructs.

"I can't help it."

"Get the monitor on her stomach, and prep her for a c-section."

Another contraction comes, making me push harder.

"We have meconium. What's the heart rate?" Doctor Morgan asks.

"Establishing baseline," Vivian says.

It's like all time has stopped. Other than my heavy breathing, and distraught thoughts, no one is talking.

"I need you to move forward," James asks. I look at him, questioning what he's holding. "We have to give you a spinal block. It'll help relax you, and the baby. But it's also there in case we need to get you into surgery."

"Okay." I sit forward. Following all his instructions is hard to do when contractions keep happening one on top of the other.

"Baseline is at ninety-eight," Vivian says.

"Get her ready. We need that block in," Doctor Morgan instructs.

"Nearly in."

The needle is painful, but nothing like the intensity of the contractions.

I look over to Mom, she's standing back, her eyes flitting between all of us. But I can see the worry inching across her face. She squirms as the needle goes into my back, but she straightens her shoulders. But I can see, she's just putting on a brave face for me.

"Ninety-seven," Vivian says.

"You'll feel cold going down your back."

"I can feel it," I say. It's like ice is traveling in my veins, but only from my mid-back down. I sit, resting for a moment. "I'm not having a contraction."

"You are, but we've turned the dosage up quite high, so you'll feel very little with the contractions."

"I can't believe how fast that's worked."

"It only takes a few moments," James says.

"Ninety-five," Vivian says.

"Give it another few moments," Doctor Morgan says.

"How are you feeling?" Mom asks.

"Tired," I answer candidly.

The room feels so quiet. Doctor Morgan is not saying anything. Vivian is watching the monitor and James is checking my vitals.

"Ninety-one," Vivian says.

Doctor Morgan stands, turns to me and says, "We need to operate. The baby isn't coping. His heart rate is falling, even after the epidural block. We need to get him out. I'm going to go see which room is available, and prep."

"Operate?" I whisper. "Why?"

"The baby's heartrate is falling. We need to get him out."

"Ninety-one," Vivian says.

"Good, gives us a bit of time. I'm sorry, I have to go and prepare. Get her ready," Doctor Morgan says to both James and Vivian before leaving the room.

"Okay, let's get you down to the operating room. There's nothing to worry about," Vivian says.

"Mom! Can Mom come too?"

"Yes, she can. I'll get her ready to come in with you," James says.

Before I even know it, my legs are out of the stirrups and I'm being covered up. I'm being pushed through the hallways in the bed, my Mom closely following us.

"Let Dad know what's happening," I say.

"I already have. I've sent him a text message, and told him I'll come find him when we have our grandson.

"You're really brave," Vivian says, smiling warmly.

"I don't feel brave."

"Well, you are." She looks up, and sees where we are. "We're here, let me go in and see if the Doctor is ready for you."

"Mom, do you think I can do this?"

"I think you can do anything you want. You'll always have us here to help. And you have Alex, and Zar. Regardless of what the future holds, we'll always be here."

This does make me feel better knowing I have their support and love.

"Can you find out if Alex and Zar are close please?"

"Andy, we'll be taking you through in about five minutes. Doctor Morgan is prepping," Vivian says.

"Thank you, Vivian. For everything."

"It's been my pleasure." Mom's on the phone a few steps away. "We need to get you ready," she says to my Mom.

"I have to go," she says into the phone, before hanging up. "I'm ready."

"You need to wear the gown, and cover your mouth and nose with the mask," Vivian starts explaining to Mom. "I've got to take your Mom to get her ready," she says to me, "but she'll be inside waiting for you. James needs to get you ready now, okay?"

I nod my head.

"We need to put an IV line into your arm, we also need to put a catheter in."

I scrunch my nose. I know what that means. But it has to be done, so I'm ready for whatever is necessary. "I'm ready," I say.

"You're doing really well. I'm going to take you into the operating room to get you ready. Now, Doctor Morgan will make an incision above your pubic bone, running from side to side. It won't be large, maybe about this size." He indicates by holding his thumb and finger about five inches.

"How long will this take?"

"On average, it's about an hour. Once the baby is out, she'll stitch you up. There's internal and external stitches which are dissolvable. We'll put a curtain up so you can't see anything, and your Mom is being encouraged not to look because people can pass out from the sight of blood. Once the baby is out, we'll check him over, make sure he's doing okay, before you get him. You'll feel what feels like pulling and tugging, but you shouldn't feel pain."

"Okay, I think I've got this." My nerves take off in a different direction. I'm not so scared now. James has told me step-by-step what's going to happen, and this isn't as scary as I imagined it to be.

"You do have this. And guess what else? You have us too. And we're the best in the state," James says with a cocky smile.

I'm not sure how to respond to him. I want to agree, but I think that sounds lame. So I smile, and nod.

I've got this. *I so have this.*

"Okay, let's get this baby," James says.

"I can't wait to meet him."

He rolls me into the room, and for the next few minutes he preps me for surgery. Mom enters as he finishes inserting the catheter.

"Stay up at this end," I instruct Mom.

"I don't think I've got a strong enough stomach to see what's going on down there." Mom points beyond the curtain. Mom sits on a stool they've provided for her. She takes my hand, and smiles. "This is really exciting." She looks around the room nervously. "But truth be told, I'm absolutely terrified too."

Calm washes over me. "You know what, Mom?"

"What?"

"I'm okay. And I know Doctor Morgan, and her team will do everything possible to make sure we're well looked after."

Mom turns to look at me. She moves some stray hair from my face, leans in and gives me a kiss on the forehead. "You are an extraordinary young woman. It's been an absolute honor to watch you become this amazing person you are."

A tear rolls down my cheek. "Thank you."

This is a beautiful moment. One I never knew could ever exist. I'm so fortunate to have the life I have.

"Okay folks, we all know what's happening." Doctor Morgan enters the room. She's dressed in white scrubs from head to toe. Beside her is Vivian, and James, dressed similarly but in green scrubs. There are two other nurses who haven't introduced themselves.

Vivian moves to look at the monitor. "Ninety-one," she says to Doctor Morgan.

"Right. Andy, from you I just need you to lay back, and relax. James explained you'll feel a pulling and pushing sensation?"

"Yeah, he did."

"I'll step you through what I'm doing, so you know what's happening. Right now, I'm making an incision above the pubic bone. The incision is about five to six inches in length. It'll fade over time, but it'll never go away."

"Okay."

"I love you," Mom says.

"The abdomen is open, and now I'm going to cut through the uterus."

Thankfully I can't feel anything painful. This is the weirdest thing I've ever experienced. I can't feel pain, but I can feel the pulling and pushing. Doctor Morgan's eyes are focused on my stomach.

The room is quiet, and everyone is watching what she's doing. A part of me wants to look too, but I know I'd freak out if I did.

"Get ready," she says to James.

James is standing beside her, ready.

The room falls completely silent.

My heartrate beats frantically.

Then suddenly, the most amazing sound is echoed throughout the room.

The sound of a baby gurgling, then crying.

My son. My boy. He's here.

James takes him over to the side, lays him down on the table, and hovers over him. I desperately crane my neck to see what he's doing. "Mom, can you see?" I ask.

"No, not yet."

"You're doing really good, Andy," Doctor Morgan says.

It feels like hours pass by, before James brings over my son, wrapped in a blanket.

"It's important to have skin to skin contact," Vivian says. She pulls the hospital gown down, and James unwraps my son.

"Congratulations on the birth of your beautiful baby…"

EPILOGUE

8 years later
Christmas Day

"WHEN ARE YOU coming over?" I hear Vivian asking someone. "I'm still in LA. I won't be home for another three weeks." I instantly recognize Zar's voice.

"But I miss you, Auntie Zar," Vivian whines.

I walk into her room, and see she's Facetiming with Zarita. "What are you doing?" I ask Vivian.

"I Facetimed Auntie Zar. I'm trying to convince her to come home. I want to see her." Viv smiles at me, showing me her beautiful white teeth.

"Auntie Zar can't be home yet. She's still working."

"I'm still here," Zar says.

"Auntie Zar, I think you should leave your job and come home. I want you here." Viv points to the floor.

"Well, I can't." Viv frowns at Zarita. These two are like two peas in a pod. They're tight as anything. And boy, do they argue when they butt heads. Zar doesn't always let Viv win either.

"Give me the phone, and go help Grandpa," I say to Viv, holding my hand out for the phone.

"Bye, love you," Viv says to Zar and hands me the phone, before Zar even has a chance to respond.

"I'll be home soon. This season is nearly wrapped up. Filming is killing my mojo," Zarita says.

"I've been watching. Man, you're so good in your role. I honestly believe you're a psycho sometimes."

"I was made to play the evil villain. But, guess what?"

"What?"

She places a finger to her lips as if to tell me it's a secret and I'm not allowed to say anything. "Guess who got asked to audition for the new Summer Sloan film? That would be me." The phone moves up and down as she jumps around with joy.

Summer Sloan is the hottest director at the moment. She makes engaging, action-packed movies where the lead character is always a woman. A kick-ass woman too.

"Holy shit, are you kidding?"

"Hell no! Apparently, Summer watches Devil in the Angel, and loves it. She asked for me by name. So her people got in contact with my agent. I'm reading for her in three days."

"I'm so damn proud of you. But wait, does this mean you won't be home for a while?" I love having Zar home. But I also understand, she's forging ahead in her acting career, and she can't pass an opportunity like this up.

"If I get this role, then I won't be home 'til probably end of next year."

"Your mom will be devastated."

"Devastated? Are you kidding? She's packing her bags and ready to move out here."

"Oh." My heart sinks a little. I'm happy for Zar, but with her being so far away, it means I'm not going to see her very often.

"Hey. I've got a surprise for you though."

"Yeah?"

"Yeah. You and Viv are flying out here tomorrow, and

staying 'til after New Years. I'm taking you both to Disney Land, and Santa Monica Pier, Universal Studios, and of course, Rodeo Drive. I have the audition in three days, but other than that, I'm all yours."

"Zar! No way. Oh man, thank you so much." I tear up at Zar's generosity.

"It's my Christmas present to you both."

"I have to clear it with Alex first."

"No, you don't. Because I already did. He's cool." I love Zar, and Alex. They are such phenomenal people. "Hey, I gotta go. I'll see you and Viv tomorrow. I'll email you the tickets."

"Love you."

"Love you too."

Walking out to the family room, I sit on the armchair, smiling.

"You're happy, Mommy."

"I'm so happy. Guess what Auntie Zar got us for Christmas?"

"What?" Viv stands between my legs, leaning all over me.

"She bought us tickets so we can visit her in LA. We're flying out tomorrow."

"We're going to see Auntie Zar?" Viv's face lights up. Her eyes widen, and her smile is so large, it's like it takes up half her angelic face. "I miss Auntie Zar," she says, her eyes filled with tears.

"I know. So do I, Rocket." Vivian curls up on my lap, snuggling in to give me a kiss. She hugs me tight. Her hugs are just perfect, like she is.

"Why do you call me Rocket?"

"Because you came into this world like a rocket. You tried coming in before you were ready, and Doctor Morgan had to stop you."

"Hm," she says and adds a shoulder shrug. One day she'll understand.

"Do you remember when you thought your hair straightener

caused the fire? It ended up being the oven. Short circuited, and caught alight," Mom says, reminding me of the day Viv was born.

"Did you cause a fire, Mommy?" Vivian asks.

"No, I didn't. But I thought I did. And because of that, I went into early labor, which is when you came."

"When is Daddy coming over?" Vivian asks.

I look at my phone, and see a message from Alex. I quickly read it. "Daddy and Kira said they'd be here in about ten minutes."

Vivian smiles. "Can I open my Christmas presents yet?" she excitedly asks.

"You know we have to wait for Daddy and Kira to come before you can do that." We're interrupted by a knock on the front door.

"I'll get it, I'll get it, I'll get it!" Vivian eagerly jumps off my lap, and races to the front door. I follow behind her, knowing it'll be Alex and his fiancée. Vivian opens the door, and she lunges forward into Alex's arms. "Daddy! Merry Christmas!" she shrieks with so much joy and happiness.

"Hey there, munchkin," Alex says as he scoops her up and plants many kisses all over her face.

"Ew, Daddy!"

"Oh, what was that? You want more kisses? Okay then." He attacks her face, plastering more kisses all over.

"Daddy!" Vivian giggles.

When Alex lets go, she throws herself straight into Kira's arms.

"Come in, get out of the cold," I say as I stand back and watch the love flow between the three of them. "Merry Christmas."

"Kira, will you sit next to me when we open presents?" Vivian takes Kira's hand, not really waiting for an answer.

"Sure thing. How about I open all your presents? I wouldn't want you to get tired, or anything."

"Tired? Of Christmas presents? Who are you kidding?" Vivian asks with sass.

"Hi," I say to Kira as Vivian drags her past me. We lean in and give each other a quick kiss on the cheek. "Hey," I say to Alex, giving him a kiss on the cheek too. "Thank you for letting me have Viv for the next few days. Zar told me she called you, are you sure you're okay with it?"

Alex looks to me and smiles. "We work together, regardless of the fact we're not a couple anymore. When Zar called and asked, I was totally fine with it. Look, how about I take Viv when you return for two weeks? Kira and I want to go to Washington for a few days. See her family. We can take Viv with us."

"Oh yeah, she'd love that. Anyway, how have you been?" We head into the family room, where Kira and Viv are already sitting together talking about something.

"I can't believe how busy it's been. I haven't stopped at work. But you're looking at one of a team who are running trials for a new drug for type one diabetes." He beams proudly.

The fact Alex is happy and proud, makes me happy and proud for him. "That's fantastic. Wow." I clutch my chest, so incredibly proud of the man he's become. And the father he's become. He's stepped up and been so phenomenal. Never missing any milestone, or any special occasion. Choosing his daughter over and over again.

"Hi Alex, how are you? Is Kira with you?" Mom looks over her shoulder, and sees Kira sitting with Vivian. She quickly gives Alex a kiss on the cheek, then goes to Kira to give her a kiss too. Mom, Kira, and Vivian all sit together, talking.

"How's school?" Alex asks.

"Who knew becoming a midwife would be so difficult? I had no idea. I'm nearly finished, and I've got a job with Doctor Morgan. Thank God for Mom and Dad, and you. I wouldn't have been able to do this without everyone's help."

"Does that mean you'll be working with Vivian? I know how

close you two have become."

She's one of my best friends. "Sadly for me, no. She's now studying to become a doctor. She's keeping crazy hours. But she and Jayden should be here soon. Actually, I meant to ask and I forgot. Can I bring Viv over tonight? We're going to see Clarence and Arthur, and I totally forgot to ask if I can keep Vivian until after we see them."

"Yeah, that's no problems at all. Just bring her when you're done."

"Thank you. I'm not sure what time our flight is tomorrow, but can I let you know and pick her up on the way to the airport?"

"Absolutely! Or, Kira and I can bring her to the airport?"

"Thank you." I lean in, giving Alex a tight hug.

"Who's ready for presents?" Dad asks from the living room. "Oh, Alex, Kira, you're here. How are you?" He shakes Alex's hand, then gives Kira a kiss.

"We're doing well," Alex responds.

"Presents!" Vivian shrills.

She really is a perfect combination of both Alex and myself. She has the most beautiful skin, and long brown hair. Her expressive, dark brown eyes always tell us how she's feeling. But her most perfect trait is her kindness and acceptance.

"Here, Viv, open this present first," Alex says as he hands her a small square object.

"What is it?" Vivian rips the paper open, and stares at the present, unsure of what it is.

I recognize it immediately. I can't help but beam with irrefutable joy.

"Merry Christmas, munchkin. You're going to be a big sister," Viv reads aloud.

She looks up to her Daddy, her eyes gleam from the water gathering. She jumps up, and bear hugs both him and Kira.

"I'm going to be a big sister," she says, happy and enthusiastic.

Our family is not conventional. But I suppose, being pregnant at fifteen wasn't conventional either.

But we make it work.

Not because we have to, but because we want to.

Family is important.

And we choose to cherish every moment.

THE END

ACKNOWLEDGEMENTS

Writing *A Bump in the Road* started as an idea to tell the pressures of a young woman who accidentally falls pregnant.

While writing this story, my life turned upside down. My mum (Vivian) became sick, and passed away. Her passing is still shocking to me. How is she gone?

But, it's okay. Don't get me wrong, I'm not saying her death is fantastic, it's far from it. But death is certainly a part of life.

In the midst of my loss, I also went through turmoil with my family. My days were covered by darkness, catastrophe and a heavy oblivion that felt like it was never going to end. However, I pushed through it and continued to tell the story of Andy, who while she felt like she had the weight of the world on her shoulders, she still managed to persevere.

Like Andy, I have an amazing support system who got me through the blackest time of my life. And for that, I'll be eternally grateful.

Thank you to these beautiful people for all their help with A Bump in the Road.

Debi Orton, my editor.

Tami Norman, my formatter.

Kellie Dennis, my cover artist.

Terry, Anna, Sam and Mandy, my proofreaders.

You're all so valuable to me, and I cherish everything you do for me.

And of course, to you, my precious reader. Without you, I could never do this. Thank you for sticking with me.

Keep reading for Previews of:
Luna Caged
The Gift
Addiction

Luna
CAGED

New York Times Bestseller
Margaret McHeyzer

PROLOGUE

Ducking my head, I hope my hair hides my face.

"Luna, what are you doing?" the Elder asks.

"Gettin' in line," I explain. "I want to go where they go." I point to the line of boys in front of me.

The Elder laughs and shakes his head. He leans down to look at me. "Girls don't go where the boys go." He points to the line. "Girls don't need to be taught anything but how to cook, clean, and look after the men."

I stare up at him. I can feel my bottom lip quiver and my eyes well with tears. "But I want to learn too," I say in a small voice.

He places his big hands on my shoulders and turns me around. "Off you go. Get back to your chores," he says as he pushes me then gives me a light smack on the bottom. Not a hard one, just hard enough to hurry me along.

I do a small jump when he smacks me, and turn to look at the line as it advances into the building. There's a word above the door, but I don't know what it says, of course. I can't read. Girls aren't allowed to read. It's one of the Elders' rules. Mommas and

Sisters can't read, neither can any girl. But I want to learn, and the Elders always tell me I don't need to. I just need to learn how to clean properly, how to cook, and how to look after the men.

Turning, I notice Cain, shuffling along at the back of the line. He keeps looking at me, then back at the line. His brows are scrunched together as the line continues. "Elder Tom, why can't Luna learn with us?" he asks the Elder who hurried me away.

"Because we're men, and the men need to learn. But the girls aren't smart like us. They don't require it."

Cain lowers his head, and steps forward before lifting his face to look at Elder Tom. "Are they different than us?" he asks.

"Yes. They're girls. They don't have the same intelligence as us."

Cain lowers his head again.

"But why?" I ask, a little too loud. "Why aren't we as smart as you?" I quickly cup my hand to mouth, ashamed for asking.

"Luna." Elder Tom's face is angry when he notices I'm still here. He strides to me in deliberate, large steps. He grabs my shoulders, and shakes me as he pulls me forward to meet his angry stare. "Even if we *did* want to teach you, you're too dumb to learn. You proved it, because you obviously can't follow instructions. Girls are girls, and not as smart as men. Now get out of here!"

My shoulders droop. "Am I stupid?" I ask.

"All girls are," he responds in an even voice. "But we're men, and it's our job to look after you." A tear breaks free, and rolls down my cheek. "Go. I don't want to have to report this." He touches my nose slightly, smiles and turns. "Now class," he states to all the boys as he walks back toward the line, "let's go."

Cain looks toward me and sees me struggling to hold in my tears. He looks sad too. My shoulders slump and I turn to walk away. Why can't I learn? It's not fair.

I head back to the big house and find Sister Lorraine. She's on her hands and knees, scrubbing the floor. I'm still sad, but I can't really do anything about it. "Do you need help, Sister?" I ask as I automatically begin helping her without an answer.

"Thank you, Luna." She smiles at me, then quickly goes back to scrubbing the floor with the big brush.

My mind is going everywhere but here. I sit back on my heels and stare out to the common area, in front of the big house. "What's that?" I ask as I gape at the big round piece of wood sticking up in the middle of the dirt oval.

"You always ask too many questions, Luna. Best get back to work," Sister Lorraine says as she continues cleaning the floors.

"But no one ever tells me anything and I've always wondered what that is."

Sister stops for a moment, and carefully looks around. She leans in and whispers as quietly as possible, "It's a whipping post. But the Elders haven't had to use it for a while."

A whipping post? I don't know what that is. "What's a whipping post?" I ask with a tone matching hers.

"If we do something wrong, they tie us to it, and hit us."

I gasp as I flinch back. "I don't want to do anything wrong. Will they hit me?" More tears sting my eyes, but I do my best to hold them in.

"Not if you're a good girl. Come on now, we have to hurry up." She urges me with her eyes to keep scrubbing the floor.

When the floor is done, I help Sister up and we start toward the kitchen. I follow so I can help her.

"Luna!" I hear from behind me.

"Hi Cain," I reply as I turn to see him standing with a huge grin on his face.

"Let's go play," he says and bounces on the spot.

"I can't. I have to help Sister Lorraine."

"Cain asked you to go, Luna. He's a man, so you have to go," Sister says.

"Okay." I shrug my shoulders.

Cain is already running out the door, and I'm close behind him. He keeps running, until we reach the edge of the meadow. There's a huge wall there that's as tall as the sky. If I look up, I can't see where it ends. "Where are we going?" I ask. Cain stops, and he's puffing. He pulls out a little book from inside his pants and gives me the goofiest look on his face. "Is that a real book?" I ask, my eyes bulging with excitement. Cain's told me about them. I'm so excited.

"It is." Cain's smile is as big as what mine feels like.

He sits beneath one of the large trees, and starts flipping through the book. In my eagerness, I can barely sit still. "Can I touch it?" I ask as I hesitantly reach out to feel it.

"Here. I'm going to teach you how to read."

My mouth falls open, and I'm so happy I start to cry. I want to hug Cain, but the Elders would be angry if I did that. Boys and girls aren't allowed to touch unless the men are disciplining the girls, or unless we're serving the Elders. "Really?" I ask.

"Yeah, here." He flips the first page open, and there's a picture of an apple and a word.

"That's an apple," I say.

"Yep. Apple starts with A, the sound A makes is like this. *Ah… ah.*"

"*Ah,*" I mimic him.

"That's so good, Luna. Now this here is a bus."

"A what?" I ask staring at the strange yellow picture on the page.

"A bus. The first letter is B and the sound it makes is like *ba*, like a sheep."

"Oh, *ba. Ba. Ba,*" I practice.

"Yes!" he says and claps when I get the sound right.

"But what's a bus?" I ask.

He shrugs his shoulders. "The Elders didn't tell us. I asked once, and the men in the class started snickering. The Elders said we don't need to know right now."

"Oh." My gaze drifts away from the page, and I look toward the wall. "I want to know what a bus is, and what it does. Don't you?"

He shrugs again. "I don't know. Maybe."

Standing, I head straight to the wall. Leaning against it, I huff in frustration. "Why are they always telling us not to ask questions?"

"Luna." Cain stands and dusts off his dirty pants. "Stop it. You're going to get into so much trouble."

"But I want to know what's happening out there. I can hear noises. Sometimes at night, when it's quiet, I can hear things happening. All I want to do is go out there and see what's making the noises."

Cain's shaking his head. "You can't. There are only bad people out there. They'll kill you. Or hurt you. Please, Luna, don't ask any more questions. The Elders will get angry."

Something inside me shrinks, like it always does when I'm told to stop asking questions.

"What is going on here?" the voice is deep and booms from across the field. I look up to see Elder Steven coming toward us. His strides are large and angry. His face, even though he's not close, is red and furious. "What is going on?" he blasts again.

I don't like Elder Steven. He scares me the most out of all the Elders. "Noth-nothing," I stutter as I cower with my back against the wall.

"What's this?" He snatches the book out of Cain's hands, but his livid eyes are set on me. He flicks through the book. "What is this?" The rage in his voice now matches his face.

"We were just…" Cain starts saying, but Elder Steven silences him with a glare.

"I'm not asking you, son. I'm asking this witch," Elder Steven says in a gentler voice to Cain. He flips his anger back to me. "What are you doing?"

These tears are because I'm terrified of Elder Steven. "I'm sorry," I offer without even knowing what I'm sorry for.

Elder Steven steps forward, grabs me by the arm and starts marching me back to the main house. He's walking so fast, I have to run to keep up with him. Cain is closely following us.

"It's not her fault, Elder Steven. I wanted to show her what a book is," he tries to explain.

Elder Steven is furious. "It's alright, son. I know it's her fault."

I want to say something, but the hard hand on my arm tells me to remain quiet and not complain or cry. But I can't help the tears. They're falling on their own.

We get to the main house, and Elder Steven shoves me toward the whipping post. I fall to my knees, scraping them on the hard-packed earth.

"I'm sorry," I cry as I bury my face into my hands.

"Men and girls!" Elder Steven summons. Peeking out between my fingers, I notice everyone is gathering around us. What is happening? Why is he yelling for everyone? "Go and tell the other Elders we're about to have a whipping," Elder Steven says to some of the other men.

Crying, I try and stop my shaking. "I'm sorry," I keep saying.

Everything is happening in slow motion. Everybody is making their way out to the center.

"Get up," Elder Steven snaps at me.

Slowly, I stand to my feet but refuse to look up at anyone. I don't want to meet their eyes. *I'm so afraid.*

"What we have here is a girl who thinks she has the right to learn to read."

I hear a collective gasp. Looking up, I see the men standing to one side, and the girls are standing on the other.

"We have rules. And the rules are easy. Girls are to look after the men and the house. No girl has the intellect to understand what we do." The men snicker and nod their heads. The girls do the same thing. "Turn and face the post." Slowly, I turn. "Wrap your hands around it." I try, but I can't reach all the way around. "If you move, you'll get three more strikes."

My tears are falling fast now, and I'm sobbing in fear. I don't know what's going to happen.

"This is why the girls don't get an education."

The sound is what happens first. The slam of something on my back happens second. I scream in agony. It stings, and it's hurting. It feels like a hot rod is melting into my back. I barely catch my breath, when it happens again.

And again.

And again.

I'm just barely standing, and my back is burning in pain. "You will not try to trick another man into teaching you how to read, will you, Luna?" Elder Steven asks.

The stinging is so severe and I'm sobbing so hard, I can't catch my breath. I shake my head in reply.

"Girls are not able to learn. That's why we've created this God's Haven for you, so you're not taken advantage of out there where only death, poverty and disease is waiting for you. We are your family. Beyond the wall is death. Beyond the wall is evil. You will die if you leave. Only we can protect you," he says loudly.

Everyone is nodding.

"Next time you use your girlish charm to trick a man, I'll have you stoned to death."

"I'm sorry," I cry again. I'm still not sure what I did. All I know is I've been punished for it.

Elder Steven leaves me heaped on the ground in an absolute mess. Sister Holly comes over to me, and helps me up. "You brought this on yourself, Luna." She shakes her head as she helps me walk into one of the smaller houses. She takes me into a bedroom, lays me on my stomach and tends to my wounds. "You have to know, we're not like the Elders. We're not as smart as they are. Anyway, why do you want to learn? Learning is only for the men."

"Sister Holly?" I hear Cain's voice from the door.

Turning, I see him watching me.

"Yes, Cain?" Sister replies.

"I need to talk to Luna."

Sister Holly stands, gives him a nod, and leaves. He rushes over to where I'm lying, and gently reaches out to me. "I don't want to get in trouble again," I say pulling my hand back when he's nearly touching me.

He quickly retracts his hand, and lowers his eyes. "I'm sorry, Luna. I tried to tell them it was my fault, but they said as a man, it's never our fault. I'm sorry, really sorry." I watch as a tear falls by his feet.

"Please…" I say as I turn my head. "Just go."

I hear him back away. Then he says in a small voice, "I don't care what the Elders say. I'm going to teach you to read, because I know it's the right thing to do. I promise. But I'll figure out a way to do it so we never get caught again."

I blink the tears away and don't respond.

Why is it so bad to learn?

I don't understand.

THE GIFT

New York Times Bestseller of Ugly & Mistrust

Margaret McHeyzer

PROLOGUE

Who could have known my life would be so drastically altered?

I didn't know. My parents didn't either.

It was a few weeks before my seventeenth birthday when everything changed. I was rushed into the hospital in the back of an ambulance, unconscious.

I got there just in time.

My appendix erupted, causing poison to leak into my blood stream. The doctors operated on me and removed it before the toxins could contaminate my other organs and kill me.

They said I had a brush with death. They said I was lucky.

When I woke I felt… *different*. Something inside me had changed.

I knew it from the moment I opened my eyes. Something felt weird.

Something was wrong.

Or maybe something was right.

This is how I received my gift.

… Or maybe it's my curse.

Addiction

I CAN STOP ANYTIME I WANT

MARGARET MCHEYZER

Prologue

"Is she dead?"

Groaning, I try to roll over so I can see where the voice is coming from.

"She's moving. We have to help her," someone else says. Their voice is breathy, sounding panicked.

My limbs are heavy, my head is fuzzy, and I swear I can hear my mother's voice.

"Hannah, are you high?" She aggressively holds my chin and stares into my eyes.

"No, Mom," I respond, and giggle.

"Your eyes are bloodshot, and you're barely looking at me."

"I'm just tired," I say and giggle again.

"What's so funny?" she asks as she lets go of my chin and steps backward.

Shrugging, I look around the room.

"We need to call an ambulance," someone says, reminding me that my mother isn't here with me.

My vision is blurry. I can't focus on anything at all. Turning my head, I look straight into the eyes of a girl. She's probably around my age, but I bet she hasn't seen half the stuff I have. She kneels beside me, and behind her are another two girls and three guys. One of them looks bored; he's scrolling on his phone.

"What do you want?" I bark toward her, but my voice comes out broken, and slurry.

"Jasmine, she's a junkie. Look at her. Just leave her. She's not our problem," the bored guy says.

"We can't just leave her," she snarls back at him.

Suddenly, my stomach starts contracting, and my breathing becomes challenged. Gasping for air, my body tightens with spasms, trying to get oxygen into my lungs.

"Shit, she must be overdosing. We gotta get out of here before anyone finds us," bored guy says.

"I'm not leaving her. She's just a kid."

"She ain't my problem. I'm outta here," the bored guy says and takes off, the others going with him.

The girl stays with me, and as I try to focus on her, all I can see is the pretty chain around her neck. It looks like it's worth a lot, I'm sure I could give it to Edgar for some crystals. Man, maybe a few days' worth. I need money big time.

"I'm going to call an ambulance," the girl says as she takes her phone out of her pocket and dials it. "What have you taken?" she asks.

Everything is fuzzy. Her voice sounds disjointed and almost robotic.

Reaching for my pipe, I scream in pain. But she doesn't seem alarmed by my screams, maybe I'm actually not moving. Everything hurts.

"I need an ambulance…" her voice is frantic as she tells the operator where she is.

My eyes keep drifting shut, and she screams at me to open them again.

"She's frothing at the mouth, and she's barely moving."

I try to turn over, but whatever those fuckers gave me was strong. It's weighing me down. I can barely move.

"Her breathing is shallow…"

If I can just get up, I'll find my way back to Edgar's. He'll look after me. He always does. Sometimes he asks me to do stuff for him. "I'm alright," I mumble.

"She's trying to say something," the girl says into the phone. "Okay, I won't touch her." Her eyes are filled with pity and sadness. I stare up at her, and can see how concerned she is. I can see her. Can she see me?

"There's a syringe beside her. I think she might have injected something. There's a pipe, too. Maybe she smoked crack or meth?"

Yeah, baby. Crystal meth. Meth. Crystal. Ice. Tina. Glass. I love it. I love getting iced. It's the best feeling in the world. Being invincible, even when there are a million people in the room. Being free. Floating. That floating is what I love best. Anything can be happening around you, and when you smoke a bit of ice, you're floating above everyone. Free and happy and high.

"I'm here!" The girl jumps up and waves her arms frantically.

"Thank you for calling, we'll take it from here," another woman says to the girl.

The girl steps back and continues to stare at me. I'm being rolled over, and talked at by someone in a uniform. "What's your name?"

"Hannah," I respond.

"She's unresponsive," the woman says as she looks up to someone. She presses into my chest plate with her knuckle, and a shooting pain rips through me. "She's barely coherent. Heart rate is down, pulse is weak. She's overdosing."

"Get me back to Edgar's," I say.

"She's crashing. Administering Narcan."

There's a tightness in my chest. Pain soars through me, every part of me is like someone is stabbing multiple sharp knives into my body.

A darkness overtakes me.

A blanket of warmth is thrown over my entire body. My last breath escapes past my chapped lips.

Suddenly, I feel weightless. This must be what heaven feels like. It's so peaceful.

"We're losing her!" I hear someone yell.

Who's losing who? What's happening?

"ETA sixty seconds," someone else says in a calm voice.

I'm not sure what's happening, all I know is I like the quiet.

"Breathe, damn it, breathe!"

"Great, another dead junkie," someone snickers.

"I haven't lost her yet."

"She's just a junkie, Sally. Who cares if she dies? It's another one off the streets."

"Hey, she's someone's daughter. You want to be the one to knock on her parent's door?"

I hear a grumble from behind me. More like a pained sigh.

Who's talking?

What the hell is happening?

As it turns out, this is far from the end of my story.

ALSO BY
MARGARET MCHEYZER

Luna Caged

I often stare at the walls and wonder what's beyond them.

The Elders tell me that nothing but sin, sadness, and disease lie beyond the wall.

Sometimes I hear things, noises that are strange to me. They're often faint, and when I ask the Elders what those sounds are, they tell me they are the tortured souls of thousands of people behind the gates of hell. I don't know what they mean.

I dream of leaving these walls, but the Elders insist this is the only place we're safe. They talk about danger, hatred, and the devil himself waiting just beyond. They tell us the walls were built to keep us safe.

Although I believe the Elders, I want to see the outside world for myself.

But there's no way out.

Or so I thought...

Luna Freed

I often stared at the walls and wondered what was beyond them.

After my first escape, I realized that everything I'd believed, everything the Elders told us, and everything I thought I knew were all calculated lies.

Now I know the truth will set me free.

Addiction

Drugs ruin people's lives.

I should know, they destroyed mine.

I'm Hannah and I got hooked on ice. What started as a trickle, ended with a tsunami washing everything away; my family, my life.

I'm not sure you're ready to read my story; it's real and confronting.

Open the book, read the pages and see how easy it is for anyone to get addicted.

Ice affects all types of people. It doesn't discriminate.

It will SCREW. YOU. UP.

Drowning

I'm a cutter.

I cut because I find solace in it.

I cut because it helps calm my frantic mind.

I cut because the voice inside my head tells me to.

I cut because this is the only way I know how to handle life.

The Gift

I have something people want. I have something they cannot take or steal. I have something they'd kill for.

The something I have, isn't a possession, it's more.

Much, much more.

It's a gift.

It's part of me.

The Curse

It's been the butterfly effect.

I changed the course of my life because I warned a man.

I thought what I had was a gift, but it's quickly turning into my curse.

Now I realize I'm much more than a girl with an ability.

Because now... I'm becoming a weapon.

Dying Wish

I have three major loves in my life: my family, my best friend Becky, and ballet. Elijah Turner is quickly becoming the fourth.

He's been around as long as I can remember. But now he's much more than just the annoying guy at school.

My life was working out perfectly...until it got turned upside down.

Mistrust

I'm the popular girl at school.

The one everyone wants to be friends with.

I have the best boyfriend in the world, who's on the basketball team.

My parents adore me, and I absolutely love them. My sister and I have a great relationship too.

I'm a cheerleader, I have a high GPA and I'm liked even by the teachers.

It was a night which promised to be filled with love and fun until...something happened which changed everything.

Ugly

This is a dark YA/NA standalone, full-length novel. Contains violence and some explicit language

If I were dead, I wouldn't be able to see.

If I were dead, I wouldn't be able to feel.

If I were dead, he'd never raise his hand to me again.

If I were dead, his words wouldn't cut as deep as they do.

If I were dead, I'd be beautiful and I wouldn't be so...ugly.

I'm not dead...but I wish I was.

Chef Pierre

Holly Walker had everything she'd ever dreamed about – a happy marriage and being mum to beautiful brown-eyed Emma - until an accident nineteen months ago tore her world apart. Now she's a widow and single mother to a boisterous little 7-year-old girl, looking for a new start. Ready to take the next step, Holly has found herself a job as a maître d' at Table One, a once-acclaimed restaurant in the heart of Sydney. But one extremely arrogant Frenchman isn't going to be easy to work with...

Twenty years ago, Pierre LeRoux came to Australia, following the stunning Aussie girl he'd fallen in love with and married. He and his wife put their personal lives on hold, determined for Pierre to take Sydney's culinary society by storm. Just as his bright star was on the upswing, tragedy claimed the woman he was hopelessly in love with. He had been known as a Master Chef, but since his wife's death he has become known as a monster chef.

Can two broken people rebuild their lives and find happiness once more?

Smoke and Mirrors

Words can trick us.

Smoke obscures objects on the edge of our vision.

A mirror may reflect, but the eye sees what it wants.

A delicate scent can evoke another time and place, a memory from the past.

And a sentence can deceive you, even as you read it.

Grit

Recommended for 18 years and over

Alpha MC Prez Jaeger Dalton wants the land that was promised to him.

Sassy Phoenix Ward isn't about to let anyone take Freedom Run away from her.

He'll protect what's his.

She'll protect what's hers.

Jaeger is an arrogant ass, but he wants nothing more than Phoenix.

Phoenix is stubborn and headstrong, and she wants Jaeger out of her life.

Her father lost the family farm to gambling debts, but Jaeger isn't the only one who has a claim to the property.

Sometimes it's best to let things go.

But sometimes it's better to fight until the very end.

Yes, Master

My uncle abused me.

I was 10 years old when it started.

At 13 he told me I was no longer wanted because I had started to develop.

At 16 I was ready to kill him.

Today, I'm broken.

Today, I only breathe to survive.

My name's Sergeant Major Ryan Jenkins and today, I'm ready to tell you my story.

A Life Less Broken

On a day like any other, Allyn Sommers went off to work, not knowing that her life was about to be irrevocably and horrifically altered.

Three years later, Allyn is still a prisoner in her own home, held captive by harrowing fear. Broken and damaged, Allyn seeks help from someone that fate put in her path.

Dr. Dominic Shriver is a psychiatrist who's drawn to difficult cases. He must push past his own personal battles to help Allyn fight her monsters and nightmares.

Is Dr. Shriver the answer to her healing?

Can Allyn overcome being broken?

My Life for Yours

He's lived a life of high society and privilege; he chose to follow in his father's footsteps and become a Senator.

She's lived a life surrounded with underworld activity; she had no choice but to follow in her father's footsteps and take on the role of Mob Boss.

He wants to stamp out organized crime and can't be bought off.

She's the ruthless and tough Mob Boss where in her world all lines are blurred.

Their lives are completely different, two walks of life on the opposite ends of the law.

Being together doesn't make sense.

But being apart isn't an option

HiT Series Box Set

HiT 149

Anna Brookes is not your typical teenager. Her walls are not adorned with posters of boy bands or movie stars. Instead posters from Glock, Ruger, and Smith & Wesson grace her bedroom. Anna's mother abandoned her at birth, and her father, St. Cloud Police Chief Henry Brookes, taught her how to shoot and coached her to excellence. On Anna's fifteenth birthday, unwelcome guests join the celebration, and Anna's world is never the same. You'll meet the world's top assassin, 15, and follow her as she discovers the one hit she's not sure she can complete – Ben Pearson, the current St. Cloud Police Chief and a man with whom Anna has explosive sexual chemistry. Enter a world of intrigue, power, and treachery as Anna takes on old and new enemies, while falling in love with the one man with whom she can't have a relationship.

Anna Brookes in Training

Find out what happened to transform the fifteen-year-old Anna Brookes, the Girl with the Golden Aim, into the deadly assassin 15. After her father is killed and her home destroyed, orphan Anna Brookes finds herself homeless in Gulf Breeze, Florida. After she saves Lukas from a deadly attack, he takes her in and begins to train her in the assassin's craft. Learn how Lukas's unconventional training hones Anna's innate skills until she is as deadly as her mentor.

HiT for Freedom

Anna has decided to break off her steamy affair with Ben Pearson and leave St. Cloud, when she suspects a new threat to him. Katsu Vang is rich, powerful, and very interested in Anna. He's also evil to his core. Join Anna as she plays a dangerous game, getting closer to Katsu to discover his real purpose, while trying to keep Ben safe. Secrets are exposed and the future Anna hoped for is snatched from her grasp. Will Ben be able to save her?

HiT to Live

In the conclusion to the Anna Brookes saga, Ben and his sister Emily, with the help of Agent rescue Anna. For Anna and Ben, it's time to settle scores…and a time for the truth between them. From Sydney to the Philippines and back to the States, they take care of business. But a helpful stranger enters Anna's life, revealing more secrets…and a plan that Anna wants no part of. Can Anna and Ben shed their old lives and start a new one together, or will Anna's new-found family ruin their chances at a happily-ever-after?

Binary Law (co-authored)

Ellie Andrews has been receiving tutoring from Blake McCarthy for three years to help her improve her grades so she can get into one of the top universities to study law. And she's had a huge crush on him since she can remember.

Blake McCarthy is the geek at school that's had a crush on Ellie since the day he met her.

In their final tutoring session, Blake and Ellie finally become brave enough to take the leap of faith.

But, life has other plans and rips them apart. Six years later Blake and his best friends Ben and Billy have built a successful internet platform company 3BCubed, while Ellie is a successful and hardworking lawyer specializing in Corporate Law.

3BCubed is being threatened with a devastatingly large plagiarism case and when it lands on their lawyers desk, it's handed to the new Corporate Lawyer to handle and win.

Coincidence or perhaps fate will see Blake and Ellie pushed back together.

Binary Law will have Blake and Ellie propelled into a life that's a whirl wind of catastrophic events and situations where every emotion will be touched. Hurt will be experienced, happiness will be presented and love will be evident. But is that enough for Blake and Ellie be able to live out their own happily ever after?